DEFIANT HEART

MARTY STEERE

PENFIELD PUBLICATIONS
2533 Eastwind Way
Signal Hill, California 90755

Cover illustration by Edward Lum
Cover design by Ben Lizardi
Layout and typesetting by Guido Henkel
Published by Penfield Publications

ISBN: 978-0-9854014-4-3

For Martha

1

May 1941

From the top of the slope, the sergeant watched flashlight beams reach out through the darkness, occasionally crossing one another as his patrol officers picked their way through the underbrush at the bottom of the embankment.

Lightning flashed, followed a second later by the crack of thunder, and the ground beneath the sergeant's feet shook momentarily. In the instant the hillside was illuminated, he saw the car clearly. It had come to a stop halfway down the incline, about thirty yards below where he now stood, its fall arrested by the trunk of an immense oak. The garish light briefly exposed mangled metal and shattered glass, and it appeared as though the entire frame of the vehicle had been twisted at an impossible angle.

In the pool of light cast by his own flashlight, his corporal appeared near the top of the ridge. The man planted a foot against an exposed tree root and held on to a low hanging branch to avoid sliding back down the hillside. Raising his voice so he could be heard above the sound of the rain, he said, "Three people. A man and a woman. Thirties or forties. And a boy, maybe seventeen, eighteen."

"They're all..." the sergeant paused with the sudden irrational thought that by uttering the word he would somehow dictate the outcome.

"Dead," the corporal confirmed. "Afraid so. No one could have survived that."

A shout from the bottom of the hill drew the sergeant's attention, and, as he watched, the beams below converged on a single spot. One of the patrolmen called out, his voice faint against the roar of the storm. "Found a body."

After a moment, he added, "He's alive."

A miracle, thought the sergeant. Must have been thrown from the car as it had rolled down the embankment. He'd seen that happen in bad accidents before. Fate could be so random.

"Sergeant," his patrol officer shouted from below. "The kid's asking about his parents and his brother. What do I tell him?"

The sergeant closed his eyes for a moment. Oh, God, he thought. Poor kid.

#

As the train whistle blew, the green of the trees that had been sliding by the windows slowly fell away, and a small wooden building came into view. A sign on the structure read "Jackson, Indiana." On the platform in front stood the solitary figure of an elderly woman.

The door at the front of the passenger car opened, and the conductor stepped through.

"Jackson," he called out, starting down the aisle. When he got to Jon, he nodded and said, "We're here."

Jon raised a hand in nervous acknowledgement, then stood as the train came to a stop and gave a slight backwards lurch. Steadying himself, he reached into the alcove above the seat and retrieved a large brown suitcase. It was old, the sides badly scuffed and the four lower corners worn and discolored. He collected the brown paper sack from the seat next to him. It contained two apples and half a sandwich wrapped in wax paper, all that remained of the food that was in the bag when the lady with the sad eyes had handed it to him as he'd boarded the train in Penn Station. He took a deep breath and squared his shoulders. Then, hefting the suitcase, he made his way down the aisle to the door at the rear of the car.

As he stepped out onto the sunlit platform, he saw that the elderly woman was still standing where he'd first noticed her. Though she was looking directly at him, she made no gesture of greeting. He took a few hesitant steps toward her, set down the suitcase, and asked, uncertainly, "Grandma Wilson?"

The woman seemed to wince. She looked away for a moment. Then, gathering herself, she turned. Over her shoulder, she said, "It's not far," and she began walking. Surprised, it took Jon a moment to react. Not sure what else to do, he lifted the suitcase and followed.

They crossed the dirt-packed road in front of the train station and, after a short distance, started up a paved commercial street. The woman walked briskly, and it was an effort for Jon to keep up with her. He was still favoring his left leg. With each step, the suitcase banged into his right knee.

She spoke without turning her head or breaking stride. "You will address me as 'ma'am.' Understood?"

"Yes, ma'am."

They turned onto a tree-lined street. When they came to a small white clapboard house, trimmed in blue, the woman climbed the steps to the porch and entered without saying a word. Jon stopped to catch his breath, then, with some effort, slowly limped up the steps and entered the dwelling.

He paused in the foyer. To his left was a living room, the far wall dominated by a fireplace with a large wooden mantle. By the front window stood a baby grand piano. The other furnishings were spare. To the right was a dining area, with an opening beyond which he could see a kitchen. A hallway off the foyer led to the rear of the house.

A framed photograph on the piano caught his attention. It was an old ferrotype, featuring a man and a woman. The woman was seated in a straight back chair, wearing a white dress with a high collar and full sleeves, her hair swept up and pinned in an elaborate bun. The man stood to the side and slightly behind, one hand resting on the back of the chair. Dressed in a high-buttoned suit and looking stiff and slightly uncomfortable, he held a hat in his other hand.

There was something familiar about the picture. Jon couldn't quite place it. And then he remembered. On her dresser, his mother had kept a small photograph in a silver filigreed frame. It was the same man, in the same suit, holding the same hat. A slightly different pose, yes, but the same stiff and uncomfortable bearing. His Grandpa Wilson.

Jon had a vague memory of Grandpa Wilson. Not the man in the picture, but an older man, with gray hair and rough hands, a mischievous smile and a twinkle in his eyes. Jon and his brother, Sandy, were in a park with a big lake. They were feeding the ducks. Hundreds of ducks. And one big swan…

"Your room is the first one on the left." The woman was standing in the entrance to the kitchen. She'd removed her hat and tied an apron around her waist. "Dinner is at five sharp."

"Yes, ma'am," he said, picking up his suitcase.

The room was tiny, the space almost completely filled with a writing desk and a small bed, not much more than a cot really. Folded neatly and lying on the bed were a pair of sheets, a blanket and a towel. A cedar chest at the foot of the bed offered the only storage. The walls were devoid of pictures. The desk was empty, as was the chest, which he discovered when he lifted the lid. There was simply nothing to indicate that anyone had ever lived in the room before. It was as sterile as he imagined a prison cell would be.

Jon closed his eyes and took a slow, deep breath, concentrating as he did on keeping his body steady. Try as he might, though, his chest still rattled, both on the intake and exhalation.

As it had many times since the accident, something his father once said came back to him. They'd been gathered for the shiva following the funeral for Grandpa Meyer, and his father had put his arm around his shoulders. "I know you're sad, Jon, and that's ok. But he wouldn't want you to be too sad. Better to celebrate the time you had together." Jon had understood that then. And he'd accepted it. Though his grandfather had been a magnificent part of his life, it had been time for him to go.

But his mother and father? That made no sense. And what about Sandy? Sweet, wonderful Sandy. Under the circumstances, how could Jon possibly celebrate anything? It simply wasn't fair. Everything that had been his life had suddenly gone away. Not temporarily. Not for a long time.

Forever.

As he formed the thought, he was again overwhelmed by a tremendous guilt. He squeezed his eyes tight, willing away the odious thoughts.

He felt a tear escape the corner of one eye and trace a path down his cheek.

After a moment, he opened his eyes and, with the back of a hand, roughly brushed away the offending drop. He would not feel sorry for himself. He would be strong.

He lifted the suitcase, placed it on the bed and opened it. Lying on top of his clothes were a series of books. One by one, he removed them and lined them up carefully on the desk.

As he was putting the last of his things in the chest, he heard voices from the front of the house.

"Honestly, Dick, I would expect you of all people to feel empathy…"

"I do. Of course I do. But when is it appropriate to put our people's lives at risk? We did it once before, remember, and what did it get us? They're at it again. It's a never-ending cycle. I submit to you, Tom, that the world will be better off if all of Europe is united."

"Well, then you'd better start practicing your German, Dick, because Hitler isn't going to be satisfied with just Europe."

Jon stepped into the hallway and saw two men in the foyer. The shorter man wore a dark suit with a minister's collar. The shorter man spotted him.

"Hold that thought, Tom," he said, stepping forward and putting out his hand. "Jonathon, I'm Reverend Mayfield, the pastor at St. Luke's here in Jackson." He gripped Jon's hand and pumped it enthusiastically. "I've known your grandmother for fifteen years. I also knew your grandfather. A fine, fine man."

"Tom Anderson," said the other man, also offering his hand. "Welcome to Jackson. Sorry about the circumstances." Anderson spoke with a deep, gravely baritone. "Do you prefer 'Jonathon,' or is it 'Jon' or…"

"Jon. I much prefer Jon."

"Jon it is then," said the reverend.

Before anyone could say anything further, his grandmother's voice called from the kitchen. "Dinner is served."

#

As a lawyer, Tom Anderson had encountered all manner of people in stressful circumstances. Out of occupational necessity, he'd become something of a student of human nature. Over the years, he had, for example, developed a strong and fairly reliable instinct for when a client or a witness was being evasive, telling half truths or, far too frequently for his taste, outright lying. He had a keen sense for emotions. They included the more base passions such as fear and anger, but he also had an uncanny ability to ferret out more subtle undercurrents.

Through this prism, he found the interaction between Marvella Wilson and her teenage grandson fascinating.

He had known Marvella for many years, and she was one of the most enigmatic persons he'd ever encountered. She was a brittle, opinionated dynamo who had never lost the toughness that came with growing up on a farm. Yet, she had won the heart of Ernie, who had been one of the most endearing men Anderson ever had the privilege to know. Ernie and Marvella had made such an odd pair. And, yet, they had adored each other, she in her way, and he in his.

Anderson could see little of Marvella in her grandson. To him, the boy was the spitting image of Ernie.

Watching her now with the young man was a challenge. As incomprehensible as it was, something in her demeanor told him there was an aspect to Jon that she found unacceptable, even, God forbid, repulsive. It seemed, under the circumstances, to be so out of place.

When they had all taken their seats at the table, the reverend cleared his throat and said, "Let us give thanks."

Anderson noticed that, as Marvella bowed her head, she gave her grandson a sideways glance.

"Lord," the reverend began, "we thank you for allowing us to welcome Jon Meyer to this fine house, and we pray that you will help look over him in these difficult times. We thank you for giving our sister, Marvella, the strength and wisdom to take in Jon. And we pledge ourselves as your humble servants to do what we can to make Jackson a place Jon can truly call home."

He concluded with, "In the name of the father, the son and the holy spirit. Amen."

"Amen," they all repeated, and Anderson again noticed Marvella giving Jon a look out of the corner of her eye.

"So, Jon," Anderson said, folding his napkin and placing it in his lap. "Have you been following the events in Europe?"

"I have, yes sir."

"And what do you think we should be doing about Mr. Hitler?"

Jon paused a moment before answering. "Sir, he's a monster. I think we should be doing everything we can to stop him now."

Nodding, Anderson said, "But what about those who say it's none of our business? Why should we get involved?"

Again, Jon paused briefly. "I don't think it's a question of if, but rather when, we'll become involved. We won't have a choice. Like it or not, we'll be dragged in." He stopped for a moment, searching for the right words. "Eventually, it'll come down to us versus them. The longer we wait, the stronger they'll get."

"And who is 'us'?" Marvella asked sharply.

The intensity of her look clearly shook Jon. "Us, all of us… Americans," he stammered.

There was a brief, uncomfortable silence.

"Well, I happen to agree with that," Anderson said. "But just to play devil's advocate for a moment, why do you believe," he asked, throwing a meaningful look at Mayfield, "that Adolph Hitler won't stop with just Europe?"

Clearly grateful for the opportunity, Jon turned to Anderson. "Because he said so in his book."

"You're talking about *Mein Kampf*," Mayfield said. "I've heard of it."

Jon nodded. "Hitler wrote it before his rise to power. According to him, it's all about world domination, and he intends for Germany to rule the world."

"How do you know that's what it says?" Mayfield asked. "Don't tell me you've read it."

"I have. Yes, sir."

The reverend sat back, a surprised expression on his face.

"That's very impressive," Anderson said. "But, still," he added, thinking about it, "if you're reading a translation, you're getting one man's interpretation, don't you think?"

Jon hesitated a moment, then nodded. "I think that's probably right, yes, sir."

Obviously picking up on Anderson's point, Mayfield asked, "So what makes you think world domination is really what Hitler intends? Wouldn't it be a convenient way to whip up support for the war if the English translation were skewed in that direction?"

Jon considered that, then replied slowly, "It could be. I haven't read the English translation, so I don't know how accurate it is."

Not sure he had followed that, Anderson asked, "You're not saying you read the book in German, are you?"

Jon nodded.

Startled, Anderson said, "You know how to read German. How in the world?"

"My grandfather." Jon stopped suddenly, glancing at his grandmother, then clarified, "My father's father. He was born in Bavaria, and he came to the United States as a young man. He worked in a bakery in Chicago. But he was very educated. He had a degree in literature from the University of Munich. When I was nine, he came to live with us. He started teaching me one day. It was fun, and we just kept at it. He'd bring home books for me, simple ones at first. I'd read them, and then we would go for long walks and talk about them. In German.

"He died," Jon said, the words catching in his throat, and everyone was silent. "He died a little over a year ago," he continued. "I'm just, I guess, lucky to have known him."

No one spoke for a few moments. Then Mayfield broke the silence. "Do you speak any other languages we should know about?" he asked, with a smile.

#

In the morning, Jon discovered he was alone. He took a few minutes to wander through the house. At the end of the hall, he opened the door and stepped into the back yard.

To one side was a trap door to a basement and on the other a lean-to shed, about ten feet by ten feet, with a tin roof and wood siding. The door to the shed was secured by a simple latch that lifted easily when Jon tried it. The door opened with a squeaking protest from the hinges, and he was greeted with a dry blast of stale air.

Jon stepped up into the shed. To his left was a broad work-bench, to his right a pegboard wall on which hung a series of tools. At the rear were dozens of small drawers laid out in neat rows and columns. Selecting one at random, he opened it and found that it contained a collection of nuts, all the same size. He opened the drawer next to it and found it also contained nuts, these slightly larger than the first. The drawers immediately above each contained bolts with diameters corresponding to the nuts in the drawer below. The lengths of the bolts increased as he moved up the column of drawers.

The person who worked here—his Grandpa Wilson, obvi-ously—had been extremely neat and organized. To Jon, there was an undeniable elegance in the way his grandfather had organized his workplace.

A noise outside caused him to start. Moving quickly to the front of the shed, he stepped out and closed the door behind him. He saw no one in the rear yard, and there did not seem to be any sound coming from the house.

He would talk to his grandmother about the workshop when she returned.

#

Vernon King grabbed the keys hanging on the nail embedded in the wall, pushed open the screen door and stepped outside. The truck, he saw, was parked next to the barn. He was relieved to note that the bed of the vehicle was empty.

Absently tossing the keys in the air with the open palm of one hand and catching them with a downward snap of the same hand, he strolled across the dusty yard. He was reaching for the handle to the driver's side door when he heard his father.

"Where do you think you're going?"

Vernon turned and saw the man standing by the corner of the barn. He had been pushing a wheelbarrow full of manure and now set it down.

"Out," said Vernon.

"Don't you have chores?"

He did, at least by his father's reckoning. But he also had something else he wanted to do, and the two conflicted. He'd made the decision that the one outweighed the other. And, if he'd had more time, he might have been willing to engage in a more lengthy discussion about it. But he needed to get going and therefore opted for a much shorter response.

"Nope."

His father came around the wheelbarrow and took a couple steps in Vernon's direction. He had a look on his face Vernon knew all too well. It was one that had terrorized Vernon from the time he was old enough to remember until about three years earlier, when, at the age of fourteen, Vernon had, almost overnight it seemed, grown four inches and added about thirty pounds, all of it muscle.

As a youngster, Vernon had been a tall, gangly boy. He'd gotten his size from his father, who stood almost six foot three inches and was built like a locomotive. All of Vernon's other physical attributes he'd inherited from his mother, a pretty petite blond who'd been forced to marry his father when she'd become pregnant with Vernon at the age of fifteen. Several years younger than Vernon's father, she had, for almost ten years, put up with the man's abuse, both verbal and physical, until one day, without warning, she'd simply left. Her parting words had been scribbled on a piece of paper she'd impaled on the nail from which Vernon had just retrieved the keys. They read, "I can't take it no more. I'm going where you won't never find me. Good bye. PS. Go to Hell."

With his mother gone, Vernon had borne the brunt of his father's cruelty. Even after he'd grown to be the same height as his father, he'd been thoroughly cowed by the man. Then came the miraculous growth spurt. It roughly corresponded to the time Vernon had begun playing basketball.

Everything came to a head one winter evening. The Jackson High School basketball team had played an away game, and Vernon arrived home several hours after sundown. His father, who had been waiting up for him and had been working himself into a rage, aided in no small part by a pint of bourbon, shoved Vernon the moment the boy walked in the door. Vernon, who was still smarting after the loss his team had suffered that evening, shoved back without thinking. His father fell backwards and sprawled on the floor.

Vernon was amazed at his own temerity. What had been more amazing, however, was the look on his father's face. It was mostly surprise. But there was something else.

Fear.

It was a revelation for Vernon. Though his father, particularly after he'd sobered up, continued to intimidate him, it was never quite the same as it had been.

He considered his father for a long moment. Then he took a couple steps in the man's direction. His father involuntarily took a step back. Vernon snorted. "Like I told you," he said, "I'm going out." He tossed the keys in the air and caught them, this time with a sideways snap of his hand that looked almost like a punch.

His father said nothing.

Vernon turned and casually walked to the truck. He slipped behind the wheel, fired up the engine and pulled away. In the rear view mirror, he could see his father still standing in the same spot.

#

With nothing better to do, Jon decided he might as well take the opportunity to explore the town. Leaving by the front door, he turned right and retraced the steps he'd taken the previous afternoon following his grandmother. He came to the commercial street on which he'd been the day before.

As he was trying to decide which direction to take, the door to a beauty salon across the street opened, and three women walked out. The small figure in the middle caught his attention. It was his grandmother.

She was talking to the woman on her left when she did a double take and looked directly at him. He raised his hand and waved. To his surprise, however, she gave no acknowledgement, instead turning and striking up a conversation with the woman on her right. The three continued down the sidewalk without a further glance in his direction.

Confused and a little hurt, Jon headed the other way.

#

The town of Jackson, Jon learned, was not much larger than what could be seen standing at the only intersection. The primary commercial drive, referred to in town as Main Street, was actually part of State Route 26, a highway that ran the width of central Indiana. The town, with a population of fewer than 300 people, served a large rural area in the northern part of Winamac County and a portion of nearby Clark County.

This information came from a garrulous old man whose sole function it seemed was to defy the laws of gravity by balancing on the back two legs of a chair planted in front of the small garage of the service station located on one corner of the intersection, while spitting sunflower seed husks with remarkable accuracy into a paper cup sitting on the ground near his feet. In the time he spoke with the man, Jon counted zero automobiles entering the station and several dozen bull's-eyes in the cup.

"So, young fella," the old man said, working a sunflower seed around his mouth with his tongue before expelling the broken shell and scoring a direct hit on the cup, "are you new in town, or passing through?"

"I just arrived yesterday. I'm staying with my grandmother."

"Oh yeah?" he said, popping another seed into his mouth. "Who's that?"

"Mrs. Wilson. Marvella Wilson."

"Ah, Ernie's widow." Another spit, and another direct hit on the cup. "Didn't know she even had any relatives."

"My mother was her daughter."

Brows furrowed, the old man leaned forward and allowed the front legs of his chair to touch the ground for a moment while he fished around in the pocket of his coveralls and pulled out another handful of seeds. Leaning back, he squinted his eyes and scrunched his face in thought. Then he snapped his fingers. "Sure, I remember. Claire, right?"

Jon nodded.

"Yep, I do remember her. Pretty girl. Smart too. So," the man said, shuffling through the seeds in his gnarled left hand, "you've come back for a visit."

"Actually, I've come here to live."

"Really?" he asked with a renewed interest, looking Jon up and down. "You play basketball?"

"No."

"That's a shame," the man said, returning his attention to the sunflower seeds. "We've got a darn good team up at the high school." Plucking a seed and tossing it into his mouth, he added, "Especially for a town this small. Went to the regionals last year. Would've won, too, 'cept for a lucky last-second shot by that guard from Muncie. Thank God he's graduated."

The old man leaned his head back and this time sent the shell in a high arc so that it dropped straight down into the cup. "Yep, just like that," he said, shaking his head sadly.

He sat quietly, apparently lost in the memory. After a moment, he shook himself and jerked his thumb. "High school's about a mile up the road. On the right. Elementary's on the left. Gym's in the back of the high school."

Jon said his thanks, and, with no better plan, started off in the indicated direction, leaving the old man still perched precariously on his two-legged throne, mouth working sunflower seeds.

#

"Come on Judy," Vernon said. "You know you want it."

They were in the back seat of the big Oldsmobile that belonged to Judy Swisher's father. It was parked in a small clearing several miles east of town. The clearing was accessible down a narrow lane that led off the highway, and it was used as a parking area by hunters during deer season. In June, of course, with hunting season months away, it would normally be deserted. This afternoon, however, there were two vehicles parked beneath the canopies of the large trees that encircled it. One was the Oldsmobile Judy had borrowed from her father. The other was the pickup truck that Vernon had taken.

Judy and Vernon had been dating for almost a year, and she had quite willingly and regularly succumbed to his charms in the past. Today, however, to Vernon's surprise, he was getting nowhere. He'd been trying for about ten minutes, and she was having none of it. She had her legs crossed and her arms folded over her chest.

"I'm not that kind of girl."

"Not that kind of girl?" Then he grinned. "Well, you sure were when we were out here last week."

She flushed at that. "Don't you want to talk?"

"Talk? Talk about what?"

"I don't know. What about the future. Don't you ever think about the future?"

"Sure," he replied, leaning in again. "In fact, I'm thinking about the next ten minutes right now."

She turned her head away.

He sat back. He was starting to get annoyed. "What the hell is this about, Judy?"

She was quiet for a long moment. Finally, she said, "I think we need to talk about us, our relationship, and where it's going."

"Well, it doesn't look like it's going anywhere at the moment."

Judy turned to him. "That's not what I mean. We're going to be seniors. We'll be graduating in less than a year. Shouldn't we start making plans?"

"Plans for what?"

"You know. I think it's time we ought to, maybe, think about," she hesitated a second, then concluded, "getting married."

"Married!" Vernon exclaimed, and Judy flinched. "Are you crazy?"

She looked at him, but said nothing.

"You're serious."

She nodded, but still said nothing.

"Well, I'm not. There's no way I'm tying myself down."

She looked away, her arms still folded. There was a long silence. Then, without turning, she said quietly, "In that case, I think we should stop seeing each other."

That surprised Vernon. Sure, he'd been thinking about breaking it off with Judy anyway. In fact, he'd figured today's liaison would probably be their last. But it was supposed to be his decision. He was, after all, the King. And, in any event, he'd been looking forward to a little action this afternoon. He considered her for a long moment, resentment beginning to build.

"All right," he said. "If that's the way you want it." He grabbed the handle and yanked open the door. He stepped out, turned and looked back, fully expecting that she would say something to stop him. She continued to stare out the other side of the car and said nothing.

That was the last straw. He slammed the door and stalked to the truck. Gunning the engine, he threw the vehicle in reverse and backed up a few feet, the tires skidding in the dirt. Then he put the truck into gear, and, with the rear wheels kicking up dust, pulled out of the clearing and shot down the narrow lane, headed for the highway.

Angry thoughts roiled in Vernon's mind. Who the hell did Judy Swisher think she was anyway? She wasn't even that pretty. Sure, she was blond and had an ok body. But, really, Vernon was so much better looking than her. He knew it. She knew it. Everyone knew it.

Driving much faster than the lane was ever intended to be traveled, he flew down the narrow path, the truck bouncing over the rutted surface. When he reached the highway, he didn't even look to see if there was oncoming traffic. He slewed the pickup onto the paved surface, mashed down on the accelerator, and began the long ride back to town. His thoughts were black. He was mad, and he was ready to take it out on somebody.

#

Jon discovered that, up around the bend from the intersection where he'd had the conversation with the service station attendant, the town pretty much petered out, giving way to large homes set back from the road. Soon, he found himself walking past fields planted in crops he didn't recognize. Beyond a long thicket of trees that pressed in on either side of the road, he emerged to find the two schools exactly as the old man had indicated. With students out on summer break, the structures sat quiet, with no activity in the adjacent parking lots.

As he stood looking at what would be his new school, he felt drops of moisture on the back of his neck. Glancing up, he saw that, though he was still standing in sunlight, a large, solid block of dark clouds was rolling in, bringing the promise of quite a storm. The shadow crossed over him, and then the rain came in earnest.

Breaking into an awkward gait, he ran with a limp across the lot in front of the high school, dodging puddles already forming in the uneven surface. He found a spot against the building under an overhang. Standing with his back pressed against the wall, he was able to stay just out of the downpour.

Growing up, he and his brother, Sandy, had loved to play in the rain, the heavier, the better.

"Bet you can't jump over this one!" Sandy's face, glistening with moisture, had grinned back at him. "Bet I can," Jon had exclaimed, and, pumping his five-year-old legs as hard as he could, Jon had taken a mad dash at the large puddle and flung himself across, landing well short of the far edge, the galoshes on his feet sending up a mighty splash in all directions. Laughing, Sandy had jumped in next to him, and the two of them had stomped madly at the water, shrieking hysterically. Then Sandy had turned to him, his face alive with excitement. But now Sandy's face began to fade, and, as it did, it became serious, somber, and, just before it was gone, there was an overwhelming sadness.

Jon shuddered, and the familiar nausea rose in him, just as it had ever since the accident, the sound of rain and the sight of drops landing in puddles turning his stomach and giving him chills. He huddled forlornly against the brick wall and tried to ignore the hissing made by the water as it struck the loose gravel covering the parking lot.

After a few minutes, he began to detect another sound, this one higher pitched, faint, as if a great distance away. One moment, it was there. Then it faded into the noise of the rain. Then it returned. As he strained to identify the source, the sound grew much louder, deepened, and morphed into a roar.

Emerging from the shroud of rain, a Model A pickup truck came barreling down the highway, water jetting out to either side and a plume of mist rising behind it as it raced by. Suddenly, there was a squeal of rubber skidding along wet pavement. Fishtailing back and forth across the highway, the truck gradually came to a stop a hundred yards beyond the school. The driver threw the truck into reverse, and, incomprehensibly, backed the vehicle up to a point opposite the place where Jon stood, heedless of the possibility that another vehicle might be traveling down the road in the direction it had come.

The driver turned the truck into the high school parking lot and drove it to a spot about thirty yards from Jon, where it sat facing him, engine idling and rain dancing on the hood. Jon could tell there was one person in the cab. At that distance, however, with the rain as heavy as it was, he could not make out the features of the driver.

Just as Jon had resolved to push himself off the wall and walk to the truck, the driver put the vehicle into gear, swung the wheel to the left and, as Jon watched, drove slowly to the far end of the parking area. He then turned, drove across the highway into the lot in front of the elementary school, turned left again and began retracing his route, picking up speed as he did.

When he pulled even with Jon's position, he made a hard left and gunned the engine.

The truck lurched and jumped across the highway. Engine roaring, it came flying directly at Jon, who stood frozen, too shocked to move. At the last possible moment, the driver yanked the steering wheel and slammed on the brakes, causing the tail end of the truck to swing around and come to rest just a few feet from Jon. The driver then hit the accelerator, the rear wheels bit into the soft, wet ground, and Jon was showered with a wave of mud and gravel.

Jon instinctively threw his hands up in front of his face, and bits of gravel dug into his open palms and forearms. Then the deluge from the truck subsided as it pulled away across the lot and veered back out onto the highway, speeding off toward town.

#

The long walk back to his grandmother's house was painful. Though the rain had let up, it was heavy enough that most of the town was still indoors. The few people Jon passed on the street stared, but he kept his head down and avoided eye contact. He had wiped off much of the blood from his hands and arms, but the wounds continued to ooze, and his clothes were covered in mud.

When he stepped through the front door, his grandmother was sitting at the piano next to a boy of nine or ten. They both looked up and froze. The boy's eyes widened to the size of small saucers, but his grandmother's narrowed, and her lips pursed. She slowly took in the sight of him, then sighed.

"Please go clean yourself up."

"Yes, ma'am," was all he could say, and, with as much dignity as he could muster, he walked quickly down the hall, not wanting her to see the tears that suddenly filled his eyes.

2

"You're going to Hell, and you don't even know it."

Amused, Mary Dahlgren lowered the book she was reading and looked at the dark-haired girl who had just made the statement. Typical Sam.

Samantha Parker was stretched out on a wicker chaise lounge, concentrating intently on the right foot of Gwendolyn Barnes. Gwenda, in turn, had Sam's right foot in her lap and was carefully brushing nail polish onto Sam's large toenail. The polish was a vivid red.

As Mary watched, Sam delicately dipped a brush into a bottle of the polish and, with exaggerated care, touched the tip of the brush to Gwenda's smallest toenail. Then she held the brush away and lightly blew on Gwenda's foot, slowly turning her head side to side. Everything Sam did had to be theatrical.

"Hell seems pretty dire," Mary observed.

"Oh, I don't mean Hell in the religious sense," Sam said, without breaking her concentration. "You know what I'm talking about. You're losing sight of the really important stuff. You sit around all day reading things that nobody else cares about. In the meantime, life is passing you by. One day, you're going to wake up, and you'll be an old maid. And then you'll say, 'Hey, why didn't I listen to Sam when I had the chance?'"

Mary suppressed a smile. This was one of Sam's favorite topics. Sam was bound and determined to mold Mary into her image of the modern woman. The fact that Mary would have none of it was a constant source of distraction for Sam.

"Is this about my not painting my nails?" she asked innocently.

"It's not just about that, but it'll do for starts."

Mary, Sam and Gwenda had been friends for as long as Mary could remember. They had just always been together. For Mary, an only child, the two girls had filled the void left after her mother had passed away when Mary was six years old, leaving her alone with a father to whom she had never been very close. The two girls were, for all intents and purposes, her family.

It wasn't that Mary didn't love her father. She did, after a fashion. And she certainly admired and respected him. But, in the ten years since his wife's death, Jim Dahlgren had never been able to allow himself to show real affection. To anyone. He'd dated a few women, but none had stuck around for long. There had never been one that Mary could get close to. Without Sam and Gwenda, Mary's would have been a very lonely existence.

Mary, however, was as different from her two friends as night was from day.

Sam, the extrovert, was obsessed with her appearance. Her hair was always coiffed in the latest style. She would spend hours on her makeup. With subscriptions to several fashion magazines, she was invariably up on all the hot trends. To Sam, being the perfect young woman took second place to only one thing: Finding the perfect man.

Gwenda was much more low-keyed, but no less anxious to present the picture of the well-put-together young woman. In Gwenda, Sam had found the ideal acolyte. Ironically, it was Gwenda who'd had the greater success with boys. For the past several months, she had been going steady with Billy Hamilton, one of their classmates and a stand-out on the Jackson High School basketball team.

To Sam's mortification, Mary had no interest in fashion. As the daughter of one of the town's most successful merchants, Mary could easily afford fine clothing. However, she preferred simple outfits. She eschewed fashionable curls and wore her honey blond hair in a simple, tousled style. Lipstick, mascara and the current object of the girls' attention, nail polish, were items Mary rarely used.

"Look at yourself," Sam was saying, the nail polish temporarily forgotten. "You are, by a mile, the prettiest one of us. Yet you do nothing to call attention to your assets."

"My assets? Like what?"

"Like your *ass*-et," blurted Gwenda, and she and Sam dissolved into a fit of giggling.

"Fine," Mary said, with feigned indignation, "I'll just leave you kids alone," and she made a show of returning to her book.

"No, seriously. And here's why it's so important now," Sam said, lowering her voice and looking suddenly conspiratorial. "I have it on good authority that Vernon and Judy are on the outs."

"Really?" asked Gwenda.

"Finished," Sam said.

She and Gwenda turned and looked expectantly at Mary.

"What?" Mary asked, after a moment.

"What to you mean, what?" said Gwenda. "We're talking about King Vernon, here. The hottest thing in three counties."

"And he's *available*," added Sam.

"Then you go after him."

"I would if I could," Sam replied, "but I'm not a blond. Everybody knows the King only likes blonds."

"Oh, applesauce," said Mary, "And, in any event, I don't give a hoot about Vernon King. Never have."

#

In the weeks following his arrival in Jackson, Jon and his grandmother had settled into an uneasy routine. She was rarely around when he awoke, returning to the house only in the early afternoon. On most days, she would then give piano lessons.

Mondays were the exception. On those days, his grandmother brought out a pair of folding card tables from her bedroom, carefully arranged chairs around them, and set out refreshments. A group of women descended on the house, and they spent hours playing bridge.

His grandmother made it clear to Jon that he was not welcome during these activities. Jon would have to go for a walk or retire to his room and read. Despite his vow not to dwell on his situation, there was no avoiding the bitter sting of this rejection.

Jon and his grandmother ate one meal together, always at 5:00 sharp. They were uncomfortable affairs, his grandmother making no attempt to initiate conversations, her replies to his comments or questions typically short, inviting no follow up. The only time he got any kind of rise from her was the one time he mentioned the work shed.

"You stay away from that place," she snapped, her eyes flashing. After a moment, she asked, "You haven't tried to go in there, have you?"

Jon shook his head quickly.

"Good. It's not a place for you. Just leave it alone."

After that, they retreated to their usual awkward silence.

#

On the Fourth of July, there was to be a parade down Main Street, followed by a barbeque hosted by the chamber of commerce. Jon had seen flyers advertising the celebration posted about town. On the day of the event, he waited until his grandmother left, then followed a few minutes later.

Compared to parades Jon had seen in New York, this one was small—a few classic Model Ts decorated with flowers and crêpe paper, a marching band, and a large float built on a flatbed trailer and towed by a fine set of six white horses, their manes braided with flowers. But what it lacked in volume was more than compensated by the enthusiasm and general merriment of the crowd. The town was decked out in an explosion of red, white and blue. The population seemed to have swelled to a multiple of its size, as families poured in from the surrounding countryside. The parade route was lined with people waving American flags. Young children darted about, laughing and swirling sparklers.

The barbeque was held in a field just to the north of town. After waiting patiently in line, Jon accepted a hot dog from one of the volunteers manning the grills and, still favoring his bad leg, slowly made his way over to a line of trees. He found a spot next to a large sycamore and sat down in the shade, his back against the uneven bark.

He was certainly no stranger to crowds of people he didn't know. He'd been to the city many times with his parents. He and his brother had attended baseball games at Ebbets Field with his father. Two years earlier, his parents had allowed him to accompany his brother, on their own, to the World's Fair in nearby Flushing Meadows, where the two boys easily mingled with the mass of people that filled the vast grounds. Never in his life, however, had he felt as isolated as he was now, so completely alone. He even found himself yearning for a glimpse of his grandmother.

His grandmother. She clearly did not like him. From the moment he'd set foot in Jackson, she'd made no secret of her antipathy. Countless times, he had asked himself, Why? Weren't they family? Didn't family stick together? Most nights, he'd laid awake in his tiny room, a crushing loneliness constricting his chest. And it had taken a while. But he'd finally come to a rueful conclusion. Here he had been, wallowing in his own self-pity, so willing to lean on the only remaining member of his family that he had, for weeks, overlooked a fundamental truth.

He was a burden. And a terribly unfair one at that.

His Grandpa Wilson had passed away several years ago. To make ends meet, his grandmother gave piano lessons. At her age. Then, out of the blue, along came another mouth to feed, a selfish one, contributing nothing and, in the process, disrupting her life.

He felt ashamed.

He was mulling over ways in which he might address the problem when his attention was drawn to a figure in the crowd. It was a young man who stood a head taller than anyone else and was therefore impossible to miss. His back was to Jon. A sleeveless t-shirt revealed muscular shoulders and a thick neck, and his head was covered with light blond curls. He was talking to someone, and, as he did, he gestured and turned slightly. The movement afforded Jon a line of sight to the person with whom he was speaking, and, instead of focusing on the young man, Jon found himself staring at the most beautiful girl he had ever seen in his life.

#

"That's nice of you to ask, Vernon," Mary said, "but my friends are here, and we're having a good time."

Vernon smiled easily and cocked an eyebrow. "It would just be for a little bit. You know I'm pretty busy these days. We may not get another chance to spend time together."

"Well, I think I'll take that risk."

"Suit yourself," Vernon shrugged with a carefree nonchalance. He looked past Mary and, apparently making eye contact with someone in the crowd, nodded.

"See you around." He stepped past her and strolled off, a study in practiced indifference.

Sam, who had been lingering a short distance away, now came stomping up to Mary.

"Are you crazy? Vernon King wants to make time with you, and you're too busy having 'a good time with your friends'? 'Oh, I'm terribly sorry, my social calendar is full at the moment. Perhaps you can check back with me later.' What are you thinking?

Are you holding out for Cary Grant? Because I've got a breaking news bulletin for you. Cary Grant isn't coming to Jackson any-time soon. What do I have to do to get some sense into your stubborn head? You can't play hard to get with the King. He likes you, but he won't wait around."

"Oh, Sam," Mary said, laughing, "I love your passion. But, in this case, you're just wrong. I've known Vernon all my life. And I can tell you he only likes two things: Basketball and Vernon King, and not necessarily in that order."

"But, he's the King..."

"And I have no interest in being the queen. Come on, let's go find Gwenda. Then the two of you can gang up on me."

#

Jon watched the two young women have a spirited conversa-tion, the dark-haired girl waving her arms in dramatic fashion, while the blond laughed gaily. Then the two linked arms, turned, and melded into the crowd. For a moment, he contemplated get-ting up and following, but realized he had no idea what he would say if he found them. He strained to catch another glimpse of the blond girl, but she and her companion were lost in the multitude.

Sitting back against the trunk of the tree, he turned his mind to the problem that had been vexing him. How, he asked himself, could he help alleviate the burden he represented? How could he make it up to his grandmother?

#

The placard in the window simply read "Help Wanted." There were no further details. Jon took a deep breath and stepped into the hardware store.

"Can I help you?" asked the heavyset man behind the counter. Jon swallowed, then took a step forward.

"I'm here about the job."

"Ah," said the man, amiably. "The owner's not in now. You wanna check back later?"

"Sure," Jon replied. Then he added, "Can you tell me what the job involves?"

"Cleaning. Stocking. Helping out with the customers when things get busy. It's not a full time job, but the pay's decent. The guy who had it before just joined the navy. You know about tools and hardware?"

Jon hesitated briefly, then admitted, "No, not a lot. But I'm I fast learner and a hard worker."

"At least you're honest," the big man said. "Say, you're not from town are you?"

"I am. I moved here a few weeks ago. I'm living with my grandmother, Marvella Wilson."

"You're Ernie Wilson's grandson? Well, that's gotta be worth something. Ernie, he was a regular in here. You know," he said with a smile, "your granddaddy was something else. If it was broke, he could fix it. I never saw nothing like it. I asked him once how he did it. You know, how he could fix something he never even seen before. He says 'Walt'—Walt's my name—'You know how you got to know how something works before you can fix it, right?' Well, to tell the God's truth, I didn't know that then. Course, now I do. So, anyway, he says, 'I don't know how it happens, but if I look at something long enough, I can figure out how it works.' He could just see it. You ever heard of anyone who could do that?"

Jon shook his head, truthfully.

"Me neither. It was the damnedest thing. You remember," he began, then amended, "nah, you're probably too young to remember, back when refrigerators first started comin' out."

Actually, Jon remembered the old ice box that his family had before they purchased their first refrigerator when Jon was about eight. Before then, the iceman would make deliveries, and Jon had fond recollections of retrieving ice chips from his wagon on hot summer days.

"Refrigerators was suddenly a hot item. I'd say in one year, half the town went out and bought one. Now you talk about your technical things. Even Ernie had a hard time understanding how they worked. And, of course, they started breaking down, just like everything does.

"Well, Ernie writes away to the folks at General Electric, and they was nice enough to send him a manual. Seems the guys they trained to fix the things was stretched to the breaking point. So they was happy to have someone learn on his own how to fix 'em.

"And then, sure enough, one day, Ernie says to me, 'I got it now.' Just like that."

At that moment, the front door opened, the tinkling of a small bell announcing the presence of someone new. They both turned as a woman Jon had never seen before entered the store.

"Oh, hey, Mrs. Cartwright," Walt called, cheerily.

"Morning Walt," she said. Then she turned and strolled up the first aisle.

"Well," Walt said, turning back to Jon, "I guess maybe I better let you go. Mr. Dahlgren should be here this afternoon. You wanna come back then?"

"I will."

"OK, see you later. Say, I enjoyed the conversation."

That struck Jon as funny. To his recollection, he hadn't contributed anything to the conversation. "Me too."

#

Jim Dahlgren returned to his hardware store in the late afternoon. As the mayor of Jackson, he would be presiding over the city council meeting later that evening. He had a number of things on his mind, so he didn't respond when his assistant, Walt, called out, "Hey boss, you're back early."

With a cursory wave of acknowledgement, Dahlgren headed straight for the narrow stairs leading up to the second floor office he maintained above the original section of the store. Before he could ascend, however, Walt said, "Say, I got good news."

Dahlgren turned and looked at Walt.

"I think we maybe found a guy to replace Bobby. You'll never believe who it is, either. Ernie Wilson's grandson. We had a nice chat today. He's a hard worker and a fast learner. And he's honest," he added.

Dahlgren nodded in a distracted way. "Well, tell you what. If you're happy with him, then it's fine with me."

And with that, Jon had a job.

#

To Jon, Dahlgren's Hardware offered more than mere employment. It was a refuge from the cold environment of his grandmother's home. And it came with the first person Jon could call a friend in Jackson.

Walt Gallagher had grown up on a farm, the youngest of eight children, all of whom, with the exception of Walt, were girls. Walt's father, in turn, had been one of seven children. Walt's grandfather had fled Ireland with his two half-brothers at the peak of the potato famine in the middle part of the prior century and had settled in Clark County. There were Gallaghers spread throughout Central Indiana. Walt, it seemed, had more relatives than he could possibly count.

With little interest, and even less aptitude, for farming, Walt had come to work at Dahlgren's when he was not much older than Jon was now. That was almost twenty years ago. He'd never married, had never been outside the state of Indiana, and, near as Jon could tell, had no regrets.

The small bell on the front door tinkled, and a stooped, white-haired man entered.

Walt looked at Jon and winked. "Good morning, Mr. Hardisty," he bellowed at the top of his lungs.

"Eh?" said the man, shuffling over to the counter. "Eh?"

Walt waved a hand in greeting and repeated, "Good morning!"

"Good morning to you, Walt," Mr. Hardisty said in response. Then he turned to Jon and observed casually, "I'm deaf as a goddamn post."

Jon had no idea how to respond to that, so he simply smiled.

The man fished around in a canvas sack he was carrying, and, after a moment, produced a flashlight that, with slightly shaking hands, he placed on the counter. "Can't get this goddamn thing to work," he announced.

"Maybe it needs new batteries," Walt said.

"Eh?"

"Batteries," Walt repeated.

"Batteries. Yes. Just put a whole new set in. Didn't help."

Walt picked up the flashlight and clicked the on/off button. Sure enough, nothing happened. He unscrewed the back and allowed three dry cell batteries to slide out onto the counter. He and Jon leaned over and looked at them, then at each other. Walt cocked an eyebrow. Slowly, Jon reached out, gripped the middle battery between thumb and forefinger, and deliberately turned it around. He then looked back at Walt and cocked his own eyebrow.

Walt nodded, then slid the three batteries back into the case and re-screwed the end piece. This time, when he clicked the button, the light came on.

"That's it. By God, you fixed it," exclaimed Mr. Hardisty, looking at Jon.

"Actually, all I did was…"

"You're a goddamn genius." He looked at Walt. "He's a goddamn genius."

"Yep," Walt said, agreeably. "You know who he is, don't you?"

"Eh?"

"You know who he is?" Walt repeated.

"Who?"

"This is Ernie Wilson's grandson."

"Ernie Wilson? Well that explains it," Mr. Hardisty said, reaching out a palsied hand and patting Jon on the shoulder. "Ernie was a goddamn genius. And you're a goddamn genius."

The man turned to Walt. "What do I owe you?"

Walt raised both hands and shook them. "No charge today, Mr. Hardisty."

"Eh? No charge? Well that's damned nice of you, Walt. You're a goddamn nice guy." He carefully put the flashlight back in his sack and started slowly for the front door. "And he's a goddamn genius," he said, waiving in Jon's direction. "A goddamn genius."

When the man was gone, Walt and Jon burst into laughter.

"You're a goddamn genius," Walt cried out in a passable mimic of the old man.

Jon shrugged in an elaborate show of modesty. "I do what I can."

#

At quitting time, Mr. Dahlgren descended the stairs with two envelopes in his hand. When Walt saw him, he jumped off the stool and said, "Hot diggidy dog. All this fun, and we get paid too."

Jon was too embarrassed to count the money in front of Mr. Dahlgren, so he simply said thanks and put the envelope in his pocket. He bid Walt and Mr. Dahlgren good evening, promised to see them on Monday morning, and walked home without touching the thing, nevertheless aware at every moment of its presence. As soon as he was in his room, he pulled it from his pocket and emptied the contents on the desk, spreading the currency in front of him.

His salary was thirty-five cents an hour. In the past week, he had worked twenty-eight hours. He counted the money, and it came out to $9.80. Exactly what it should be. He'd never held this much money before. After a moment of thought, he removed $1.50 and transferred it to the pocket of his coat, which he then refolded and returned to the bottom of the cedar chest. He placed the balance of his clothes back on top of the coat and closed the chest. The rest of the money he returned to the envelope.

#

The soft glow of twilight illuminated Elm Street as Marvella Wilson approached the house. She had opted to take a walk after dinner.

As usual, Claire dominated her thoughts.

Claire. Her miracle.

After two miscarriages, the doctors had said Marvella would never be able to carry a child to term. Then, against the odds, she'd had the little boy. The poor thing hadn't lasted two hours. Always just "the little boy." He never had a name. She and Ernest couldn't bring themselves to give him one. It was just too hard.

They'd resigned themselves to being childless, so it came as a shock when, two weeks shy of Marvella's fortieth birthday, old Doc Anderson announced, with more than just a little concern, that she was pregnant once again. It posed a terrible risk to her health, and Doc Anderson hinted at alternatives. But she and Ernest desperately wanted a child. And seven and a half months later, to the surprise of everyone, Claire came bounding into their world, vibrant, full of life, mischievous, curious, irrepressibly happy. A true blessing. Claire made up for all the pain, all the longing. She was a gift from God. She lifted the clouds and brought the sunshine.

And that man had no right to take her.

It was in the summer of 1919. Or was it 1920? So many years ago, now. Claire, a young woman, yes, but still a child in Marvella's eyes, had been anxious to get out and "see the world." Ernest, rest his soul, agreed that it might be a good thing for Claire to experience life outside of Jackson.

"She won't be happy until she does," he pointed out, always so pragmatic. "You know how she is. If we don't let her go, she's liable to up and go on her own."

Of course, Ernest had been right. So, while Marvella argued against it, in her heart she'd known it was no use.

It was decided. Claire was to stay with Ernest's cousin, Nancy. Widowed when her husband, who had shipped out to France with the 79th Infantry Division, had failed to return from the Argonne Forest, Nancy had converted her home on the south side of Chicago into a boarding house. She reported that there were jobs to be had at the Mercantile Exchange where two of her boarders were employed.

Claire had worked hard on her shorthand, and had spent hours on the old Munson typewriter that Ernest had found and restored. Countless evenings, after Marvella and Ernest went to bed, Claire sat at the dining room table banging away at the keys, the click-clacking producing a surprisingly comforting lullaby to which she and Ernest would nod off.

And so it was that, over twenty years ago now, Claire bid her goodbyes and boarded the train for Hammond, with connections to Chicago. Marvella's last image of Claire had been a beaming face in the frame of the Pullman window, eyes bright with excitement and anticipation of the journey ahead.

Claire was a good correspondent, her letters full of details. On the weekends, Claire and her new friends would go to the White City Amusement Park, or they would hop the "L" and take it into the city. Or they would cram into a convertible owned by the brother of one of the other residents and head off to Clarendon or Wilson Avenue Beach. Each day brought new adventures, which Claire recounted with relish.

After a few weeks, references to "Frank" began to appear in the pages of Claire's letters. Claire was effusive in her descriptions. Frank was so smart. Frank was so handsome. Frank was so witty. You should have heard Frank go on the other night.

"Who is this fellow Frank?" she asked Ernest one morning, peering over the pages of the letter that she was reading for the third time since it had arrived the afternoon before.

Ernest, who never spoke without first gathering his thoughts, paused in mid-bite, then deliberately finished chewing and swallowing his food before responding.

"Sounds to me like Claire's got a beau," he said in his laconic Midwestern drawl. "Don't see anything wrong with that."

"But do you think it's proper for her to be running around Chicago with a man we've never met? And unchaperoned at that?"

With the hint of a smile tickling the corners of his mouth, Ernest raised one eyebrow and said, "Well, now, I don't seem to recall you being too concerned about chaperones when you and I were courting. And, if I'm not mistaken, you were younger than Claire is now."

Looking at him teasing her, with that twinkle in his eye, she softened for a moment. But then she raised her chin and squared her shoulders.

"That doesn't change anything. I know you. I don't know this Frank person. I think we have a right to be concerned."

"We?"

"Yes. Our daughter... *your* daughter, is gallivanting around the city with a man we know nothing about. We've never met him. We don't know anything about his family. He could be married, for heaven's sake."

Ernest looked at her for a moment, then nodded with exaggerated solemnity. "If it's gotten to the point that gallivanting is involved…"

"Ernest."

He knew that tone and raised his hands in mock surrender.

"I'll send a wire to Nancy and ask her if she can tell us something about this gentleman."

The letter from Nancy arrived a week later. As Ernest handed her the envelope, she saw that it had been opened. She looked closely at Ernest's face to see if it betrayed any emotion, but he was as unreadable as always.

She carried the envelope into the parlor, sat, and retrieved the single sheet of paper.

"Dear Ernie and Marvella," Nancy began. "I hope this letter finds you well. Words cannot express what a joy it has been having Claire here. She is a wonderful young woman, and you have every right to be proud of her.

"You have asked about Frank. He and Claire have become quite close, and they make a handsome couple. Now, because you have inquired, I feel it is my duty to be as forthcoming as I can. First, let me tell you that Frank is an extremely polite young man. He is quiet at first, but when he lets his guard down, he can be very funny. He is intelligent without being overbearing. He has been studying law in New York, and I understand he has only one more semester before he will graduate. About his family, I don't know much. His sister, Rachel, has been a boarder with me for the past two years, and I have had no complaints with her.

"Now," she continued, "I will tell you one thing that you must know. I mention this not because I find it to be an issue myself, but only because I think you would consider it important and would want to know."

Marvella felt a chill, and her grip on the page tightened.

"Frank is of the Semitic race. You would not know it to look at him. His features are a little dark, but he appears normal to me.

His sister, by the way, is quite fair, and I had no idea she was a Jewess until she mentioned it last Christmas. Now, as I say, I have no objections to this type of thing. But I know that it can be a problem for others…"

She allowed the letter to fall into her lap.

After a moment, Ernest crossed the room and gently retrieved the sheet of paper. Taking a seat across from her on the divan, he fixed her with a level gaze. They sat that way for at least a minute, neither saying anything, the stillness broken only by the rhythmic tick-tock of the pendulum clock.

Ernest cleared his throat, but, before he could speak, she interjected.

"Don't you start with me, Ernest Wilson. You know that Jew murdered my father and stole his farm."

Ernest sighed and looked away for a moment. When he looked back, there was a sadness in his eyes.

"Nobody murdered your father. He died in his sleep."

"He died because of what that man did to him."

She and Ernest had been married for less than a year when they learned that her father had borrowed money from a man named Goldman. To secure repayment, her father had pledged his farm as collateral. When Goldman foreclosed on the mortgage, it left her father homeless. A broken man, he died just six months later.

"Your father didn't have to take out that loan," Earnest said, softly. "It was his choice. Then we had three straight drought years. Who could have predicted that?"

"He was an honest man. He would have paid it back."

Nodding, Ernest said, "He was an honest man. And yes, I believe he would have moved heaven and earth to pay it back. But Mr. Goldman was being threatened with foreclosure on his own farm. He was within his rights…"

"No! That farm was my father's life. And that man took it from him."

41

Ernest ran a calloused hand through his graying hair, then rubbed his chin.

"Ok," he said, in a placating tone. "That's in the past. Let's focus on now."

"Yes, let's," Marvella said. "We need to nip this thing in the bud. I will not have Claire consorting with Jews. She's a good girl."

She looked at Ernest, sitting there on the divan, elbows on his knees, a sad expression on his face. Ernest. Always so forgiving. So trusting. Bless his heart, sometimes so foolish.

"I didn't make the world the way it is," she said with finality, closing off the conversation. "I'll do what I have to do to protect my daughter."

That evening, she had written to Claire. She had not minced words. Marvella was not one to do that. Claire was to stop seeing Frank. She had a reputation to maintain. It was for Claire's own good. The issue was not open for discussion. If Claire refused, she would no longer be welcome in Marvella's home. She would no longer be her daughter.

There had been no reply from Claire.

Claire and Frank had been married and living in New York for a year before Marvella learned of it. She'd suspected both, but had no details and had sought none. She'd known that Ernest kept in touch with them. That couldn't be helped. But he'd known better than to speak of it.

In October 1929, just days before the crash that marked the beginning of the Great Depression, Ernest had boarded a train for New York. He told Marvella he was going to visit an old relative from his side of the family who was ill, and she allowed that fiction to go unchallenged. He returned a month later with first hand stories of chaos and panic on Wall Street and in the other cities where the train had stopped and taken on passengers.

On his first night back, Ernest went into the basement and retrieved the bottle of Jack Daniel's that he had hidden years before on the eve of Prohibition. As he carried it out to his workshop, he said to her, "You should know that you have two beautiful grandsons."

By the morning, the bottle was empty, and Ernest had nothing more to say about New York.

In early 1934, Ernest began experiencing chest pains. Marvella accompanied him to the regional hospital in Terre Haute, where they saw a heart specialist who gave them the bad news. Always able to fix everything, Ernest had finally found something he couldn't repair. On the evening of February first, Ernest went to bed, and, in the morning, he did not wake up.

With Ernest gone, there had been a terrible emptiness in Marvella's life. Though she tried hard not to dwell on it, Claire was never far from her thoughts. How, she would ask herself, could that man have taken her daughter and left her now so utterly alone?

Indeed, that had been the very question she was asking herself on the morning the telegram arrived. The message had been to the point: "Regret to report on 5 May Frank Claire and Sanford Meyer killed in automobile crash Glen Cove stop Request you contact Nassau County Police re Jonathon Meyer."

She had sought the assistance of Tom Anderson, old Doc Anderson's son, and the lawyer who'd helped put their affairs in order before Ernest had died. Anderson tracked down the details regarding the accident that had taken the lives of Marvella's daughter, son-in-law and eldest grandchild. Her other grandchild, sixteen-year-old Jonathon Meyer, had been the only one to survive the crash.

"You are his only living relative," Anderson had explained to her. "Perhaps," he had said gently, "you should take responsibility for the boy."

They'd been sitting around her dining room table. Reverend Mayfield had accompanied Anderson to lend support.

"That can't be," she said. "What about Frank's family? I know he has a sister."

Consulting his notes, Anderson said, "He had a sister. Rachel Meyer. Unfortunately, she died of tuberculosis in 1925. His parents are also both deceased."

She sat back, contemplating a spot on the far wall.

"I can't do it," she announced after a moment. "Look at me. I'm eighty years old."

"Marvella, you're the most spry eighty-year-old I've ever known," Reverend Mayfield said. "We're not talking about something that's going to last forever. The boy will be an adult soon enough. He just needs a guardian for a couple of years."

Turning toward him, she said, "There's more to it than that."

"What is it?" he asked, cocking his head.

Suddenly, she had trouble meeting the reverend's eyes. Unable to find the words to explain her unwillingness to take in the young man, she allowed the question to hang there. And now, on this fine summer evening, it was still hanging there, unanswered.

Today, for the first time since his arrival in Jackson, her grandson had missed the evening meal. She wasn't exactly sure how to feel about that.

On the one hand, of course, she was put out that she'd made a meal for the boy, and he had not told her he wouldn't be eating with her. That was simply rude. But, she had to admit, it was also unusual. Say what she would about everything else, he had generally made an effort to be polite.

On the other hand, though, at least for one evening, she had been spared the discomfiting silence and the awkward role playing that accompanied their meals together. Yet, even that was oddly unsatisfying, and it troubled her in a way that she could not readily identify.

She reached the stoop and slowly climbed the steps to the front porch, pausing at the top. She seemed a little more tired these days. Simple activities took a toll that she didn't remember. Must be the heat, she decided.

As she entered the kitchen, she noticed an envelope on the counter. Looking inside, she saw that it contained money, a little over eight dollars. She turned the envelope over in her hands. It had no writing, and there was no accompanying note.

That's odd, she told herself, and she stood there for a long moment. Then, uncertain what else to do, she reached into the pantry and retrieved the coffee can from its place on the top shelf. Looking inside, she saw that it still contained the few bills and change that remained following Ernest's funeral, the last time she'd felt a need to draw from what she and Ernest had called their "emergency account."

So many years, she thought, fingering the can. What, she asked herself, would Ernest do if he were here now. What would he tell her? God, she missed him. A wave of emotion washed over her. Sadness. And something else. Something that she was loathe to acknowledge. And, when the admission finally came, it was with an unusual and unexpected tinge of self-doubt. Regret. She felt exhausted.

Finally, she deposited the envelope in the can, reattached the metal lid, and returned the container to the pantry shelf.

3

It was a Monday, his grandmother's bridge day. Even though Jon got off work at 3:00, he knew not to return to the house immediately. He passed the time taking a walk.

His grandmother had been angry with him for missing dinner on Saturday. She'd had a point, there was no denying it. But he'd simply not realized in advance that, on Saturdays, Dahlgren's stayed open until 6:00, and he was expected to stay until closing time. He apologized, but when he began to explain the circumstances, she would have none of it. Adding to his consternation was the fact that she said nothing about the money he'd brought home as part of his pay. She didn't even acknowledge it.

The problem with his grandmother, it seemed, was not going away easily.

As he entered the house, Jon could hear voices from the kitchen.

"Can't you just order a replacement part?" his grandmother was asking.

"Well, that's the rub," came the sound of a man's voice, one that Jon did not recognize. "I wouldn't know what part to order."

Stepping into the dining room, Jon could see through the kitchen door that the refrigerator had been pulled away from its usual spot against the wall. A man Jon had never seen before was in the process of returning tools to a wooden box.

"The problem is with the compressor," the man continued. "Those are specialized pieces of equipment. You'll need to contact an authorized service provider. Maybe someone can come up from Terre Haute."

"So what you're telling me is you don't know how to fix it."

"Ma'am, I don't think even Ernie would have known how to fix it."

His grandmother made a snorting sound, but said nothing further.

At dinner that night, his grandmother was more voluble than she'd been since he'd arrived. The failure of the refrigerator was distressing, and it had her fretting about the imminent spoilage of the food it contained. But to Jon it seemed she was more upset at the handyman for his suggestion that his grandfather would not have known how to make the necessary repairs.

"As if he has any idea," she harrumphed, more to the room than to Jon.

#

The next morning, after confirming that his grandmother was not in the house, Jon slipped out the back door and entered the work shed. It has to be here, he told himself. His grandfather was far too organized not to have kept it. On a shelf near the door, he found a series of catalogues. Electrical supplies. Plumbing fixtures.

And there it was.

In large block letters on the cover it read "General Electric Monitor Top Refrigerator, Manual for Repair and Service."

He slid the manual out and re-straightened the remaining volumes on the shelf. Then he did a brief check to make sure he had left no evidence of his entry, and he quickly exited the shed. He returned to his room, where he closed the door, sat down at the desk, and opened the manual to the first page. As he scanned the introduction and took in the technical jargon, he realized this was not going to be easy. He took a deep breath, cleared his mind, and set to work reading.

#

Tom Anderson was just finishing a phone call when he heard the front door to his office open, and he called out, "Come on back." When Marvella Wilson walked in, he rose, came around the desk to great her, and held a chair for her to sit.

Anderson knew better than to try to make small talk with Marvella, so, returning to his seat, he retrieved a manila folder and said, "I've got your file right here. First, let me say that settlement of the estate was easier than I thought it might be. I'm very impressed with how thorough and organized your son-in-law was."

He could see Marvella's lips tighten at this.

"The house has been sold," he said, consulting his notes. "The proceeds, after payment of the mortgage and closing costs, have been placed in the trust account I set up for you. Same thing with the furniture. A second-hand dealer took the whole lot. Pursuant to your suggestion, clothes and other personal items were inventoried and donated to the Red Cross.

"Frank and Claire had one investment, a few shares of stock in the Pennsylvania Railroad. Those have been sold. There were two life insurance policies, a small one for Claire and a more substantial policy for Frank. Payments have been issued directly into the account.

"After deducting my expenses and fee, the total amount in the account stands at just a little over $29,000."

It was a staggering amount of money, more than most men would make in ten, maybe twenty years, and he could see that she was surprised. Though she endeavored to maintain her stoic pose, the rapid blinking of her eyes gave her away.

#

Jon had been reading for a couple of hours when he suddenly stopped and sat more upright. He flipped back a couple of pages. It can't be that easy, he asked himself, can it?

Shaking his head, he got up and walked to the kitchen. The refrigerator was still plugged in. He unplugged it. Then he leaned back and twisted his torso so he could put his ear next to the large round compressor assembly on the top of the cabinet while reinserting the plug into the wall socket. As soon as the plug was in, he heard a short, low hum, then a click. He stepped back from the unit, seized with a nervous excitement.

He returned to his room, took a notebook from the desk and opened it to a blank page. Referring to the manual, he made a notation. Then he tore out the page, folded it and put it in his pocket. He opened the cedar chest, removed a stack of clothes, and placed the manual at the bottom of the chest. From his coat, he retrieved the $1.50 he had stashed a couple days before, and he put the money into his pocket next to the folded note.

#

"This is what you want to order?" Walt looked at Jon with a bemused expression.

Nodding, Jon replied, "That's it."

A grin split Walt's face. "Ok, I got it. I mean, I don't got it, but I get that there's something I should get."

"No, I'm serious. I need it as soon as possible, too."

"All right," Walt said equably. "I can get the boss to order it, and we can have it in a day or two. But you know, even though the part won't cost much, the rush will add a lot of expense."

Jon reached into his pocket, pulled out the dollar bill and placed it on the counter. "Will that cover it?"

"Oh, yeah. That's more than enough."

Walt fixed him with an impish look. "You sure you're not just fooling with me?"

"Yes, I'm sure."

#

The last of her students had gone, and Marvella Wilson sat at the piano, absently tapping out a melody with one hand. She felt spent. It had been a trying afternoon, and she had found it difficult to concentrate.

Earlier, she'd had a testy telephone conversation with the owner of the home appliance store in Ridley, the nearest General Electric dealer. Apparently, no one would be able to look at her refrigerator for several days. And then they'd have to come all the way from Indianapolis.

It was a while before she even realized what song she was playing on the piano.

It was one of her own compositions, something she had written many years ago, primarily as an exercise for her students. It was a simple tune in the key of C minor, but it had a pleasing lilt and could be played with either hand in slight variations. When performed with both hands, it was quite beautiful, even she had to admit. It was a relatively easy piece to play, and, over the years, she had taught it to all of her students early in their lessons.

She'd never been able to complete it, however. The problem was finding the right transition for the bridge. Try as she might, she was unable to piece together a combination of chords that would do justice to the melody. As a consequence, the tune was simply a never-ending refrain, one that could be played as a round with alternating hands.

She called it "Claire's Song."

For a moment, the years fell away, and she was sitting on the bench next to Claire. The little girl was hunched over the keys, an intense expression on her face as she struggled to mimic the motions of her mother's hand. The small pink tip of her tongue protruded between her front teeth as it always did when Claire was concentrating. Marvella could smell the faint scent of lilac on the child's freshly shampooed curls.

A movement on the other side of the room shattered the moment, and the music came to a crashing halt as she dropped all five fingers onto the keyboard.

Her grandson was standing in the entrance to the hallway.

"I'm sorry," he said, immediately. "I didn't mean to interrupt. It's just that I heard the song you were playing. It's always been one of my favorites."

"Always?" she asked, after a moment.

"Well, ever since I can remember, yes. My mom taught me how to play it. But," he added, "I'm not very good. My brother, Sandy. Now, he was a whiz. You should have heard him. He could play anything."

She thought about that. "And your mother taught you this song?"

"Yes. The part you were playing just now I can play well. It's the rest I find hard."

She wasn't sure she had heard that correctly. "The rest?"

He nodded. "The next part. The bridge."

Eyes blinking rapidly, she said, "Can you show me?"

A look of surprise crossed his face, but he stepped forward without hesitation. "Sure. I'm a little rusty, but I'll give it a go."

Feeling a bit shaky, she slid off the bench and stepped away. With obvious self-consciousness, her grandson took a seat. He opened and closed both hands, flexing the fingers, then placed their tips on the keys. He stayed that way for a moment, head nodding in thought. Then, slowly, softly, he began to play.

He had a light touch, and she couldn't help but notice his technique was quite good. She followed along absently.

Suddenly, she realized what he was playing was different. Not completely different, she amended. A transposition of the original chords, but it worked, and it slid seamlessly from and back into the original melody, staying faithful to the tune, while providing a logical and interesting transition. Hearing it played now, it was so obvious to her.

How could she have missed it?

She stepped back, her legs catching on the front edge of the divan, and she sat down heavily. After some time, it dawned on her that the music had finished and her grandson was looking at her. She took a deep breath. "Did your mother have a name for that?"

"She just called it 'Mom's Song.' I've never heard it anywhere else. We didn't have sheet music for it." He paused, then looked at her with concern. "Are you ok?"

She squared her shoulders. "I'm fine. Really. Just a little tired. I'm going to sit here for a few minutes. Then I'll get dinner."

He nodded, rose, and started walking toward the hallway.

"Thank you," she said, softly.

He stopped, turned, and looked at her with an earnest expression.

"You're welcome."

#

When Jon entered the store late Friday morning, Walt was behind the counter as usual. Holding up a small item, he called out, "One relay switch, as you ordered, Mr. Meyer."

A jolt of excitement shot through Jon. Excitement tinged with trepidation.

"Thank you, Mr. Gallagher," Jon said, affecting a calm he did not feel. "Excellent service. I guess I won't have to drive down to Ridley Hardware after all."

"Bite your tongue, sir. Say, are you ever going to tell me what this is for?"

Jon accepted the small device from Walt and turned it over in his hand. "It's for a project I'm working on," he said. Then, as much to himself as to Walt, he added, "I'm not a hundred percent sure it'll work."

"So, what's the project?"

"Oh," Jon said with a slight smile, "that's top secret."

"You mean like one of those military things?"

Jon nodded. "Exactly. You know how it is. If I told you…"

"Then you'd have to kill me," Walt concluded. "Well, ok, Admiral. But don't keep ol' Walt in the dark too long, you know?"

"No, I won't," Jon replied, again fighting nagging doubts.

#

Jon had spent considerable time making his plans for the attempted repair of the refrigerator. He'd studied the manual carefully and identified the tools he would need. Earlier in the week, when his grandmother was out of the house, he again slipped into the work shed, located each of the necessary items and set them aside on a corner of the bench. All was ready for Saturday morning.

When he arose that morning, however, he found that his grandmother was still at home, a rare occurrence. He spent an anxious half hour in his room, hovering just inside the slightly open door, listening to the sounds made by his grandmother as she moved about the front of the house. With some misgivings, he eavesdropped on a pair of phone calls, one to a friend with whom she planned to get together, and another to the manager of an appliance store. Apparently, she had previously spoken to the manager, and, from the half of the call Jon could hear, he was not able to tell her when a service technician would come out and look at the refrigerator.

Finally, he heard his grandmother gather her things from the table and leave by the front door. He waited a few seconds. Then, stepping quietly from the bedroom, he tip-toed to the front window, lifted back the curtain, and watched as she turned up Main Street.

Now, it was time.

He went to the shed, retrieved the small collection of tools he had previously assembled, and carried them to the kitchen, where he arranged them on the counter. Then he unplugged the refrigerator and, with a small screwdriver, carefully detached the decorative ring surrounding the base of the compressor unit and pulled it away. Loosening the screws holding the unit to the cabinet, he lifted the assembly, located the terminals cover, and removed it, exposing the starter relay.

He referred briefly to the manual, and then, one by one, he disconnected the wires holding the relay to the compressor terminals, noting the locations for each. When he'd loosened each one, he gave a firm yank on the old relay, and it came away. Turning the piece over in his hand, he could see a slight deformation on the back. Upon closer inspection, the flaw appeared to be the result of copper melting into the housing. His spirits lifted.

He positioned the new part in the same location as the old, and, being careful to match the connections, attached the wires that dangled from the new unit to the compressor terminals. He then straightened, closed his eyes and said a quick prayer.

Holding his breath, he reached down and reinserted the plug into the electrical socket. After a tantalizing second, the compressor motor began to hum, there was a slight gurgling sound, and the hum settled into a steady rhythm. Jon released the air that he'd been holding in his lungs in a long, grateful expulsion.

He had done it.

He reached down once again to unplug the refrigerator, and, with a renewed sense of purpose, he methodically reassembled the compressor unit and reattached it to the top of the cabinet. When he was finished, he wiped down all of the surfaces with a soft cloth. He then plugged in the cord and stepped back.

The only evidence of his handiwork was the wonderful sound of an operating refrigerator.

#

Marvella Wilson led the young man from the market up the steps and held the door for him. He stepped past her, turned sideways and eased through the opening with a large box full of groceries.

"Just set it on the counter," she said briskly, taking off her hat and placing it on the dining room table next to her purse. "The refrigerated items will need to go down in the basement. There's an old ice box at the foot of the stairs." One finger at a time, she began removing her white gloves.

"Why don't we just put them in the refrigerator?" the young man called from the kitchen.

She made a sour face. "Unfortunately, the refrigerator is not working." She shook out the gloves, positioned them so that the fingers were matched up, and laid them across the top of the purse. "We'll have to make do."

"Seems ok to me," came the reply.

She turned and straightened. "What did you say?"

"I said it looks like it's working fine to me."

She walked to the kitchen door, where she saw the young man bent down in front of the refrigerator, one hand on the open door, and another inside the empty space, waving back and forth.

"It's plenty cold."

Eyes blinking rapidly, she stepped over to where the young man stood. She could feel the cold air escaping from the refrigerator.

"Oh my," was all she could say.

#

While Jon's meals with his grandmother continued to be awkward affairs, the overt hostility he had sensed when he first arrived in Jackson had faded over time, replaced by what Jon could only characterize as studied ambivalence. It seemed to Jon almost as if his grandmother was trying hard not to show any emotion. He, in turn, had learned to match her mood as a defensive mechanism. They'd essentially found an equilibrium, and neither was willing to upset the status quo. Their evening pas de deux might even have been comical, Jon reflected, if it hadn't been so downright uncomfortable.

His grandmother still hadn't acknowledged the money he'd been bringing home each week now for almost two months. Not that it bothered him terribly. While the cash represented a lot of money to Jon, he suspected it was not nearly enough to fully compensate her for the cost of taking him in. At least, he told himself, he had the knowledge that he'd made a reasonable attempt to lessen the financial burden he represented.

She had also never acknowledged his repair of the refrigerator. That, too, was ok with Jon. Had the matter come up in conversation, it would have necessitated addressing the question of where Jon found the tools to effect the repair. He'd not known for sure how he would handle that. Ironically, he had the sense she also did not know how to deal with it and had decided that silence on the subject was the safer, more expedient course of action.

Then, one evening late in August, to Jon's surprise, his grandmother actually initiated a conversation.

"I understand school will be starting in two weeks," she said as she spooned some peas onto her plate at dinner time. "Have you given any thought to how you'll get there?"

Surprised by the question, it took Jon a moment to react.

"I guess I'll walk. It's not that far."

"The school is over a mile away. You do know that, don't you?"

He nodded. "It's not a problem. I can walk. It's really not that far."

They ate in silence, and Jon assumed the conversation was over. After a couple of minutes, however, his grandmother spoke again.

"You know," she said, "there may be an alternative. I'll show you after dinner."

#

When they had cleared the dishes, Jon's grandmother motioned for him to follow her. She walked to the back door, stepped out, and went immediately to the work shed, Jon nervously in tow. At the door, she paused, and it appeared to Jon as though she was debating with herself. Then, as he had seen her do so many times, she squared her shoulders. Lifting the latch, she pulled the door open.

She flipped on the lights and stepped up onto the threshold, where she again paused. After a long moment, she strode purposefully to the back of the shed, turned around and pointed to an object resting against the pegboard wall opposite the workbench. Jon had previously noticed it, a shapeless form covered by an oilcloth, but he had not paid it much attention.

"What do you think of this?" she asked.

Jon stepped up into the shed and looked from his grandmother to the object and back. He made an inquiring gesture with his hands, as if to lift the cloth, and she nodded. He gripped the cloth with both hands and pulled it up and over.

Beneath the cover stood an old bicycle on two flat tires.

"I was thinking that, perhaps," she said slowly, "you might be handy enough to get this old thing back in running condition."

He could not be sure, but Jon thought he might have detected just a bit of wry humor in his grandmother's tone. He certainly wasn't going to take any chances.

"I'd like to try. Thank you."

"Good," she said with finality. "I believe you'll find all the tools you could possibly need right here in this shed."

#

Jon's dad had not been particularly handy about the house. He could hang pictures and, in a pinch, unclog a drain. But most repair jobs he left to "people who know what they're doing." That is, with one major exception. From the time he was a child, Frank Meyer had worked on bicycles.

Some of Jon's earliest memories were of sitting with his father, watching him repair bikes. And not just his own. It seemed that, whenever anyone in the neighborhood had a problem with a bike, it eventually made its way to the small garage behind the Meyer home, where Frank would spend hours in the evening after dinner happily tinkering.

When Jon and Sandy were old enough to ride bikes, they accompanied their father to the dump out past Great Neck, where, for a couple of dollars, the supervisor let them pick through a collection of discarded junk until they found two likely candidates and an ample collection of spare parts. Then Frank, with Jon and Sandy assisting, rebuilt both bikes. Over the next several years, with their father's help, Jon and Sandy retrofitted their prize possessions with whatever was the new rage, from balloon tires to aerodynamic fins, from headlights to speedometers. Somewhere back on Long Island, Jon reflected sadly, were a pair of bicycles that had been the envy of Nassau County.

His grandfather's old bike was certainly no Schwinn. It was a basic utility vehicle for a working man. Behind the seat, his grandfather had rigged a large, sturdy frame to hold a set of canvas saddlebags in which, his grandmother informed him, he had carried his tools and materials. Jon could tell the bike had been well-maintained at one time, but years of sitting untouched in the work shed through a succession of hot summers and frigid winters had taken a toll. In addition to the two flat tires, a couple of the wheel spokes had sprung, and the insidious onslaught of rust had spread to most of the metal surfaces.

Jon first disassembled the bike, separating the major components. He removed the tires and checked the tubes for leaks. One was fine, but the other had to be patched. The tires themselves were still in decent shape, so he cleaned those and set them aside. From Dahlgren's, he ordered replacement spokes with corresponding nipples, and, when they came in, he restrung and trued the wheels. The saddlebags were too worn and frayed to be of further use, so he discarded them and their support structure.

He spent several evenings laboriously scrubbing rust from the frame and priming the freshly cleaned surfaces. At the moment, he was in the process of repacking the bearings in the rear hub. It was a very messy job.

Jon could not remember the last time he'd been so happy.

A noise at the door of the shed caused him to pause and turn. His grandmother stood just outside the opening, illuminated by the soft light spilling from the structure.

"Do you mind if I come in?" she asked.

"Of course not."

As she planted a foot on the threshold, Jon pointed a greasy finger at the bicycle frame he had mounted on a makeshift stand just inside the door. "Careful, there are still some wet spots."

She stepped up into the shed, holding her robe close so as not to rub against the freshly primed metal. She stood straight and squared her shoulders. With an intent expression, she slowly surveyed the interior. Jon could see it was not the look of someone viewing something new or unfamiliar. Instead, it was the frank, appraising gaze of someone who knew what she was looking at and what she was looking for.

Finally, she nodded and said softly, "This is good." She turned in a complete circle and nodded again. "Yes. He would be pleased."

She made as if to leave, but, with one hand on the door, she turned slightly.

"Don't stay up too late. You need your rest."

"Yes, ma'am," Jon said. But she was already gone.

#

On Sunday, it was ready. Jon had reassembled all the parts, adjusted the brakes and checked the wheels for proper alignment. As a final touch, he had painted the frame a glossy black, using a pint of enamel he'd found under the bench in the shed. The black made the freshly polished metal of the spokes and crankset stand out. Though it was still just a utility vehicle, it had what Jon considered a snazzy look. Without admitting it to anyone else, he was as proud of this bicycle as he had been of anything he'd ever possessed.

He wheeled the bike around the side of the house, through the wooden gate and up to the curb in front of the stoop. His grandmother had left earlier for church, and the street was deserted, so there was nobody to observe him. It didn't matter to Jon. He didn't know anybody anyway.

He took a deep breath and swung a leg up over the seat, planting a foot on the raised pedal. He looked in both directions, suddenly uncertain where he should go. Then, for no reason other than the fact that the bike was already pointed that way, he shifted his weight from the foot resting on the curb, stepped down hard with his other foot, and allowed the bike to roll in the direction opposite the town.

Jon was immediately engulfed in a feeling at once familiar and unfamiliar. As his speed increased, the air washed over him, and it felt like a cleansing breeze. He had the sudden, irrational feeling he was escaping, as if a great, unseen force had somehow reached down and begun stripping away cobwebs and tentacles he'd not realized had been holding him.

Before he knew it, he was on a two-lane highway, pedaling at a rapid clip, fields and pastures whizzing by on either side, and not another vehicle or person in sight. The sense of freedom and exhilaration was overwhelming.

Through the euphoria, Jon only vaguely realized he was crying.

4

When Jon awoke on the morning of the first day of school, a thin shaft of light was peeking through the edge of the window shade and had splayed itself across a portion of the wall above his bed. It carried the promise of a bright, sunny day. With a sense of nervous anticipation, he hoped the weather would be a harbinger of good things.

Though it was a Monday, and, therefore, bridge day, Jon was surprised to find that his grandmother was not in the house when he emerged from his room. Unperturbed, he served himself breakfast. When he was finished, he cleaned his dishes, retrieved a notebook and a set of pencils from his room and made his way to the work shed.

The bike was sitting as he had left it the evening before, propped against the side wall. However, as he stepped up into the shed, he noticed something different. Hanging from the handlebars was an old khaki knapsack. Curious, he opened it and saw that it contained a brown paper bag. He pulled out the bag and looked at the contents. On top, he could see a sandwich neatly wrapped in wax paper. Beneath the sandwich he found an apple, and, nestled against the apple was something Jon hadn't seen in a long time. It was a package of one of his favorite treats, a Twinkie bar.

Jon shook his head in wonder. His grandmother had packed a lunch for him.

#

The ride to school took Jon no more than five minutes. Though his first sight of the building brought a momentary unpleasant memory of the encounter with the pickup truck, it passed quickly. The scene that confronted him this morning was completely different. What had been an empty parking lot in the rain was now a beehive of activity on a sun-splashed day.

Jon steered the bike into the lot and picked his way carefully across the uneven gravel surface to the front of the building, where he found a rack in which a half dozen other bicycles of myriad colors and styles had already been parked. After placing his bike in the rack, he shrugged off the knapsack, retrieved its contents, and hung it from the handlebar. He then followed a group of students up the broad steps to the large double doors.

In the vestibule just inside, Jon found a series of tables had been set up around the edges of the large entryway. He located the table with the letters "K—M" taped above it. Seated behind it was a wiry, athletic looking man who, at the moment, was sharing a laugh with two boys standing to the side of the table.

A line of students had formed in front of the table, and they were waiting for the man to finish his conversation with the two boys. Jon stepped up to the back of the queue and looked at his surroundings.

Light banter, punctuated by occasional outbursts, echoed off the tiled floor and marbled walls with a natural amplification that made a sound much louder than it would have been in a more open area. The faces of some of the students, particularly the younger ones, reflected varying levels of anxiety, but, for the most part, there was a sense of gaiety. It was not so different, Jon reflected, from his old school. He found that, by squinting and blocking out all but the general shapes in the milling crowd, he could believe he was back in Glen Cove.

As he reopened his eyes and focused, he was surprised to see another pair of eyes staring back at him from across the room. They were a pale, iridescent blue, almost transparent. Eyes like

Jon had never seen before. They were so mesmerizing, in fact, that it took Jon a second to realize they belonged to the girl with the tousled blond hair, the one he'd seen on the Fourth of July. She stood calmly looking at him. Not in a judgmental way. Not in a curious way, either. She was just looking at him.

They both stood that way for a long moment, eyes locked. Then someone near the girl said something, and she turned, laughing as she did.

A movement next to him drew Jon's attention. A boy about Jon's age was gesturing with one hand. He pointed past Jon and said, "Line's moving."

Jon saw that, indeed, the line had grown shorter. In fact, there was only one student ahead of him, and she was just turning away from the table with an envelope in her hand. Jon took a step forward. Suddenly, something very large and solid was in the space between Jon and the table, and Jon was staggering sideways, his lunch bag and school supplies falling in a scattered pattern on the hard floor. Jon was able to catch himself before he also hit the floor, his right hand reaching out in an instinctive gesture and grazing the tiles as he shuffled his feet to avoid falling. As he regained his balance and straightened, he found himself looking up into the face of the blond boy he'd first seen on the Fourth of July. The boy was at least ten inches taller than Jon, and, with his broad shoulders and sturdy build, he towered over him.

"You don't mind if I cut in, do you?" Without waiting for a reply, he added, "Of course you don't," and turned his back on Jon.

Without thinking, Jon tensed and was about to take a step toward the bigger boy when he felt a hand on his shoulder. Turning reflexively, he saw the face of the student who'd previously spoken to him. It was a ruddy face, with full cheeks dotted by freckles. The boy increased his grip on Jon's shoulder and gave a barely perceptible shake of his head.

"Nice pick," he heard a voice say, and, turning, he realized it was the man behind the table who was speaking. "But watch that rear foot sliding over. Wherever it is, plant it before the contact. Then, when you lean into the defender, don't make it so obvious."

The blond laughed and said, "Hi ya, Spitz,"

"King, good to see you," the man replied. "Been workin' out like I told you?"

"You bet."

Jon kneeled and collected his belongings from the floor. When he stood again and faced the table, the giant was sauntering away. The man seated behind the table gestured impatiently.

"Name?" he barked.

"Meyer. Jonathon."

"Meyer," the man repeated, leafing through the box of envelopes on his table, until he found the right one.

"Oh, yeah," he said, glancing up and, for the first time meeting Jon's eyes. "You're the new kid." He leaned forward and looked at Jon more carefully. "You play basketball?"

Jon let the question dangle for a moment. Then, with as much calm as he could muster, he replied, "No." And, after a beat, added, "Sir."

The man's eyes narrowed and he stared at Jon for a long moment. "Your loss," the man said, finally, tossing the envelope down on the table in front of Jon.

#

From across the hall, Mary watched the exchange between the new boy and Vernon, and the reaction, or, more to the point, the non-reaction of the teacher, and it made her angry.

"I honestly don't know who's the bigger bully," she said to Sam, without turning, "Vernon or Mr. Spitzman."

"Oh, I get it," Sam said. "You want to get run out of town on a rail, is that it?"

Mary looked at Sam. "No, that's not it. I just think there's too much importance placed on the basketball team. It's great that the town has something to be excited about. And I'm all for school spirit. But sometimes I think people get a little too carried away. And," she added quietly, "I don't think much of Mr. Spitzman."

"Well, he's only the most successful coach we've ever had. Everyone's saying we have a real chance this year to go to the state finals."

"Believe it," said a voice behind them, and they both turned as Billy Hamilton walked up, Gwenda at his side, her right arm linked protectively around Billy's left.

"This is our year," Billy said, proudly. "We've got all five starters returning. Most everybody else lost important players, including just about every school in our division. We can do something really special this year. Put Jackson on the map, maybe."

Mary nodded. "That would be special," she acknowledged.

Turning back, she watched as the new boy and Mr. Spitzman spoke. "Does anybody know who that guy is?"

Sam shook her head. "Never seen him before."

"I do," said Gwenda. "Missy Lambert told me he's from back east. He moved here this summer to live with old Mrs. Wilson. Must be a relative or something. She said she saw him there when she was taking piano lessons."

"He's been working at your father's store," Billy added. "I noticed him a few weeks ago."

Mary turned, surprised. "Really?"

Sam looked at Mary. "Your father never mentioned it?"

Mary gave Sam a sideways glance.

"Oh, right," Sam said. "Never mind."

"He's in our class," Gwenda said. "Or at least *our* class," she amended, squeezing Billy's arm and gesturing toward Sam. "Isn't it great we're all going to be in the same classroom again?"

"Yes," Mary agreed. The Jackson High student body was so small that the seventh and eighth graders shared classes, as did the ninth and tenth, and the eleventh and twelfth graders. Early the previous year, Mary's teachers had realized that, as a freshman, she'd been exposed to and had already mastered the sophomore curriculum. Their solution was to move her into the upper class, and she'd been separated from Sam and Gwenda. Now, that she was in twelfth grade, and other girls were in eleventh, they would once again be sharing the same classrooms.

Taking in the group, Mary smiled brightly and added, "This is definitely going to be a special year."

#

The first thing Agnes Tremaine did after entering her classroom was check the contents of the two boxes that had been left on the floor by her desk. Satisfied that the boxes contained the correct number of books, she took a seat at the desk, opened her leather folio and extracted a stack of papers. On top was a master roll. In addition to her normal task of teaching English for each of the six grades at Jackson High, she would be serving this year as the home room teacher for the combined eleventh and twelfth graders.

She scanned the list of students and noted a couple she did not expect to see in her classroom, if at all, until later in the semester. They were boys who lived on farms well outside of town and would almost certainly not appear until after the corn harvest was in.

The names on the list she knew well. This was Agnes' eighth year teaching at Jackson, a job she'd taken shortly after her graduation from Bryn Mawr. She had taught each of these students from the seventh grade on. There was only one unfamiliar name: Jonathon Meyer, the transfer from New York. She had been given a copy of his transcript, and he appeared to be a very good student. He was one of the two subjects occupying her thoughts this first morning of school.

The other was Mary Dahlgren. What was she going to do with Mary this year?

That Mary was a superb student was beyond question. The problem, or, better yet, the challenge, Agnes reflected, was going to be finding a way to keep Mary engaged. The year before, Mary had devoured not only the readings for the eleventh graders, but she'd taken it upon herself to read each of the works on the twelfth grade reading list. When she had sat for her final exam the previous spring, she'd done something unprecedented, taking both the eleventh and twelfth grade exams at the same time. Moreover—and, frankly, this had come as no surprise to Agnes—Mary had posted the highest scores on each exam. And it wasn't even close.

Over the summer, Agnes had corresponded with Julius Crittendon, the former superintendent of the school district. Dr. Crittendon had taken a keen interest in Mary's progress, and, even though he'd moved on to a new position in California, he had expressed a desire to remain engaged in her advancement.

From her stack of papers, Agnes withdrew the reading list that Dr. Crittendon had compiled. His suggestion to Agnes had been to put Mary on a course of independent study, utilizing the works on the list. It was quite an impressive collection of books. Some of them even Agnes had not read, and she was looking forward to the challenge.

She scanned the list again. Among them, Joyce, Dostoyevsky, Austen, Wilde, Tolstoy, Wharton, Brontë. The last name made Agnes chuckle. Not because it didn't belong on the list. Of course it did. But Dr. Crittendon, who should have known better, had listed Emily Brontë as the author of *Jane Eyre*. That classic novel, however, had been written by Emily's sister, Charlotte Brontë.

Activity at the door caught her attention, and she looked up as her students began to make their way into the classroom. She spotted Mary and called out to her. Mary said something briefly to Sam Parker, then turned and walked over to Agnes' desk.

"Good morning, Miss Tremaine."

"Good morning, Mary. Did you have a nice summer?"

"I did, thank you,"

Agnes was once again struck by just how poised and mature Mary acted. She actually seemed older than the other girls, though Agnes knew she was one of the youngest in the class.

"Mary, I've given some thought to your course of study this semester, and I'd like to show you a reading list I've compiled."

She plucked the sheet from the top of the stack on her desk and held it out. With a curious smile, Mary accepted the sheet and began reading it. Over Mary's shoulder, Agnes saw a face she did not recognize in the doorway. She was about to call out, when Mary said, "Excellent."

"I'm sorry?" Agnes said, refocusing her attention.

"This is a great list of books," Mary said, handing it back. "The only thing I would change is the entry for *Jane Eyre*. That was written by Charlotte Brontë, not Emily."

Agnes began to say something, then stopped. She looked at Mary, who returned her gaze with a frank openness. "Mary, you've read all of these, haven't you?"

"Oh, yes, and I think they're wonderful. I've got a couple of other suggestions, if you're interested."

Again, Agnes opened her mouth to speak, then changed her mind. She looked back at the list, then at Mary. Finally, she said, "Yes, let's talk about that later."

"Ok," said Mary, cheerfully. "I'll just grab a seat?"

Agnes nodded, and the girl turned and made her way down one of the aisles.

Shaking her head slowly, Agnes reached for another set of papers on her desk. This was the master reading list for each of the six grades that comprised the student body at Jackson. They were bound by a clip, and Agnes slipped the supplemental reading list she had shown to Mary behind the others.

Looking up, she made eye contact with the new boy whom she'd seen a moment earlier. He was standing just inside the doorway, looking uncertain. She beckoned for him to join her.

"You must be Jonathan."

"Yes, ma'am. Jon. Jon Meyer."

"Welcome to Jackson High, Jon. I'm Miss Tremaine, and I look forward to having you in my class. You're with the eleventh graders, so you'll want to take a seat on that side of the classroom," and she indicated the side nearest the door.

Jon took a step in that direction, and Miss Tremaine said, "Jon, wait just a moment." She held out the master reading lists. "The literature we'll be studying this year builds on themes we've explored in prior years. Because you're new to the school district, I don't want you to be disadvantaged. Do you mind taking a moment to look at the lists here, and let me know what you have and haven't read?"

"Of course," Jon said, accepting the proffered pages.

Agnes was about to point out to Jon that he need only look at the first four pages, representing the reading lists for grades seven through ten, but she was distracted by a sudden loud noise. She looked up as the room went still and saw that everyone had turned in the direction of the far aisle, where Vernon King stood over a desk already occupied by another student. She could barely make out the curly hair of Charlie Morris behind a large canvas bag sitting on the top of the desk. Agnes guessed the noise she'd heard had been the bag being dropped on the desk with some force.

"I think this is going to be my desk this year," Vernon said casually, looking at Charlie.

"Now hold on just a moment," Agnes began, but, before she could say another word, Charlie had scrambled to his feet and backed quickly away from Vernon.

"Vernon," she called, "you can have any unoccupied desk on this side of the room." She indicated the half of the classroom that was closest to the window. "But Charlie has already selected that desk."

"I don't mind." Charlie's voice was an octave higher than normal. "He can have it."

"No," Agnes said, but Vernon interrupted.

"That's ok, Charlie. Miss Tremaine is absolutely right. You've already selected this desk. And I've changed my mind anyways. I think I like that desk better," and he pointed to an empty desk in the next row over.

He picked up the bag and took a step in Charlie's direction. Charlie retreated further, as Vernon slid easily between the desk recently vacated by Charlie and the one behind it.

Agnes grimaced inwardly. Vernon King had never been a model student, but he'd become progressively more difficult to handle over the years. She could tell he was going to try her patience this year. Oh well, after this year, she would be done with him.

She turned her attention back to Jon, who was holding out the reading lists.

"I've read them."

"All of them?"

"Yes, ma'am."

"Oh, good," she said. "That'll make things easier."

He nodded in agreement. "One thing, though."

"Yes?"

"*Jane Eyre* was written by Charlotte Brontë, not Emily."

Agnes opened her mouth to speak, stopped, then let out a slight chuckle. "You're right. Of course. Thank you for pointing that out."

She watched as the young man located an empty desk and took a seat. Oh, boy, she thought to herself. This year was going to be interesting.

#

On the second day of school, things for Jon went very bad very quickly.

The third class each day was health and physical education. It was the one class for which the boys and girls were separated. The boys' class was taught by Mr. Spitzman, the basketball coach. On the first day of school, Mr. Spitzman had handed out textbooks, assigned reading to the class, and then proceeded to take aside what amounted to almost half the boys for a raucous chat session. Mr. Spitzman was anything but subtle. For him, there were two types of students: Those that played on the basketball team and those that didn't.

After class on the first day, Jon had sought out the ruddy faced boy who had been behind him in line that morning. His name was Doug Larson.

"Has it always been like this?" Jon had asked.

"Yep," Doug had replied, "ever since Spitz got here. And that's been about four years, now."

"How does he get away with that?"

Doug had laughed. "Are you gonna tell him he can't? I wouldn't try if I was you. Look," Doug had added, with a serious expression, "Spitz is like a god around here. And so are the players on the basketball team. You don't want to cross them. You won't get any sympathy from anyone, and he'll make your life miserable."

On the second day, the boys did not convene in the classroom. Instead, with a growing sense of concern, then alarm, Jon followed his fellow classmates to the gymnasium. Each of the other students had retrieved gym bags or rolled towels from their lockers. Jon had nothing other than his textbook. No one had told him he needed gym clothes, and it had simply not occurred to him that he would.

#

"Where the hell are your gym clothes?"

They were in the boys' locker room, a narrow, rectangular space, with open lockers lining the walls, in front of which sat a series of small wooden benches. The other boys had changed into shorts and t-shirts, several of them giving Jon surreptitious glances as he sat nervously waiting for Mr. Spitzman. When the latter arrived, Jon had immediately stood and approached him, intending to explain himself.

"Sir, I don't have any. I wasn't aware I needed them for this class…"

"You didn't think you needed gym clothes for gym class?"

"Sir, I…"

"Not another word." Mr. Spitzman looked around the room. "Does anyone here think it's ok that Meyer doesn't have gym clothes for gym class?"

No one spoke, though there were a few sniggers. Jon could see that several of the boys were avoiding eye contact, but a few seemed to be enjoying the confrontation.

"Fletcher, what do you think we should do about Meyer?" Mr. Spitzman asked.

Jon looked at the subject of Mr. Spitzman's inquiry. Jeff Fletcher was a twelfth grader, a year older than Jon, though he seemed even older than that. Fletcher feigned deep concentration for a moment. Then he said brightly, "Medicine ball."

"Medicine ball," repeated Mr. Spitzman. "Outstanding."

"Larson," Mr. Spitzman said, looking at the freckled faced boy, "go get one of the medicine balls out of the equipment room."

The boy nodded quickly, jumped up and left the room.

Mr. Spitzman returned his attention to Jon. "You. Follow me."

He led Jon out onto the main floor of the gymnasium and indicated a spot against the wall. "Stand there."

Doug Larson appeared, carrying what looked like an oversized basketball. Mr. Spitzman took the object and held it up in front of Jon.

"Hands over your head."

Jon complied. Mr. Spitzman cradled the ball in one hand, raised it up over Jon's head and placed it between Jon's hands.

"Grab it."

Jon did as he was told, gripping the ball on either side. It remained there, with both Jon and Mr. Spitzman supporting it. Then, Mr. Spitzman let go, and the ball slipped and almost fell. Jon had to squeeze hard, then regrip in order to avoid dropping it. This was no basketball, he realized. A basketball, Jon knew, weighed about a pound and a half. This thing weighed several times that.

"Now," Mr. Spitzman said, leaning in and putting his face inches from Jon's. "You will hold this ball above your head for the duration of the class. You will not drop it. In fact, you will not allow it to go below where it is now. Do you understand?"

Jon nodded.

"I didn't hear that," Mr. Spitzman said.

"Yes, sir."

"Good." Mr. Spitzman turned his back on Jon and faced the other boys. "Since Meyer has decided he doesn't need to follow the rules, we'll have to stay indoors today."

A few of the boys booed or hooted in contempt.

"All right," Mr. Spitzman called out over the noise, "let's split up into two teams for dodgeball. King and Fletcher, you select."

After a few minutes, Jon's arms and shoulders began to ache. In an effort to find relief, he experimented with the position of the ball. He discovered that, by sliding his palms beneath it, he could take some of the pressure off his upper arms. But his shoulders still throbbed, and, soon, the throbbing morphed into a burn. After a time, all he could focus on was the excruciating pain radiating down from his wrists, through his arms and shoulders and across his back. His world having shrunk to a small, agonizing place, he closed his eyes and squeezed them tightly, trying to force out all thought. Starbursts of light exploded on the backs of his eyelids in synch with the sharp stabs of pain that came now with increasing frequency.

The ball in his hands seemed to weigh at least a hundred pounds. His head drooped, and his chin touched his chest. He could feel sweat running down his face, soaking the front of his shirt and dripping off the tip of his nose. A shaking began in his arms and shoulders. He tried to still it, but he could not control himself. Slowly, inevitably, his hands began to sag.

Suddenly, he was struck in the midsection by something hard. His eyes flew open in time to see a soccer ball ricochet off his body, land on the floor and bounce away.

"You better not drop that ball, Meyer," Mr. Spitzman yelled.

The teacher was standing a few yards away, Vernon at his side. Through the pain fogging his mind, Jon wondered who had thrown the ball that struck him. Something cold and raw stirred within him. He raised his chin. His arms stopped shaking. Slowly, deliberately, he pushed the medicine ball upwards until his elbows locked. He stared back defiantly.

"All right, that's it," Mr. Spitzman said, turning away after a moment. "Time to shower up." The rest of the boys filed toward the locker room.

The door at the far end of the gym swung open, and the girls began to enter. Several of them pointed at Jon, and he could hear laughter. Holding his chin high, he looked straight ahead and kept his expression stoic. From the corner of his eye, he saw Mary Dahlgren come through the door. Though she looked in his direction, she neither pointed nor laughed. He took irrational solace from that. Gritting his teeth, he swore to himself he would not drop the ball.

Eventually, a quiet descended on the gymnasium. Several minutes passed before he heard a door open and footsteps approached. Doug Larson came into his field of vision.

"Spitz says you can put it down now."

Jon looked at him, uncertainly.

"I'm serious," Doug said, reaching out with both hands. "Here, let me help."

With a jerky motion, Jon began lowering the medicine ball. He'd gotten it down no more than a foot or so when it slipped from his hands, and Doug caught it. He continued lowering his hands until they were down at his sides. He felt lightheaded, and he was struck with a wave of nausea. He staggered. Doug moved as though to catch him, but Jon was able to retain his balance. He put his hands on his knees and took several deep breaths.

"The department store in Ridley is where most everyone gets their gym clothes," Doug said, quietly. "But, if you can't get there after school today, you should be able to find some at Molly's Thrift Shop on Main Street, next to the hardware store."

Hands still on his knees, Jon looked up and nodded. "Thanks."

"Sure," said Doug. He stood awkwardly, holding the medicine ball against his hip with one hand. Then he tilted his head in the direction of the locker room. "I gotta put this back."

Again, Jon nodded, and he watched as the other boy walked away. With difficulty, he straightened and slowly followed.

#

When Mary came downstairs for breakfast, her father was at the kitchen table, reading the paper. She served herself a bowl of cereal and sat down across from him.

"Dad?" she asked as she poured milk into the bowl.

"Hmm?" he muttered without looking up.

"Dad," she repeated.

Head still buried in the paper, he reached for his coffee cup and raised it to his lips. In mid-sip, there was an inchoate sound that might or might not have been a response.

"Dad!"

Her father lowered the paper and looked at her. "Yes?"

"Good morning."

"Good morning," he replied. He sat back and gave her an inquiring look. After a moment, he asked, "Is everything ok at school?"

"Everything's great." Sifting a spoonful of sugar into the cereal, she asked casually, "Is everything ok at the store?"

Her father cocked his head. "Fine. Why do you ask?"

She looked up and smiled. "Oh, just curious. You never talk about the store these days."

He returned the smile. "Well, honey, everything is just fine."

She took a bite of cereal and chewed it slowly. After a moment, he lifted the paper and resumed reading.

"So who's working there these days? I mean, besides Walt."

Her father lowered the paper and gave her a quizzical look. "Well, you know Bobby left at the end of June. So I hired a new boy to replace him."

"Oh, really?" she said, studying her spoon with sudden interest.

"Yes." He arched an eyebrow. "As a matter of fact, you probably know him from school."

"Oh? Who would that be?"

Smiling slightly, he replied, "That would be Jonathon Meyer."

"Oh, yeah? The new guy. How about that."

"How about that."

She took another bite of cereal. Rather than resuming his reading, however, her father left the paper on the table and looked at her expectantly.

"So," she said, finally, "he still works there now that school's started?"

Still smiling, he replied, "He does. Same hours as Bobby. After school and Saturdays. Why the sudden interest in Jonathon Meyer?"

"Jon," she said quickly. "I'm pretty sure he likes to be called Jon."

"I didn't know that." He nodded thoughtfully. "He probably prefers 'Jon' to 'the new guy' too, huh?"

He was having fun with her now. She decided it was time to change the subject. "That was quite a storm we had last night, wasn't it?"

"Yes, quite a storm."

She ate in silence, and he sipped his coffee, also in companionable silence. After a few minutes, she got up from the table, washed her bowl and utensils and turned to leave.

"Honey."

She stopped at the door. "Yes, Dad?"

"I think Jonathon...Jon...is a nice boy."

"Oh, ok," she replied with an airy nonchalance. "That's good to know." As she walked into the hallway, she could hear her father chuckling softly to himself. She felt her cheeks flush, but she was not angry. No, she was definitely not angry.

#

Mr. Hanson was like no teacher Jon had ever known. He was not as old as Jon's grandmother, but still pretty old. Of course, that didn't make him all that much different from other teachers. It wasn't his age that set him apart. It was the way he taught.

First of all, he sat while teaching, with his feet up on the desktop, exposing the soles of an old pair of shoes that looked to be just about worn through. Even that, though, wouldn't have merited much note. It was what he did next that Jon found fascinating.

While seated with his feet on his desk, Mr. Hanson leaned back in his chair with a piece of chalk gripped between the middle and ring fingers of his left hand, and, with the palm of his hand facing forward, he wrote on the blackboard behind him. His handwriting was a little sloppy, granted, but no worse than the handwriting of most teachers. To Jon, it was incredible he could write at all in that position, as he was effectively writing upside down and backwards. Apparently, Mr. Hanson had been doing it for so long it was second nature to him.

It was Wednesday morning, and they were in Mr. Hanson's second period math class.

"Who can tell me the sine of angle A in this right triangle?" asked Mr. Hanson.

Among the twelfth graders, only one hand went up.

"Yes, Mary?"

"The sine would be three fifths, or point six oh."

"And you got that how?"

"By dividing the length of the side opposite the angle by the length of the hypotenuse."

"That's right," said Mr. Hanson, reaching behind himself and, without looking, scrawling "Sin A = O/H = .60" on the blackboard.

"Now, who can tell me the cosine of angle A?"

No hands came up immediately. After a moment, Mary again raised her hand.

Mr. Hanson made a show of peering out around his battered oxfords, rotating his heels so he could look first to the left of his toes, then to the right. Finally, he splayed the tips of the shoes and looked intently between them, his eyes slowly taking in the entire side of the room occupied by the older students. Still, the only hand in the air belonged to Mary. He affected a dour expression.

"Let me rephrase the question. Who, *other than Mary*, can tell me the cosine of angle A?"

Mary lowered her hand and seemed to duck her head in embarrassment. At least that's the way it appeared to Jon, who, though hunched over the piece of paper sitting on his desk, was covertly watching the twelfth graders being taken through the basics of trigonometry.

The paper on Jon's desk contained a series of problems that were designed to test how well the eleventh graders had absorbed their first couple of lessons in advanced algebra. It had taken Jon less than ten minutes to complete the calculations. Much of the subject matter he'd already covered in his freshman algebra class at his old school.

Four fifths, he said to himself. Point eight oh.

With about ten minutes to go in the class, Mr. Hanson assigned reading to the twelfth graders, unfolded his lanky frame from his desk seat, stood and began writing in a conventional way on the blackboard. What he wrote was a long arithmetic formula with symbols Jon had never seen before. When he was done, he turned and motioned to Mary.

"Mary, I'd like you to write this down. This is going to be your assignment for the next week. I want you to either solve for 'x' or tell me why it can't be solved. Everything you need for that is in the first three chapters of your textbook. However, you'll need to do some independent thinking about how to get to the answer from where we're starting."

Mary took out a sheet of paper, and she began transcribing the problem Mr. Hanson had written on the board.

Mr. Hanson then collected the quiz papers from the eleventh graders and released the class. As soon as Jon had turned in his paper, he pulled out another sheet, and, as the rest of the class filed out, he quickly scribbled down the problem on the board, finishing just as the last of his classmates exited the room.

Jon hastily stuffed the paper in his notebook, stood and gathered his things. As he was leaving, he glanced at Mr. Hanson, who had resumed his normal spot at the desk and was reviewing the papers he had collected. Mr. Hanson looked up at Jon over the top of the papers and gave him an enigmatic smile.

#

The boys rounded the last turn and began the run in toward the finish line. A few sprinted ahead. Jon could see they were all members of the basketball team. At the finish, Billy Hamilton just managed to edge out his backcourt mate, Cyrus Clayton.

Jon was content to pace himself. The run they were completing had taken them around the large field behind the school three times, about a mile and a half by Jon's estimation. It had served as a reminder that he'd not been exercising over the summer. He was a bit winded.

As each boy reached the finish line, Mr. Spitzman consulted a stopwatch and recorded their times. After Jon crossed the finish, he slowed to a walk and put his hands on his hips, drawing in deep breaths. Several of the other boys bent over with their hands on their knees.

Jon was dressed in the clothes he had purchased the prior afternoon, a pair of navy blue shorts with white piping and a white t-shirt with the initials "JHS" stenciled across the front. He was wearing a pair of canvas athletic shoes he had brought with him from New York. The clothes were the closest fit he'd been able to manage given the limited selection at Molly's. The shorts weren't too bad, but the t-shirt was at least a size too big. He had tucked as much of the excess material of the shirt into the waistband of his shorts as he could. It wasn't pretty, but it was a heck of a lot better than being without gym clothes and incurring Mr. Spitzman's wrath.

"All right," the gym teacher called out, striding toward the door to the gym, "hit the showers."

The boys who had been bent over straightened, and the group began following. An instinct told Jon to hold back, and he waited as the others entered the building. Then, as he reached for the door, he heard voices. A moment later, the girls came around the corner of the building. They were each carrying some sort of wooden stick that Jon had never seen before.

With his hand on the knob, Jon stepped back and held the door open for them. As they filed past, a few gave him friendly looks and murmured thanks.

"You are most kind, sir," Sam Parker said with a dramatic wave of a hand.

She passed through, and Jon saw, with a start, that the last girl was Mary Dahlgren. As she approached the doorway, she gave Jon a direct look. He wasn't sure, but he thought there might have been a smile playing at the corners of her mouth. At the threshold, she paused, held the look for a long second, then stepped into the building.

Jon inhaled deeply. His heart seemed to be beating faster than it had at the end of the run. He held the breath for a moment before letting it out slowly. Then, with a renewed sense of energy, he swung around the door and made as if to step into the building. He was immediately brought up short. Filling the doorway, was the imposing figure of Vernon King.

Vernon reached out one of his big hands, laid it on Jon's chest and pushed hard. Jon stumbled backwards a few feet. Vernon stepped out of the gym, allowing the door to close behind him.

"What are you doing?" Jon asked.

"What am *I* doing? I think the question is what are *you* doing."

Puzzled, Jon said, "I don't know what you're talking about."

"I'm talking about Mary."

"Mary?" Jon repeated, his confusion deepening.

"That's right. Mary." Vernon took another step toward Jon. Speaking slowly, he said, "You leave her alone."

Jon shook his head, as if to clear it. "I wasn't…"

But Vernon had again planted a hand on Jon's chest, and again he gave Jon a hard shove.

As before, Jon staggered backwards. Anger flashed in him. "That's the last time," he said, raising a finger.

A nasty smile spread on Vernon's face. "Oh yeah?" He stepped closer and put his hand out. This time, however, before he made contact, Jon pushed his hand to the side. Without thinking about it, Jon lowered his head and charged at Vernon. His shoulder drove into Vernon's chest, and, somewhat to Jon's surprise, the bigger boy went down.

Jon crouched, facing Vernon, uncertain what to do next. Vernon made a growling sound and began scrambling to his feet. Instinctively, Jon stepped toward him, thinking only that it would be a bad idea if Vernon got up. Suddenly, Jon felt pressure on his back as someone grabbed a handful of his t-shirt. With a ripping sound, he was yanked hard, and he found himself stumbling backwards. He windmilled his arms, trying to keep his balance, but failed, finally landing on his behind, stunned. When he looked up, Mr. Spitzman was glowering down at him.

#

Over the years, Ed Spitzman had developed several highly successful athletic teams by employing a simple set of rules, rules that he enforced with an iron discipline. He'd found that, by making it clear what was expected of each team member and by rigidly adhering to that code of behavior, he could mold a group of disparate young men into a cohesive and effective unit.

One of his rules was no fighting.

He looked down at the new kid, Meyer. He'd already had to discipline the boy once for not being prepared. And here he was again, breaking another of Spitzman's essential principles. He stared at the boy for a long moment. Then he turned to King. "Who started this?"

"He did," both boys said at once.

Spitzman whirled on Meyer. "When I'm ready to hear from you, I'll let you know." Returning his attention to King, he said again, "Who started this?"

"He did," King repeated, nodding toward Meyer. "I don't know why. I think there's something wrong with him."

One of Spitzman's other rules was loyalty to your teammates. It was one of the most sacrosanct. He considered King for a long moment. He wanted to believe him. He almost did. Finally, then turned and looked at Meyer. "All right. Give me another lap."

The boy was clearly stunned. "Why? Don't you want to know…"

"You want to go for two?" Spitzman shot back.

The boy blinked. He didn't immediately move, and Spitzman thought he might try to defy him. Then, slowly, the kid stood. He looked between Spitzman and King, hesitated, then turned and began jogging toward the field.

"Thanks, Spitz," King said.

"Not now. Hit the showers."

After King had gone, Spitzman watched Meyer run the course. There was something different about the boy. He couldn't put his finger on it, and it bothered him. Meyer finished his lap and, without a glance in Spitzman's direction, jogged to the door and entered the gym. Spitzman continued staring out across the field. What was it, he asked himself, but the answer still eluded him. After a couple of minutes, he shrugged, turned and entered the gym.

He crossed the floor of the basketball court and was on his way to his office when the door leading to the boys' locker room opened and Cyrus Clayton stepped halfway out, his hair wet and a towel wrapped around his waist.

"Hey Spitz, you might want to come take a look at this."

Annoyed, Spitzman nevertheless followed Clayton into the locker room. The boys were in various stages of dressing, and water still ran in the showers. Clayton motioned for him to step over to the shower room entrance. It led to a space even smaller than the locker room, bare, save for a series of shower heads placed a few feet apart along the tiled walls.

There was only one person in the shower, standing under the spray from one of the nozzles. At the moment, the kid had his head tilted back, rinsing shampoo out of his hair.

Spitzman was about to ask Clayton why the hell he'd called him in. Then he didn't need to.

Spitzman had played his college ball at Notre Dame and had stayed two years following graduation as an assistant coach. After that, there had been a succession of high school coaching jobs in Ohio and Pennsylvania. It wasn't until the year preceding his coming home to Indiana and taking the job at Jackson that he'd seen a circumcised penis. At the time, he'd been coaching at a small school in Maryland, and there were two Jews on the team, neither of whom was any good. He'd run them off pretty early on.

So that was it. None of the boys here had ever seen a Jew. Until now.

Meyer had turned and was looking at him. They held eye contact for several seconds. Then Spitzman hawked, spat on the floor and walked out.

5

Marvella Wilson set her knitting aside, reached over and turned off the radio. Too much talk of war. It had once seemed so far removed, that conflict raging an ocean away, confined to images in newspapers and magazines, terrible to be sure, but still of no immediate threat. These days, however, it was impossible to avoid the notion that, as inconceivable as it was, America might find itself drawn into the horror. Every day brought a higher level of belligerent discourse. Just a week earlier, President Roosevelt had gone on the radio and accused the Nazis of trying to control the seas by ruthless force. He'd likened Germany to a rattlesnake poised to strike and had exhorted the nation not to wait until it had done so before crushing it. The image was chilling.

In the hallway, Marvella paused by the door to her grandson's room. It was open, and she could see the room was empty. He must be in the work shed, she told herself. A glance out the rear door window confirmed her suspicion. Light from the open shed illuminated a patch of the rear yard.

He had been unusually reserved that evening at dinner. There was clearly something wrong. She had been tempted to ask him about it, but she'd held back. She stood peering out for a long time. Finally, she pulled the ends of her shawl together, opened the door, and stepped out into the cool evening air. At the entrance to the shed, she paused.

He was sitting on one of the stools, bent over the workbench, his profile a study in concentration. Whatever he was working on she couldn't see from this angle. Something about the whole tableau, however, was extraordinarily familiar, and it triggered a strong emotion. What was it? She felt she should know.

And then it hit her.

His posture, the way he held his head, tipped just so, the furrowed brow, the set of his jaw. She caught her breath. My God. He looks just like a young version of Ernest. She stared in wonder, then shook her head. How had she failed to notice that until now? Or had she noticed it and chosen to ignore it?

Shaken, it took her a moment to recover. Then she knocked lightly on the door frame.

He turned, a look of surprise on his face. Surprise and something else. Was it guilt? No. Embarrassment maybe?

"Hi," he said, quickly. "You surprised me."

She noticed that he leaned a little toward the door, which had the effect of placing his body between her and whatever he had been working on.

"May I come in?"

He hesitated a split second, before replying, "Of course."

Once she was up in the shed, she could see what was on the bench in front of him. A piece of clothing of some kind. Next to it was a pair of scissors and a spool of thread. Lying across the top of the garment where it had obviously just been dropped was a sewing needle. A length of thread was inserted in the needle, the longer end of which ran to a point in what appeared to be a hem. She looked more carefully at the object and realized it was a t-shirt.

"You're sewing."

"Yes, ma'am."

"May I see it?" she asked, reaching out a hand, and, again, for a brief moment, he hesitated. Then he reached down, picked up the needle with the fingers of one hand, lifted the shirt with the other, and handed everything to her.

With a practiced gesture, she slipped the needle through the fabric so as to keep it from falling, held the shirt up and shook it out. It was torn in two places. The seam in the right shoulder had separated and the fabric itself was ripped at a spot in the middle of the back. She could understand a seam coming loose, but it would have taken a lot of effort to tear the fabric. She turned the garment around, noticed the initials on the front, then noticed something else.

"Is this yours?" she asked.

"Yes, ma'am."

"This is much too big for you. Where did you get it?"

"At Molly's Thrift Shop."

"And you need this for school?"

He nodded.

"Tomorrow?"

Again, he nodded.

She was about to ask him how it became torn, but there was something in his expression that made her stop. Instead, she studied the stitches her grandson had already made and shook her head.

As handy as Ernest had been, he couldn't sew worth a lick. Apparently, her grandson suffered the same shortcoming. She folded the shirt loosely, and, holding it in one hand, reached out and plucked the spool of thread off the workbench. "This won't take me but a few minutes."

He opened his mouth to protest, but she gave him a look, and he stopped. "Thank you," he said, simply.

#

Things were slow at the hardware store on Thursday afternoon, so Jon took a seat on one of the stools and opened a book he'd checked out of the library. It was the same trigonometry text that the twelfth graders were using in Mr. Hanson's class. The school, he'd discovered, kept a few extra copies of the textbooks in the library.

He was trying to figure out the problem Mr. Hanson had assigned to Mary. He'd been noodling it all day, whenever he had a spare moment.

"Whatcha reading?" asked Walt, as he stepped through the back door. Walt had taken advantage of the lull to use the toilet in the storeroom.

Jon held up the book so Walt could see the cover.

"Trigonometry," Walt grimaced. "That hurts my head just saying it." He stepped up to the counter and leaned against it with one elbow. "Is that your toughest class?"

"Not really. I won't be taking this class until next year."

"You're not even in the class, and you're reading the book?" Walt asked incredulously.

Jon laughed. "It's kind of hard to explain."

"You like to read a lot, huh?"

"I love to read. Don't you?"

Walt shook his head solemnly. "Let me put it this way: Ol' Walt has never met a book he couldn't ignore."

"Don't you like stories?"

"I love stories."

"You're missing out on so many good stories by not reading. Here," Jon said, pulling one of the books from the stack on the counter and holding it out. "I just read this for the second time. It's a great story."

Walt took the book from Jon and turned it over in his hands. "*The Mayor of Casterbridge*," he read. "Hey, sort of like the boss."

"Well, the main character *is* a mayor. But it's about a lot more than that."

"Got a lot of action, huh?"

"It depends on what you mean by action. But, sure, there's a lot that happens."

Walt looked again at the book with a dubious expression. Finally, he shrugged and said, "Ok. What the heck."

He came around the counter and placed the novel on the shelf. Glancing over Jon's shoulder, he pointed to the sheet of paper on which Jon had transcribed Mr. Hanson's problem. "What is that, a code?"

"Well, sort of. Each one of these symbols has a meaning"

Walt picked up the sheet and held it closer to the light. He turned it upside down. Then, apparently deciding it didn't make any more sense that way, turned it back again. Finally, he returned it to the counter.

"So, what does it say?"

"That's kind of what I'm trying to figure out. What I don't understand is why or how this part," and Jon pointed to the last line of the equation, "equals zero."

"Well, it's a cinch I don't know," Walt said, sliding his stool over to the counter. "So what good is any of this stuff anyway?"

"Oh, believe me, you can do a lot of things with this."

"Yeah? Like what?"

Jon thought for a moment. "Ok, you know that big elm tree by the funeral parlor?"

"Sure."

"Would you be able to figure out how tall it is?"

"Oh yeah, piece o' cake."

Bemused, Jon asked, "How?"

"I'd climb it," Walt said, as he struggled to pull himself up on his stool, "with a measuring stick." Settling onto the seat, he gave Jon a self-satisfied look.

"You would climb the tree," Jon deadpanned.

"I've climbed lots of trees."

Jon looked at Walt skeptically. "Have you climbed any lately?"

"No."

John chuckled. "Well, ok. Let's say you climbed the tree. While you were climbing the tree, I could sit at the bottom and eat my lunch."

"Why would you be eating your lunch?"

"I'm just making a point. While you're doing all that work climbing, I'm not working at all," he said, then added, "I don't have to be eating lunch."

"You could be eating lunch if you wanted to."

"Right. The point is this. Long after you started climbing the tree, but before you got to the top, I could stand up, pace out fifty feet from the trunk, take a reading from my protractor here," he held up the small plastic device, "and, with a couple of calculations, I could tell you exactly how tall the tree is. It would take me all of one minute, and I would never need to leave the ground."

"Why fifty feet?"

"It doesn't have to be fifty feet. It could be sixty feet."

"Well, which would it be? Fifty or sixty?"

"Oh, for heaven's sake, Walt. It doesn't matter."

"I know. I'm just havin' fun with you," Walt said, laughing. "Here's the thing though," he said, affecting a serious look and speaking with an exaggerated solemnity. "I am never, ever, in a million years, gonna wanna know how tall that tree is." He arched his bushy eyebrows and grinned. "So, I guess I don't need to know trigonometry now, do I?"

Jon was about to respond when the bell above the front door tinkled, and Mary Dahlgren stepped into the store.

#

Mary had spent the previous half hour across the street at the diner. She'd seen no customers enter the store, so it didn't surprise her to see Jon and Walt sitting alone at the counter.

"Hey, Mary," Walt called out, "haven't seen you here in, gosh, I don't know how long."

She paused, just inside the door. For the hundredth time, she asked herself just what in the world she was doing. For the hundredth time, she had no ready answer. She took a deep breath, smiled brightly, and said, "Hi. I, um, just stopped by to surprise my dad."

"Oh," Walt said, "he's not here right now."

She knew that. In fact, she knew exactly where he was. It was Thursday afternoon, so he would be at the city hall, going over paperwork and getting ready for the city council meeting that evening.

"He's not? Gee, that's too bad."

She was still standing just inside the door, not having taken a step since entering. She could see that Jon was looking at her in that intense, curious way he had, with his head slightly tilted. She realized she had to do something. She stepped over to the counter and set down the books she'd been holding across her chest.

"Hey," Walt exclaimed immediately, "look at that. You've got the same trigonometry book as Jon."

Jon seemed to flinch at Walt's words. The comment also struck her as odd, but she didn't immediately focus on it. Then she cocked her head and said, "Trigonometry?"

"Yeah, yeah," said Walt, "the secret code." He snatched the sheet of paper off the counter a fraction of a second before Jon could reach it. "See," he said, laying it down in front of Mary. "We're having trouble figuring out why this part equals zero," and he punched the last line of the equation with a stubby finger.

She looked down at the page and the familiar equation. When she looked up, Jon's cheeks had reddened.

"Yes," she said, "I'm having trouble with that as well."

There was an awkward pause. Then Jon said, slowly, looking intently at the page and avoiding eye contact, "I think it has something to do with the cosine having an even function."

She was about to ask him why he had the same equation that Mr. Hanson had assigned to her when what he had said caused her to stop. "Of course," she said, "that would mean the coefficients for all of the odd powers have to equal zero." She slipped a pencil out of her notebook. "What if you assume this," and she made a notation on the sheet.

Jon looked at what Mary had written and furrowed his brow in concentration. "Then," he said thoughtfully, reaching out and rotating the page, "multiplication of the denominator and substitution of the series would yield this," and he scribbled out a new line on the page. He turned the sheet back around and showed it to Mary, looking up at her, his hazel eyes now bright with enthusiasm.

She felt an intense excitement. Glancing back and forth between the page and his eyes, she concluded, "And, the only possible result is zero. Oh my God, that's it."

She stood there, looking at him, her heart racing. This time, he did not look away.

Walt beamed. "Isn't this great? Anyone want to go measure some trees?"

The bell above the front door tinkled again, and all three of them turned to look. This time, it was Jim Dahlgren who walked through the entrance. Obviously in a hurry, he made immediately for the stairway, then he suddenly pulled up short with a classic double take.

"Mary, what are you doing here?"

For the hundredth and first time, she had no answer to that question. "Well," she said, after a moment, "I actually came to surprise you."

"But," he said, a confused expression on his face, "today is Thursday. You know I have city council on Thursday. I only came back because I left a file in my office."

"Oh, today is *Thursday*," she said, as though it had just dawned on her. "Of course. What am I thinking? I don't know where my head is at," she continued. She was speaking too rapidly, she knew, but she was unable to stop herself. She quickly gathered her books from the counter and hugged them to her chest. "It must be everything going on at school."

She turned toward Jon and Walt and, bouncing lightly on the balls of her feet, said cheerfully. "Well, it was good seeing all of you. Bye now."

She hurried to the door. "I'll see you later Dad," she trilled, and she was gone.

#

On Friday morning, Jon arrived at school a few minutes early. He hurriedly parked his bike and took the front steps two at a time. For reasons he couldn't explain even to himself, he wanted to be in Miss Tremaine's classroom before Mary arrived.

In the entryway at the top of the stairs, he turned left and walked quickly down the main corridor. It was lined on both sides with metal lockers bolted to the walls. As he approached his locker, he slowed. Something was out of place.

All of the lockers were painted a gunmetal grey. This morning, though, Jon could see red at the end of the row on the right. The color stood out starkly against the drab uniformity of the lockers. It wasn't until he was within a few feet of the end of the hall, however, that he realized what he was seeing. With a sudden intake of breath, his stomach constricted, and bile rose in the back of his throat, bitter, almost metallic tasting.

Across the face of his locker in large block letters, someone had painted the word "JEW." The paint had run, and there were long scarlet trails extending from the bottom of the word almost to the floor in a macabre suggestion of blood.

"What the hell?" said a loud voice behind him, and he turned to see Mr. Mabry, the school janitor. The man was wearing a pair of overalls, and he had a broom in one hand and a dustpan in the other. Jon had seen him around the school a couple of times.

"You do that?" Mr. Mabry asked. Then, without waiting for a reply, he said, "No, 'course not. Wouldn't be standin' here if you did."

With the handle of the broom, he pointed. "That your locker?"

Jon nodded.

The janitor studied the messy graffiti, mouthing the word. He then looked at Jon. "Just what I don't need," he said, finally. "That's gonna take me some time to clean off." He shook his head. "Just what I don't need," he repeated. Then, as if to hammer the point home, he said, loudly, "Damn," and he turned and stalked off.

Jon watched him leave. Returning his attention to the locker, he reached out, tentatively, gripped the handle and opened the door. A foul odor assaulted him.

Someone had urinated in his locker.

He stood there a moment longer, gathering his wits. Then, wrinkling his nose against the smell, he leaned forward and peered at the shelf that ran across the width of the locker. His books were still sitting where he had left them the afternoon before. He had nothing hanging on the two hooks below the shelf, and, because it was Friday, his gym shoes that might otherwise have been sitting at the bottom of the locker were back at his grandmother's house.

He took a breath, held it, and reached into the locker, putting his hands around the books and pulling them out. Awkwardly, he arranged them, large to small, bottom to top, and he placed them under one arm. He took one last look at the locker. Then, leaving the door open, he turned and trudged heavily down the corridor in the direction of his first class.

At the door to Miss Tremaine's class, he paused. He could see there were just a few students in the room. Mary was not one of them. All of the students who had arrived before him were sitting at their desks with the exception of one of the eleventh grade girls, who was standing beside the teacher's desk, hunched over, her finger on the page of an open book. She and Miss Tremaine were studying the book intently.

Vernon King was sitting at his desk, his back to the entrance. He was talking to Jeff Fletcher, who occupied the desk behind him. Vernon was usually the last person through the door in the morning, so his presence in the classroom now was unusual.

Jeff spotted Jon standing in the doorway. He tapped Vernon on the arm and inclined his head in Jon's direction. Vernon turned quickly. As Jon stepped through the door, both Vernon and Jeff suddenly squinted their eyes and crinkled their noses.

"Ah," they said in tandem, drawing the word out as if holding back a sneeze. "Ah," they repeated, a little louder and longer, each tilting his head back and contorting his face as though the coming sneeze were putting him in great distress. "Ah," this time almost yelling. Then, together, they threw their heads forward and exclaimed, "A Jew!"

Vernon sat back, a vicious smile on his face. Jeff made a show of wiping his nose as though it was running.

"Goodness," Miss Tremaine said, looking up from the book on her desk. "Are you boys coming down with colds?"

"Oh, no, Miss Tremaine," Vernon said. "I think there must be something in this room that doesn't agree with us."

"Really?" she replied, a mixture of confusion and concern playing on her face. "Well, I don't know what it might be."

"It's ok, Miss Tremaine," Vernon said quickly. "We'll be fine."

"Yes," Jeff said. "We can manage. But thank you, Miss Tremaine."

Jon walked slowly to his desk and sat down, feeling that he was being watched. When he glanced up, however, the only ones looking in his direction were Vernon and Jeff. They both had smug expressions. Vernon winked.

Jon looked back, holding their gaze. After a long moment, Jeff looked away, but Vernon continued to stare, his expression becoming more serious. Then, after a few more seconds, he smirked and looked away as well. Only then did Jon turn his attention to the classroom door.

A long minute passed, and then Mary entered the classroom. As she did, she gave a quick sideways glance in the direction of Jon's desk. He felt a jolt of adrenalin, but, the instant their eyes met, she turned away. The bile began to rise again in the back of his throat.

After a second, however, Mary pivoted, looked directly at him, and gave him the most wonderful smile he had ever seen.

#

"Are you going to tell me what's up?" Sam asked.

Mary continued staring into the distance. After a long moment, she said, "Do you think it's possible they could be any more puerile?"

"Puerile?"

"Childish. Immature."

"Do I need to carry around a dictionary when we're talking?"

Mary didn't reply. The two of them were sitting at one of the long benches in the outdoor eating area adjacent to the school cafeteria. Though it was a slightly windy, overcast day carrying the threat of rain at any moment, they'd chosen to sit outdoors, rather than in the main indoor area, which could be quite loud when full of students.

Sam studied Mary carefully. Mary had been distracted all morning. At the outset of the day, she'd been cheerful. Her mood, however, had soured quickly. Given her most recent comment, Sam wondered if it might have something to do with the developments concerning the new boy, Jon Meyer.

The school had been abuzz with the revelation that Jon was a Jew. To Sam, it seemed much ado about nothing. So what if the guy was Jewish? Why should that bother anyone? Apparently, however, the opportunity to engage in mischief at the expense of another had been too much for one or more of her classmates to resist. The vandalism of Jon's locker had been shocking. And, yes, immature. But Sam knew the whole thing would blow over in a day or two. After all, who cares?

Perhaps, however, it had struck a chord with Mary. She was uncharacteristically subdued. There were worry lines around her pretty blue eyes, and her usual smile was gone, lips instead tightly compressed in a contemplative frown. No, Sam thought, whatever was bothering her friend had to be really significant. It couldn't just be Jon Meyer.

She was about to probe further when there was a movement, and Gwenda slid onto the bench next to her.

"I've got something really important," Gwenda said, looking at Mary. When Mary did not react, Gwenda turned to Sam and gave her a quizzical look. Sam shrugged, then leaned forward and waved a hand in front of Mary's face.

"Hello, anybody home?"

After a moment, Mary refocused and looked at Sam. "Hmm?"

Sam extended an index finger and, with an exaggerated motion, pointed it at Gwenda, who was leaning forward, a look of excitement on her face. Mary looked at Gwenda.

"You know about the dance tomorrow night, right?" Gwenda asked. It was a rhetorical question. Of course they all knew about the dance. Gwenda would be going with Billy, but Mary and Sam planned to tag along. It was the first dance of the school year, and they'd been looking forward to it.

"Well, I just talked to Billy," Gwenda continued, "and he told me Vernon wants to go with you. Isn't that great!" She put an emphasis on the last word so it came out almost as a squeal.

Mary blinked a couple of times. Finally, she said, flatly, "Oh."

Sam and Gwenda exchanged glances. After a moment, Sam said, "Oh? That's your response? Gee, let's try to contain our enthusiasm. I mean, you don't want to be too easy. God forbid anyone gets the wrong impression."

Mary looked back and forth between Sam and Gwenda. Sam could see that Gwenda had a shocked expression on her face.

Mary suddenly reached out and cupped Gwenda's hands with hers. "Oh, Gwenda, I'm sorry. I just have a lot on my mind right now. Thank you for letting me know."

Her excitement returning, Gwenda asked, "So I can let Billy know you're planning to go with Vernon."

"No."

"No?" repeated Gwenda. "Why not?"

"Hmm," Mary said, leaning back and looking up. "Why not, indeed? Let's see, where do I start?" She adopted a pensive look, compressed her lips and took a deep breath through her nose, letting it out slowly. "Why don't we start with the fact that he didn't have the nerve to ask me directly? Heck," she said with a dismissive wave of her hand, "he didn't even ask you directly. He had to go through two people."

"Well," Gwenda started to say in a half-hearted way, but Mary cut her off.

"Oh, I know. The King is just too grand to be asking girls out in person. That simply won't do for someone of his prominence. But let's set that aside," she continued, "and talk about what's really important. The fact of the matter is Vernon King has got to be the most mean, arrogant, self-absorbed, inconsiderate..." She paused, searching for words.

"Puerile?" suggested Sam.

"Yes, good," Mary said. "Honestly, I would sooner poke my eyes out with a knitting needle than go the dance with that ape."

There was a look of shock on Gwenda's face now. Shock coupled with something almost akin to fear. She looked to Sam for help, but Sam merely shook her head.

"What do I tell Billy?" Gwenda asked.

"Tell him I already have a date," Mary replied.

Sam started. "You do?"

"No," Mary said. "I would have told you, of course." Turning to Gwenda, she said, "But he doesn't have to know that."

"Won't it be obvious it's not true when you show up at the dance without an escort?"

Mary made a noncommittal sound, then said, "We'll cross that bridge when we get to it."

Gwenda again looked at Sam, then back at Mary. She puffed out her cheeks and expelled a big breath of air. "Ok," she said, uncertainly. "I'll tell him." She hesitated a second, then rose, and walked back into the building.

Sam watched her go, then turned her attention to Mary. "Seriously, are you going to tell me what's gotten into you?"

"What? Because I don't want to go to the dance with Vernon?"

"No, I get that. But there's something else going on, right?"

Mary looked away, and Sam waited patiently. When Mary turned back, there was a new look in her eyes. "What do you think of the new boy, Jon?"

Sam shrugged. "He's Jewish?"

"Apparently," Mary said, with a touch of sarcasm. "Either that, or someone got pretty worked up for nothing. But that's not what I'm talking about. What do you *think* of him?"

Sam looked at Mary, who stared back with an expectant expression.

And then it finally hit her. It had only taken Mary sixteen years to become interested in a boy, but it had actually happened. Sam took a deep breath. "Well it's about time," she said.

#

Walt Gallagher was in high spirits when he opened the store on Saturday morning. He had gotten used to having Jon around, and, when Jon started school, Walt found himself missing his company during the day and anticipating the late afternoon hours when Jon would join him at the store. Today, Jon would be working most of the day.

He set his knapsack on the floor behind the counter and pulled out the book Jon had given to him. He'd finished the first chapter and was looking forward to talking to Jon about it.

Things got busy for the first hour or so, and there was no opportunity for them to speak. As the morning rush died down and the last of several customers walked out, Walt settled himself on his stool, reached for the book and set it down on the counter. He tapped it with a finger and looked at Jon. "I read the first chapter," he said proudly.

"And?"

"The guy gave away his wife and his daughter. How could he do that?" He fixed Jon with a serious look. "So, is he gonna get 'em back?"

Jon arched his eyebrows and looked from Walt to the book and back.

"Oh, I know what you're sayin'. I gotta read the book. And I'm gonna, 'cause I wanna know what happens. But…"

The front door opened and Mr. Dahlgren came in. He glanced briefly in their direction, but said nothing.

"Hey boss," Walt called out. Mr. Dahlgren did not reply. He made straight for the stairway and ascended the steps.

Walt made a face. "I don't think the boss is in a good mood today."

Mr. Dahlgren was back in less than two minutes with an envelope in his hand. He walked directly up to the counter, set the envelope down in front of Jon, and said, "Here's your pay for the week. I even included an amount for the entire day today. I'm letting you go."

Walt experienced a sensation, like a fluttering. Thinking that he had misunderstood what Mr. Dahlgren had said, he looked quickly at Jon, then at Mr. Dahlgren. Jon's face had a bewildered expression. Mr. Dahlgren's was stern and resolute, and he was staring intently at Jon.

"No, wait," Walt blurted.

"You stay out of this, Walt," Mr. Dahlgren said, his focus still on Jon. "This is none of your concern."

Jon blinked. He opened his mouth as if to say something, but then closed it again.

Mr. Dahlgren pointed to Jon's books, which Jon had set on the side of the counter when he'd come in that morning. "Gather your things and go now."

Jon looked at his books, then at the envelope on the counter. A few seconds passed. Then, wordlessly, Jon slid off the stool and collected his books. He started to turn, stopped, and reached out to pick up the envelope. Walt could see there was a tremor in Jon's hand. Jon tucked the envelope inside one of the books, stepped around the counter and walked to the door.

"One more thing," Mr. Dahlgren said. Jon stopped and turned.

"I want you to stay away from Mary. You leave her alone. Do you understand?"

Jon hesitated, then nodded, silently. He looked past Mr. Dahlgren and met Walt's gaze. There was a deep sadness in his eyes. Then he turned and walked out the door.

Walt stared at Mr. Dahlgren's back, waiting for him to turn around. When he finally did, Walt asked, plaintively, "Why boss?"

Mr. Dahlgren took a deep breath. "Walt, I had to do that."

"But why?"

"You probably didn't know this. I just learned it myself. Turns out Jon is a Jew."

"No he's not," Walt said, quickly. "He's a good guy. He's honest and he's a hard worker."

Mr. Dahlgren gave Walt a puzzled look. Then, as if a light were coming on, he nodded. "I don't mean it that way, Walt. When I say he's a Jew, I mean he's a member of the Jewish race. I'm not saying he's a bad person, I'm saying he comes from a group of people that others don't want to have anything to do with."

"Because they're bad people?"

"Well," Mr. Dahlgren started to reply, then stopped. After a long moment, he made as if to speak, then stopped again. Finally, he said, "It's complicated. Let's just leave it at that."

Mr. Dahlgren turned and headed toward the stairs.

Walt started to make a response, but bit it back. He had never, ever crossed Mr. Dahlgren. Involuntarily, his mouth opened. Before any sound came out, however, he clamped it shut. He cursed himself. Mr. Dahlgren had reached the bottom of the stairs. Walt balled his hand into a fist and punched himself in the leg. He opened his mouth again to speak, and again he froze. Mr. Dahlgren was climbing the stairs. He shut his eyes and squeezed them tight.

"Boss!"

Mr. Dahlgren stopped. Stepping backwards, he descended to a point where, bending down and leaning out, he could look at Walt.

"Boss, you know I always agree with you. And that's because you're always right. Every time."

Mr. Dahlgren looked at him, but said nothing.

"Every time," Walt repeated. "Except now."

Speaking rapidly, Walt continued. "I don't know about this Jewish race thing, but I know this. Jon is not a bad person. He's not. He's actually a good guy. A really good guy. He's good for the store, too. The customers like him. A lot. And he's smart. He's really, really smart. But he doesn't make you feel bad about that. And, he's fun to work with. And... and..."

And he had run out of things to say.

Mr. Dahlgren was silent for a few seconds. Then he leaned closer, squinted and asked, "Are you crying Walt?"

Walt rubbed a sleeve across his face. "No boss."

Mr. Dahlgren tapped the handrail absently. "Well," he said, after a moment, "like I told you, it's complicated." Then he straightened and resumed climbing the stairs.

#

Mary had given this a great deal of thought. Thursday afternoon had been too unplanned, too unstructured. She did not want a repeat of that. She had mapped out a strategy. She knew her lines. She had responses ready, including options, depending on his responses. Victory would be Jon's invitation to her to accompany him to the dance. Partial victory would be his accepting her invitation to join the group. The latter was a little risqué, she knew, but she didn't care.

At the front of the hardware store, she took a deep breath. Then she pushed the door open and stepped in.

Walt was sitting behind the counter, but there was no sign of Jon. Fortunately, there was no sign of her father, either. That was a complication she was prepared for, but she was happy to avoid it. She walked confidently up to the counter, a bright smile on her face. As she did so, out of corners of her eyes, she checked the aisles. Still no sign of Jon.

Walt gave her a desultory wave of his hand. "Hi, Mary."

Mary looked at Walt carefully. His face was drawn, and his shoulders were hunched. He looked back at her through bloodshot eyes. She had known Walt all her life. He was invariably cheerful and talkative. She had never seen him like this.

"Walt, what's wrong?"

"I'm not too happy with your father right now."

"Why? What did he do?"

Walt sighed heavily. "He fired Jon."

"He what?" She reflexively looked over her shoulder in the direction of the stairway, then back at Walt. "Why?"

"Something about the Jewish race. I don't get it." He shrugged. "It's supposed to be complicated."

Mary set her jaw. She tilted her head up and looked at the ceiling. "Is he here?"

Walt nodded.

"Well, we'll see about that." She whirled, marched to the stairs and climbed to the top, where she paused briefly in front of her father's office door.

She was tempted to barge in, but she decided against it and knocked instead. She heard the muffled voice of her father calling out. She turned the knob and stepped into the room.

Her father had the telephone receiver to his ear. He motioned Mary to one of the chairs in front of his desk. She sat down heavily, folded her hands and stared at him.

He looked back at her with one eyebrow raised. "Sounds good," he said to whomever was on the other line. "Listen, Burt, something's come up here that I need to attend to. Will you be around later this afternoon?" He listened for a moment. "Ok, I'll call you then."

He set down the receiver and folded his own hands in front of him on the desk.

"Why did you fire Jon Meyer?" she asked, without preamble.

"It's good to see you, too, Mary"

She would not be deterred. "Why did you fire Jon Meyer?"

He looked away for a moment, sniffed, then turned back to her. "It's complicated."

"Oh, no. That might work on Walt. Actually, I'm not sure it *is* working on Walt. But it's not going to do it for me."

"No, honey, it really is complicated. Let me explain, ok?"

She shrugged her shoulders angrily, but nodded.

"I haven't told you this, because I didn't want to trouble you prematurely. I'm planning to run for Congress next fall. And I have some very strong backing. The gentleman I was just on the phone with works for General Wood, the president of the America First Committee. They're going to sponsor me.

"There are certain people," he continued, "who are opposed to the AFC, people who want to see this country enter the war. One of the most powerful groups among them is the Jews, and the AFC has drawn a line in the sand. The Jews are on one side, we're on the other. That's just a political reality."

"So what are you saying," she interjected, "Jon's the enemy?"

He shook his head. "No, that's not it at all. It really has nothing to do with Jon personally. He's sort of a, I don't know," he searched for the word, "a casualty, if you will. It's the group of people he represents. And," he raised a finger as she was about to interrupt. "And it's about how others view that group of people. If I thought I could continue to employ Jon and not have it affect my campaign, I would. But I know I can't. The AFC has done some polling, and a candidate who takes a firm stance against the influence of Jewish groups on the media and the government will likely win next fall. Like it or not, I have to be seen as that candidate."

"Well, I don't like it," she said, angrily. "Come on, Dad, you don't have to do this." She pointed to the telephone. "Call them right now and tell them to get someone else."

He took a deep breath. She could see his entire demeanor change. "This is something I need to do. I'll never have another opportunity, and I am not going to pass this one up. You're going to have to accept that."

Suddenly, she felt very small, very helpless. It was as if she were six years old again. Her mother was gone. She was all alone, except for her father. And her father... what?

Her father didn't care.

"Now," he was speaking again, "I'm pretty sure you're not going to like this either. But you're going to listen to me, and you're going to obey me."

He fixed her with a stern look. "You will not have anything to do with Jon Meyer. I can't afford a scandal. And, I'm sorry, but if my daughter were dating a Jew, I'd be dead before I started. That's also a political reality. So you'll leave that boy alone. And he'll leave you alone."

She started to say something, but he cut her off. "That's not open to discussion. He's already agreed to it."

She sat back, stunned.

"Look," he said, in a placating tone. "There are plenty of other fish in the sea. You'll find a boy in due time. It just won't be this one. So," he continued, "do we have an understanding?"

She had an overwhelming sensation of being lost, as if she had fallen into a deep hole, with smooth, steep sides. The top was a long distance away, represented by a tiny circle of light. She couldn't climb out. She couldn't call for help. No one would hear her.

Slowly, she nodded.

#

Jon sat on the edge of his bed, disoriented, adrift. How long he had been sitting there he couldn't really say. He barely remembered the walk home from the hardware store. His grandmother had not been at the house when he'd arrived, and he was grateful for that. He had not wanted to face her just then. The embarrassment was too great.

What, he asked himself, would he do now? Without the income from the store, he couldn't contribute to the cost of his overhead. His grandmother would be upset. And it was happening just when she had started to treat him like something other than a deadweight.

He buried his head in his hands.

As bad as that was, it wasn't even the worst part. Not by a long stretch. No, the worst part—the thing that was causing the ache in his stomach—was losing Mary. And even that thought made him feel foolish. How can you lose something you never had?

He had honestly believed, though, that there was a spark between them. She had given signals that she was interested in him, hadn't she? Hadn't she? And, even with the awful things happening at the school, he had held out hope that maybe…

What was he thinking?

But to be fired? Hadn't he been doing a good job? Mr. Dahlgren had seemed pleased with his work. What had changed?

Mr. Dahlgren had seen him with Mary at the store. Had she told him about… well, about… the awful things?

Was that what this was about?

Was she laughing at him now?

He raised his head and looked around at the bare walls in his small room. He so desperately missed his home. He and his brother, Sandy, lying on their beds, with the old radio between them, listening to the broadcast of the Dodger game. His mother and father in the kitchen, talking about the day, sharing a laugh.

Suddenly, he had to get out, get away, go anywhere. He couldn't stay in this place. Without thinking about it, he was up, down the back steps, at the door to the work shed. Then, before he knew it, he was on his bike, trees and fence posts a blur on either side of him, wind and tears stinging his eyes.

6

It was a Thursday, and, though it was still early, the weak afternoon sun was losing its battle with the coming night chill. The trees by the side of the road cast long shadows across Jon's path. It was a reminder that, as October drew to a close, the days were getting shorter. He would have to start back soon, but he didn't want to let go of his freedom just yet.

Over the past month, his rides in the countryside had become his refuge, an escape from the claustrophobic existence that awaited him back in town. As he formed that thought, though, he realized, with a little rueful self-deprecation, that it was perhaps a bit of an exaggeration. While his grandmother still maintained her distance, at least the hostility was gone. He had been pleasantly surprised when she had made no mention of the fact that his pay from the hardware store had stopped. She'd just never brought it up. Better still, even without the money, she was not treating him like a complete inconvenience.

School, however, was a different story. From the day word had gotten out that he was Jewish, Jon had been subjected to an insidious isolation. Apparently, members of the basketball team, led by Vernon, had decided Jon needed to be shunned. One day, shortly after the locker incident, he had tried to strike up a conversation with Doug Larson. Doug had been frank and to the point.

"I can't talk to you. It's not safe. I'm sorry." To Doug's credit, he did appear to be sincere about being sorry. But it didn't matter. He still joined the others in giving Jon the cold shoulder.

As a result, Jon came and went without acknowledgment. He ate his lunch alone. And he endured a painful silence whenever school activities required that he be in proximity with fellow students.

Among the few people at the school Jon could talk to and who would talk to him were his teachers, with the notable exception of Mr. Spitzman, who appeared to have decided to join the students in freezing Jon out. That actually met with Jon's approval. Better to be ignored by the man than to have to deal with his bullying.

Other than the coach, Jon did like his teachers. He was particularly fond of Miss Tremaine and Mr. Hanson. She had a good heart and genuinely cared about her students. He was just an incredible educator, and Jon was learning a lot from him. Mr. Hanson had even taken to assigning Jon advanced problems, both in algebra and trigonometry, having realized early on that Jon was head and shoulders above the others in his class.

The interaction with his teachers, however, only went so far. It represented but a fraction of what should have been the normal intercourse with the people at his school. The vast majority of Jon's day involved a careful navigation of treacherous waters, anticipating and avoiding as much as possible situations that could become tense or unpleasant. On his best days, it was merely inconvenient. Those days were few and far between. Most of the time, he lived in a fragile bubble that could be pierced at the drop of a hat, whether by a crass comment or simply a boorish turn of the head.

As bad as all of that was, though, there was still one more thing he had to endure. It was the thing that really hurt, that literally caused him physical pain when he thought about it. That thing was the impenetrable wall between him and Mary.

After the shock of being fired from Dahlgren's, he had still clung to a desperate hope that she would somehow transcend the craziness, that they could nevertheless be friends. But, of course, he had been wrong to hold out that hope.

From the first day back at school after the firing, Mary had gone out of her way to avoid him. She hadn't been mean about it, but her intentions had been unmistakable. Out of respect for her, Jon had, in turn, made it a point not to put her in the awkward position of overtly snubbing him. As a result, they traveled parallel paths, never actually coming in contact with one another, not an easy thing to do in such a small environment.

With no job and, therefore, time on his hands, Jon had taken to the road. Every day after school and on the weekends, he mounted his bike and set out down the various routes surrounding Jackson. He'd started his explorations within a relatively small radius around the town. As he'd became more familiar with the territory, he'd expanded the circuit, eventually traveling several miles in each direction.

His rides gave him a true appreciation for just how in the middle of nowhere Jackson really was. There was simply nothing around but farms, meadows and woods. The one exception, he found, was the river that flowed a few miles to the east of town. He had followed it downstream to a point where it passed through a gorge near the town of Middleburg, which, amazingly, was even smaller than Jackson.

On this Thursday afternoon, Jon had ventured to the west of town and had ridden further than he had on any previous outing. The road he was on meandered through a series of wooded areas, intermittently broken by open fields. At the moment, he was approaching a slight rise, so he picked up the pace in order to generate sufficient momentum to carry him over.

Just as he was cresting the rise, he was startled by a sudden noise behind him. It grew from a mild hum to a loud roar in the span of about three seconds. As it reached its crescendo, a large object passed directly overhead, no more than a hundred feet above him. The pace at which it was traveling was so fast that he scarcely had time to register its existence before it just barely cleared a line of trees ahead of him at a right-hand bend in the road, and it was gone, the sound diminishing from a roar to a hum, and then to nothing, in about the same three seconds it had taken to achieve its loudest point.

It was an airplane. That much was obvious. What kind, he couldn't say. This one, he'd noticed, had an upper and a lower wing, a biplane, he knew. In the short span of time he'd had to observe, it looked to Jon as though the cockpit was open. He was sure he had seen a helmeted head poking above the fuselage.

The angle at which the plane had been flying suggested to Jon that it was in the process of landing. Anxious to see where, he stood up out of the saddle and bore down on the pedals. Shortly after the bend in the road, he spotted a track that led off to the left at a ninety-degree angle. He leaned into the turn and guided the bike down a narrow lane. It took him through a thick stand of trees. Then the left side opened up to reveal a large field.

Ahead, in the distance, he could see a pair of structures. As he approached, he realized that the building nearest him was a small house with a shingled roof and a chimney. Beyond the house, separated by a large open area, was what appeared at first to be an oversized barn. The door to this structure was on the side facing in his direction, and it was open, revealing an aircraft sitting on three wheels. This was not the plane Jon had just seen. It had only a single wing and a closed cockpit. It was also painted white. The one that had flown overhead had been yellow.

Jon slowed to a stop before he reached the end of the drive, stepped off and set the bike carefully against the trunk of a tree. There was a small knoll on the right side of the road, and he climbed it to get a better look.

He heard the plane a moment before he saw it. It had been shielded from his view by what Jon now realized was a hangar, but, when he reached the top of the knoll, he could see the thing rolling across the field toward the structures. He took a seat on a patch of wild grass and watched.

The surface of the field was obviously not completely level, and, as the craft bumped along, the tips of the wings alternately lifted and dipped. The pilot headed for the open area between the hangar and the house. At a spot just in front of the large open door, the tail suddenly swung around, and the sound of the engine stopped.

Now Jon could see that there were actually two cockpits, one in front of the other. As he watched, two men slowly climbed up and out of the openings and jumped to the ground. They stood by the side of the plane and spoke for a few minutes. It appeared to Jon that one of the men was giving instruction to the other. Finally, they shook hands, and the man who had been the recipient of the instruction walked to a car parked by the hangar and drove off.

The other man spent a few minutes walking deliberately around the aircraft. From where Jon sat, he appeared to be an older gentleman, with a head of salt-and-pepper hair, more salt, actually, than pepper. He seemed fit and energetic.

He disappeared into the hangar and reappeared a moment later pulling a wheeled object that looked vaguely like a wagon. He rolled it up to the tail of the plane. With an ease that Jon would not have expected, the man lifted the tail of the craft and set it on the device. Then, with more effort this time, the man pulled on the handle, and he slowly rolled the wagon and the plane into the hangar to a spot next to the other aircraft.

The man walked out of the hangar and around the far corner of the structure. He appeared a few seconds later, pulling on a cord attached to a large door that rotated at the corner of the building. A mild creak of protest from hinges reached Jon. The door closed with a bang. The man then walked into the hangar through a smaller door on the side of the building.

A quiet descended, and Jon belatedly realized he was running out of daylight. He stood and scrambled down the hillside, retrieved his bike and turned it to face in the direction he'd come. He took one last look back and was surprised to see the man again, standing outside the hangar just in front of the large door. He was wiping his hands on a rag, looking at Jon, and, after a moment, he raised a hand in an amiable gesture. Jon waved back.

Then, with a renewed sense of urgency, Jon stepped down on the pedal and began the ride home.

#

On Friday morning, Mary was at the kitchen sink, washing her breakfast dishes, when she heard the front door open. Sam's voice came echoing down the hallway.

"For saints have hands that pilgrims' hands do touch, and palm to palm is holy palmers' kiss."

Mary smiled. Sam had been given the lead in the school play. She would be Juliet to Charlie Morris' Romeo. Rehearsals would start in a couple days, and Sam was learning her lines.

Mary called back, "Have not saints lips, and holy palmers too?"

Sam appeared at the kitchen door, striking a melodramatic pose. "Ay, pilgrim, lips that they must use in…" she paused for a long beat, then said, breathlessly, "prayer."

Mary laughed. "I don't think it's supposed to be quite that lascivious."

Sam sauntered in and shrugged. "I'm just adding a little flair."

"Well, you add too much of that flair and the whole production is going to be banned before it opens."

Sam stuck her tongue out at Mary.

Mary laughed again. "Nice stagecraft."

After drying her hands, Mary collected her books from the kitchen table, and she and Sam walked around to the side of the house where her father's Packard sat. Mary climbed behind the wheel, and Sam slid into the passenger seat. Mary cranked the engine, eased the car out onto the highway, and they began the short drive to the high school.

"I have to meet with Mrs. Bell after study hall," Sam said. "We're going over the rehearsal schedule. It'll take about half an hour. Is that ok?"

Mary nodded. "Sure. I need to talk to Mr. Hanson anyway about the last problem he gave me, so that works out well. We'll meet at the car when we're both done."

Mary started to say something else, but she suddenly stopped, her attention arrested by a sight ahead of her on the road. It was a solitary figure, peddling a bicycle. He was hunched over the handlebars, working to get the bike up over the last hill before the school. She knew immediately who it was.

The Packard easily overtook him, cruised past and proceeded down the road, rapidly putting distance between itself and the cyclist. Mary pursed her lips and fought the urge to look in the rear view mirror. She felt Sam's eyes boring into her.

"What?" she asked, after a moment.

"I didn't say anything."

They drove in silence for another minute. Finally, Sam said, "Do you want to talk about it?"

"No," Mary said immediately. "I told you there was nothing to talk about."

"Ok." Sam turned and looked out the window. Without taking her eyes off the passing scenery, she said, "I'm here when you're ready."

They pulled into the school parking lot, and Mary steered the car to a spot near the front entrance. As she did, she noticed that a group of boys and girls had congregated in an area to the side of the building's front steps. In their present position, she saw, with some concern, they were between the bicycle rack and the steps.

Vernon King was part of the group. His blond head towered over the others. When she pulled up, she also recognized Jeff Fletcher and at least two of the other boys from the basketball team. It took her a moment to realize that the girl who was standing with her back turned to her was Gwenda. As usual, Gwenda was hanging on the arm of Billy Hamilton.

Mary shut off the engine, but remained seated, one hand still on the steering wheel.

"We're going to sit here for a while?" asked Sam.

Mary nodded.

"Ok," Sam said, lightly.

Jon arrived a couple of minutes later. His attention seemed to be focused on avoiding the large ruts and dips in the gravel surface of the lot, and it did not appear that he noticed the group of students until he was at the bicycle rack. He looked up, stared at them for a moment, then dismounted and rolled the front wheel of the bike into a slot between two of the bars.

"Hey, look," Vernon called out, loud enough that Mary could hear him from the car, "it's a kike on a bike," and he laughed at his own witticism.

The others turned in Jon's direction and joined in the laughter. Jon's shoulders seemed to hunch, but he made no acknowledgement. He slid his knapsack off, reached in and pulled out a stack of books. He put them under one arm, turned and walked stoically past the crowd to the front steps. Someone in the group said something Mary couldn't hear, and they all laughed again. Jon paused at the foot of the stairs but didn't turn. Slowly, he climbed the steps and entered the building.

Mary watched him the whole way. After the doors had closed behind him, she remained in the same position for another couple of minutes.

Sam said nothing.

#

After school, Jon had turned his bike in the direction of the airfield he'd discovered on his last ride, and he now sat on the same patch of grass at the top of the knoll.

Unfortunately, there was nothing happening. The large door to the hangar was closed, and Jon could see no activity in or around either of the structures. He passed the time reading, but finally concluded that he would see nothing today. He was just about to get up and leave when the hangar's small door opened, and the man he had seen the previous day walked out.

The man started across the open space between the hangar and the house. He had his head down, as though in thought. Suddenly, he stopped, raised his head, and looked directly at Jon. Then he turned and began walking in Jon's direction. Surprised, all Jon could do was sit and watch him approach.

Jon's original impression of the man was reconfirmed. Though he was not young, he radiated an undeniable vitality. He had a strong jaw, a prominent chin, and a rugged face that was pleasantly lined with small creases at the corners of both eyes and mouth. It gave the impression of someone who smiled a lot. Though, at the moment, he wasn't smiling, he wasn't frowning either. He stopped in the middle of the roadway and gave Jon a frank look.

"You found your way back," he said, casually. There was something calm and reassuring about his voice.

Jon nodded. "Yes, sir."

"Are you interested in airplanes?"

"I am," Jon replied. "I've never been around planes before, but I find the whole theory of flight fascinating." He held up the book he'd been reading. "What I know so far, anyway."

The man squinted and looked at the book, then at Jon. He was quiet for a long moment. Finally, he said, "Are you prepared to match reality with theory?"

Puzzled, Jon said, simply "Sir?"

The man waved a hand in the direction of the hangar. "Would you like to go up?"

"Oh, I would. Yes, of course. But," he said, trying to keep the embarrassment out of his voice, "I don't have any money."

The man continued looking at Jon for several seconds. Then he said, "Tell you what. Give me a couple hours of work around this place and we'll take the Jenny up. Eight o'clock tomorrow morning?"

Jon was nodding before he'd even thought about it. "Yes, sir."

"Good. I'll see you then." The man turned and, without another word, walked away.

Jon watched him for a moment. Then he made his way down the knoll and retrieved his bike. It wasn't until he was halfway home that it occurred to him he didn't even know the man's name.

#

Ben Wheeler walked into the small house, closed the door and paused. He was not a man given to impulse. Yet, he had to admit, what he'd just done had been impulsive. He rubbed his jaw. He wasn't sure why he'd asked the boy to come back and offered to take him up in the old Jenny.

He looked around the small living room. It was a masculine place, with a lot of wood and leather. It hadn't seen a woman's touch in a very long time. And it was, as always these days, quiet.

Maybe I ought to get a dog, he mused absently. Then he dismissed the thought.

He walked toward the kitchen. As he passed by a large oak cabinet, he stopped. A photograph in a frame sat on the top shelf. He opened the glass door, reached in, and pulled it out. He then continued into the kitchen, where he set the photo down on the small table. He poured himself a glass of milk and took a seat.

Sipping the milk, he studied the picture as if for the first time. It was a picture of him, standing outside a church. He was wearing his suit. It had been brand new at the time. Hell, he thought, it's still practically brand new, hanging in the closet, covered by the garment bag it came in. He hadn't worn the thing even a half dozen times in the eight years he'd owned it.

In the picture, he was standing between two boys, his arms draped over their shoulders. Ben, Jr. had been fifteen, and Tommie had been thirteen. All three of them were smiling broadly. He looked at the picture for a long time.

#

When Jon arrived at the airfield on Saturday morning, the large hangar door was open, and he could see the pilot standing on a stepladder, his head hunched over the exposed engine of the white plane. Jon wheeled his bike to the side of the structure and leaned it against the wall. Then he walked around to the front and called out, "Good morning."

"Morning," the man replied, his head still down, and Jon could now see that he had his arms in the engine and appeared to be straining to tighten something. After a moment, he lifted his head and withdrew his arms, revealing a tool in each hand. He tossed the tools down on a mat he'd laid out below the aircraft and wiped his brow. As his hand came away, it left a streak of oil across his forehead.

He climbed down from the ladder and pointed to the yellow plane. "Grab the handle on the wagon and let's wheel this thing out."

Jon moved to the rear of the biplane and lifted the bar on the device he'd previously seen the man use. The man took up position along the side of the fuselage, and, together, they pushed the craft out into the open area in front of the hangar.

The man walked into the hangar and emerged a moment later carrying a broom and a dust pan. He motioned for Jon, then pointed to a trash container in the corner.

"Why don't you tidy up here while I go clean myself," he said.

"Yes, sir," Jon said, taking the broom and dust pan.

The man went into the house, and Jon set to work sweeping. When he finished, he collected the pair of tools that had been left on the mat below the white airplane and returned them to the workbench that ran along the back of the hangar. They were full of grease and oil, so he cleaned them with some solvent he'd noticed earlier. Then, since he was at it, he cleaned the other tools, many of which were filthy, and he organized them in a way that seemed logical.

As he was finishing, the man reappeared, carrying a leather jacket. The man tossed the jacket to Jon and said, "You'll need this."

Jon started to put the jacket on, and the man said, "Not yet. Let's go over a few things first."

The man walked to the rear cockpit of the biplane and motioned for Jon to come around to the other side. When Jon looked in, he could see a seat with another jacket laying on it. In front of the seat, situated much like the dash of a car, was a small panel. There were three dials mounted on the panel. The man pointed to one of them.

"This is your altimeter," and he looked at Jon.

Jon nodded and said, "Tells you how high you are off the ground."

"Right," said the man. He pointed to the other two. "Direction and airspeed. For basic flight, that's really all you need to know. Now, to control the aircraft, you have to understand the way the plane moves on three axes."

He put his right hand out and held it level. Then he pointed with his left hand to a small wheel that protruded from the panel. "This is the yoke. You can turn it left or right." He rotated his right hand so that one side came up and the other down. Then he rotated it back the other way. "You're turning on the roll axis. Push it in." He dipped the tips of his fingers on his right hand. "Or pull it back." He raised the tips of his fingers. "And you're turning on the pitch axis."

He leaned further over and pointed with his left hand down at the floor, where there was what looked like a bar with two pedals. "That's the rudder."

"Which controls rotation along the yaw axis," Jon finished.

The man looked at him. "Very good." He rotated the tips of the fingers on his right hand, left and right, as if the palm of the hand was balanced on the tip of a stick.

"The last control you need to know about is the throttle," the man continued, and he pointed to a metal lever with a knob on top of it that was located on the right hand side of the cockpit. "This controls the fuel mixture and makes the plane go faster or slower."

Stepping back, he said, "Now you're ready. Go ahead and put on that jacket and climb up into the front cockpit. There's a helmet on the seat. Put that on and strap yourself in."

Jon slipped on the jacket. It fit perfectly. He then stepped up onto the wing and, contorting himself slightly, eased into the front cockpit. As the man had indicated, there was a leather helmet on the seat. When he picked it up, he found that it was attached by a cord to an outlet on the panel. He swung the cord up and around so it was out of his way, and he sat down. There were straps on both sides of the seat and one beneath the seat between his legs. He pulled up the one between his legs and realized the ends of the two shoulder straps would attach to it by means of a buckle. He made the connections and adjusted the straps, Then he fit the helmet on his head, fastened the strap, and slid the goggles down over his eyes.

While Jon had been doing that, the man had been walking around the plane, gripping the flaps and giving them little shakes. Now, he stepped up on the wing and bent down over Jon, checking the connections on the straps. Apparently satisfied, he walked around to the front of the plane, put two hands on the wooden propeller and slowly rotated the blades counter clockwise through a full turn. He repeated that three times. Then, he took a firm grip on the curved edge of the propeller, lifted one leg, and, using his own weight, pulled down hard.

There was a putt, putt, putting noise as the engine fired to life, and the propeller began to turn on its own. To Jon, the sound was like a car engine that was out of tune. Looking forward on either side of the exposed engine, Jon could see a series of what looked like giant metallic praying mantises dipping their heads up and down in random fashion.

The man came around the wing and hauled himself up easily into the rear cockpit. Jon could see that the man was putting on his jacket and a helmet. Looking forward, Jon studied the controls in his cockpit. They were identical to those the man had pointed out to him in the rear cockpit.

"Can you hear me ok?" came a voice, and it made Jon almost jump out of his skin. It sounded as if it had come from inside his own head.

"Relax," came the voice again, with the hint of a chuckle. He realized it was the man speaking, though his voice sounded distorted and tinny, as if it were being broadcast from an inexpensive radio.

"I've got a microphone back here, and you've got speakers in your helmet," the man continued. "You can hear me, but I can't hear you. So, if I ask you a question, either nod or shake your head. Ok?"

Jon nodded.

"If you get sick or feel like you need to come down for any reason, you tap the top of your head. Understood?"

Again, Jon nodded.

"Ok, let's get this show on the road."

The sound of the engine changed. It became deeper, the rough putt, putting noise settling into a regular thrum, and then they were moving.

The man guided the airplane to one end of the field and turned it so it was facing down a long open stretch.

"If you'd like," came the man's voice, "you can put your hands and feet on the controls. But do it lightly. Just to get a sense of how they work. I don't want you to fight me. If I say 'off,' take your hands and feet away. Understood?"

Jon nodded. He placed his right hand gingerly on the knob of the throttle and his left hand lightly on the small wheel the man had referred to as the yoke. He set his feet so they were barely touching the pedals of the rudder.

The noise of the engine grew even louder as his right hand—the one gently holding the throttle—moved forward involuntarily, and the plane started rolling down the field, the bouncing becoming more pronounced as the speed increased. The bouncing abruptly stopped, his left hand came back slightly, and, with a sudden feeling of exhilaration, Jon realized they were in the air.

#

Ben Wheeler eased the craft up through a lazy left turn, climbing slowly. For years, he had been giving rides to people who had never been in airplanes before, and he knew to keep the maneuvers gentle. He set a course roughly due east that would take them just south of the town of Jackson, and he brought the plane up to eight hundred feet. Out of habit, he looked around, but there was nothing else in the air.

What was it about this boy?

The kid was smart as a whip. That was for sure. But that wasn't it.

Ben was almost embarrassed to admit to himself he'd awakened that morning looking forward to spending time with the young man. I must be getting old, he said to himself. That's got to explain it.

He scanned the instruments, and took another look around. Then he made a decision. He reached for the toggle on the microphone.

"You want to take a shot at flying it yourself?"

He expected some hesitation, but there was none. The boy's head jerked up and down enthusiastically.

"Ok. I'm going to let go of the controls at the count of three. Don't worry, though. I'm right here, and I'll take them back the moment there's any problem. Understood?"

The boy's head again moved up and down.

"Here we go. One, two, three," and he took his hands and feet off the controls.

The left wing dipped, the nose dropped, and they started to lose altitude. He was about to grab the controls when the wings suddenly leveled and the nose came up. Not bad. He checked the altimeter. They had lost about fifty feet. As he was looking, however, they started to climb. They came back up to eight hundred feet and leveled out. In a moment, they were flying exactly as they had been, on the same setting.

What the hell?

He tapped the microphone. "Good recovery."

He glanced around, then reached again for the microphone. "Ok, see the railroad tracks coming up?"

The boy nodded.

"When we get to them, I want you to turn south. Put them on your left and follow them until they get to the gorge by Middleburg. Then, turn to a heading of two eighty. Understood?"

Again, the boy nodded.

Shaking his head, Ben tensed for the next maneuver. Banking slightly, the boy eased the plane through the turn, compensating for the inevitable loss of lift by pushing the throttle forward, then, as they came out of the turn, bringing it back to where it was. When he had completed the turn, they were exactly where Ben had told the boy he wanted to be. And they were at the same altitude.

What the hell?

They flew in silence for a few minutes. Below them appeared the river, then, in the distance, the spot where the sides of the river grew steep, and the course was spanned by the railroad bridge. As the bridge slid below them, the plane again banked, and the boy executed a perfect turn, leveling out and heading exactly on a course of two hundred and eighty degrees.

Ben just shook his head.

They were now on a line that would take them back home. Ben allowed the boy to fly for a while. As they approached the airfield, he got on the microphone again.

"Ahead at eleven o'clock is the field we took off from. Do you see it?"

There was a moment's hesitation, as the boy looked, then nodded.

"We're going to land in the same direction we took off. But we'll circle it first. Stay on this heading. When I say turn, bring the plane onto a course parallel to the line we want to use when landing. Understood?"

The boy nodded again.

Ben had taught hundreds of students in his day. He had never allowed a novice pilot to land a plane on his first flight. Well, he said to himself. There's always a first for everything.

Ben talked the boy through the final turns, getting him lined up on the roadway.

"Bring the altitude down slowly. I want you to be at a hundred feet when we hit the point where the road turns. Got it"

Another quick nod. The boy was concentrating hard. Good.

Ben had his hands and feet in place, ready to throttle up and take the plane around again if necessary. They dropped down through two hundred, then one hundred fifty feet. As they reached the point where the road turned, they were at exactly one hundred feet. The last line of trees passed quickly below them.

"Ease back on the throttle and let gravity do the work, nice and gentle."

The ground was coming up.

"Just before we touch down, raise the nose slightly and throttle back."

The ground began rushing by. Then the two wheels touched down with a barely perceptible bounce, the tail settling onto the ground a split second later.

The kid had made an almost perfect three point landing on his first flight ever.

"I got it from here," Ben said, and he took control of the plane, bringing it rapidly to a near stop and wheeling it around to head back to the hangar. As they taxied back, Ben asked himself if he had ever seen anything like this before.

Nope. Never.

When they reached the hangar, Ben rotated the Jenny and killed the engine. Then he removed his helmet, swung his legs up over the edge of the cockpit and dropped to the ground. A moment later, the boy did the same.

"That was extraordinary," the boy exclaimed.

Ben looked at him, standing there by the side of the plane in that leather jacket, his smiling face radiating excitement. "Ben," he said, without thinking about it.

"Sir?" the boy said, a look of puzzlement mingling with the animation on his face.

Ben realized what he'd said and recovered quickly. "Ben Wheeler," he replied, putting out his hand.

Understanding replaced puzzlement, and the boy reached out to shake his hand. "Jon Meyer." Ben noticed that his grip was firm.

"Well, Jon, that was an excellent job of flying. You're absolutely certain you've never flown before?"

"Yes, sir. Believe me," he grinned, "I would have remembered that."

#

Ben set Jon to work washing down the Jenny and walked into the hangar to retrieve a wrench. He'd noticed a wobble in the undercarriage. He opened the drawer where he kept his socket set and reached for the wrench, then froze and stared in surprise. The wrench, universal joints, extenders and sockets all gleamed back at him. They looked new. He opened a couple of other drawers. Same thing. He stood back and shook his head.

The kid had cleaned his tools.

Jesus, he thought, I told him to do a little tidying up. But this is crazy. He turned and looked out the entrance of the hangar. As he watched, the boy dipped the sponge into the bucket of soapy water and began assiduously scrubbing down the side of the fuselage.

Ben chuckled to himself. Then he closed the drawer. The undercarriage would wait.

He walked out of the hangar and headed for the house. "I'm hungry," he called out. "Let's get a bite to eat."

Jon looked up, surprised, and watched as Ben walked into the house. Then he dropped the sponge into the bucket, wiped his hands on the side of his pants, and followed.

"How about some scrambled eggs," Ben called from the kitchen when he heard Jon enter.

Jon appeared at the entrance to the kitchen and said, "Sounds great."

Ben pulled down the skillet from its hook, lit the burner on the stove top, and retrieved a bowl from the cabinet. He grabbed a handful of eggs from the basket that had been dropped off earlier that morning, cracked them one at a time and emptied the contents into the bowl.

"Are these two boys your sons?"

Ben looked back and saw that Jon was leaning over the kitchen table studying the photograph that he'd taken out of the cabinet the previous evening. He had meant to return it to its usual place, but forgot. Damn.

He turned back to the counter. "Yes," he said, as he whisked the eggs. "The one on the right is Tommie, and the one on the left is Ben, Jr."

After a moment, Jon asked, "How old are they now?"

Ben paused before answering. "Tommie turned twenty-one a few months ago. Ben would have been twenty-three in a few days."

"Would have been," Jon repeated.

Ben took a deep breath. He really hadn't wanted to have this discussion, but he'd foolishly left the damn thing on the table. "Ben died," he said simply. Then, realizing that was a little abrupt, he added, "It was a week before his eighteenth birthday. Complications from pneumonia. That's what the doctors called it."

"I'm sorry," Jon said simply.

Ben shook his head. "No need. Not your fault. Nobody's fault, really. Just one of those things that happens."

"Still, I bet you miss him."

If you only knew, Ben said to himself. Out loud, though, he said, "Of course."

After a minute, Jon asked, "So, where is Tommie?"

Ben shut off the heat, lifted the skillet, and began transferring the eggs to a pair of plates he'd previously laid on the counter. "I don't know."

He turned with the plates, and, when he saw the shocked look on Jon's face, he laughed. "Oh, I didn't mean it like that. The army's got him." He set one of the plates down in front of Jon and the other in front of the chair across the table. "They're supposed to be teaching him how to fly. Thing is, he's been flying all his life, from the time he and his brother were tall enough to see out of the cockpit."

He stepped over to the refrigerator and removed a bottle of milk. "Of course, the army'll teach him how to fly the army way." He poured the milk into two glasses. "Which, in this case, might not be all that bad a thing."

"What's the army way?"

Ben laughed again. "You know, I was in the army, and I can tell you there are about a hundred answers to that question. Most of them are not appropriate to repeat in polite company." He set the two glasses of milk on the table and sat down. "I think," he continued, "if Tommie gets anything out of the army, it should be a little discipline." He raised his fork and waggled it from side to side. "Not that Tommie is completely undisciplined. It's just," he paused, thinking about the best way to put it. "It's just that he has a little too much of his mother in him."

Jon looked as though he was going to say something, but he didn't.

Ben smiled wryly. "You were going to ask about his mother, right?"

"I don't mean to pry. I've already asked a lot of personal questions."

Ben shook his head. "It's ok. That part of my life is ancient history." He took a sip of milk. "I got married when I was in the army. I joined right after we entered the war. Nineteen-seventeen. I had this notion I would go over there and single handedly take on the Hun. The army had other ideas, though. They thought I was a little too old to be flying their precious planes. They wanted younger guys. I was thirty-four at the time. So, instead of going to France, I went to Mississippi, where I taught a lot of those younger guys how to fly."

"You taught them the army way," Jon said, with a smile.

"I taught them the army way," Ben agreed, smiling as well. "Or my version of it."

He took a bite and chewed it, remembering. "I met the boys' mother at a dance sponsored by the Magnolia Society, or some such grand thing. She loved my uniform. I was the dashing army officer she'd been waiting for all her life. She was ten years younger than me, but she didn't think I was too old for her, and I didn't think she was too young for me." He paused. "Turns out, we were both wrong.

"Shortly after we got married," he continued, "the war ended. The army had no more use for me. Which was fine. I'd pretty much had my fill. I took my discharge, and we moved back here."

"You were originally from here?"

"Yep," said Ben. "You're sitting on land that's been in the Wheeler family for over a hundred years. What you see is just a small part of it. The place is big enough that there are three families farming on it. Tenants. The rent they pay keeps me in this luxury you see," He waved his hands around the kitchen. "That, and eggs.

"So, anyway," he said, picking up the thread of the story, "I brought my new bride home. She was pregnant by then, with Ben. It was hard for her living out here. This place has never been the center of anywhere, and it was a shocking change from the garden parties and social circles of Biloxi. Eighteen months after Ben was born, Tommie came along. And that was it for her. She just up and told me one day. She was through being a mother, and she was through with living in Indiana. She'd done her duty, given me two fine sons, and she was moving on."

Jon looked at him incredulously. "She left?"

Ben nodded.

"How could she leave her boys?"

Ben spread his hands, palms up. "Not everybody is cut out to be a parent."

Jon thought about that. "Where is she now?"

"I don't know." Then he smiled. "This time I really mean it. Last I heard, she was in New York. She couldn't go back to Mississippi. The scandal would be too great. She managed to wrangle a divorce. I'm not sure how she paid for it. I signed the papers the day they arrived. I'm guessing she's probably still in New York.

But I don't really know. I haven't heard from her in," he thought for a moment, "eighteen, nineteen years."

"That's kind of sad."

Ben shrugged. "Water under the bridge." He gave Jon a level look. "So, now that you know my life story, what's yours?"

Jon blinked, and, to Ben, he seem to draw into himself.

"Not much to tell," Jon said, somewhat vaguely. "I live in Jackson with my grandmother."

Ben nodded slowly. It was clear to him that Jon wasn't anxious to give details about himself. He wouldn't push it. Hopefully, they would have time.

"You know," Ben mused, "I'm thinking it would be a damn shame if you didn't take lessons and really learn how to fly. And it just so happens I've got a little time on my hands. What do you say?"

Jon's eyes shone. "Oh, yes. Yes, sir."

7

"You make a compelling case, Jim," said Bob Chapman, wiping the corner of his mouth with a napkin. The older man sat back to allow his plate to be taken away. Then he leaned forward again. "And I'm ready to get behind someone I think can take the damn seat away from the Democrats. But it's all about the money. Do you have any idea how expensive it would be to mount this kind of challenge? We're not just talking about an incumbent. We're talking about a guy who's spent practically half his life in Congress. Hell, he raises money going to the toilet."

Jim Dahlgren nodded soberly. Inside, however, he was excited. He had carefully led Chapman to this point through the entire dinner. Just a little bit further.

"So," Dahlgren said, thoughtfully, "you think if I could match Barker in fundraising, you'd be in a position to put your support behind me?"

"In a heartbeat."

Bingo.

They were dining at the Lodge. Unfortunately, it was too cold to sit out on the veranda, so they were in the main room, a comfortable, wood-paneled space that nevertheless provided an expansive view of the river through a series of large windows, or at least it had until the sun had set. Chapman had accepted Dahlgren's invitation and had made the almost hour and a half drive from Ridley.

A private club, the Lodge was situated on the site of the former Olmstead estate. The Olmsteads had been the first known settlers in the region, and they had built their home on a spot where the Winamac River made a wide lazy turn around a spit of land that jutted out and interrupted its largely southward course. Dahlgren had been part of the original founding group that had acquired the site after the last of the Olmsteads passed away. It had been one of his best investments. The value of his member-ship had quadrupled in nine years. People from as far away as Terre Haute wanted to join, which, to some folks, seemed ex-traordinary, given the fact that the only thing the club offered was an opportunity to dine in a spectacular setting. There were no other facilities to speak of, though it was possible to reserve one of three suites of rooms for overnight stays. For the substantial initial investment and the significant annual dues, it seemed to many not to be worth it.

However, the real attraction of the Lodge, the one that those who couldn't see themselves making the investment also couldn't appreciate, was its exclusivity. Members of the club represented the elite from the three county area. They were people who could afford the indulgence for a chance to rub shoulders with one an-other.

For Dahlgren, the Lodge now offered him a base from which he could launch his campaign for Congress. For the past few weeks, he'd been carefully selecting and inviting influential peo-ple to spend an evening dining on fine food while being skillfully courted for their support in the upcoming primary election. Bob Chapman was one of those people. He was a city councilman in Ridley, a former mayor, and a prominent voice in county politics. His support would provide a big boost to Dahlgren's efforts to get himself elected.

And he had just said he would give that support if Dahlgren could show him he had the money. Dahlgren had one last big gun to fire.

They left the table and, befitting their fine meal, strolled casu-ally toward the entrance. Quietly, Dahlgren said, "Bob, there's something I'd like to tell you, but I need your assurance you'll keep it confidential for a short time, just a few weeks."

Chapman looked intrigued. "You have my word."

"I'm not jumping into this race completely on my own. I have the full support—financial support—of the America First Committee. General Wood himself has asked that I run. The AFC will foot the lion's share of the cost. Mine is one of a handful of candidacies that the AFC has decided to back in an effort to shake things up in Washington in a more direct way."

Chapman thought about that, then nodded. "You know, I've been wondering when the AFC would start getting more political. It just makes so much sense." He stopped and gave Dahlgren an appraising look. "You're very fortunate, Jim."

"I am," Dahlgren agreed. "Particularly," he added, with a smile, "if I can count on your support."

Chapman put out his hand. "You've got it."

Dahlgren took his hand with both of his and shook it. "Thank you, Bob."

As they entered the grand foyer, an open space with a large staircase that led up to the rooms on the second floor, Dahlgren noticed a trio of men standing near the foot of the stairs. They were in conversation, but they stopped abruptly when they spotted Dahlgren. He had the immediate sense they'd been waiting for him.

After seeing Chapman off, Dahlgren walked over to the three men. Mort Fletcher, the president of the Farmers Bank, and Everett Crane, a prominent Jackson businessman, were close acquaintances of Dahlgren. It was the third who was the most intriguing.

Charlie Harper was one of the wealthiest men in the county and an influential figure in local politics. Dahlgren and Harper had never been close.

His voice sounding a little strained, Fletcher said, "Jim, something has come up, and we'd like your assistance. Can we step in here for a moment?" He indicated the adjoining parlor.

Dahlgren nodded, and he followed the three into the small room. They were alone.

The three of them looked at one another, and Dahlgren waited. Finally, Harper spoke. "Last night, there was an incident at the diner involving several of the boys from the high school basketball team. They apparently got their hands on some alcohol." He glanced quickly at Fletcher, who looked away. "Things got a little out of control. Some of the tables and chairs were damaged, and they didn't pay their bill. Patsy Langdon is fit to be tied. She swore out a warrant for the arrest of several of the players."

Surprised, Dahlgren asked, "Were they arrested?"

"Not yet," Harper replied, again looking at Fletcher. It occurred to Dahlgren that Fletcher's son, Jeff, must have been one of the boys involved.

"Bill Jansen's sitting on the warrant right now," Crane said. "As a favor," he added.

Jansen was the Winamac County sheriff. Dahlgren knew him well.

Fletcher had found his voice again. "Look, Jim, he won't hold off for long. The only way the boys aren't going to be arrested is if Patsy can be convinced to withdraw the charge. I tried to talk to her, and she wouldn't give me the time of day."

"Jeff is one of the boys?" Dahlgren asked, knowing the answer.

Fletcher nodded ruefully. "Yes," he said, unable to hide the embarrassment. "Obviously, I don't want to see my son go to jail. But there's more to it than that."

"This will absolutely destroy the basketball team," Crane said. "It'll ruin what should be an amazing season, and it'll devastate the town."

Dahlgren looked at each of them. He did not reply immediately. The wheels were turning in his head. Finally, he said, "What do you need me to do?"

A look of hope passed across Fletcher's face. "Talk to Patsy," Fletcher said. "Convince her not to push this. Look." He pulled an envelope from his pocket. "This will cover the damages and then some. I know she'll listen to you."

Dahlgren accepted the envelope and looked inside. There were several bills in a neat stack. He looked back at the three men. Again, however, he did not say anything. He considered each of them in turn, Harper being the last.

As if reading Dahlgren's mind, Harper spoke. "Jim, each of us would consider this a big favor. We'd owe you one in return."

It was what Dahlgren was waiting to hear. He nodded. "You can count on me."

#

Jim Dahlgren was waiting at the entrance to the diner on Monday morning when Patsy Langdon opened for business.

"Mr. Mayor," she said with surprise. "You're up awful early."

Patsy was a tough cookie. She and her husband, Al, had purchased the diner in 1916. Shortly thereafter, Al went off to France with the American Expeditionary Force. When he returned eighteen months later, he was missing an arm, most of a leg, and his eyesight. Patsy had done her best to care for him, but he never really regained any semblance of a life, or, for that matter, any real desire to live. Six months after he got back, he managed to locate the service revolver the army had allowed him to keep when he was discharged. He loaded it with a single bullet, crawled into the bathtub and put the bullet through his brain.

Patsy had forged on. With the help of her younger sister, she had operated the diner now for twenty-five years. It was a hard life. She was up before dawn to open the doors, and she generally stayed until they closed at nine o'clock. She was a no-nonsense type of person. She would extend some credit, but not a lot. She ran a clean kitchen. The food, though basic, was generally good and always served hot.

As Dahlgren entered the diner, he glanced to the rear sitting area and could see tables and chairs stacked in the corner. Patsy saw him looking that way. "Sorry for the mess. We had a little problem Saturday night. You might have heard."

Dahlgren nodded. "Actually Patsy, that's what I'd like to talk to you about." He took a seat at the counter.

She looked at him for a long moment, then poured two cups of coffee and slid one in front of Dahlgren.

"If I'd thought about it, I would have realized they'd send you."

Dahlgren didn't answer right away. He took a sip of the coffee. Then he gave Patsy a frank look and nodded.

"Well," Patsy said, in a matter-of-fact tone, "it's not going to do any good. I respect you, Jim. But those boys deserve to be punished."

"I'm not going to argue with you, there," Dahlgren said immediately, his tone reasonable. "What they did was wrong, and they deserve to be punished."

Patsy looked surprised, and, for a moment, pleased. Then she narrowed her eyes, gave Dahlgren a suspicious look, and said, "But?"

"But, does the whole town deserve to be punished?"

She was silent for a long time, considering him. Finally, she said, "So, that's where you're going with this. You want to make me out to be the villain. My establishment gets wrecked, I get cheated, and, yet, I'm the bad guy because I complain. Is that what you think?"

Dahlgren chose his words carefully. "No. That's not what I think. No rational person will either. But here's the thing. People don't always think the way they should. They get emotional. They let their prejudices take over. They do the wrong things, sometimes terrible things. I don't want that to happen."

Patsy's eyes flashed. "What kind of '*things*' are you talking about?"

Dahlgren had not wanted to go there. But he'd anticipated that he might have to. "I don't know for sure. But you know how excited everyone has been since last year. People absolutely believe the basketball team is going to the state finals. It's been the collective dream of this town for months. If that dream gets crushed, they'll want a scapegoat."

"Then they can blame those boys," Patsy said, angrily, and she pointed toward the back of the diner, "and what they did."

Dahlgren winced, and nodded. He reached into his coat pocket and took out the envelope Mort Fletcher had given him the night before. He set it on the counter.

"In here," he said, tapping the envelope, "is more than enough to cover the repairs, the bill they didn't pay, and your trouble. It's a very generous sum."

She looked at him hard. "What kind of '*things*'?" she repeated.

Dahlgren looked away, then shrugged and said, "I don't know. Maybe they stop eating here. Maybe they try to find other ways to hurt your business."

"Like what?"

Still not meeting her eyes, he said, "Who knows. I've seen strange ordinances proposed at the city council. Limits on hours of operation, building upgrade requirements, things like that."

She laughed, but there was no humor in it. "That would be illegal. We both know that. And, anyway, you could stop it."

He looked at her again. "Maybe I could, maybe I couldn't." He took a deep breath. He was committed. Meeting her eyes, he said, "Then again, maybe I would, maybe I wouldn't."

He braced himself for her response. But, instead of anger, what he saw on her face was sadness. And something else. Pity?

She pursed her lips, eyed the envelope lying on the counter, then slowly looked at him. She was silent for a long time. Finally, she said, "All right. If that's the way it has to be. I'll take the money. And I'll call Bill Jansen."

Dahlgren nodded. Awkwardly, he reached in his pocket, pulled out some change and put the coins on the counter. "Thank you, Patsy," he said.

He rose and turned to go, but she called after him. "If they get away with this, what kind of message does it send? That they can get away with anything? What do you think they'll do next?"

He had no answer for that.

#

At lunch on Tuesday, Jon was sitting at one of the benches in the outdoor seating area. He was alone, which was not unusual. When he was in a charitable mood, Jon actually found it almost funny the way he could clear a table in the cafeteria just by sitting down.

It was a little chilly today to be outside, but Jon figured, if he was going to take up a whole table, it might as well be one of these. And, truth be told, he preferred not to advertise his isolation in the public manner that sitting alone in the main dining area entailed.

The door leading from the cafeteria opened, and he glanced up to see Jeff Fletcher and one of the other boys from the basketball team, Caleb Pratt, step outside. They were speaking in hushed tones. Caleb spotted Jon and nudged Jeff, who glanced in Jon's direction, made a face, then turned back, shaking his head. Jon wondered what they were up to, then realized a moment later when he heard the telltale scratch of a match and almost immediately smelled the tobacco.

Jon turned his attention back to his sandwich and ignored the two boys as they smoked their cigarette in violation of school rules. It was none of his business what they did.

"I wouldn't worry about him. He's a pansy."

Jon glanced up. It was Jeff who had spoken. He and Caleb had taken a few steps toward Jon's table. Jeff had the cigarette between two fingers. He casually held it up to his lips, took a drag, then blew the smoke in Jon's direction. "Isn't that right, Jew boy. Aren't you a pansy?"

Jon looked at Jeff, but said nothing. He knew the toughness was, in large part, the result of Caleb's presence. He'd observed Jeff over the past couple of months. For all his bravado, Jeff was a coward. Still, the boy was a good two to three inches taller than Jon, and he had at least twenty-five pounds on him. Jon had no desire to provoke a fight. He took a bite of his sandwich and chewed slowly.

Jeff's mouth curled into a sneer. "Yep. Like I said. Pansy." He looked back at Caleb, who shrugged.

The school bell rang, signaling the end of the lunch period and indicating the next classes would start in five minutes. Watching Jeff carefully, Jon rose.

Jeff whipped his head back around. "Where do you think you're going?"

Keeping his voice level, Jon replied, "Same place you are. Science."

Caleb tapped Jeff on the shoulder, turned and started toward the door. Uncertainty played across Jeff's face. He hesitated, then turned, and started walking toward the door as well. Cautiously, Jon followed.

Just before he reached the door, Jeff wheeled and stepped toward Jon. He was now close enough to reach Jon. Jon tensed, watching Jeff's eyes.

They stood, facing one another.

Jeff's eyes narrowed. "What?" he said, loudly. "What did you call my mother?"

"I didn't..."

Jon never saw the punch coming.

There was a sudden flash of light and a startling dizziness. Then Jon realized vaguely that he was lying on his back, though with no recollection of having gotten there. It took a moment for his brain to register pain, but, when it came, it was intense, radiating out from his left temple and cheekbone, a sharp, burning sensation. He felt confused. He tried to focus, but images swam in front of his face. In the background, he could hear voices.

"The son of a bitch insulted my mother. I'm not gonna to repeat what he said. It was disgusting."

Jon tried to raise himself, but he slipped and fell back. He opened his mouth to speak, but that made the pain worse, so he immediately clamped his jaw shut.

Someone was leaning over him. Or maybe it was more than one person. There seemed to be several heads swirling in the space above him.

"If you insulted his mother, then you got what you deserved."

The faces disappeared. Then the voices dissipated and were gone as well. Jon lay on his back, stunned, the only sound the rustle of tree branches swaying in the breeze. Cold from the ground began to seep up through his trousers and coat.

#

Ben Wheeler walked to the small hangar door, stepped partially out and looked up at the sky, which was, for the most part, clear. Though it would be a little chilly, they would still be able to get in a short flight. But only if they got going soon. He checked his watch again. It was a good half hour later than the time Jon had arrived the day before. Unbidden, a feeling of anxiety passed through Ben. He chided himself and dismissed the emotion. The boy will get here when he gets here. Ben resolved to wait. He did not, however, return to the relative warmth of the hangar. Instead, he remained at the door, peering down the road.

Another twenty minutes passed before a small figure appeared at the far end of the road and, as it neared, transformed itself into Jon on his bicycle. The boy was pedaling slowly, as if laboring, and it took him a full two minutes to cover the distance to the hangar.

When Jon reached a spot a few yards from the building, he swung off the bike and began walking it, choosing to go around the back of Ben's truck rather than making straight for the door. His head was down, and the way he was holding himself gave Ben the sense that he was trying to avoid looking in Ben's direction. Jon set the bike against the outside wall and slid the knapsack off his back. He then walked toward the door, head still down and turned slightly away.

"Sorry I'm late. I was delayed a little at school."

Ben stepped back to allow Jon to enter the hangar. However, he remained just inside the door, so that, as Jon stepped over the threshold, he was brought up short. Ben reached out, put his hand under Jon's chin, and gently turned the boy's head to face him.

Encircling the outer two thirds of Jon's left eye was a huge shiner.

Nodding, Ben said, conversationally, "That's a good one. Head still ringing?"

Jon looked down and said carefully, "I'm ok."

Ben let go of Jon's chin and stepped back. He did not say anything, but continued to regard Jon.

After an awkward silence, Jon ventured, "We were playing dodgeball." He made a vague gesture toward his face and added, "I got hit by a lucky shot."

Ben was silent for a moment longer. Then he asked, "That's what happened?"

Jon nodded, but did not meet his eyes.

Quietly, Ben said, "You're not a very good liar, son." Walking to the door, he added, "Follow me."

In the house, Ben gathered ice from the small compartment in the refrigerator and wrapped it in a towel. He instructed Jon to sit at the table and tilt his head back. Then he placed the ice pack on Jon's face and had him hold it in place.

Ben returned to the refrigerator, took out a bottle of milk and poured two glasses. He set one down in front of Jon and the other on the opposite side of the table, where he took a seat.

"So," Ben said, "did you even see it coming?"

Jon shook his head.

"Sucker punch, huh?"

Jon nodded.

"Did he give you a reason?"

Still looking up at the ceiling through his good eye, Jon replied, "He said I insulted his mother."

"Did you?"

"No, sir," Jon said, immediately, taking the ice pack away and looking directly at Ben.

Ben motioned for Jon to re-place the ice. Jon leaned back again and returned the cloth to his eye. After a moment, Ben said, "Can you think of a reason why he might have felt it necessary to punch you out?"

Jon didn't reply. Something about his silence seemed odd to Ben. He took a sip of milk and studied the boy. After a minute, he said, "There's more to this story, isn't there?"

Jon hesitated, then gave a half shrug of his shoulders and a vague nod of his head.

Ben sat back. "Why don't we start at the beginning."

It took some patient prodding, but, slowly, a picture began to emerge. Jon had somehow managed to cross the most important clique of students at his new school, the players on the school basketball team. He had, for several weeks now, been turned out and ostracized by a large part of the student body, the others being motivated either by the same thing inspiring the basketball team or because they were simply afraid of the players on the basketball team.

Ben could understand the latter if Jon's black eye was any indication of how those boys dealt with people they didn't like. What he couldn't understand, however, and what made the whole thing so mysterious, was how a kid as likeable as Jon could possibly wind up so at odds with so many others. Thus far, Jon had been reluctant to give details.

"Jon, you haven't told me why they're treating you like this. You do know, don't you?"

Jon had sat up and set the ice pack aside. Ben had let it be. In response to Ben's question, Jon nodded, hesitantly, a sad expression on his face.

Ben waited, patiently. Slowly, Jon looked around the room. He glanced at Ben, but his eyes darted quickly away. Finally, he fixed on a spot in the middle of the table and stared at it for a long quiet moment.

Then, in a small, barely audible voice, Jon said, "I'm Jewish."

Ben was not sure he'd heard correctly. He was about to ask Jon to repeat himself when the words sunk in.

He looked at Jon, who was still staring at the center of the table. And then the full impact of the boy's words dawned on Ben. Here was Jon, sitting across from him, afraid that Ben would think less of him.

Ben asked, quietly, "Do you think the fact that you're Jewish makes a whit of difference to me?" he asked.

Jon looked up at him, a mixture of uncertainty and hope playing across his face.

"Well, it doesn't."

When he saw the look of relief on Jon's face, he had to fight the urge to reach out to the boy.

Slapping the table with his palms, Ben said, "Tell you what. We're not going to fly today. It's late and it's too cold anyway.

Take that ice and meet me out in the hangar. I need to get something."

#

When Ben entered the hangar, he was carrying an old canvas bag. Stenciled in large white letters along the side, Jon could see, was the name "Wheeler." Setting the bag down on the workbench, Ben took a seat on one of the stools. He gestured for Jon to do likewise.

"I'm going to tell you a little something about my younger days," Ben said. "I'll be honest with you up front. I'm not proud of every part of it."

Jon settled onto a stool. Ben had his attention.

"When I graduated from high school," Ben began, "I couldn't wait to get out of this place. Back then, if you can believe it, Jackson was even smaller than it is today. I felt there was just nothing here for me. I needed to see the world. That didn't make my dad very happy. He wanted me here to help out on the farm. And I think he wanted my company. I was an only child, and we were pretty close. But I was headstrong. We argued a little. He finally agreed to let me go because he knew deep down I'd go anyway.

"For a few years, I bounced around a lot. I guess you could say I was a bit of a ne'er do well. I held jobs, but none for long. I didn't have the inclination or the discipline to stick with anything. I'd make just enough money to keep from starving. I treated life as one adventure after another. I wanted to go everywhere, try everything. And, to me, the more danger involved, the better. I was a daredevil. Heck, you had to be a little crazy to strap yourself to some of the planes I flew before the war.

"One night, when I was in Baltimore, a buddy invited me to go with him to a local prize fight. It was in a dicey part of town, but they drew a damn good crowd. The top of the card turned out to be a couple of tomato cans who whaled on each other for a half an hour before one of them walked into a wild right hook and went down for the count. When I found out what the purse was for the winner, it got me thinking.

"You see, my dad had taught me how to box starting when I was a lot younger than you are now. He'd learned boxing from his father. I have no idea where my grandfather learned it. But my granddad, he had a reputation as no one to be trifled with." Ben gave Jon a wry look. "He knew what to do in fight.

"Anyway, there I was in Baltimore watching a couple of rubes I knew I could beat easily, and it turned out they were making more money in a half an hour than I was making in a week. Well, it didn't take me long, and I had a new gig, as a prizefighter. I knocked out the first couple of guys I fought and started drawing attention. A couple more knockouts, and I was moving up the cards. One thing led to another, and, eventually, I got offered a title bout. I was going to fight Bob Bollman. They called him Bobo. At the time, he held the middleweight title for the whole mid-Atlantic."

"Wow."

Ben nodded.

"What happened?"

"It never came off. I walked away from the whole thing. It was just time to move on." Ben made a dismissive gesture. "Truth is, I knew I'd probably gone as far as I could. I wasn't exactly a spring chicken by then. America was getting into the war. So, I signed up to fly with the army. Seemed like a good idea at the time. And anyway," he said, laughing, "Bobo probably would have taken my head off."

"So you never went back to boxing?"

"Nope. Never boxed again professionally. But," he indicated the bag, "I held on to this thing. When the boys were old enough, I dragged it out and taught them how to defend themselves."

Ben unbuckled the straps that held down the cover to the bag, reached in and withdrew a pair of leather gloves that looked to Jon like overstuffed kitchen mitts. He laid them on the workbench.

"And I'm going to do the same thing for you."

#

Dick Mayfield was seated in his favorite chair, his feet up on the ottoman. It was Sunday afternoon. After the effort that went into preparing for church services, the services themselves, and the inevitable busy aftermath, this was his moment to relax.

He'd pulled down a book from the shelf to read and had lit a fire in the fireplace. The kids, he knew, were playing in the yard, and his wife was in the kitchen, shelling peas. Through the open kitchen door, the soft strains of classical music from the radio drifted in. He'd read a few pages from the book, but his lids were getting heavy, the warmth of the fire and the comfort of the chair luring him into a nap.

He'd set the book on his lap, closed his eyes and was just drifting off.

"Dick!" his wife called out in alarm.

Mayfield's heart jumped. His first thought was of the children. One of them must have fallen. He was out of his chair and across the room in two seconds. At the door to the kitchen, he saw his wife sitting at the table in front of a mound of unshelled pods and a bowl full of peas. She had a stricken look. She'd lifted one hand to cover her mouth. With the other, she was pointing to the radio on the counter.

He could hear the ending notes of an orchestral piece, followed by polite clapping. An announcer began to introduce the piece. Tchaikovsky, it sounded like. He looked at his wife with a questioning expression.

She lifted her hand away from her mouth. "They said the Japanese…"

Suddenly, the radio went silent. Then a new voice started speaking.

"This is John Daly speaking from the CBS newsroom in New York. Here is the Far East situation as reported to this moment. The Japanese have attacked the American naval base at Pearl Harbor, Hawaii, and our defense facilities at Manila, capital of the Philippines. The first disclosure of this news was made by Presidential Secretary Stephen Early by telephone at approximately 2:25 in Washington. I read the text of this historic announcement at a little after 2:30."

Mayfield sagged against the door frame. The announcer went on to provide what details were known. There were confirmed strikes on American ships, a naval engagement was in progress off the shores of Honolulu, police had been called out in case of revolutionary activity, declarations of war were imminent.

In a shaky voice, Mayfield said, "It's begun. God help us all."

#

Marvella Wilson buttoned her coat slowly. The cold exacerbated the arthritis in her fingers, so it was not an easy task. On the dresser next to her sat her favorite hat. It was the one she had purchased the previous Christmas as a gift to herself. Not a person given to fashion whims or frivolous expenditures, Marvella had acquired the chic item in a moment that was completely out of character. But, she'd reasoned, it had been Christmas, and that was a special time. And, in any event, she was looking forward to wearing it tonight.

For Marvella, the midnight Christmas service was the essence of the holiday season. Nothing meant Christmas more than the celebration for which she was getting ready. Every year of her life had included this special event.

As she walked down the short hallway, she noticed her grandson's door was open and the room was empty. Odd, she thought, given the late hour. When she entered the parlor, she found him sitting on the divan. He was wearing a nice pair of slacks and a clean white shirt she'd never seen on him before. His coat was in his lap. He stood as she walked into the room.

"Oh," she said, uncertainly. "What's this about?"

He looked a little self-conscious and hesitated before responding. "I was wondering if it would be ok if I went with you to the midnight service."

She thought she'd stopped being surprised by the boy, but this took her aback. She considered what to say next, but couldn't quite find the right way to put it. The two of them stood there awkwardly for a long moment.

Finally, he volunteered, "I know what you're thinking. But every year since I can remember, we always went to the midnight service. My dad said it was something my mom insisted on from the time they were married. It was always a special thing, and it wouldn't be Christmas without it. And I was just hoping," his voice trailed off.

Marvella blinked a few times. Then she nodded and said, formally, "Yes, we'll go together."

The boy's face brightened. He moved quickly to the door, slipping on his coat as he did. He opened the door and held it for her. As she stepped past him, she said, "Thank you."

They descended the steps and, side by side, walked up the darkened avenue.

The church had been done up in splendid fashion. Boughs of evergreen had been tied with red ribbon and mounted at the end of each row of pews. The theme had been carried up into the sanctuary, where hundreds of candles had been placed among the branches, the flickering of their flames causing the panes of the stained glass window to shimmer in a constantly changing and seemingly infinite variety of patterns. The church organ was softly playing "Away in a Manger."

Marvella found a spot near the front, and she and Jon took their seats, each picking up one of the mimeographed sets of Christmas hymns that had been laid at regular intervals along the bench. Precisely at 11:45, the music came to an end, and Reverend Mayfield ascended the short steps to the altar. He gave a brief blessing, then invited everyone to join in the first hymn.

After a short opening flourish, the organist settled into the familiar strains of "Oh Come All Ye Faithful," and the congregation took up the song. Someone with a fine, clear voice was singing near her, and it took Marvella a moment to realize that the voice belonged to her grandson. Without turning, she studied him from the corner of her eye. He had a joyous expression on his face and was unabashedly belting out the tune. She shook her head slightly and smiled.

Over the next hour, the Reverend Mayfield interspersed the story of the Nativity with familiar Christmas hymns, and the service concluded with a rousing rendition of "Joy to the World."

As they were filing out of the church, a voice called out to her. She turned to see Everett Crane working his way through the crowd. She and Jon stepped to the side and waited for him.

Crane and his wife, Cynthia, had been long-time acquaintances of Ernest and Marvella. The two men had been close friends, and, before Ernest's death, the four of them had socialized on a regular basis. Cynthia had been a member of Marvella's bridge group until she had passed away two years earlier.

When he caught up to them, Crane said, "Merry Christmas, Marvella. You're looking quite fashionable this evening."

Despite herself, she flushed. "Thank you, Everett, and a very merry Christmas to you. How have you been?"

"No complaints," he replied, and then he said with a smile, "at least none that are going to do me any good."

"Have you heard from your son?" Crane's son, Charles was an officer in the navy, and he was stationed on an aircraft carrier in the Pacific. After the attack on Pearl Harbor, there had been a few anxious days before word got back that he was fine.

"I have," Everett replied, his smile broadening. "He's gone back out to sea, but, before he left, he was able to put a phone call through from Hawaii."

"Really?"

Crane nodded. "It wasn't a very good connection, and he couldn't talk long, but it was wonderful to hear his voice."

"That was a nice Christmas present."

"Yes," he agreed. Turning to look at Jon, Crane asked, "And who is this young man?"

After only a brief hesitation, Marvella said, "This young man is my grandson." Then she added, "Jonathon."

Crane put out his hand and said, "Merry Christmas, Jonathon."

Jon took his hand and replied, "Merry Christmas to you, sir."

After exchanging a few more pleasantries, they parted, and she and Jon began the walk home. It was a cold, clear night, and the sky was resplendent with stars. The quiet was broken only by the soft crunch of their feet on the day-old snow lining the side of the road. Notwithstanding all the talk of war, Marvella felt an odd sense of peace.

8

"I'm sorry, sir, but Mr. LoBianco is not in the office at the moment."

Jim Dahlgren couldn't be sure, but it sounded like the voice of the woman who'd answered the phone the last few times he'd called. "Can you tell me when you expect him back?" he asked.

There was a pause, then the woman said, "I really don't know."

He gave the woman his number, for what had to be the fifth or sixth time, and hung up. He sat back in his chair, raised his fingers to his temples, and rubbed gently. What the hell is going on, he asked himself, not for the first time today, and certainly not for the first time in the past two weeks.

On December 11, a few days after the attack on Pearl Harbor and the declarations of war against Japan and Germany, the America First Committee had issued a statement announcing it was disbanding, declaring, "Our principles were right. Had they been followed, war could have been avoided. No good purpose can now be served by considering what might have been, had our objectives been attained."

It was a potential body blow to Dahlgren's candidacy. At a minimum, it meant an already organized constituency had just vanished into thin air. That was bad. What was worse, however, was the possibility that the funding on which Dahlgren had been counting was no longer available.

"Damn it," he said to himself, not for the first time that day, and not for the first time in the past two weeks.

There was a knock on his door. He composed himself, and called out, "Come in."

The door opened, and Mary entered. "I'm ready to get going," she said. "Do you have the final list?"

Dahlgren looked at his daughter. For the past two or three months, he had noticed a change in her disposition. Mary had always been one of the most vibrant, alive persons he had ever known. She took after her mother in that respect. But the Mary standing before him now was very different. She was quiet, reserved. Behind her uncharacteristically veiled eyes, there lurked something he couldn't quite put his finger on. She seemed, for lack of a better term, sad. He'd made a couple of attempts to talk to her about it, but she'd deflected him, and, to tell the truth, he'd been so busy organizing his campaign, he hadn't really pursued it.

"Mary, will you please tell me what's wrong?"

She gave him a wan look. "Nothing, other than the fact that I need to get going so I can make it back before the storm hits."

Mary, who was out of school for the Christmas holiday, would be driving to Parkersville to pick up some checks from donors. There had been reports that a major winter storm would be rolling into the area in the late afternoon or early evening. It was projected to bring a great deal of snow and would likely close most of the roads in the area.

"There's time. You and I both know that something's wrong. Let's have it."

Mary didn't reply right away. She looked at him, then looked away. She seemed to be debating with herself. Telling himself he needed to be patient, he waited.

Finally, she gave him a direct look, and asked, "Why are you doing this?"

He spread his palms. "Doing what?"

"Well, for starters, running for Congress."

He sat back, a little surprised. "Why would you even have to ask? It's an incredibly important and prestigious thing to be a United States Congressman."

Mary thought about that. "Prestigious? Maybe. But how important is it really? Is it worth what you're doing? Is it worth what you've," she stopped, her eyes dancing around the room, before settling again on him, "become?"

Puzzled, he repeated, "What I've become."

She suddenly seemed uncertain, but she nodded.

"What," he asked, "have I become?"

"Dad, it's like you're a different person. I'm not sure you even see it yourself. You've been doing things I'd never have expected you to do. And the way you treat people," she paused, apparently searching for the right words, "it's as if everything has to be weighed in terms of how it'll affect your chances of being elected. And, if it means you have to step on someone's toes, or worse, these days you just do it."

"Now, hold on a minute," he said, leaning forward. "That's not fair. Yes, I'll admit the campaign has become very important, and, yes, I've been a little distracted. But I'm still the same person. I haven't done anything wrong."

"Really?" Mary asked, a little fire returning to her eyes. "Didn't you threaten Patsy Langdon's business if she refused to drop the charges against the boys who damaged the diner?"

That caught Dahlgren by surprise. "Who told you that?"

"What difference does it make? Did you or didn't you?"

"No," Dahlgren said, shaking his head. "No," he repeated, "it wasn't like that. And, in any event, what I did was for the town."

"If you weren't running for Congress, would you have done that," and she allowed sarcasm to creep into her voice, "*for the town?*"

Before he could respond, she continued. "Let me help you there, Dad. The father I knew would never have tried to strong-arm Patsy. I don't know what you got out of it, but I know it had something to do with the election. And, it's disgusting."

He was shaking his head again. "That was an isolated incident…"

"No it wasn't. Didn't you vote to exclude Lodge membership to a man from Ridley just because he's Jewish?"

That caught him up short. It was true. Dahlgren had pulled strings to prevent the admission of a businessman from Ridley as the Lodge's first Jewish member. He'd been concerned that, if word got out Dahlgren was the member of an exclusive club that included Jews, with whom he would be seen as associating closely and sharing confidences, it would devastate his candidacy. How, Dahlgren asked himself, did Mary learn about that? Membership committee deliberations were supposed to be secret. Damn, he thought, would that whole thing backfire on him? He'd have to do some checking and maybe rebuild some bridges.

Mary emitted a dry laugh. He detected a tinge of scorn. "Are you doing political calculations right now? Trying to figure out if this is going to hurt your campaign?"

Hoping his guilt didn't show, Dahlgren replied, "No, of course not. Look, honey," he said, trying to sound reasonable, "that's not the kind of person I am."

"It's not? Didn't you fire Jon Meyer just because he's Jewish?"

Dahlgren now regretted bringing up the conversation, and he was desperate for a way out. With this latest comment, he saw an opening. "Is that what this is all about?" He narrowed his eyes. "You haven't been seeing that boy, have you?"

This time there was no hiding the distain. "No, I haven't. Just like you ordered. And," she added, "it hasn't been all that difficult to do, because he's certainly ignored me."

Despite himself, he felt a touch of anger. "And you blame me, right?"

"Why not? I'm sure he thinks we're both monsters. And he may be right."

Dahlgren bit back a retort. He took a deep breath and put out his hands in a placating gesture. "Look, let's calm down. You're angry with me. Ok. I've been distracted by the campaign. Maybe I haven't been exactly myself. But this will pass. We'll get back to normal. You'll see. Everything's going to be fine."

The veil had dropped down again over Mary's eyes. After a long moment, she nodded and shrugged. "Do you have the list?"

Dahlgren looked at her silently. Then he picked up the sheet that contained the names and addresses of donors from whom Mary would collect checks, and he held it out to her.

Wordlessly, she took the paper, turned and walked to the door.

"Mary?" he called after her.

Her hand on the knob, she stopped and turned slightly, but she did not look at him.

"Drive carefully, please."

She nodded, walked out, and closed the door behind her.

Dahlgren sat back, his mind a swirl of contradictory thoughts. On one level, he understood Mary's anger. Politics, he had come to discover, could be a dirty business, and she was seeing some of the seamier parts. But, he knew, much of that was simply necessary in order to be able to be in a position to do good things. And he was prepared to do good things. He just had to get from here to there, and, in the meantime, keep his eye on the big picture. Mary would eventually understand. He'd make it up to her.

The ring of the phone caused him to start.

"Jim," came the voice on the other end, "it's Burt LoBianco."

Relief flooded Dahlgren. Keeping his voice steady, he said, "Tell me what's happening Burt."

"Well, you know we disbanded the committee. Had to. We'd have just been throwing gasoline on the fire if we'd kept on. And, we'd have gotten everyone mad at us in the process. What we said in the announcement was about as far as we dared go in this climate."

LoBianco hadn't yet gotten to the important part. Dahlgren remained silent. He wanted LoBianco to bring it up.

"Anyway," LoBianco continued, "I'm not telling you anything you don't already know. I suspect what you care about is the impact on your campaign. Am I right?"

"You are."

There was a long quiet on the other end. Then LoBianco said, "I'm afraid it's not good news, Jim. We've shut it down completely. We're doing no further fundraising. In fact, we're having some trouble with contributors who want their money back."

Dahlgren felt a pain in his stomach. More out of frustration than anything else, he said, "So what do you suggest I do now?"

"It's your decision, of course. I'd certainly understand, we'd understand, if you chose to stop now. Here's the thing, though. That seat is still vulnerable. I think Barker can be beaten. I've always thought you were the right man to do it, and everything I've seen and heard about the efforts you've been making leads me to believe I was correct in my initial assessment."

That made Dahlgren feel better. Not a lot better, but some.

"Listen," LoBianco continued, "I've got to run. I'm fielding calls from disgruntled contributors, and I've got a few more guys like you I have to talk to. If you do decide to move forward, stay the course. I think you've got a good strategy. Keep the message clear and avoid controversy, ok? Good luck."

After they'd hung up, Dahlgren spent several minutes in quiet contemplation. Of the money he'd raised, most of it he'd already spent or committed to expenditures that couldn't be cancelled. He could repay that money, though. It would set him back, but he could do it.

The problem was, he didn't want to. He looked around the room that had been his office for almost twenty years now. There was nothing to it. He rarely had meetings here. It was a room above a hardware store, for heaven's sake. He'd now had the chance to contemplate a more grand existence. He wanted the trappings. He wanted the spotlight.

After a few more minutes of thought, he came to a decision. He would figure out a way to make it work.

#

Jon had known a big storm was coming, and he had started home from Ben's place a little after 1:00. When he'd left, the snow had been only a swirl of light flakes.

He'd barely traveled a mile, however, when the snow started falling in earnest, large, heavy flakes that clung to him and his bike and began to accumulate on the road. After he'd gone another mile, the wind had picked up. By the time he'd covered about half of the twenty miles to town, the snow on the road had become simply too heavy for him to keep riding. He had dismounted and continued on foot, half walking and half jogging, wheeling the bike alongside.

He was now still a good six to seven miles from town. About a mile back, he'd picked up the bike and started carrying it. The drag of the wheels through the snow had been too much for him to continue pushing it. The added weight on his shoulder had slowed him to a crawl.

He knew he'd have to abandon the bike soon. The thought was devastating. Even though he'd have a chance of finding it after the spring thaw, he hated the prospect of doing without for months. Moreover, he knew there was a possibility he might never see it again. He was becoming dreadfully tired, and a mild panic was beginning to overtake him. At the rate he was going, and at the rate the snow was falling, he was beginning to fear he might not even make it himself.

The snow had the effect of deadening most sounds. The only thing Jon could hear over his own labored breathing was the wind. For that reason, he didn't even know the car was approaching until it pulled up alongside him. He caught the movement out of the corner of his eye, and the shock made him stumble and almost drop the bike. Through the fog of his exhaustion, he registered what the object was and he took a step toward it.

Suddenly, however, a warning sounded in his head. He stopped. Images flashed before him. A spray of mud and gravel. Blood dripping down a locker. Awful things. He recoiled. Instinctively, he turned away from the vehicle and began staggering up the road in the direction he'd been traveling. His breath was coming in wheezes now.

There was movement to his side. The car. Then it was in front of him, and it was no longer moving. He lurched to a stop, and stood there panting, too fatigued to do anything else. The driver's side door opened, and a figure emerged from the car. His heart was pounding.

He peered through the snow. Whoever it was had put his hands on his hips. Jon could hear the muffled sound of the engine.

Finally, a female voice said, "Are you so pig-headed you'd rather stay out here and die than accept a ride from me?"

#

Mary squinted and peered ahead at the snow-covered road. The wipers were struggling now, snow having built up along the base of the windshield, hampering their movement and causing them to stick each time they swung downward. She was driving slowly, taking clues from the trees and other vegetation along the sides in an effort to stay in the middle of the roadway.

They had managed to get the bike in the back of the car. To fit it in, Jon had removed the front wheel with a wrench he'd retrieved with some difficulty from his knapsack. As he'd placed the tool and turned it, Mary had needed to hold his hands steady, they were shaking so badly. Once in the car, Jon had tried to speak, but the shaking had overtaken him. He was curled up and leaning against the passenger door. Mary could hear his teeth chattering.

Through the swirling snow, a structure appeared on the right hand side of the road. A moment later, there was one on the other side. They were on the outskirts of town. They crossed over the railroad tracks, and Mary turned the car onto Elm Street. As she pulled up in front of Mrs. Wilson's house, she could see the outline of the woman standing by the front window, a shawl wrapped around her shoulders.

Mary jumped out of the car and hurried around to the passenger side. She opened the door. "Jon," she said urgently, "you need to get inside."

Still shaking, Jon slowly pulled himself out of the car, where he stood, swaying side to side. Mary lifted one of his arms and placed it over her shoulder. Then she reached around his back and got a grip on his torso.

With Jon leaning against her, they stumbled up the front steps. Mrs. Wilson had opened the door, and she pointed down the hallway. "First door on the left."

Mary guided Jon into what turned out to be a small bedroom. She helped him on to the bed, where he curled up into a fetal position. She touched his forehead. He was burning up.

Mrs. Wilson came in carrying a blanket and towels. "I'll take care of him," she said and began unbuttoning Jon's coat. "You get home now, Mary Dahlgren, before you catch your death of cold."

Mary nodded. Slowly, she backed her way to the door, looking around the room. It was bare, save for a series of books and a framed picture on the desk. She couldn't make out who was in the picture. She was about to leave when Mrs. Wilson straightened and turned. "Thank you," she said.

#

On New Year's Day, Jon was finally able to get out of bed under his own power.

Of the prior three days, he had limited recollection. He remembered most of what had happened to him up to the moment when he first saw the car in the snow. After that, things were hazy. He could vaguely recall his grandmother feeding him some sort of broth and a man prodding him and listening to his breathing through a stethoscope.

He knew that Mary had driven him home, because his grandmother told him so, but he had no memory of it. For some reason, however, he was able to recall with a startling clarity the image of Mary's face hovering above him, her eyes clouded with concern. When, where and how that occurred, he had no idea. He wasn't even sure he hadn't dreamed it. Still, he couldn't get the image out of his mind. It both haunted and thrilled him, and it left him with the feeling that he had to do something.

At a minimum, he knew, he needed to thank Mary. But, more than that, he was hoping it would lead to something else. What, and perhaps more importantly, why, he couldn't say. On the first day back at school, Jon was seated at his desk in Miss Tremaine's first-period class when Mary entered. He watched her closely. She was subtle about it, but he noticed that she glanced in his direction before taking her seat. He opted to accept that as an encouraging sign.

The opportunity he'd been waiting for came sooner than he thought it might, at the end of second-period math, when Mary stayed behind to discuss an assignment with Mr. Hanson. Jon exited the classroom but lingered in the hallway as the other boys and girls headed in opposite directions to the separate classrooms they attended for health. He crouched down across the corridor from the door to Mr. Hanson's room and pretended to tie a shoelace. He'd been in that position for a couple of minutes when the door finally opened.

As Mary walked out, Jon stood and took a step toward her. She glanced up, saw him, and, without a word, whirled and strode quickly down the corridor in the direction of the girls' classroom, the clicking sound of her heels echoing off the walls of the now empty corridor.

Feeling foolish, Jon watched her until she turned the corner and the sound of her steps receded to nothing. The rest of the day was a blur, the disappointment so crushing that Jon couldn't wait to get away.

When the bell sounded at the end of study hall, his last class of the day, Jon remained seated as he always did, waiting for the other students to leave. He had his elbows planted on the desk, his chin resting in his hands. A book lay open in front of him, turned to the same page it had been when the class started. As the other students filed by his desk, Jon morosely looked past the book and contemplated their feet. Soon they were gone, and the sound of their voices faded.

Something brushed by his shoulder, and a small object landed on the pages of the book in front of him. Startled, he looked at it for a moment. It was a folded piece of paper. Without taking his chin off his hands, he raised his eyes just in time to see Mary's back as she passed through the door. As quickly as he'd noticed her, she was gone. His eyes dropped down again to the open book.

He sat up straight and looked around. He was alone. He looked back at the paper, lying where it had come to rest in the crook formed by the two open pages. Tentatively, he reached out and picked it up. He started to unfold it, then reflexively looked around again. Still alone.

The paper was a small white square, its sides no more than two inches in length. It had been folded twice. When he opened it, he found that, in small neat handwriting on the inside face, it read "Meet me at the bluff on the road to Middleburg. M."

Jon knew the spot. He'd discovered it early in his rides through the countryside. It was about two miles south of town, a few hundred yards past the point where the road to Middleburg split off from Ridley Road. It was not a heavily traveled route, and the spot was fairly isolated. It afforded a nice view of the river.

Heart suddenly beating fast, Jon closed the book on his desk, stood and hurried out of the room.

#

Ed Spitzman had a problem.

It had nothing to do with how the team was playing. On that front, all was going exceptionally well. Jackson was undefeated, having now won its first eight games. Spitzman's problem was that he was about to lose two of his best players. He'd received word that morning that Vernon King and Jeff Fletcher were flunking English. That bitch, Agnes Tremaine, was going to give the two of them failing grades for their first semester work. Pursuant to the district rules, they would both have to be placed on academic suspension.

He knew the boys were ignoring their schoolwork. They were barely passing their other courses, and Spitzman guessed some of the other teachers might also have failed them were it not for subtle pressure that had been brought to bear to keep the team from suffering. Unfortunately, not every teacher could be persuaded to look the other way. He'd anticipated problems with Bob Hanson, and, to make sure they didn't fail trigonometry, he had, at the beginning of the year, given two of his other seniors the responsibility for doing the homework for King and Fletcher. He realized now he should have done likewise for English.

He was going to have to find a way to convince Agnes to alter their grades.

He'd instructed the boys to scrimmage and left them alone in the gym. As he walked down the empty corridor, he racked his brain for a solution. He'd come up with nothing by the time he reached her classroom.

The door was open, and the woman was sitting at her desk, writing. "Agnes?"

"Yes?" she said, looking up with a smile on her face. The smile froze when she saw who it was. "Oh, hello, Ed."

"I hope I'm not interrupting," he said, as he walked into the classroom, knowing, of course, full well that he was. She did not reply, which, under the circumstances was probably best. He pretended to look around, feigning interest in a couple of study aids she'd hung above the blackboard. When he reached her desk, he planted his feet and clasped his hands behind his back. He gave her what he hoped was a winning smile.

"Is there something that you need from me?" she asked.

Having no better plan, he decided to take a direct approach. "Yes, I need you to give Vernon King and Jeff Fletcher passing grades for the first semester."

She set her pen down, folded her hands and asked, "Why would I do that? Considering," she continued, conversationally, "that neither of those two has turned in a single assignment, they've each failed every quiz I've given, and their performances on the final exam were, in a word, pathetic. Or maybe," she added, "you think I should give them passing grades just because they're such nice guys."

Spitzman shrugged. "Well, you have to admit they are that."

"They are what?" she asked, acidly.

"Nice guys."

"Oh, really," she said, arching her eyebrows. "So tell me, which one of them gave Jon Meyer the black eye?"

"Black eye?" Again he shrugged. "I'm not sure what you're talking about."

She snorted. "He *is* one of your students, Ed. Are you blind?"

It wasn't, he had to admit, the smartest response he could have made. "Look, I don't care about Meyer."

"Obviously."

Something in the way she said it gave him the germ of an idea. "I don't mean it that way, Agnes. I care about all of my students, of course. Right now, I'm worried about King and Fletcher passing English. Just as I'm sure you're worried about Meyer passing health and physical fitness."

It seemed to take her a moment to process what he'd just said. Then she narrowed her eyes and pursed her lips. "You cannot be serious," she said, a slight quiver coming to her voice. "Are you that unprincipled?"

"I'm very serious," he replied, innocently. "As for principle, don't you think it's wrong to fail students just because you don't like them?"

"What?" she exclaimed.

"That's right," he said, taking a guess, "you don't like King and Fletcher because you think they're picking on Meyer."

"That has nothing to do with it."

He had guessed right.

"Oh, really," he said, warming to the challenge. "Do you deny that you're angry about Meyer being picked on?"

She didn't answer, but he could see he'd scored a hit.

"Do you deny that you think King and Fletcher have something to do with it?" he continued, beginning to enjoy himself.

Again, she was silent. He could see she was fuming.

"In fact, you blame King and Fletcher for what's happened to Meyer, right?"

"No," she spat, angrily, and it caught him by surprise. In a voice practically dripping with venom, she said, "I blame you. You and your nauseating double standard. Not only do you let those boys get away with murder, you encourage it. You have no business being in education. You have no business being around young people. You, sir, disgust me."

It took him a moment to get over the shock. Then he stepped toward her and put his hands on her desk, resting on his knuckles. She instinctively leaned back. In a quiet voice, he said, "That's your opinion, and your entitled to it. Just like I'm entitled to think your opinion is worthless. Now," he said, leaning in, "if you don't want Meyer to flunk my class, you'll pass King and Fletcher. And, if you think for one moment I can't flunk Meyer—or worse—guess again. Those are my terms. And they're not negotiable."

She stared at him. Gone was all pretense of civility. She was breathing hard. He thought for an uncomfortable moment she might actually try to strike him, and he wasn't sure how he was going to handle that. But then she blinked and looked away. A long moment passed. Finally, still contemplating something outside the window, she said, "Not for you, and certainly not for those boys, I'll let them pass this once." She returned her attention to him and, to his surprise, leaned forward. He had to fight the sudden instinct to pull back. Her face inches from his, eyes blazing, she added, "You will give Jon Meyer an A, because we both know he deserves it. And you will keep your boys away from him. Those are *my* terms. And they're not negotiable."

They remained in that position for several seconds. Then Spitzman stood up straight and took a step back. He'd gotten what he needed. He couldn't care less what grade Meyer got. The important thing was that he'd just saved the season.

"Done," he said, and, without another word, he turned and walked out of the classroom.

#

As Jon approached the point where the road to Middleburg veered off from Ridley Road, he slowed. He'd been pedaling furiously from the moment he'd left the school, but he was suddenly beset by doubt. In a moment, he would be able to see the spot where Mary had told him to meet her. Would she be there? Or would this have simply been a joke, something that she could laugh about with her friends?

A small rise hid from view the bend in the road where he was headed. As he crested it, he saw an automobile parked on the side of the road, facing in his direction. It was a blue Packard. When he was about thirty yards from the car, he could make out the silhouette of a single occupant. His breath caught. It was Mary.

Mary had rolled down the window as he'd approached. He detected what seemed to be a look of worry on her face.

Uncertain what to say, he asked, "Did I make you wait long?"

She shook her head. She pointed toward the rear of the car. "Why don't you park your bike behind the car? I'll slide over, because I think the other door is blocked by the snow."

He did as she'd suggested, dismounting and wheeling the bike behind the car, where he set it against the mound of snow piled on the side of the road. He walked back, opened the driver's side door and slid into the front seat, thinking absently as he did that it was the first time he'd ever sat behind a steering wheel.

Mary had rolled the window back up and had moved across the bench to the passenger side, where she sat with her left knee up on the seat, turned toward him, her hands folded in her lap. Jon could smell a faint scent of soap. It occurred to him that it was one of the most incredible things he'd ever smelled.

He looked at her and realized he had no idea where to begin. She seemed to have the same problem, and they stared at one another for a long moment. Finally, he swallowed, took a deep breath, and, hoping his voice wouldn't betray his nervousness, he said, "Thank you for helping me in the storm."

As he'd started to speak, she had leaned forward slightly in anticipation. His words, however, seemed to deflate her, and she slumped back. She gave a slight nod and shrug of her shoulders.

He continued, quickly, afraid of what she might say. "I know I'm different from everyone else. I don't know why it's important, but I get that it is." He paused, then decided to take the plunge. "It's just that I was hoping there was a chance we could…"

"I'm so sorry, Jon."

He felt like he'd just been punched in the stomach, but he said, immediately, "Oh, I... I understand."

He couldn't meet her eyes, so he focused on her tightly clasped hands. There was a long silence. Then he heard her say, "What?"

He looked up. She was leaning forward again, staring at him intently. Confused, he asked, "What?"

"What did you say?" she asked, a tinge of excitement in her voice.

He thought for a moment. "I said I understand."

"No," she replied, with a quick, firm shake of her head, and Jon could swear her eyes were sparkling. "What you said before that. Something about how you were hoping there was a chance. Right?"

Her excitement was palpable.

"Say that part again," she told him. "And finish it this time, please."

Heart pounding, Jon said, haltingly, "I was just hoping that, maybe, there was a chance we could be," he shrugged, awkwardly, "friends."

Her eyes bore into him, and he felt as though he were on a precipice. Slowly, she reached her hands out, placing them on the seat between them, palms up.

He looked at them, then at her face. Hesitantly, he reached out with his own hands, and their fingers brushed. As soon as they touched, she clasped one of his hands in both of hers, squeezing tightly. He instinctively folded his other hand around them. Her hands were warm. They felt small in his.

And they felt wonderful.

9

When Jon finally returned to Ben's place on Saturday, almost two weeks had passed since he'd last been there. A week of that was attributable to his recuperation. The past week, however, had been all about Mary.

Jon and Mary had been together every afternoon following school, and Jon had never been so happy in his life.

They'd settled on a meeting place more proximate to the school, down a long private lane that branched off the highway about a mile east of the school. The lane led to a farm occupied by an elderly widower whom Mary knew to be extremely reclusive. The likelihood of their running into anyone coming up or down that lane was remote.

They spent quite a bit of time just sitting and talking. Mary explained to Jon in detail the whole situation with her father and his campaign and apologized so many times that he finally had to put a finger to her lips. It didn't matter. He did not blame her at all.

Jon told her about his trips to Ben's and learning to fly. Mary asked if she could come out to watch. They took drives, and Jon got a glimpse of places that had been too far for him to travel on his bike. The first time they ventured out, Mary offered to let him take the wheel and was flabbergasted when he told her he didn't know how to drive.

"Really?" she asked, laughing. "You know how to fly an airplane, but you can't drive a car?"

She resolved to teach him, and he learned quickly, the only real challenge being the timing required for the release of the clutch. It occurred to Jon that, if Mr. Dahlgren had any idea Jon was learning how to drive in his car, he'd have a fit. But, then again, how much worse would it be than if Mr. Dahlgren learned that he and Mary were spending all their free time together?

When they parted on Friday, they made plans to meet at their regular rendezvous on Saturday afternoon, Jon explaining that he needed to see Ben Saturday morning and let him know all was well. Neither was anxious to part, and they lingered until Jon finally said, "I really have to go, or I'll be late for dinner." He turned to open the door, and, before he realized what was happening, Mary leaned over and kissed him on the cheek, quickly sitting back, an impish expression on her face. He was so surprised, he didn't know what to do or say. The sensation stayed with him the entire ride home. When he arrived at his grandmother's, he honestly couldn't recall even turning the pedals.

When Ben saw Jon on Saturday morning, he put on a show. Tapping his forehead and gazing up, he said, "Your face is very familiar. I'm sure it's going to come to me."

A little embarrassed and not sure how to respond, Jon simply smiled.

Ben looked at him thoughtfully. "If I didn't know any better, I'd say there might be a young lady involved."

Jon felt his face flush.

Ben gave a knowing nod. "And who might this lucky young lady be?"

"Mary Dahlgren," Jon said.

"Jim Dahlgren's little girl? Boy, I haven't see her since she was," he thought for a moment, then put a hand out about three feet above the ground, "here."

He thought about it further. "I knew her mother, though. She was a beautiful woman. If her daughter takes after her at all, you're a lucky man."

Ben reached over to the bench, grabbed a pair of boxing gloves and tossed them to Jon. "You can give me the details later."

As they did on occasion, Ben and Jon sparred at half speed. It was an exercise Ben used to demonstrate punch combinations and footwork. Throughout, Ben kept up a running commentary.

"Step forward on the jab. Use your rear leg like a spring. Extend, extend. Good. Quick snap back and cover."

They circled around the "ring," which was really just a corner of the hangar Ben had cleared of equipment.

"Ok," Ben said, "Now I step in with a jab," and he put his left hand out, "and come immediately with the right like this." He brought his right hand over, pivoting slightly.

"That would be a mistake."

"Show me why."

"I slip the jab," Jon said, moving his head slightly. "Then I block the right." Jon wedged his right elbow against his chest, catching the punch with his hand. "Your elbow has dropped, and I can come over the top with a left hook."

"Excellent," said Ben, drawing back and reestablishing his stance. He tapped his chest with both gloves. "Eyes here. See my whole body. Anticipate what I'm going to do next. If I'm not careful, I tip off my next move. If you're looking up at my face, you won't see it."

Ben rotated and came in with a straight right. Jon rolled with the punch and looked for the combination. Ben came back immediately with another straight right. Jon was almost fooled. The counter he was going to throw would have rendered him badly exposed to a hard left. Instead, he rotated and danced away.

"Good move," Ben said. "You don't want to press if you've lost the advantage."

Jon stepped in with a left-right combination. Ben parried and counterpunched, landing a decent shot to Jon's body. Jon had steeled himself for it, however, and he took advantage of the momentary opening to tap Ben on the head with what would have been a deadly right cross at full speed.

Ben stepped back, smiling. "Where did that come from?"

Jon smiled in response and tapped his chest with his gloves. "Eyes here."

Ben laughed. "All right, smart guy."

Suddenly, Ben stepped back, looking alert, his eyes focused nowhere in particular. He tilted his head. Taking the end of one of his glove laces in his teeth and pulling quickly, he said, "Let's go," and strode rapidly to the door. Jon followed, also loosening his laces.

When he stepped outside, Jon realized what it was Ben had heard. It was a distant rumble. Jon's initial thought was that it might be a large truck.

Ben started walking toward the field, his head up, his eyes now looking eastward.

The rumble was more distinct now, more of a throaty roar. Certainly not a truck.

Then it was upon them. Above the trees lining the east end of the field, an aircraft flying at a jaw-dropping rate of speed appeared, just barely clearing the top branches. It came whipping straight over the field at a height of no more than a hundred feet, accompanied by a sound louder than anything Jon had ever heard before. And then it was gone, the roar fading, though not completely. In the distance, Jon could still hear the thrum of its engine.

Jon had only had a couple of seconds to observe it. It was a single wing aircraft, the wing set below the fuselage. The propeller was encased in a nose cone that came to a sharp point at the front. Immediately behind and below the propeller was what appeared to be a large air scoop. The fuselage tapered back from that point to a slightly rounded tail. The cockpit was set well back along the fuselage, glass surrounding the pilot everywhere but immediately behind him, the top of the glass blending into the top of the fuselage aft of the cockpit. It gave the craft a sleek, modern look. The plane was painted an olive green. Stenciled on the side of the fuselage behind the cockpit was a large white five-sided star inside a blue circle, the ends of a white bar extending out from either side of the circle. Jon knew it was a military aircraft.

They both stood there a moment, listening to the distant sound of the engine. Then Ben pointed to the south. "There," he said. "I'll be damned. He's going to try to land it here."

"I wonder who it is."

Ben grunted, and Jon looked at him. Something about Ben's expression struck Jon. "You think you know who it is?"

Ben nodded. "I have an idea. Part of me says I hope I'm right. Part of me says I hope I'm wrong."

Surprised, Jon turned back and scanned the sky for a sight of the aircraft. "Do you think he'll be able to land it here?"

"If it's who I think it is, yep."

After another minute, the sound began to increase again, though, this time, when the plane appeared above the tree line, it was traveling much slower. Landing gear had appeared below each wing, Jon only now realizing he'd seen no undercarriage on the plane as it had passed by initially.

The plane dropped quickly, flaring at the last moment, and settling gracefully onto the field, the two front wheels and a small wheel below the tail making contact at the same moment. It bumped along the surface until it was near the far end, turned and taxied back to a spot just beyond the open area between the hangar and Ben's house, stopping about fifty feet from where Ben and Jon stood.

The pilot shut the engine down, and a relative silence descended. A portion of the cockpit glass slid back, and a figure appeared, standing, then gripping the frame of the cockpit canopy and easily swinging his legs up and over the edge of the fuselage, landing for a moment on the back of the wing, then jumping to the ground. He was wearing khaki trousers and a dark brown jacket. On his head was a light brown fabric helmet that bulged at the ears. A pair of goggles had been pushed back onto his fore-head.

He came jogging toward them, and Ben stepped forward. When the pilot reached Ben, he threw his arms around him, and Ben reciprocated with a bear hug. They stayed that way for several seconds. When they stepped back, both appeared to have moist eyes.

"Good to see you, Pop," the pilot said, slipping the helmet off of his head and revealing a mop of wavy black hair.

Ben took a deep breath. "I'm happy to see you, too, Tommie. But, I'm also a little concerned." He pointed to the plane. "Something tells me the army didn't order you to land here."

Tommie grinned, revealing a set of even, white teeth. "You're right about that. They're expecting me at Chanute Field, where I'm supposed to refuel in," he consulted a watch on his wrist, "thirty-two minutes."

"Chanute? Over in Rantoul?"

Tommie nodded.

"If you hadn't stopped to land here, you'd be there by now."

"Yep," said Tommie, "I hightailed it from Buffalo. Got off a little early and kept the throttle open the whole way. I figured, when the army told me to fly practically right over this place, it was really telling me to stop in and see my pop. Who, by the way, I haven't seen in almost a year. You remember how the army works, right?"

Ben shook his head, but he was smiling.

Tommie seemed to notice Jon for the first time. "Tommie Wheeler," he said, putting out a hand.

Jon stepped forward and shook his hand. "Jon. Jon Meyer."

Tommie nodded toward the boxing gloves that Jon had forgotten he was still holding. "I see my pop is teaching you how to box. Has he shown you the Widowmaker yet?"

Jon looked at Ben, who laughed. "Not yet. We'll get to that soon enough."

Tommie adopted a boxing stance, moved his fists side to side for a moment, then threw a big overhand right at no one in particular.

"You tipped it off," Ben said, and this time it was Tommie's turn to laugh.

"You know, Pop, I really need to hit the head. I'll bet you've got some cold milk in the fridge. Why don't we sit down for a few minutes and catch up." He put his arm around Ben's shoulder, and the two of them started walking toward the house.

Jon was unsure what to do, but Ben looked back and jerked his head in the direction of the house, indicating he should follow.

Ben had poured three glasses of milk, and he and Jon were sitting at the kitchen table when Tommie came in and sat down.

"So tell me, Tommie," Ben said, "what's the army got you doing now?"

"Right now," Tommie said, taking a sip of milk, "I'm a glorified truck driver. That P-40 you see out there just came off the line in Buffalo. I'm taking it to Los Angeles. From there, I understand it's on its way to China or someplace like that."

"You're not going with it?"

Tommie shook his head. "Nope. Like I said, glorified truck driver."

Ben seemed relieved. "Well, I can think of worse things."

"I know, Pop," said Tommie. He looked at the table and absently ran his fingers along the grain of the wood. Then he looked up. "The thing is, there's a war going on. I can't just be ferrying planes around the country. Heck, the army's starting to train women to do that."

Ben spread his palms. "If I recall correctly, the army doesn't usually ask you what you want to do. It tells you what you're going to do."

Nodding, Tommie said, "That's right. It hasn't changed much. But," he leaned forward, his face animated, "they're pretty desperate right now to fill aircrews for the European bombing campaign. Heavy bombers. B-17s and B-24s. They've been asking for volunteers. It's a quick ticket to the show."

Ben frowned. "Why would you want to fly one of those if you can strap yourself to something like that fighter out there?"

"Because it's the only way I'm guaranteed to get into the mix. I want to get there before it's all over."

Ben expelled a breath. "I don't think you have to worry about that, Tommie. This war isn't going to be over any time soon. Maybe you should just let the army use your skills the way they see fit."

"Too late," Tommie said. "When I get to L.A., I've got orders sending me up to Idaho. I start training in a week."

Ben was quiet for a long time. Tommie broke the silence by turning to Jon. "Have you been flying?"

Jon nodded. "I have, yes. In the Jenny."

"Figured. I saw the picture in the cabinet." It was a picture Ben had taken just after Jon had soloed for the first time. Ben had set his camera on a tripod and snapped it using a remote cord. They both had broad smiles on their faces. Ben had his arm around Jon's shoulder.

"Jon took right to it," Ben said. "I let him land the Jenny the first time he went up."

"Really?" Tommie said, looking impressed. "Had you ever been flying before?"

"No, sir."

Tommie arched his eyebrows and looked at Ben. "A natural, huh?"

Ben nodded.

Tommie returned his attention to Jon. "Meyer. I don't remember that name. Are you new to the area?"

"Yes, sir. I came this past summer to live with my grandmother."

"Jon's parents passed away," Ben added. "His mother was Claire Wilson, Marvella's daughter."

"Huh," Tommie said, "I didn't know Mrs. Wilson even had any kids. Sorry to hear about your folks Jon."

Jon nodded. "Thanks."

Tommie looked at Ben. His expression became somber. "Pop, don't worry about me. I'm going to be fine."

Ben said nothing, but he nodded.

Pushing himself up from the table, Tommie said, "I'd better get going before the army realizes they're short a pilot. And, worse, a plane."

The three of them walked out to a spot a few feet from the aircraft Jon now knew was a P-40. Tommie turned to Ben, and they embraced, holding it for a long moment. Stepping back, Tommie wiped his eyes with his sleeve and walked to the plane. He had a foot up on the wing when he stepped back, pointed to Jon and motioned him over.

Jon jogged over to where Tommie stood. Tommie reached out his hand, and Jon took it. "Jon, it was a pleasure meeting you. You know," he added, "my pop is a really good judge of character, and he obviously thinks a lot of you."

He reached over with his left hand and put it on Jon's shoulder. Squeezing both hands at the same time, he said, "Be well. And look after my pop, ok?"

"Yes sir."

Jon and Ben stood together and watched as Tommie fired up the engine and went through a quick check of the control surfaces. He taxied out to a point near the tree line, ran the engine to maximum revolutions, and then, releasing the brakes, he sent the aircraft hurtling down the field and into the air. In a matter of a few seconds, it was gone, the sound receding to nothing.

Ben stood very still for a long time, and Jon waited patiently.

Finally, Ben turned and put a hand on Jon's shoulder. "I'd say maybe it's time I showed you the old Widowmaker. What do you think?"

Jon nodded, and together they walked back to the hangar.

#

Jon told his grandmother he would not be eating dinner with her that evening. She assumed he would be eating with Ben, and he said nothing to correct that misimpression. He and Mary drove to Ridley in the late afternoon. It was the first time in seven months Jon had been anywhere with traffic signals and street lights.

They had dinner at a restaurant Mary knew. She had to convince Jon it was ok for her to pay, finally sealing the deal when she noted the money was an allowance from her father, and, in reality, her father was treating them to the meal, something Mary felt he owed Jon many times over.

After dinner, they walked to the Orpheum to see *Babes on Broadway* with Mickey Rooney and Judy Garland. They shared popcorn and held hands through the entire movie.

Jon drove back, and, just before they reached Jackson, he pulled off the road to retrieve his bike from the rear of the car. With the front wheel re-attached, he stood and faced Mary. She looked up at him, reflections of the moon sparkling in her eyes. It was a still night. No breeze ruffled the tree branches, and Jon could hear no sound other than the muffled pounding of his own heart.

Mary took a step closer to him. As she did, he reached out and gently touched her shoulder. She leaned in, and, instinctively, he did likewise. When their lips touched, a warm, thrilling sensation flooded his body.

Mary put her arms around his neck, pulling him closer, and he encircled her with his. He couldn't say how long they stayed that way. When they did finally separate, however, it was only for a brief moment. They looked each another, and immediately fell back into a kiss.

Finally, out of breath, they stopped. Mary put her head against his chest, and Jon leaned his face against the top of her head, drinking in the scent of her hair. After a moment, he realized she was crying. Alarmed, he pulled back to look at her. She seemed embarrassed.

"What's wrong?" he asked.

She shook her head and laughed softly. "Nothing is wrong," she said. "Absolutely nothing. I'm just so happy."

Jon let go of her with one hand and reached up, running a finger tenderly across her cheek where tears had run. She grasped his hand with hers, turned it and gently kissed the back of it. "Will I see you tomorrow?"

He nodded solemnly. "Nothing is going to keep us apart."

#

On Sunday morning, Jon and Mary drove to Ben's place. Jon and Ben had made plans for Ben to take Mary up in the Jenny. As they pulled up, Ben was out by the hangar waiting for them, and, when Mary got out of the car, he stepped forward and gave her a hug. Ben and Jon rolled the Jenny out of the hangar. Ben gave Mary the leather jacket to wear, and she was quite a sight in it. The garment was almost twice her size, but she pushed the sleeves up and had a good laugh about it at her own expense.

Her eyes bright with anticipation, Mary climbed into the front cockpit and allowed Jon to strap her in. Jon rotated the propeller and fired up the engine. He then watched as Ben taxied out to the field and lifted off.

When they returned, Mary was even more animated than usual. Her cheeks a rosy red from the cold and her impossibly blue eyes positively dancing, she recounted the adventure with breathless excitement.

Before they left, Ben gave Mary another hug. As Ben straightened, Mary took him by surprise, standing on her toes and planting a kiss on his cheek. "Thank you for everything," she said. "Especially being here for Jon."

Ben's cheeks reddened slightly and he seemed at a loss for words. Still, he looked pleased.

Jon leaned over and said, "I know exactly how you feel."

#

"Ok, what's that look supposed to mean?" asked Mary, chuckling. The expression on Sam's face was priceless.

"At some point you *are* going to tell me what's turned you into the happiest person on the planet, right?"

Mary laughed.

They were sitting in the outdoor eating area at school. It was the first week of March, and, though it was still cold, it was a rare sunny day. Mary had convinced Sam to bundle up and eat lunch outside. The only other person in the outdoor area was Jon, who was, as usual, alone, seated two tables away from where Mary and Sam sat.

Jon had become something of an invisible man. Nobody seemed to pay attention to him any more, other than, of course, Mary, who was always keenly aware of his presence. She hadn't told Sam that Jon was one of the reasons she'd been so insistent on eating outdoors today. When she and Sam sat down, Mary had taken the seat facing in Jon's direction, and Sam sat with her back to Jon. From their respective positions, Mary and Jon were able to see each other and exchange covert looks.

"Seriously," Sam continued, "I'm thinking it has to be either a guy or a lobotomy."

Mary shook her head. Fortunately, Sam had been so busy the past several weeks with the school play she hadn't noticed anything unusual in Mary's comings and goings. Mary and Jon had arranged their schedules so that, when Sam was available to do things with Mary, Jon spent time with Ben. It had worked well, and Sam had not yet caught on.

"Have you seen me hanging around with any guys lately?" Mary asked with a smile.

Sam thought about that for a moment. Finally, she said, "So, how much did you pay for that lobotomy, anyway?"

Mary was about to reply, when a shadow fell across the table between them. She and Sam both looked up.

Vernon stood at the end of the table. He was in shirt sleeves. "Do you mind if I join you?" he asked. He paused a beat, and, when there was no immediate response, he slid onto the bench next to Sam.

"Aren't you a little cold?" Sam asked.

Vernon shrugged. "Not a problem for me."

Sam turned to Mary, who returned her look with a shrug of her own.

"Sam," Vernon said, with a forced politeness, "would you mind terribly if I had a word in private with Mary?"

The reaction on Sam's face mirrored Mary's, a mixture of surprise and annoyance. Sam gave Mary an inquiring look. Mary had no desire to talk to Vernon. But she knew Vernon, and she didn't want a scene. She gave a slight nod, hoping Sam would not go far. Sam collected her lunch items, lifted her legs and pivoted around. She stood and, from behind Vernon, gave Mary a look and pointed to the cafeteria door as if to say that she'd be waiting inside. Mary nodded.

When Sam had left, Vernon folded his hands in front of himself and gave Mary a brilliant smile. She had to admit, he was very good-looking. Most anyone who didn't know Vernon would be instantly attracted to him. Mary, of course, knew it was a thin veneer. She returned his look without smiling.

"Mary," he said, effusively.

"Vernon," she replied, politely.

He continued to give her that winning smile.

"Well," Mary said, "now that we've established our identities…"

"This Saturday evening," he interrupted, "there will be a party to celebrate our victory in the regional championship."

"You won the regional championship?" Mary asked, innocently.

Vernon's brow furrowed momentarily. "No, not yet. But we will on Saturday. And when we do, we'll be celebrating at the Lodge. Where, by the way, my father's now a member."

"Congratulations."

"Yes, well, I was wondering if you would do me the honor of accompanying me. As my date."

There was no way, Mary thought, she would accompany Vernon. Anywhere. Ever.

Keeping her tone exceedingly polite, Mary replied, "Vernon, that is such a kind invitation. I appreciate it very much. However, I respectfully decline."

Vernon looked confused. He glanced away, obviously thinking hard. Then he looked back at her. "Why not?" he asked, the forced civility having been dropped.

Mary gave him a level gaze. "Because I don't want to."

Vernon stared at her for several seconds. She could see his mood darken. "What is it with you?" he finally asked, annoyance in his voice. "Any girl at this school would jump at the chance to go to this party with me. It's the regional championship, for god's sake. Why wouldn't you want to be there? With me?"

Unable to resist, Mary asked, "Do you really have that high an opinion of yourself?"

"Don't you?" he fired back immediately.

"The answer is no, Vernon. Thank you. But, no."

His expression soured. "You stuck up bitch."

Jon was halfway out of his seat. Mary gave him a direct look and shook her head. Keeping her voice light, she said, "Sticks and stones, Vernon. Sticks and stones."

Vernon stared at her, breathing hard. Jon, thank God, sat back, but he looked alert.

"Well, goodness, Vernon," she said, as if they were at a garden party, "it was nice talking to you. But, really, you should get inside before you catch a cold."

He continued looking at her for a long moment. Then he put both hands on the table and violently pushed himself back, knocking over the bench on which he'd been seated. Without a word, he turned and stalked to the cafeteria door, where he grabbed the handle and yanked it open. Sam, who had obviously been leaning against the door, came stumbling out past him.

"Well, ok," Sam said, flustered. "Thank you."

Vernon passed through and slammed the door behind him. Sam looked at Mary with a questioning look.

Mary shook her head and gave a slight wave of one hand. "Everything's fine," she said, as much to Jon as to Sam.

#

Monday had been an odd day at school. On Saturday evening, the basketball team had, to the shock of everyone, lost in the regional championship game, a heart-breaking defeat for the second year in a row. The basketball players were uncharacteristically subdued. Mary had heard that Mr. Spitzman had not even shown up at school.

Gwenda was distraught. Apparently, Billy had taken the loss particularly hard and was refusing to have anything to do with anyone. And that, at least for the moment, included Gwenda. She had come to Mary and Sam in tears after school. They were in Sam's bedroom in the apartment that she and her mother shared above the beauty shop her mother owned and operated.

"I've never seen Billy like this," Gwenda said.

Sam handed her another tissue. "You know he'll get over it."

Gwenda blew softly into the tissue, and then, folding it, she used it to dab her eyes. "I guess," she said. "It's just that he hurts so bad, and I hurt for him."

Mary leaned forward, put a hand on Gwenda's knee and squeezed lightly. "That just means you're meant to be with him."

Gwenda thought about that for a moment. Then she nodded and said, "I guess I am meant to be with him. And he's meant to be with me. Really, we're so perfect for each other." She smiled weakly. "When we're not together, I just don't feel as happy as I do when we are."

"There you go," Mary said. "You just need to give Billy a little time to get over the disappointment. He will. Soon enough, everything will be back to normal."

"You think?" Gwenda asked, hopefully.

"Absolutely."

Gwenda dabbed her eyes again. Taking a deep breath, she looked around the bedroom. "You know, it's been such a long time since we've been together like this. It's nice." She looked at Mary and Sam. "I've been so wrapped up with Billy, I don't even know what's been going on with you two."

Mary and Sam looked at each other and shrugged.

Sam said, "You haven't missed much. I've been busy with the school play." She looked at Mary. "And, of course, Mary's turned into the happiest person on the planet."

Gwenda turned to Mary. "Really? What's happened?"

Mary shook her head. "Nothing."

Gwenda looked at Sam.

"Yep," Sam said, "that's pretty much all I've gotten out of her myself. I've concluded she must have had a lobotomy."

Returning her attention to Mary, Gwenda peered into her eyes. After a long moment, she said, slowly, "No, that's not it. It's a boy."

"See, that's what I thought, too," Sam said. "But it would have to be the most top secret thing in the history of romance, because I've never seen her with any boys."

Gwenda had not taken her eyes off Mary. "It is, isn't it?"

Mary felt her cheeks flush.

"I'm right, aren't I?" She was boring in now.

Mary looked away.

"Ah, hah," Gwenda declared triumphantly. "I am right."

"She is?" Sam asked.

Mary didn't reply.

"You little devil," Sam exclaimed. "You've been holding out on me."

Now both Gwenda and Sam were looking at her. Mary thought about what she might say to cover things up. Then she realized they'd see through anything that wasn't true. After a long pause, she gave a slight nod of her head.

"Oh my goodness," Sam said, excitedly. "Out with it. Now."

Mary looked down at her hands, then back at her two friends. "You have to swear to keep this a secret," she said.

Both girls nodded.

Mary took a deep breath. "I've been seeing Jon Meyer for the past two months."

"The Jewish boy?" blurted Gwenda.

Sam was quiet for a moment. Then she nodded. "That makes sense."

"But he's Jewish," Gwenda insisted.

Sam turned to Gwenda. "What difference does that make?"

Gwenda looked confused. "I… I don't know. I guess," she hesitated, looking back and forth at Mary and Sam. "Well, maybe…" Brow knitted, she looked away, chewing on her lip. Finally, she turned back. "I guess it really doesn't matter?"

"That's right," Sam said, turning back to Mary, reaching out and taking Mary's hands in hers. "What's important is that Mary is happy." She looked intently at Mary. "And you are happy aren't you?"

Mary nodded. "Very much."

"Then I'm happy for you," Sam said.

Tentatively, Gwenda reached out. Mary removed one hand from Sam's, grasped one of Gwenda's, and pulled it toward her so that they were all holding hands. Gwenda put her other hand on top, and they all three laughed.

#

When the boys gathered for gym class on Tuesday, there was uncertainty as to whether Mr. Spitzman would show. He'd not been at school on Monday, and nobody seemed to know where he was.

They milled about in the gym just outside the locker room. After a few minutes, a door slammed, and the boys all stopped and turned at the same time. Mr. Spitzman had emerged from his office and was walking toward them, an equipment bag in his hands.

He reached them, dropped the bag on the floor and planted his feet.

To Jon, the man looked horrible. His eyes were bloodshot. His face was haggard, and it looked as if it had a green tinge to it.

"Listen up," Mr. Spitzman announced, his voice sounding hoarse and gravely. "Today, you boys are going to learn about boxing."

Jon perked up.

"I'm going to need a volunteer," he continued. He pointed at Jon. "Meyer, you just volunteered."

Surprised, Jon stepped forward. It was the first time in months the teacher had even acknowledged him.

The man reached into the bag, rummaged around a bit, then pulled out a pair of old boxing gloves. He threw them at Jon. "Put these on." He pointed to Doug Larson. "Larson, you help him tie the laces."

Jon slipped the gloves on. They felt the same as the gloves he'd been using at Ben's. Doug stepped over, and Jon turned his hands palms up. Doug pulled the laces tight and started to tie a knot. "No," Jon said, quietly, "like you were tying your shoes."

Doug looked at him, surprised, but he did as Jon instructed. When he was done, Jon tested the gloves, punching his fists together. They felt good. He looked at Mr. Spitzman, who was in the process of having a pair of gloves tied by Cyrus Clayton.

"All right," the teacher said, smacking his gloves together, "pay attention." He pointed a glove at Jon. "Meyer, stand like this," and he adopted a boxing stance. Jon did as he was told.

"Now," he continued, "there are four basic punches. The first is the jab, which, if you're right handed, you make with your left hand," and he waved his left hand. "Let me show you."

He crouched in a boxer's stance. Without warning, he snapped his left hand and caught Jon square on the nose with a hard punch. Jon staggered backwards and almost fell. He was just barely able to keep his feet under him and retain his balance. He straightened and shook his head to clear it. When he rubbed his forearm under his nose, it came away smeared with blood.

Jon could hear murmuring among the other boys.

"You have something to say, Larson?" Spitzman asked.

"No sir," Doug said, immediately.

"How about you, Morris. It looked like you might have something to say."

"No. No, sir."

"Good." The man returned his attention to Jon. "Assume your position."

Jon took a boxer's stance, again. This time, however, he was fully alert, his eyes on the teacher's chest.

"The next punch," Spitzman announced, "is the left hook," and, with the word "hook," he threw a vicious left aimed at the side of Jon's head that, had it connected, would certainly have sent Jon to the floor and might have knocked him out. However, Jon was ready for it. Without dropping his guard, he leaned his head back. Spitzman's fist sailed harmlessly by and he staggered after it.

There were audible snorts from the other boys. The man regained his balance and looked hard at the group for several seconds. Apparently unable to single anyone out, he rolled his shoulders and turned back to Jon. There was undisguised anger on his face now.

"The next punch," he began, but he was already throwing a straight right directly at Jon's chin. Jon moved his head slightly to the left and easily slipped it. Again, Spitzman staggered.

Now there were open guffaws from the boys. Straightening, Spitzman moved his head as though stretching his neck muscles. He ignored the other boys and looked at Jon with a baleful expression.

"All right. You want to go? Let's go."

He crouched in an alert stance, his head moving side to side. The other boys had fallen quiet.

Spitzman stepped forward with a jab that Jon easily deflected. The man danced to his right. Jon shifted his feet, but held his ground. Spitzman tried a quick left-right combination, but Jon parried it and, shuffling quickly, re-established his position. He had yet to throw a punch, biding his time as Ben had taught him.

Spitzman looked frustrated. He feigned a move to his right, then bounced back, looking for an opening. Jon wouldn't give him one.

They circled each another, the look of frustration on the man's face deepening by the moment. Just to establish the range, Jon threw a couple of jabs. Spitzman blocked them both, but, in the course of doing so, he left his guard down. If he had wanted to, Jon could have attacked, but he held back.

Finally, Spitzman stepped in with a ferocious volley. Nothing connected squarely, but it was clear he wasn't pulling any punches. Jon pivoted away, moving lightly on the balls of his feet. He knew now this was for real. He watched for an opening.

Spitzman gave him one right away. The teacher snapped a couple of jabs, but Jon could see he'd cocked his right arm and was ready to throw a hard right. Jon waited patiently for it. Spitzman drew his right hand back slightly, then lunged forward. Instead of slipping the punch by moving to the left, Jon pivoted on his left foot and brought his right foot around a hundred and eighty degrees. Spitzman went sailing by like a bull passing a matador, and, as he did, Jon clipped him on the jaw with a left hook.

The punch staggered the man, and it was a testament to his athleticism that he didn't go down. Spitzman turned, enraged, and threw a another hard right. This one Jon blocked with his right glove and, while Spitzman's elbow was down, Jon came over the top with another left hook to the chin. Then, for good measure, Jon pivoted his body and, throwing his entire weight behind it, gave the man a hard shot to the stomach.

Instinct told Jon to jump back, and he did so just in time to avoid being splattered with the vomit that came spewing out of Spitzman's mouth, soaking the man's legs and feet. As he watched, the teacher's shoulders heaved a second time, and he deposited another bilious load down his front.

Jon slowly lifted one of his gloves, grabbed the end of the lace between his teeth, and released the knot. He slid the glove off, undid the other lace, and removed the second glove. He tossed both gloves in the general direction of the equipment bag lying a few feet away. Then he turned and began walking toward the locker room.

Between Jon and the door stood Caleb Pratt and Billy Hamilton. Jon walked straight up to the two boys, stopped and arched his eyebrows. Silently, they each took a step to the side, clearing a path. Calmly, Jon stepped between them and continued to the door leading to the locker room. With his hand on the knob, he turned and looked back. Spitzman was still bent over, hands on his knees, his head drooping and a long, viscous line of drool hanging from his mouth. The other boys were all looking at Jon. Without a word, Jon opened the door and passed through.

10

The school parking lot took longer than usual to empty out on the Friday before spring break. There was a general sense of festivity in the air, the prospect of time off lightening the mood. Students lingered, sharing plans or making arrangements to get together during the upcoming week.

Vernon King sat in the cab of his father's pickup truck. Billy Hamilton was next to him in the passenger seat. They were waiting for Jeff Fletcher, who had been sent to the principal's office for talking during study hall.

"You doing anything special this week?" Billy asked.

"Not really," Vernon said, with a shrug. "I might give Darlene a shot. She's been hanging around a lot." He turned and gave Billy a salacious wink. "I think she's ready for me."

"Really? Darlene?"

"Why not? A man's got to do what he's got to do."

Billy chuckled.

"How about you?" Vernon asked. "You and Gwenda, right?" He waggled his eyebrows in a suggestive way.

"What?" Billy said, then he immediately shook his head. "No, Gwenda's not like that."

"Not at all?"

Billy's cheeks reddened slightly.

"That's what I thought," Vernon said, with a coarse laugh. He returned his attention to the front of the school building. The door opened, but, instead of Jeff, Mary Dahlgren emerged and began walking down the steps. She was carrying a couple of books that she held against her chest. She smiled and waved to someone in the parking lot.

"Now there's a skirt I wouldn't mind getting under," Vernon said, tipping his head in Mary's direction. "Problem is, I think she's one of those girls who's not interested in guys at all, if you know what I mean."

Billy looked at Mary and shook his head, chuckling slightly. "Nope."

Vernon looked sharply at Billy. "What?"

Billy winced. "Forget it."

Vernon snorted. "Forget it?" He squinted his eyes and gave Billy a hard look. "What do you know?"

Billy looked away. Vernon waited.

After a long moment, Billy turned back. "I shouldn't have said anything. I promised Gwenda I wouldn't. Let's leave it at that."

"Let's not and pretend that we did. Come on, Billy. Out with it."

Billy took a deep breath and puffed his cheeks as he blew it out. "Gwenda swore me to secrecy. If I tell you, you have to swear to me you won't tell a soul."

"You know you can count on me to keep a secret."

Billy hesitated. Then he said, "All right. But not a word to anyone else."

Vernon held up a hand, as if he were swearing an oath.

Billy nodded toward Mary, who was getting into a blue Packard. "Mary's been going out with Jon Meyer."

"You're kidding me."

"No," Billy said, shaking his head. "They've been seeing each other for months."

Vernon sat back in the seat. He watched the Packard as it pulled away. It circled around the parking lot and turned onto the highway.

He'd been trying to get Mary to go out with him since, when? Since the summer. So many opportunities he'd given her. She'd rejected him every time. He'd never been able to understand why. He knew it couldn't be that she had no interest in him, and he'd finally consoled himself with the thought that Mary had no interest in guys at all. That, now, was apparently not the case. He felt the first stirrings of anger.

But that wasn't even the half of it. She hadn't just rejected him. No. She'd turned him down for that nobody, and, in the process, made a fool of him. The anger started to burn.

Then, he had a thought. As he rolled it around in his head, it began to take shape. He massaged it, filling in the details. Finally, he turned to Billy.

"Did I tell you about the party on Monday night?"

Billy's eyes brightened. "No. What party?"

"Out at the Lodge."

"The Lodge? On a Monday? I thought the Lodge was always closed on Mondays."

Vernon nodded. "Usually. It's a special event. For the new members." He added, casually, "You want to come?"

"Sure."

"Ok. But you've got to do me a favor."

Billy shrugged. "What do you need?"

"I need you to get Gwenda to invite Mary."

Billy frowned. "Why?"

"I need a chance to talk to her. It'll be the perfect opportunity."

"I don't know," Billy said, uncertainly.

"Look," Vernon said, making an effort to sound as sincere as he possibly could. "I'm not sure what Mary sees in Meyer. I just need a chance to convince her to go out with me. The club will be the perfect setting. I need you to do me this favor, ok?"

Billy thought about it for a moment. "Ok, I'll ask Gwenda."

"You mean you'll tell Gwenda," Vernon said. "To ask Mary," he added.

"Right."

Vernon lowered his chin and gave Billy a sober look. "It's very important that Mary comes to the Lodge on Monday night. She'll do it for Gwenda. Gwenda will do it for you. And you'll do it for me. Right?"

"Right," Billy said again.

#

On Monday evening, Jon wheeled his bike around the house and mounted it. His grandmother had been a little under the weather, and he was on his way to pick up some cough medicine. He wanted to get to the pharmacy before it closed.

He and Mary couldn't be together this evening. Mary had explained to him that she'd be attending a party at the Lodge. She didn't really want to go, but Gwenda had begged her to come, and the thought of refusing had made Mary feel bad. It was just as well, Jon reflected. He'd stay home and care for his grandmother. He and Mary would have the rest of the week to spend together. They were planning another trip to Ridley, and he was looking forward to it.

As Jon turned his bike onto Main Street, he noticed a couple walking in his direction on the other side. In the light spilling out from the large front windows of the diner, the couple was illuminated for a moment, and he was surprised to see that it was Gwenda and Billy. He was even more surprised when they turned at the door to the diner and walked in. They took a seat at one of the front tables.

That struck Jon as odd. Mary had said the party would start at seven o'clock. It was now just a few minutes before seven. Maybe, he thought, they were meeting Mary, and they all planned to go together. That had to be it. Mary would almost certainly be along shortly.

He had a few minutes to spare before the pharmacy closed. Anxious, as always, to catch a glimpse of Mary, he decided he would wait until she arrived. He pedaled his bike to a spot just across the street from the diner, braked, and put a foot down to steady himself.

Through the front window, Jon could see Gwenda and Billy clearly. Betty Langdon stopped in front of their table, took out her order pad and started writing. Why, Jon asked himself, would they be ordering if they're going to a party in just a few minutes? As soon as he'd asked the question, however, the answer came to him. They're just ordering Cokes to sip while they wait. That made perfect sense.

A few minutes went by, and there was no sign of Mary. Jon realized he would have to get going or he'd miss the chance to pick up his grandmother's medicine. Disappointed, he put a foot on one of the pedals, prepared to leave. Then he froze. Betty had appeared with two plates of food in her hands, and she set them down on the table in front of Gwenda and Billy. She returned a moment later with a pair of drinks and set those down as well. Billy picked up a hamburger and took a bite.

That made no sense. Jon watched them eat for a moment, a nagging disquiet beginning to gnaw at him. He ran through different scenarios in his mind, but nothing clicked. Finally, putting off all thoughts of the pharmacy, he stepped down on the pedal and rode the short distance to the Dahlgren house.

The house was dark, no light appearing in any of the windows. He debated with himself for a moment. He didn't want to do it, but his apprehension overrode concerns about what Mr. Dahlgren's reaction might be if he suddenly appeared on the man's front step. He walked to the door and knocked.

An anxious minute passed, and there was no response. He knocked again, this time a little louder. Still, no answer. Finally, he pounded on the door and called out, "Mary!"

The house sat quiet as a tomb. Something, Jon realized, was very wrong.

#

"Tell me again why the party was cancelled?" asked Gwenda.

Billy finished chewing the bite he'd taken and swallowed. "All I know is what Vernon told me. He said someone got sick, and they had to cancel."

"Some*one*?" she repeated. "One person gets sick, and a whole party gets cancelled? That doesn't make any sense."

Billy shrugged. "I'm just telling you what he said."

Gwenda thought about that. "And he said he told Mary?"

"Uh, huh," Billy said, his mouth full again.

"Why would Vernon be talking to Mary? More importantly, why would Mary be talking to Vernon? She doesn't even like him."

"I don't know why they would be talking."

There was something in his tone that struck Gwenda as odd. It was almost as if Billy was being intentionally vague, evasive. A troubling thought occurred to her.

"Billy, you haven't told anyone about," and she lowered her voice to a whisper, "Mary and Jon?"

Billy shook his head adamantly. "No, I told you. I haven't said a word. I promised you I wouldn't. Don't you trust me?"

Gwenda reached out and touched Billy's arm. "Of course I do. I'm sorry. It's just…" She stopped, her thoughts churning.

"It's just what?"

After a long moment, Gwenda finally said, "I don't know. It just feels like there's something wrong." She had a thought. "Hey, can we walk over to Mary's house?"

"Can I finish my hamburger first?"

"Of course."

When they were done eating, they took the short five-minute walk to the Dahlgren house. No one appeared to be at home, and there was no answer when they knocked. Gwenda saw that the car was gone. The concern that had descended on her in the diner deepened.

"I wonder where Mary is," Gwenda said, half aloud.

"Maybe she's with Sam."

Gwenda shook her head. "No, Sam went with her mother to visit her grandparents in Valparaiso. She won't be back for a couple of days."

"So," Billy said, "maybe she's with Meyer." He put his arms around her. "Come on, Gwenda. You're worrying about nothing. Everything's going to be fine."

She leaned against him and nodded. Still, the sense of foreboding would not leave her.

#

Mary steered the Packard into the parking court at the Lodge. Normally, there would be an attendant to take the car and park it in the lot out of sight just beyond the thicket of woods that lined the approach to the club. But there were no attendants to be seen. She saw no people coming or going, and the place seemed unnaturally quiet. She knew it had to be just about seven o'clock. That's when Gwenda had told her the party would start. Her foot on the brake and the engine idling, Mary leaned forward and looked out the windshield up at the main Lodge building. There were plenty of lights on, so it was obviously open. Uncertain what to do, she set the parking brake, turned off the engine and got out of the car.

Perhaps, she thought, she'd gotten the time wrong. She decided she would go in and ask. When she stepped inside, she did not hear any voices, and there was an air of desertion about the place. She could, however, hear music coming from upstairs.

"Hello," she called out.

"The party's up here," a voice replied, immediately. It was a voice she didn't recognize. It sounded muffled.

That was surprising. Mary had never been on the second floor of the Lodge. She knew there were rooms for overnight guests up there, but she hadn't realized there was an area that would accommodate a party. She climbed the stairs and paused at the top. The music was coming from down the corridor to her left. There was a door open near the end, and light from the room beyond illuminated a portion of the passageway.

She walked down the hall and stepped into the room, where she experienced a moment of confusion. This was no party room. It appeared to be a parlor or sitting room. There was a radio against the far wall, and that was obviously the source of the music. To her left, she could see another door, but it was closed. She stepped further into the room to peer to the right, and, as she did, the door she'd just passed through swung shut with a loud bang, causing her to jump.

She looked behind her at the door that had just slammed shut. Jeff Fletcher stood with his back to it, a grin on his face.

"Jeff? What's going on?"

He didn't immediately reply. There was something unsavory about the way he was looking at her.

"Hello, Mary," came a voice from behind her. She whirled and saw Vernon standing in the doorway that had been closed a moment before. He was leaning casually against the frame, his arms crossed. "Nice of you to join us."

#

Jon had never been to the Lodge, but he knew where it was. It was accessed by a road that branched off the highway about ten miles to the east of town, shortly before the highway crossed the river.

He was riding as fast as he could. Fortunately, there was almost a full moon, and he was just able to make out the road by the light filtering through the trees on both sides.

He knew there was a chance he was going to be extremely embarrassed, trespassing at a private club where he had no business. But it was a chance he was willing to take. His instinct told him Mary was in trouble, and the possibility of looking like a fool was not going to deter him.

He almost missed the turnoff. A small wooden sign bearing the words "The Lodge" sat at the point where the access road led off from the highway. It was illuminated by a shaft of moonlight, but he noticed it only as he passed. He braked quickly, turned around, and pointed his bike down the new road.

#

Mary and Vernon were in the bedroom. As soon as she had seen Vernon, Mary had turned and tried to reach for the door handle in an attempt to escape. But Jeff seized her by her arms and threw her bodily at Vernon, who caught her and dragged her into the bedroom, planting himself between her and the door.

Heart pounding and breath coming in quick gasps, Mary frantically looked about for anything she might use as a weapon. There was a small lamp on the dresser, but Vernon was closer to it than she was.

Vernon folded his arms again. He ran his eyes down her body and back up to her face.

"You know," he said, "I gave you plenty of opportunity to be with me in a more," he paused, "conventional way. But you didn't take advantage of it. Your mistake."

He took a step toward her. She tried to retreat, but her back struck the armoire, bringing her up short. He leaned in, and, as he did, she reached up and scratched him across the face as hard as she could. He jerked back, and two narrow lines of blood appeared on his cheek.

He slapped her hard, and she started to fall sideways. He reached one arm out quickly and grabbed a handful of her dress, stopping her fall. He yanked roughly, straightening her. There was a loud ripping sound, and the front of her dress tore open.

Her head was ringing from the blow, and she was dizzy. She knew her bra was exposed. Vernon licked his lips. Then he came at her again.

#

As Jon approached the Lodge, he could see lights glowing from windows on both the first and second floors. In the circular drive in front of the building sat the Packard.

He braked to a stop a few yards behind the car, jumped off the bike and raced up the front steps of the building. Inside the main door was a large foyer. To his right were stairs leading up to a short landing where they turned ninety degrees and continued up to a hallway that was open to the area below.

He stood, poised, listening. Suddenly, there was a scream from somewhere on the second floor. He took the stairs two at a time. At the top, he looked in both directions. To his left, he could see a narrow horizontal shaft of light beneath a door near the end of the hall.

He ran to the door, gripped the handle and threw it open. The first thing he saw was Jeff Fletcher. The boy was leaning against another door, this one also closed. He had his head turned sideways and an ear pressed against it.

It took Jeff a moment to realize he was no longer alone. When he did, he pushed himself away from the door and turned to face Jon. That was all the time Jon needed to reach him. Jon balled his fist, and, throwing his entire body behind it, he came over the top with the punch Ben called the Widowmaker. He caught Jeff flush on the jaw.

The taller boy's head snapped back, his eyes rolled up, exposing the whites, and he crumpled to the floor. Jon grabbed the door knob, rotated it and pushed hard, flinging it open. He stepped over Jeff and into the room beyond.

In the span of about a second, he took in everything.

Vernon King had thrown Mary across one of the beds. She was on her back, and he was on top of her. The lower half of one of Mary's arms was flailing wildly. The upper half of that arm and the rest of her body were pinned to the bed by the weight of the large boy. Vernon had one huge hand clamped over Mary's mouth and the other was up her dress. Obviously hearing the door open, he'd turned his head toward the entrance.

"God damn it, Fletcher, wait your..." but when he saw who it was, he moved instantly. He pulled the hand out from under Mary's dress, planted it on the bed and pushed himself upwards. As the hand covering Mary's mouth loosened its grip, Mary leaned her head forward and bit it.

Vernon roared. He grabbed Mary by the hair and flung her away. She staggered backwards, unable to gain her footing, and fell, the back of her head striking the corner of the dresser with a sickening crunch. Her body dropped to the floor like a discarded rag doll, and she lay perfectly still.

Vernon was upright, in a crouch and alert before Jon had the chance to make any type of move. There was a lamp on the dresser. Jon grabbed it, yanked the cord out of the wall and flung it at Vernon, who ducked. The lamp sailed over his shoulder, striking the window and shattering both the window and the lamp.

Vernon, his face a malevolent mask, came around the bed, stepping over Mary's lifeless body. He was almost a foot taller than Jon, and he outweighed the smaller boy by at least sixty pounds. Though a part of Jon's mind was screaming for him to tend to Mary, he forced himself to focus on Vernon.

Vernon advanced with both arms outstretched. Jon waited until the bigger boy was just the right distance away. Then he stepped forward on his right foot and, with all the force he could muster, swung his left up in a kick. His toe struck Vernon solidly in the groin.

Vernon staggered, an initial expression of shock giving way to a grimace of pain. Still moving forward, Vernon's hands dropped reflexively to the source of the pain, and Jon threw a hard left jab into Vernon's solar plexus. There was a whoosh of escaping air, and Vernon bent forward. Jon followed with a right uppercut, catching Vernon under the chin. Jon put so much force into the blow that it straightened Vernon up completely for a moment.

Amazingly, Vernon did not go down. He did, however, stumble backwards between the two beds. The backs of his knees struck a small table, and he half sat on it, crushing the remaining lamp and plunging the room into semi-darkness.

By the light entering through the open doorway, Jon could see that, though Vernon was not out, he was certainly down for the count. Jon turned toward Mary and took a step.

A shadow filled the doorway, and a voice said, "Stop."

He froze, and his head jerked around.

"Don't move, or I'll shoot."

Jon couldn't tell who it was. The man's face was in full shadow. But there was no mistaking the weapon he held in his hand. It was a large caliber revolver and it was pointed straight at Jon's chest. The light from the other room glinted off the barrel. The hand that held it was steady.

Desperately, Jon pointed to the body of Mary. He started to speak, but the man's thumb pulled back the hammer. It made an abnormally loud clicking sound. "The army taught me how to use this thing, and they taught me well. I won't hesitate to shoot, and I'll shoot to kill."

From the other side of the room, Vernon was trying to speak. He wheezed several times. Finally, in a strained, unnatural voice, he exclaimed, "He was trying to rape her."

#

At the bottom of the stairs, Vernon led Jeff into the darkened main hallway. Jeff was still woozy, and his knees wobbled slightly.

The doctor had arrived, and he'd ordered everyone out of the bedroom. Mr. Crandall, the Lodge caretaker, had made Jon sit in one of the chairs in the sitting room, and he still had his gun on him. Vernon had told Mr. Crandall that he and Jeff needed to use the bathroom and tend to their injuries. The old man had let them leave, but he'd told them not to go far, because the sheriff had been called, and they'd need to give statements.

When they were at a spot where Vernon was confident they couldn't be overheard, he put a hand on Jeff's chest and pushed him up against the wall. Not hard, but not easy either.

"Listen," he said. "The sheriff is going to be here any minute now. We've got to get our stories straight."

Jeff's eyes began to close and his head drooped to one side. Vernon slapped him, and his eyes flew open again.

"Come on, now," Vernon said. "Pay attention. All right?"

Jeff nodded.

"We were just finishing up our cleaning when Meyer arrived with Mary. Her father's a big shot in the Lodge, so we didn't think anything of it. Got it?"

Jeff nodded again.

"Then we heard a scream. We came into the room, and he had her on the bed. We told him to stop, and he went berserk. He kicked me in the balls, and, while I was down, the two of you started fighting. He knocked you out, so you don't know what happened after that."

Vernon punched Jeff in the chest with a finger. "You stick to that story."

Jeff looked at Vernon dully. His jaw was swollen, and it was beginning to turn several shades of blue and purple. In a monotone he said, "He'll tell them what really happened."

"So what," Vernon said, quickly. "It's his word against ours. I'll take those odds."

"Yeah, until Mary wakes up. Then we're in big trouble."

Vernon shook his head. "It's still their word against ours."

Jeff continued to look at him listlessly. Vernon let go of him and stepped back, his mind working overtime. He was missing something, an important piece. What the heck was it? Then it struck him. "How the hell did Meyer get here?" he asked.

He looked at Jeff, but the other boy was of no help.

"Come on," he said, and he walked to the front door. Jeff slowly followed.

The Packard Vernon had seen Mary driving on Friday was parked in front of the building. There was another car behind it. Vernon figured it was probably the doctor's. He walked around both vehicles. It didn't take him long to find what he was looking for.

"There." He pointed to the hedge lining the base of the veranda. A bicycle lay half propped against the shrubbery and half lying on the small patch of grass in front of it. He put a hand on Jeff's shoulder and looked into the boy's eyes. The night air had apparently helped, as they looked a little more focused. "Get rid of this. I'll stay here and cover for you."

Jeff looked from Vernon to the bike and back. He seemed to get it. Without replying, he stepped over, picked up the bike and began carrying it toward the corner of the building. He had barely rounded the corner when headlights appeared in the distance.

A vehicle raced up the drive and around the parking circle. As it entered the light cast by the windows of the Lodge, Vernon could see the sheriff's markings on the hood and sides and the single red light mounted on the roof. Two men jumped out of the car. One was in uniform. The other was wearing a pair of slacks and a pullover sweater. Vernon stepped forward.

"Where is George Crandall?" the man in the sweater asked without preamble.

Vernon pointed back toward the building. "Second floor, down the hall to the left."

The man in the sweater looked to the man in the uniform and tipped his head in the direction of the front door. Without a word, the man in uniform strode quickly up the steps and into the building.

"Who are you?" asked the man.

"Vernon King, sir."

"What happened?"

Vernon gave the version of the story he'd just outlined for Jeff. "We heard her screaming 'No, I don't want to do that.' When we entered the room, he was on top of her and she was fighting to get him off. He saw us and went crazy." He added a couple of details for flavor and filled in the part following the moment when Jeff was knocked out.

When Vernon finished, the man said, "All right, follow me." He led Vernon up the stairs and back into the sitting room.

Jon was still in the chair where Mr. Crandall had ordered him to sit. There was now a pair of handcuffs on him, Vernon saw with some satisfaction. Mr. Crandall stood to one side, and the man in uniform to the other. Vernon could see the uniformed man had a badge that read "Deputy Sheriff."

The man in the sweater looked expectantly at the deputy, who said, "The victim's in the other room with the doctor. It's Mary Dahlgren, Jim Dahlgren's girl."

The man in the sweater made a pained expression and turned to Mr. Crandall. "You're Crandall." It was more a statement than a question.

The older man nodded.

"Tell me what happened." He had taken a small notepad and pencil out of his pocket.

"I was in my house," Mr. Crandall said. "I live in the care-taker's cottage around by the back," and he pointed in that direction. "I heard a window break, so I grabbed my gun." This time, he pointed to the weapon, which was sitting on a table across the room. "I ran up the stairs, and, when I came into this room, I saw a boy lying on the floor by the bedroom door. He wasn't moving."

"Where is this boy?"

"I'm here," Jeff said. Vernon turned and saw Jeff standing in the doorway.

"Who are you?" asked the man in the sweater.

"Jeff Fletcher."

The man squinted. "Mort Fletcher's boy?"

"Yes, sir."

Vernon was glad to see that this information seemed to carry some weight.

"All right," the man in the sweater said, returning his attention to Mr. Crandall. "Continue."

The older man said, "I went to the bedroom door. I saw him," and he pointed to Vernon, "over against the wall between the beds. And I saw him," pointing to Jon. "He was near the door, and he was moving toward the girl."

"I was going to help her," Jon exclaimed. "She was already on the floor, after he," and he raised both hands and pointed toward Vernon, "threw her against the dresser. I had just fought him off, and I was going to help her."

The man in the sweater turned to Mr. Crandall. "Could he have been going to help?"

Mr. Crandall thought for a moment. Then he nodded. "Possibly. I can't rule it out."

The man in the sweater made some notes in his pad. Then he turned to Vernon and Jeff. "What were the two of you doing here?"

"I let them in," Mr. Crandall volunteered. "They were here to do some cleaning. Their fathers are member of the Lodge, and they offered to pitch in."

"Is that normal?"

The man shrugged. "No, not really. But I was happy to have the help. And," he added, "ever since my wife died..."

"Did they do the cleaning?" the man in the sweater interrupted.

"I don't know," said the caretaker. "I haven't had a chance to look."

"Do that for me please."

Mr. Crandall seemed surprised, but, after a short hesitation, he nodded and left the room. Vernon silently congratulated himself. Jeff had wanted to skip the cleaning, but Vernon had insisted that they not only do it, but that they do a diligent job of it.

The man in the sweater turned his attention to Jeff. "Let me hear your version of it," he commanded.

Jeff repeated the story Vernon had told him in the hallway downstairs, almost word for word.

Then the man pointed to Jon. "Now, let me hear your story."

Jon recounted how he'd been told there was to be a party at the Lodge that Mary was supposed to be attending and how he'd seen Gwenda and Billy, who were also supposed to be at the party. He explained his concern for Mary's safety and told of his bike ride to the Lodge. He described bursting in on Jeff, knocking him out and entering the bedroom.

"He was the one on top of Mary," Jon said, and his eyes burned with fury as he looked at Vernon. Vernon forced himself to remain calm. Jon told how Vernon had thrown Mary against the dresser, his voice choking as he said it, and how they'd fought briefly before Mr. Crandall arrived.

211

The caretaker returned. The man in the sweater made a few more notes, then looked up at him inquiringly.

"Yep," said Mr. Crandall. "They cleaned the place. Did a pretty good job, too."

The man in the sweater consulted his notes. Then he turned to Jon. "Where did you leave your bike?"

"I jumped off as soon as I got here. It's right out front."

The man glanced at the deputy. "Go down and look for the bike." The deputy nodded and left. Then he turned to Mr. Crandall. "Do you know this boy?" he asked, indicating Jon.

Mr. Crandall shook his head. "I've never seen him before."

The man in the sweater closed his notepad and tapped it absently with the tip of the pencil, obviously thinking. The deputy returned, and he looked at him.

"There's no bike down there," the deputy said.

Vernon could see Jon start. Jon raised his hands, and said, "They must have hidden it."

"That's enough," said the man in the sweater, raising a hand. Jon sat back, but he glowered at Vernon and Jeff.

The man in the sweater continued tapping his pad with the pencil for a few more seconds. Then he turned to the deputy and said, as much to himself as the other man, "We've got two boys who have a legitimate reason to be here. They've got consistent stories, and their stories are corroborated by the only other eye witness. On the other hand, we've got this boy who has no good reason to be here and who has a story that, at least so far, doesn't measure up. And, two of the others say they saw him assaulting the victim."

He slipped the notepad and pencil back into his pocket and turned to face Jon. "Son, I'm placing you under arrest."

Just then, the bedroom door opened, and the doctor stepped out. He nodded grimly to the man in the sweater. "Hello, Bill."

The man in the sweater gave a nod of acknowledgement. "How is she?"

The doctor shook his head. "I've stabilized her and called for the ambulance. But she won't make it through the night."

A loud sob erupted from Jon. Vernon let out the breath he'd been holding.

11

Taking advantage of the school recess, Billy Hamilton slept late on Tuesday morning. When he got up, he found that both of his parents had already left the house.

He was in the kitchen eating breakfast. There was a knock at the front door. When he opened it, he was surprised to find Vernon King standing on the stoop.

"Is anyone else here?" asked Vernon, without greeting.

Billy shook his head.

"Good," said Vernon, and he walked in, brushing past Billy. "We have a big problem. Things went bad at the Lodge last night."

"What things? What are you talking about?"

"Don't pretend like you don't know. You helped me get Mary out to the Lodge last night."

Vernon's whole tone and the subject matter seemed off base to Billy. "Hold on," Billy said. "You told me the party was cancelled. There wasn't anything going on at the Lodge last night."

Vernon acknowledged the statement and gave a slight motion of his hand. "Well, maybe. But Mary was still there."

Confused, Billy asked. "You didn't tell her?"

And then, after a moment, it clicked. "There never was a party, was there? You used me and Gwenda to get Mary out to the Lodge. Alone. Why?"

The words Vernon had used earlier suddenly sunk in. Things went bad, he'd said. "What happened?" Billy demanded. "What did you do?"

Vernon shrugged. Casually, he said, "As far as the sheriff is concerned, I didn't do anything."

"The sheriff?"

"Sit down, Billy. You look a little pale."

Vernon took a seat in the big leather chair that Billy's father used. He pointed to the sofa. Billy realized suddenly that he *did* need to sit. He took a couple shaky steps and lowered himself onto the sofa.

Vernon leaned forward. "Listen, why it happened, and even how it happened, is not really that important. What's important now is that the sheriff thinks Meyer did it. And he's going to keep thinking Meyer did it unless you and Gwenda are stupid enough to tell him about the party. You know. The one that never was."

Slowly, Billy asked, "What does the sheriff think Meyer did?"

Vernon spread his palms. "He thinks Meyer tried to rape Mary."

"What?"

Vernon held his hands out, palms down, and shook them. "Take it easy, Billy."

"You tried to rape Mary?"

Vernon held up a finger. "Don't say that. Don't ever say that. Unless you want to go to jail."

Billy thought about that for a moment. "Don't you have a serious problem? Don't you think Mary is going to have something to say about this?"

Vernon shook his head. "Mary's not going to be telling anybody anything. Ever."

"Why not?" And then, as the words came out, it felt as though someone had shoved a needle in his heart and pumped it full of ice water. "Oh my God. Are you telling me Mary is... dead?"

"Not as of ten o'clock last night. By now, though…" Vernon shrugged.

"Jesus," Billy said, feeling lightheaded. "How can you be so casual about it?"

"Because," Vernon said roughly, "there's nothing I can do about it."

Billy stood up. He was shaking. "No. I don't believe I'm hearing this. You're going to have to leave now."

Angrily, Vernon said, "Sit down, Billy," and, for the first time, Billy felt fear.

He sat.

"Now, this is the way it's going to be. Neither you nor Gwenda are going to tell the sheriff about any party that was supposed to be happening last night. They're going to ask you, and you're going to say you have no idea what they're talking about. Because," he added, his eyes boring into Billy's, "if I go down, you go down with me. I'll have nothing to lose at that point. I'll tell everyone you were in on it from the beginning. You were my accomplice. They'll believe me."

"You wouldn't."

"Oh, yes I would," Vernon said. And, with a sickening realization, Billy believed him.

#

The woman behind the desk in the small reception area set down the telephone receiver and said to Tom Anderson, "Mr. McAllister will see you now."

Anderson unfolded his lanky frame from the large overstuffed chair, picked up his briefcase and walked to the door leading to the private office beyond. As he opened the door and stepped in, Murray McAllister, the Winimac County Prosecuting Attorney was already coming around his desk, his hand out to shake.

Anderson had come to McAllister's office today to discuss the Jon Meyer case. Marvella Wilson had sought out Anderson the day after Jon was arrested, and he'd readily accepted the engagement.

Jon had been locked up in the county jail in Ridley for thirty-two hours without any visitors when Anderson had finally seen him earlier that morning. Anderson was an old hand at dealing with the criminally accused. He understood and accepted the fact that most of his clients were, when all was said and done, guilty of one thing or another. He'd gotten his share of them off, or, at least, gotten their charges reduced. But most deserved to be where they were when he first saw them in the county lockup.

Jon was another matter altogether. In Anderson's mind, there was no possibility Jon had done anything remotely close to the crime with which he'd been charged. The sight of the boy sitting in the small, bare cell was completely incongruous.

Jon's thoughts were entirely on Mary Dahlgren. Desperate for information about her condition, he fought back tears when Anderson told him she was still alive, though in a coma and in critical condition. Anderson struggled to keep his own emotions in check.

They went over the events of Monday evening in excruciating detail. Nothing in Jon's answers gave Anderson a scintilla of doubt regarding Jon's innocence. Anderson did his best to reassure Jon that he'd do everything in his power to get Jon released, and he explained that he would be meeting shortly with the prosecuting attorney.

In his more than thirty years of practice, Anderson had never felt the kind of pressure to see a client exonerated that he was feeling now.

McAllister, who had taken a seat at his desk, folded his hands in front of him and gave Anderson, who now sat across from him, a level look. "I hate this case, Tom."

Anderson nodded and waited for him to continue.

"I'm going to be honest with you, though you know I'll deny it if we go to trial. I have serious doubts about the charges against this kid." He opened the file sitting in front of him on the desk. "I've got statements here from several of his teachers indicating he's a model student and a solid citizen, though I do have one guy, here," and he shuffled through some pages before selecting one, "his gym teacher, who claims the kid is unstable and violent." He tossed the sheet on top of the stack. "That doesn't square with the rest of the picture I'm seeing, so I take it with a grain of salt.

"On the other hand," McAllister continued, "I've got nothing remotely approaching these kinds of accolades for the two boys who've accused him. Other than the fact that they're apparently decent basketball players, there's nothing to recommend them. Near as I can tell, they're more likely the kinds of characters to have committed this crime. And the whole case comes down to their word against his."

He gave Anderson a wry smile. "I know you, Tom. You'll get those two boys on the stand, and you'll make mincemeat of them."

Anderson started to speak, but McAllister held up a finger. "Hold your thoughts for a moment. Let me tell you the three problems I've got."

He tapped the pad of his right index finger with the tip of his left. "First, the kid says he arrived on a bike. But there was no bike at the scene. Sure, I know," he said, raising a hand in anticipation of the comment Anderson was about to make, "one of the other boys could have dumped it somewhere. They apparently had time to do it. But, it's still a problem. And, if the kid is lying about that, then he could be lying about everything else."

McAllister held out both his right index and middle fingers and tapped the latter. "Second, the kid says he was told there was a party at the Lodge that night. Says he heard it from the victim, who heard it from a friend. We've interviewed this friend." He consulted another piece of paper. "Gwendolyn Barnes. She says she never said any such thing. We've checked around, and she's apparently very close to the victim. According to the deputy who interviewed her, she was a basket case over what happened. Under the circumstances, I have a hard time believing she'd lie."

He looked hard at Anderson. "You've got to admit, Tom, that's a significant problem for your client." To himself, Anderson admitted that McAllister was right. It *was* very troubling. However, he kept his face passive and simply shrugged.

Nodding, McAllister held out three fingers on his right hand and tapped the ring finger. "Third, and I'm sorry, but this is just a hard reality, I stand for re-election this fall. If I were to drop the charges, which," he said, cocking an eyebrow, "I know you're going to ask me to do, I'll get skewered. This case is too high profile. Especially," he added, "if the girl dies."

McAllister sat back. "Now," he said, "you can have at me."

Anderson gathered his thoughts. "I appreciate your candor, Murray."

Mirroring McAllister, Anderson held out his right index finger. "The bike you've already addressed. There are huge gaps of time during which either of the other two boys could have taken that bike somewhere and stashed it. We may never find it. However, it's well-established that my client did have a bike, he went everywhere on it, and," he added with emphasis, "the bike is currently nowhere to be found."

Holding out two fingers, Anderson continued, "I don't have a definitive answer for you on the story about the party. Maybe the boy misunderstood. Maybe the girl misunderstood. But, here's the thing. Though it would be great for me to have that corroboration, because, frankly, I'd have you dead to rights, the fact that I don't just means I don't have a great defense. It doesn't, in and of itself, make your case against my client any stronger."

McAllister gave a gesture of acknowledgement. It was a good point.

Anderson held out three fingers. "This case may not be as high profile as you think. I spent an hour yesterday with Jim

Dahlgren. I've known Jim for a long time. I think you have as well."

McAllister nodded.

"I was, and am, a little aghast at what I'm about to tell you. The fact of the matter is, though, Jim doesn't want this case prosecuted. Not against my client, not against the other two boys. He wants this case buried."

McAllister leaned forward, a look of surprise on his face. "Why? Is he embarrassed because of the sexual assault?"

Anderson shook his head. "I thought that, and I spent a lot of time with him on the issue. But, it turns out, that isn't it at all."

Clearly curious, McAllister asked, "What then?"

Working hard to keep the disdain out of his voice, Anderson said, "It's because his daughter has been dating my client. Jon is, as you may know, Jewish. Jim is convinced that, if word got out his daughter had been dating a Jew, it would hurt his chances for election. And, if there's a trial, he figures it'll get out."

McAllister was no rookie. He'd seen plenty of human behavior over the years that was less than honorable, so he didn't overreact. Still, there was scorn in his voice. "You mean to tell me his daughter has been assaulted, she's clinging to life and probably won't survive, and he wants to brush it all under the rug because he thinks it'll hurt his chances for election? What kind of a father would do that?"

Anderson merely shrugged.

McAllister sat back, thinking. Then he got up and walked over to a file cabinet, opened it and retrieved a folder. He returned to his seat and removed a single sheet of paper from the folder. He consulted it for a moment, then refocused his attention on Anderson.

"I received this bulletin a couple months ago. It's from the state attorney general, and it's addressed to all prosecuting attorneys. I won't bore you with all the details. Suffice it to say it provides political cover for dismissal of certain cases that are, for lack of a better term, marginal.

"You may have heard," McAllister continued with a rueful look, "that there's a war going on. The army, apparently, is looking for bodies. According to the attorney general, I'm authorized to consider, as a factor in plea bargaining, a willingness on the part of the accused to enlist concurrently with dismissal of charges. In this case, of course, I'd need confirmation from Jim Dahlgren that he doesn't want to see your client prosecuted. If he gives me that, and if your client is willing to enlist, I'll take a recommendation of dismissal to the judge."

Now it was Anderson's turn to sit back and think. How certain was he that he could get Jon off? He was confident in his abilities as a lawyer. But he'd been in enough courtrooms to know anything could happen during a trial. He simply could not guarantee that a jury wouldn't convict.

Of course, Jon was still only sixteen, but Anderson knew his birthday was only a few days away. He also knew the army was accepting enlistees at age seventeen with parental or guardian consent. He was sure Marvella would give consent if it meant getting Jon out of jail and avoiding the possibility of prison altogether.

He looked at McAllister. "I'll recommend it to my client."

#

Ben Wheeler parked his truck across the street from the county courthouse. Inside the building, he was directed down a long corridor to an annex at the rear of the main structure. He waited in a short line, watching uniformed officers come and go. When he reached the front of the line, he gave the elderly woman at the counter his name, showed her his driver's license and told her he was there to see a prisoner named Jonathon Meyer.

He was directed to a bench where he sat for a few minutes before being called by a sheriff's deputy, who led him through a locked door and down another corridor. This one ended at a small anteroom, manned by another deputy who, when they walked up, set down a newspaper, removed a key from his pocket and unlocked one of the desk drawers. From the drawer, he retrieved yet another key which he used to unlock the heavy iron gate separating the anteroom from the series of cells beyond. He then stood to the side to allow Ben and the first deputy to pass through. As he did, he put a hand conspicuously on the butt of his service revolver. When he noticed Ben looking at it, he said, simply, "Regulations."

Ben nodded and followed the first deputy inside. Behind him, the second deputy closed the gate and locked it. The first deputy walked to the door of the cell on the far right and removed a key from his breast pocket. Speaking into the cell, he commanded, "Stand with your back to the rear wall. Hands where I can see them."

He then unlocked the door, stood back, alert, and motioned for Ben to enter.

As Ben stepped past him, the deputy said, "I can only give you a couple of minutes. I'll return shortly. If you need assistance, call for the duty attendant." He tilted his head in the direction of the other deputy.

Ben murmured, "Thank you," and entered the cell. The door was promptly closed behind him.

Jon stood in shadow at the back wall, which was all of about four feet from Ben. He looked exhausted. Ben had steeled himself for this moment, but, when he saw Jon, his reserve crumbled. He reached out, Jon stepped toward him, and Ben wrapped his arms around the boy.

After a minute, Ben stepped back, his hands still on Jon's shoulders, and looked at him more closely. The boy's face was drawn. There were dark circles under his eyes. It didn't look like he had slept in three days. Ben realized he probably hadn't.

"Mary?" Jon asked simply. There was a look of desperation in his eyes.

"I was just there," Ben said. "She's in a coma."

Pushing gently on Jon's shoulders, Ben turned him and made him sit on the edge of the hard cot. Ben took a seat next to Jon.

"I talked to the doctor," Ben said. "Probably the best thing for Mary at this point is that she *is* in a coma. That way, she can't feel pain."

"Will she get better?" Jon croaked.

Ben hesitated. The doctor had been very clear with his prognosis. He had expressed surprise she'd lasted as long as she had to this point.

"Maybe. But no guarantees."

Ben could see something new appear in Jon's eyes. The faintest glimmer of hope. He felt a little guilty, but he knew Jon needed something to hang on to.

"All we can do is wait and see."

Jon nodded.

Ben took a breath. "Have you heard about the plea bargain?"

Jon nodded again. "Mr. Anderson was here this morning. He said the judge accepted it."

Ben was relieved to see just the slightest hint of a rueful smile play on Jon's lips. "I guess," Jon said, "I'm going to learn the army way."

Ben flashed a smile of his own. "I wish I could give you some good advice about how to cope with the army, but that's something you'll have to pick up on your own. They'll show you everything you need to know. Just keep your wits about you."

Jon shrugged. "I'll be ok."

"I made some calls. A few of my old buddies are still in the army. A couple of them are pretty senior officers now." Ben smiled again. "God help the army.

"Anyway," he continued, "I got one of them to track down your file and mark you for assignment to the air corps. You won't have a chance to fly. They don't let enlisted men do that. But you'll be around planes."

"Thank you."

Ben nodded. There was a clanking sound out in the hallway, and footsteps approached. The deputy who had let Ben in appeared at the door to the cell. "I'll need the visitor to stand over here," he announced, and he indicated a spot next to the hinged part of the cell door. "Prisoner, you stand with your back to the rear wall. Both of you keep your hands where I can see them."

Ben and Jon stood. Ben turned to Jon, and they embraced. Ben squeezed tightly and said, "You be careful, son."

When he stepped back, there were tears in Jon's eyes. Ben turned quickly so Jon wouldn't see his own eyes.

The deputy unlocked the door, and Ben stepped out. As the deputy closed and re-locked the door, Ben looked back at Jon. The boy raised a hand weakly. Ben returned the gesture. Then he turned and walked down the corridor, tears now shamelessly streaming down his face.

#

That evening, Jon was led from his cell out to a patrol car. After a short drive, the car pulled up to a bus depot. There were three people waiting in front of the building. Mr. Anderson was easy to spot. He stood talking to another man whom Jon recognized as the man who'd been asking all the questions at the Lodge the night Jon had been arrested. Tonight, instead of a sweater, the man was wearing a uniform. It took a moment for Jon to realize that the third figure, standing off to the side, was his grandmother. Jon was suddenly embarrassed.

"Take off those cuffs," said the man who'd been wearing the sweater. The deputy who had driven Jon from the jail took out a key, inserted it into the lock and removed the handcuffs. Jon rubbed his wrists.

"Jon," the man who'd worn the sweater said, "the bus we're waiting for will take you to Indianapolis. There will be other recruits on this bus. At the depot in Indianapolis, there will be an officer in an army uniform. You report in and follow his orders. Do you understand?"

Jon nodded. "Yes, sir."

The man looked at him for a moment. Then he nodded and, turning to Mr. Anderson, said, "I'll wait over here." He walked over to where the deputy was standing by the patrol car, and he leaned against it.

Mr. Anderson put out a hand, and Jon shook it. "Godspeed Jon," Mr. Anderson said.

"Thank you, sir. For everything."

Anderson held on to Jon's hand for a moment. Then, he gave Jon a pat on the shoulder, turned and walked over to join the two men in uniform.

Jon looked at his grandmother and noticed for the first time that his knapsack was lying at her feet. She reached down, retrieved it and held it out for him. He took it from her.

Crisply, she said, "I put some essentials in there. Socks, underwear, toiletries. I also put in a couple of your books."

"I didn't do what they're saying I did," Jon blurted. "I didn't do any of those things."

"Of course you didn't," she replied quickly. "I don't know where you get the notion you need to tell me that."

She opened her purse, reached in and pulled out a stack of envelopes bound by a piece of string. She handed them to Jon. He looked at them. The envelopes were unmarked. He slid one out of the stack and looked inside. There were a few dollar bills and some coins, and he realized belatedly that this was one of the envelopes in which he'd brought home his pay from the hardware store. He looked at the bundle. It appeared as though every one of the envelopes he'd received at Dahlgren's was there.

"I figure you could use some spending money where you're going."

Jon started to protest, and his grandmother raised a hand. "I don't want to hear it."

Jon nodded. He took the envelope he'd removed and slid it back into the stack. Then he put the bundle into his knapsack.

There was a rumbling noise, then the sound of gears being downshifted. A block away, a bus turned the corner and headed for the depot. A backlit sign on a panel above the windshield read "Indianapolis."

"Now," his grandmother said, "the rest of your clothes and things will be waiting for you when you get back. So will I."

Jon had no idea what to say. There was a slight squeal of protest from the brakes as the bus pulled up to the curb behind him. With a metallic creak, the passenger door opened.

Without warning, his grandmother stepped forward and put her arms around Jon, pulling him to her. He dropped his knapsack and folded his own arms around her. It suddenly struck Jon just how small and frail she was. His grandmother had always seemed so fierce and indestructible to him. She squeezed him tightly, and he reciprocated.

One of the men cleared his throat, and Jon stepped back. His grandmother raised her chin and, in a clear voice, she said, "You return safely. Understood?"

"Yes, ma'am," he replied. Then he picked up his knapsack, turned, and got on the bus.

12

As she had done every weekday morning for the past three months, Penelope Radkovich paused in front of the door to room 207 and said a quick prayer before stepping in. As usual, she called upon Saint Camillus of Lellis and St. Jude Thaddeus. However, because it was a Monday, and, in particular, the Monday after a long Fourth of July weekend, she also made an appeal to the Blessed Virgin Mary, who was the namesake of the poor girl in room 207. She then made the sign of the cross and stepped over the threshold.

As had been the case every day for the last three months, the pretty girl lay motionless in the bed, attached by a series of tubes and wires to the various plastic bags and monitoring devices arranged around her. Unfortunately, no change for the better. Fortunately, none for the worse.

Penelope, known as Penny to her friends, first opened the curtains to let in the bright morning sun. Even though the nurses said it made no difference to comatose patients, Penny considered it important that there be sunlight during the day. Perhaps, she thought, somewhere in the deep place the girl's mind had gone it would have some salutary benefit.

On the chart attached to the foot of the bed, Penny wrote down the levels of liquid in the bags that provided nourishment to the girl and collected her waste. Lifting the light blanket, she massaged the girl's right leg, starting with the ankle and working up to the thigh. She did the same with the left leg. Then she put her hands under the girl's arms and lifted. Penny had grown up on a farm doing chores that would have fallen to the boys had her parents had any. With the strength she had developed on the farm, and with an experience borne from doing this work over the past five years, Penny easily turned the girl's body on its side, and she massaged her back and buttocks, checking as she did so for signs of bedsores.

When she was finished, Penny returned the girl to her original position. She delicately pushed back a lock of blond hair that had strayed across the girl's forehead. For good measure, she said another quiet prayer. Then she arranged the blanket, turned and walked to the door.

"May I have some water?"

Penny froze, unsure whether she had really heard or just imagined the sound. It had come from behind her. Barely audible, it couldn't even be said to have qualified as a whisper so much as an exhalation of breath that carried with it a hint of phonetics. Penny turned slowly. The girl still lay in the same position, motionless, nothing to indicate any change in condition. However, as Penny took a step toward the bed, she realized that, through barely opened slits, a pair of extraordinarily blue eyes were looking back at her.

#

"When will she be able to go home?" Jim Dahlgren asked.

He was sitting in the office of the chief resident of neurology at the Terre Haute Regional Medical Center. The man's tag read "Dr. Hudson." Over the past several months, Dahlgren had encountered many of the doctors at the hospital. This one was new to him.

The doctor shook his head. "Difficult to say. Recovery from a coma is usually a gradual process, and it can be complicated by physical or psychological problems. I can tell you that, at this point, Mary is making good progress. Each day, she's awake a little bit longer. She's still very confused, however. It's going to be interesting to see how she reacts when she sees you."

Dahlgren was surprised. "Why is that?"

"Often with patients awakening from a comatose state, there's some memory loss."

"You mean she might not remember me?"

The doctor tilted his head and made a gesture with one hand as if to say, Perhaps.

Dahlgren processed the information. It had been a shock when he'd received the call earlier in the week letting him know that Mary had awoken, if only for a few minutes. He'd been prepared to make the trip down from Jackson right away, but the doctor had suggested he wait a few days to see how Mary responded to treatment. It had worked well with his schedule. He was in heavy campaign mode.

Dahlgren had prevailed in the Republican primary election a month earlier, defeating his two opponents handily. For the past several weeks, he had been criss-crossing the congressional district, giving stump speeches, attending fund-raisers and meeting with prominent supporters. His poll numbers were surging. Though he still trailed the Democratic incumbent, it was a workable margin, and he had all the momentum.

"When can I see her?" Dahlgren asked.

The doctor put two hands on his desk, preparing to stand. "How about now?"

They took the stairs to the second floor, and the doctor led Dahlgren down the hall to a door marked "207." He rapped perfunctorily on the open door and stepped in. Dahlgren followed.

It was a small room, brightly illuminated by sunlight pouring in from the window. The space was dominated by a bed, the head of which was set against the wall to the left. On the far side of the bed, a woman whom Dahlgren judged to be in her mid- to late-twenties sat in a chair. She was not wearing a nurse's cap or uniform. Instead, she was dressed in a plain, white smock. She had a name tag that Dahlgren couldn't read, and a tiny gold crucifix hung from her neck.

In her left hand, the woman held a small cup with a straw. The other hand was supporting the head of the patient who occupied the bed. It took Dahlgren a moment to process the fact that the tiny figure in the bed was his daughter.

Mary's face was pale, almost the color of the white sheet on which she lay. It appeared thin and drawn. Her eyes, however, were still the same stunning blue, and when they saw him, they opened wide.

She pushed the straw from her lips with her tongue and said, "Dad."

She said it so softly, he could barely hear it. He stepped over to the side of the bed, and Mary followed him with her eyes. She did not otherwise move. Dahlgren looked back, uncertainly, at the doctor.

"Why don't you take her hand," the doctor said.

Mary's right hand rested on the top of the blanket. Dahlgren reached for it and put it between his. It felt limp at first. But then he detected just the slightest stirring. Mary's eyes crinkled slightly, and the corners of her mouth turned up in the faintest of smiles.

"Good to see you, Dad," she whispered.

He increased the pressure slightly on her hand, and she seemed to respond with a movement of her own.

"Penny," the doctor said, "will you give us a moment?"

The woman nodded. She gently lowered Mary's head to the pillow, touched Mary briefly on the shoulder and rose. Mary's eyes followed her. She gave Mary a smile, turned and walked out of the room.

The doctor stepped around to the other side of the bed, took Mary's left hand in one of his and said, "Mary, try to squeeze my hand."

He paused a moment. Then he said, "Good." He looked at Dahlgren. "She's getting stronger."

The doctor turned his attention to Mary. "Mary," he said, "do you know where you are?"

After a moment, she gave an almost imperceptible nod of her head.

"Where?"

"The hospital," she said, faintly.

"Do you know what happened to you?"

There was a long pause. Mary's eyes seemed to cloud. Finally, she moved her head slightly to the side and back.

The doctor patted her hand. "That's ok," he said. He looked at Dahlgren. "That's very common."

#

Mary reached a hand out slowly, put a finger on one of the white checkers and slid the piece diagonally.

She was sitting up in bed. Late afternoon sunshine glowed in the window and cast what looked like a halo around the hair on Penny's head. Mary chuckled.

"What's so funny?" Penny asked, without taking her eyes off the board. "You think you got me now, huh?"

Mary shook her head. "No. I was looking at the light shining through your hair."

Penny looked up and unconsciously patted her own head. "What? Does it look bad?"

"No," Mary said, and she laughed. "It looks beautiful."

Penny's cheeks reddened. "Oh, yeah. Gorgeous."

Penny, Mary knew, had some self-esteem issues. She was not, Mary had to admit, a classically beautiful woman. Her face was a little long, and her features were somewhat plain. The side of one of her eyes drooped slightly, the result, Penny had explained, of a kick she'd received from a horse as a little girl.

To Mary, however, Penny was beautiful.

The young woman had been an almost constant companion from the time Mary had awakened to find herself in the hospital. In the several weeks they'd spent together, Mary had grown extremely fond of her. Penny had one of the purest hearts Mary had ever known. She was very devout, and had at one time considered becoming a nun. However, as much as Penny loved God, she also loved her husband Andy. The two had been married at a young age, and, though they'd been unable to conceive the child they both so much wanted, they were happy together.

Andy had worked as an attendant in the mental health ward of the hospital until he'd been drafted into the army a couple of months earlier. Penny had found her calling serving as a nurse's assistant and caring for bedridden patients like Mary. It was something she'd been doing for several years now, and, for Penny, it represented a reasonable substitute for the service to God she had passed up.

Whatever the reasons that had brought Penny to her, Mary thanked God that He had seen fit to let it happen.

Penny had taken to spending time with Mary after her shift ended in the afternoon. She'd also begun coming in on the weekends. Though delighted to have her companionship, Mary had expressed concerns about monopolizing Penny's time. Penny had dismissed them outright. "Don't even start with me about that," she had said. "I can't stand sitting alone in that apartment. All I'll do is think about Andy, and then all I'll do is worry."

Penny used one of her pieces to jump over two of Mary's, and she removed the eliminated pieces from the board.

Mary concentrated on bringing her arm over and taking hold of the piece she wanted to move. Mentally, she felt strong. For a few weeks after waking up, she had been confused and easily tired. Thankfully, that feeling had passed. She still, however, struggled with physical movements, needing to think about what she was doing.

She gripped the piece she wanted, slowly raised it and moved it over the first of the three checkers she intended to jump. As she set it down on the first square, Penny slapped herself on the forehead and said, "I do not believe I did that."

Mary slowly completed the triple. She sat back and said, with a grin, "Crown me."

Penny chuckled and added the additional piece to the one Mary had just played. "When you move slowly like that, it fools me. It's easy to forget that your mind is sharp as a tack."

Mary laughed. "I'm doing it intentionally, you know."

Penny, who was hunched over the board, said, "I can believe that."

"Have you heard from Andy?"

Penny looked up and nodded. "I got a letter today. He's done with basic training. He sounded happy about that. He's not sure where he goes next." Her brow furrowed. "Or, at least, he's not telling me."

"Oh, Penny, I know. Let's just hope we stay out of the war."

Penny gave Mary an odd look.

"What?" Mary said, after a moment.

Penny continued staring at Mary. After a moment, Mary started to become concerned. She opened her mouth to speak, but Penny said, "Mary, do you remember Pearl Harbor?"

Mary thought for a moment. "I've heard of it. It's in Hawaii, right?"

"That's it?"

Mary smiled. "I've never been there, if that's what you're asking."

Penny looked down for a moment, then back up. "Do you know what month this is?"

"Sure. It's August." Penny had just celebrated a birthday the week before. August 18. It stuck in Mary's mind because it had been just one day removed from the day that had been her mother's birthday, August 19.

Penny nodded her head. "And do you know what year it is?"

The question surprised Mary. And, for some reason, it made her feel uneasy. Slowly, she said, "I think I do."

Penny arched her eyebrows.

"Isn't it," Mary said, suddenly uncertain, "1941?"

Penny blinked her eyes a couple of times. Finally, she reached out a hand and took one of Mary's. "Mary," she said, "it's 1942."

#

"There's really nothing Mary can't do at this point," the doctor explained to Jim Dahlgren. They were sitting in the hospital cafeteria. It was the same doctor Dahlgren had met when he had visited Mary in early July.

Mary was finally ready to be discharged. She'd been deemed fit to travel and capable of functioning on her own. Dahlgren had made the drive to Terre Haute that morning, and the doctor had suggested they spend some time talking before he picked her up.

"She still has a little motor impairment," the doctor continued. "Some physical activities continue to require concentration. But that'll get better, especially once she's home and in a familiar environment."

"What about her memory?"

The doctor sat back and crossed his legs. "That's the big unknown. This is one of the more severe cases I've encountered, though I've read of others like it." He shrugged. "To tell you the truth, she may never get back the time she lost."

"But she might."

The doctor nodded. "I think there's a chance she'll recover some of it. It could come back in stages. A bit here, a bit there. Or, it could come back all at once. That's less likely, I think, but it could happen."

"Will she remember what happened to her the night she was hurt?"

"Possibly, though that's even more of an unknown. Some research suggests that memory loss is, in part, a defense mechanism. Some events may be so painful or traumatic the mind simply represses them. That might be part of what's going on here."

"Is there anything we should or shouldn't do? Could it be harmful for Mary to suddenly remember things?"

The doctor shook his head. "No. There's no reason to hold back information. If her mind is suppressing memories in order to protect her, it'll continue to do so until it's time for her to remember. No reason, however, not to give it that opportunity. The best thing that can be done for Mary is simply for her to immerse herself in her old life. Let her experience things that might stimulate a recollection. A familiar event, a face, even a word can have a triggering effect. Particularly anything that sparks an emotional reaction. See that she gets back to her old routines. Let nature run its course."

Dahlgren took a sip of coffee. There were seven weeks to go before the election. Though he'd been initially concerned when the doctors had told him Mary had lost the memory of an entire year of her life, he'd quickly recognized the pragmatic silver lining in that cloud. Most importantly, she had no memory of Jon Meyer. As long as that memory didn't return, her relationship with the boy, whatever it was, couldn't adversely impact Dahlgren's chances of being elected. As an added bonus, the tension that had developed between Dahlgren and his daughter was gone. He certainly didn't mind having that clean slate, and he wasn't particularly interested in stimulating a recollection that would dredge up those painful moments.

"I understand," he told the doctor.

#

Penny finished buttoning Mary's sweater, stepped back, and appraised her.

"You look like a model," she said, and Mary blushed.

"Oh, Penny, I can't believe I won't be seeing you. I mean, I'm happy to be going home, but I'll miss you terribly."

"Well, honey," Penny said, gathering up the rest of Mary's things and slipping them into the case the girl's father had brought with him that morning, "we're not going to be strangers. We're going to keep in touch, and I'm going to come visit you in Jackson as soon as I get some time off. In the meantime, you have some catching up to do with your father. And something tells me there are a few folks back home who are anxious to see you."

Mary gave an acknowledging nod.

"I'll bet there's a special guy, too, isn't there?" Mary had never mentioned any boys, and Penny had been loathe to ask previously because she didn't want Mary to dwell on her circumstances. But she felt certain a girl as smart and pretty as Mary had to have a beau.

Mary's brow knitted, and she suddenly looked disoriented. Penny reached out a steadying hand. Mary was still vulnerable to moments of confusion.

"Mary?"

Mary looked away for a moment. Then she looked back, and, as she did, the lines on her forehead smoothed and her brilliant smile returned. "Yes?"

"Are you ok?"

Mary nodded. "Do you promise to come to Jackson?"

Penny put two hands on Mary's shoulders and gave her a solemn look. "I do."

Mary reached out her arms and they encircled Penny, drawing her close. "Thank you for everything," she said, her head pressed firmly against Penny's chest.

Penny put one hand on Mary's back and the other she rested gently against the back of Mary's head. "No, Mary," Penny said with feeling, "thank you for being part of my life."

After a long moment, they separated. Mary took a deep breath, picked up the small suitcase, and said with a mixture of excitement and trepidation, "Here we go."

She walked to the door, where she stopped and turned back. A look of concern crossed her face. "Aren't you coming?"

Penny shook her head. "No. This is where we say goodbye for now."

Penny stepped across the room and stood in front of Mary. With her right hand, she made the sign of the cross in front of Mary's face. Then she leaned over and kissed Mary gently on the forehead. "Travel safely, Mary. And I'll see you soon."

Tears welled in Mary's eyes. She looked at Penny for a long moment. Then she nodded, turned, and walked out of the room.

#

Sam Parker pushed open the door to the diner and stepped inside. She saw Gwenda immediately and waved. Mr. Dahlgren, she could see, was seated across from Gwenda, his back to Sam. She made her way over to the table and slid into the booth next to Gwenda.

"Good morning," she said.

"Good morning, Sam," replied Mr. Dahlgren. Gwenda gave Sam's hand a quick squeeze.

Sam was excited. Mary was finally home from the hospital, and Sam would see her for the first time in over five months. She had thought she might never see her friend again.

Mr. Dahlgren had contacted Sam and Gwenda the day before, after returning from Terre Haute. They'd been anxious to come over right away, but he'd suggested they wait until the next morning, to give Mary a chance to rest from the long trip. He'd asked them to meet him here at the diner before they came to the house.

Mr. Dahlgren took a sip of his coffee, then gave the girls a friendly smile. "Thank you for meeting me this morning. Before you see Mary, I just wanted to go over some things I discussed with her doctor yesterday."

Sam nodded, as did Gwenda.

"One thing the doctor stressed," Dahlgren went on, "was how vulnerable Mary is right now. Anything that might remind her of the accident must be avoided at all costs. You mustn't say anything to her about what happened."

Sam shrugged. "We don't even know what happened." She looked at Gwenda. For some reason, Gwenda looked away. Sam returned her attention to Mr. Dahlgren. "All we've heard was that she was supposedly attacked by Jon Meyer."

"Exactly," said Mr. Dahlgren. "I particularly need you to avoid any mention of Jon Meyer."

"What if she asks us questions about Jon?" asked Gwenda.

"She won't," replied Mr. Dahlgren. "She doesn't remember him at all."

Sam was surprised. "At all?"

"At all. Girls, Mary has no memory of the past twelve months. In her mind, Jon Meyer doesn't even exist. I want you to keep it that way."

Sam tried to process the information. "She doesn't remember any part of the past year?"

Mr. Dahlgren shook his head. "None of it."

"Wow," Sam said. And then, because she couldn't think of anything else, she repeated, "Wow."

"So," Gwenda said slowly, "we can't mention Jon, but we can talk about other things that happened?"

"I'd prefer you didn't," Mr. Dahlgren replied. "Anything about the past year could trigger a reminder of Jon Meyer, and that could be devastating."

A thought occurred to Sam. "How is she going to avoid hearing about Jon from others? I mean, we can hold off saying anything about him, but there's no way he isn't going to come up."

"Well, that's one of the things I wanted to explain to you. For the next few weeks, Mary isn't going to be seeing anyone other than the two of you. And me, of course. We're going to keep her sequestered for a while. Just to give her time to become reacclimated."

"She won't be going to school?" Gwenda asked.

Mr. Dahlgren shook his head.

"She can't go to parties?" asked Sam.

Again, Mr. Dahlgren shook his head.

"And how long is it going to be like this?" Sam asked.

"Just a few weeks," Mr. Dahlgren said. He smiled. "Tell you what. The election is in early November. Why don't we make that the cutoff? Until then, Mary will stay at the house. She can have the two of you as visitors, but no one else. Once the election is over, we'll let her ease back into a more normal routine. Sound reasonable?"

Not really, Sam thought. But, then again, she wasn't a doctor. If this is what the doctor wanted, she would go along with it for Mary's sake. She nodded, as did Gwenda.

"Great. So, are you ready to see Mary?"

"Yes," both girls said at once.

When they entered the Dahlgren house, Mr. Dahlgren said, "Mary should be on the sun porch. Why don't you join her out there?"

With Gwenda in tow, Sam passed through the living room. At the steps leading out to the sun porch, she paused for a moment and took a deep breath. Then she stepped into the room.

Mary was sitting cross-legged on one of the chaise lounges, facing the door, a look of bright anticipation on her face. The moment they made eye contact, she jumped up and threw her arms open. Sam and Gwenda fell into them, and they hugged tightly.

#

Ben Wheeler pushed open the door to Dahlgren's Hardware and stepped inside. Walt Gallagher was at the counter, and he called out, "Hey, Mr. Wheeler. Haven't seen you in while."

"Hello, Walt. It's been some time, hasn't it?"

Ben walked over to the counter, and took out a piece of paper from his pocket. "I need to pick up a few things, and I'm hoping I can special order a part." He set the paper on the counter and pointed to the last item on the list he'd made. It was a length of hose he needed for the fuel line on the Cessna.

Walt looked at it for a moment, then said, "Is this for one of your airplanes?"

Ben nodded. "Yep."

Walt studied it further. Then he turned around and ran a finger along the spines of the catalogues on the shelf behind him, finally pulling out the one he'd been looking for. "Should be in here," he said. He put it down on the counter and started riffling through the pages.

Ben turned and started down one of the aisles. As he did, he called back over his shoulder, "Any update on Mary's condition?" The last Ben had heard, Mary had emerged from her coma and was making progress toward a recovery. Thank God. He'd sent Jon a letter letting him know the news as soon as he had heard. Jon had replied, begging for details, but Ben had none to provide.

"She's home."

Ben turned and walked back to the counter. "Really?"

Walt nodded. "She came home about a week ago."

"Have you seen her?"

"No. The boss says she needs to rest, on account of her coma and everything."

Ben thought for a moment. Then he asked, "Is Mr. Dahlgren here today?"

"Uh huh," Walt said. "He's in his office," and he tipped his head upwards.

"Do you think he'd mind if I stopped in and said hi?"

"Heck, no," Walt replied, immediately. "Go on up. I'll get the things on your list together for you."

"Thanks, Walt."

Ben walked over to the narrow staircase and climbed the steps. At the top, he tapped on the door. He heard a voice call out, opened the door and peered in.

Jim Dahlgren was on the phone. When he saw Ben, he gave him a startled look, but then waved for him to enter. Ben stepped into the office and, when Dahlgren pointed to one of the guest chairs, took a seat and waited patiently for the man to finish his call.

Dahlgren was obviously talking about plans for a rally and fundraiser. The election would be about six weeks from now. Dahlgren, Ben knew, had raised his profile substantially in the past several months. The newspaper was reporting that he had pulled into a dead heat with the incumbent, John Barker, quite a feat for a small town mayor.

Dahlgren wrapped up his call and put the receiver down. He half stood, leaned over the desk, and held out a hand. "Ben, this is a pleasant surprise."

Ben accepted the proffered handshake and said, "Jim, it's good to see you. It's been some time. I see you're in full campaign mode."

Dahlgren nodded, settling back in his chair. "We're coming down the home stretch. Things are looking good, knock on wood," and he rapped a knuckle on the top of the desk.

"So I've heard. Good for you."

"Can I count on your vote?" Dahlgren asked with a smile.

"Absolutely."

"Well, now that we've got the most important thing out of the way, what brings you by?"

Ben gave a wave of his hand. "I was picking up a few things, and Walt happened to mention that Mary was home."

Dahlgren nodded happily. "She is. I brought her back from the hospital last week."

"How's she doing?"

"She's well. Thanks for asking. A little weak still, but gaining strength every day. The doctors think she'll make a full recovery."

"Thank God for that."

"Amen," agreed Dahlgren.

"You know, Jim, I got a chance to get to know Jon Meyer pretty well. I've been corresponding with him. I know he's anxious to hear from Mary, and I imagine she's pretty anxious to hear from him."

A palpable change came over Dahlgren's face at the mention of Jon's name. His lips pursed and there was a tension around his eyes that hadn't been there before. He did not respond immediately. Instead, he glanced away, seeming to gather his thoughts. After a long moment, he looked back and said, "I don't think that's a good idea, Ben."

Ben was surprised. "Why not?"

"That was a difficult thing Mary went through. She's in a fragile state right now. The mention of Jon Meyer brings back painful memories that she doesn't want to have to re-live." He leaned forward and fixed Ben with an intent gaze. "Ben, you need to tell the boy that she's fine, but she's moved on."

Ben was stunned, and it took him a long moment to formulate a response. Finally, he said, "That doesn't sound like Mary."

There was brief confusion on Dahlgren's face. Then he took a deep breath. "As well as you may think you know Mary, I guarantee you don't know her as well as I do."

Ben gave a nod of acknowledgement.

"As I said," Dahlgren continued, "she went through a traumatic experience. You can't possibly imagine what that was like for her. She wants to get on with her life. I'm sorry, but that's the way it's going to have to be."

Ben nodded. "Of course. I understand," though he really didn't. Poor Jon, he thought. After having his hopes raised, this news would be devastating. He sighed heavily.

Both men were silent for a moment.

"Well," Ben said. "I won't keep you any longer. I know you're busy." He rose from his seat and put out a hand. "Good luck in the election."

Dahlgren accepted his handshake. "Thanks Ben."

With a heavy heart, Ben walked to the office door. He stepped out, closed the door, and slowly descended the stairs.

#

Internally, Gwenda winced.

"Let me understand," Mary had just said to Gwenda. "You don't know exactly what happened to me, but you have a general idea, right?"

Mary and Gwenda were sitting in Mary's bedroom. School had finished for the day. Gwenda had dropped by to visit, and Sam, who was meeting with Mrs. Bell to discuss plans for this year's school play, would be along in a bit. For the moment, it was just the two of them. They'd been listening to the radio, and Mary had been peppering Gwenda with questions designed to discover the facts surrounding her injury.

It was a subject Gwenda had been much better able to deal with when Sam was around. For the past few weeks, Sam had been adamant about following the instructions from Mary's father and had simply refused to allow answers to even the most innocuous questions about the incident. Gwenda was realizing, belatedly, that she did not share Sam's discipline.

The irony was that Gwenda knew a whole lot more about what had happened to Mary than she could ever tell. Than she *would* ever tell. And, now, Mary had pulled loose a thread in the narrative, and she was exploiting it to Gwenda's great discomfort.

Gwenda had been relieved when Mr. Dahlgren had instructed them to steer clear of the Lodge incident. She continued to be beset with guilt over her role in luring Mary to the Lodge, though, in that respect, she'd been an unwitting accomplice. Her real sin had come after the fact, when she'd denied inviting Mary to the bogus party. She'd done so reluctantly, but Billy had made it clear that, if she admitted the story, he would be arrested. Gwenda had been unable to abide the prospect, so she'd lied to protect Billy. As a result, of course, Jon Meyer had been arrested. Even worse, Vernon King had gotten away with doing something horrible to her friend. She prayed Mary would never find out. And, yet, here was Mary, working hard to extract the details.

"Ok," Mary said, "do you know where it happened?"

Uncertainly, Gwenda said, "Yes."

Mary cocked an eyebrow.

"Oh, no," Gwenda said, quickly, "I can't tell you. It's your father's instructions. He said the doctor…"

"Oh, poppycock," Mary interrupted. "I know what my father said. But it doesn't make any sense."

Gwenda shook her head. "I can't tell." She gave Mary a direct look and said, plaintively, "I would if I could."

Mary's features softened. She looked down for a minute, then back at Gwenda. "Do other people know," and she paused, then said softly, "what happened?"

Gwenda didn't know how to respond, so she bit her tongue.

Mary looked distracted for a moment. Then she said, somewhat absently, "Does that seem fair? Is it right that everyone else…"

And then, she stopped, an odd look on her face. She blinked a couple of times, but her eyes did not seem to be focused on anything in particular.

"Mary?"

Mary continued to look off into nowhere. On the radio, Judy Garland was singing *How About You?*

With a sudden chill, Gwenda leaned forward and put a hand on Mary's shoulder. "Mary," she said urgently.

Mary's eyes slowly refocused, and she looked at Gwenda. "I saw him again."

"Who did you see?"

Mary's brow furrowed. After a moment, she said, "I don't know."

#

Walt Gallagher had finished the book Jon had given to him and was dying to discuss it with someone. Unfortunately, Jon was no longer around. After carrying out a spirited debate with himself over the past couple of days, he'd made his way to the high school late on a Monday afternoon, where he now paced back and forth at the foot of the front steps.

Jon had talked at length about his English teacher. She was a nice person, Walt knew. But would she give him the time of day?

Walt had arrived as the last class was getting out and taken up his vigil. The kids had now all come and gone, and he'd seen a few adults leave. A quiet had descended.

He'd worked out his greeting and was practicing it under his breath. "Hi, Miss Tremaine. My name is Walt Gallagher, and I'm a friend of Jon Meyer."

He tried it with a different inflection. "Hi, Miss Tremaine. My name is Walt Gallagher, and I'm a friend of Jon Meyer." No, that wasn't it. He was in the process of auditioning the twentieth or thirtieth iteration when the front door opened, and a woman with red hair and a pair of horn-rimmed glasses stepped out and descended the steps. When she reached the bottom, Walt took a step toward her.

"Hi, Jon Meyer. My name is Miss Tremaine, and I'm a friend of Walt Gallagher."

She looked at him curiously for a moment, her lips moving silently. Then she laughed. "If I'm following you, that would make you Walt, right?"

Walt nodded vigorously.

"How can I help you, Walt?"

Walt held out the book he'd been gripping in front of him with both hands. "Jon gave me this book to read. And I did. I finished it."

Miss Tremaine tilted her head sideways to read the cover. "*The Mayor of Casterbridge*," she said, approvingly. "That's a good book."

"Uh huh," Walt replied, quickly. "Jon said it was. He said I was gonna like it, and I did."

She nodded and gave Walt a long look. Finally, she asked, "Would you like to talk about it?"

Walt stood up straighter and smiled. "I was hopin' you was gonna say that."

#

On the morning exactly two weeks before the election, Jim Dahlgren was surprised to find Mary seated at the table when he entered the kitchen. She was in her robe, her hands folded and placed on the table top in front of her.

She sat very straight, looking up at him with a luminous expression. Her eyes were bright, and her face was alive with an excitement that Dahlgren hadn't seen since the accident. She positively radiated energy. It was an amazing transformation.

He was about to say something when the next words out of her mouth caused him to stumble and almost fall.

"Jon Meyer."

He reached for the back of the nearest chair to steady himself.

"I remember him," she said with delight. "Oh, Dad, I remember Jon. I've been sitting here remembering him. I remember his face. I remember his eyes. His beautiful eyes. I remember the way he tilts his head, just so. And the little crease he gets between his eyebrows when he's thinking." She touched her brow lightly.

"And I remember," she continued, thinking, "Oh my God, I remember his smile. I remember his lips." She paused, her cheeks reddening slightly. "Dad," she said, fixing him with a look of elation, "it's so exciting."

Slowly, Dahlgren pulled out the chair he was leaning against and sat down.

"It just came to me," she enthused. "For the longest time, I just knew there was someone. I could almost see him, but I couldn't quite make him out. And then, when I woke up this morning, there he was."

She leaned forward and gave him a dazzling smile. "Isn't it wonderful, Dad?"

Dahlgren was still processing the information, when Mary's face suddenly clouded with consternation.

"I don't remember how we met." Then brightening, she asked, "Do you know?"

He shook his head slowly, and her brows knit again. "Oh," she said. She looked down at the table and concentrated. Finally, she looked up and shook her head.

Then another thought occurred to her.

"Do you know where he is?"

Dahlgren looked away for a moment. Then he looked back and said, "He's not here, honey. He went away."

She looked crestfallen. "Oh," she said again. Then she shook her head firmly. "No. That can't be right. How can that be?"

Dahlgren reached out and put a hand over Mary's. "Honey," he said, with as much calm as he could muster, "you need to forget about Jon Meyer."

"I already did that. Once. No, no, no," she said, shaking her head in an animated fashion. "I can't forget about him. I won't forget about him."

She pulled her hands back and set them on the edge of the table. Looking around, she said, speaking quickly, "I have to find him. I have to be with him." She looked at Dahlgren and nodded rapidly. "Will you help me?"

He realized she was not going to be easily deterred. And, yet, he had to navigate the next two weeks without incident. He thought quickly. Mary would start extracting details about the boy from her friends. Could he keep her away from them for two weeks? No chance of that. The first thing she was going to learn was that Marvella Wilson was the boy's grandmother. What if Marvella knew how to contact the boy? His mind raced.

He took a deep breath. "Tell you what, let me talk to Mrs. Wilson. She's his grandmother."

"Oh," Mary said, a look of surprise on her face. Then her eyes widened. "Yes, she'll know where he is."

"I'll pay her a visit today."

"Oh, Dad," she said, standing. She came around the table and put her arms around his neck. "Thank you."

#

"How could she not know?" Mary asked, disappointment vying with incomprehension. She had been certain all day that her father would return home with information that would reunite her with Jon. She had been waiting on pins and needles. This was horrible news.

"I don't know," her father said. "I guess she doesn't care that much for him."

Mary stepped back, stunned. "How can that be?"

Her father shrugged. "I'm sorry, honey."

When she'd seen Sam and Gwenda that afternoon, she'd revealed how the memory of Jon had suddenly returned and how her father was going to find out where he was. Sam had seemed somewhat relieved. Gwenda's reaction had been more subdued.

"What else do you remember about Jon?" Gwenda had asked.

Mary shook her head, still baffled by the limited nature of her recollection. "It's the strangest thing," she said. "I remember him clearly. And I know that I love him. I know that. I just don't remember how we met. Anything we did. Where we went."

She looked intently at her friends. "What can you tell me about him?"

Sam and Gwenda filled in what details they knew. Jon was the grandson of old Mrs. Wilson. He'd come from back East and enrolled in school the prior fall. They described some of the problems Jon had experienced at school, and Mary started crying. They told her that, somehow, she and Jon had begun seeing one another around January. They further informed her, however, that she'd kept it secret from them. As a result, they had few details to share about the relationship.

When it came to revealing anything about the accident, however, they balked.

"The night you got hurt," Sam started to say.

251

"That's enough," Gwenda interjected, giving Sam a sharp look. "You know what the doctor said."

Sam nodded.

It had been frustrating for Mary, and she'd been looking forward to the information her father would provide. And now, unfortunately, she'd learned he had no information.

#

The results of the 1942 Eighth District Congressional election were the closest in the history of Indiana politics. Jim Dahlgren lost to the incumbent, John Barker, by fewer than a hundred votes.

Dahlgren had known that someone from the bank would be calling. They waited a decent two and a half weeks after the election before doing so, and, when the time came, it was Mort Fletcher who was tasked with the dirty work.

Fletcher invited Dahlgren to join him for a late lunch at the Lodge. He booked one of the private dining rooms off the main room. The two of them engaged in some desultory small talk, but both men knew why they were there. When the entrée arrived and the waiter discreetly left them alone, Dahlgren decided they'd put it off long enough.

"How bad is it, Mort?"

Fletcher finished chewing the bite he'd taken, swallowed and touched his napkin to the side of his mouth before responding.

"The board is adamant that we have a substantial paydown before the end of the month. This has been a tough year, unfortunately. I'd say about a third of the county's male population between the ages of eighteen and thirty have joined up. You take that many people out of the work force, and it's hard to bring in a full crop. Defaults have spiked this fall."

Dahlgren nodded. He was not surprised.

When the funding from the AFC had fallen through, Dahlgren had decided to press on, making up the shortfall from his own account. Unfortunately, he'd exhausted his savings just getting through the primary election. When he got the nomination, he approached the Farmer's Bank for a loan.

It had been a modest advance at first, one he knew he'd be able to repay without too much difficulty. But then his opponent started spending money like he was printing it. Dahlgren had been warned about the incumbent's ability to raise funds. By the time he learned the lesson, though, he was far too committed to the campaign. He went back to the bank for more money. The second loan was for a much larger amount.

This time, the bank needed collateral. Reluctantly, he put mortgages on the house and the hardware store building, and he pledged all of the other hardware store assets. His thought at the time was that he'd raise more money as they came down the stretch and, once elected, he'd be in a position to retire campaign debt by fundraising as the new incumbent.

The intensity of Barker's own fundraising and spending thwarted the former plan. Dahlgren needed every penny he could raise to match the effort of his opponent. The election results dashed the latter plan.

The promissory notes he'd signed for both loans were demand notes. They could be called at any time. If the bank required payment of everything at once, Dahlgren would be wiped out.

"When you say substantial, what exactly are you talking about?"

Fletcher hesitated before replying. "They're looking for twenty thousand."

Dahlgren felt the blood drain from his face. Heart pounding, he forced himself to remain calm.

"Mort, I don't have that kind of money. Not right now. Can't you buy me some time?"

With a sad expression, Fletcher shook his head. "Believe me, Jim, I tried. I also tried to get them to go with a smaller principal reduction. Unfortunately, the board is adamant."

Dahlgren took a deep breath. "Isn't there anything you can do?"

Fletcher tilted his head slightly. "There's one thing."

Dahlgren felt a glimmer of hope.

"However," Fletcher added, "you're probably not going to like it."

Reluctantly, Dahlgren motioned for Fletcher to continue.

"Earlier this month, we consulted with Tom Anderson regarding our rights and remedies. He's the bank's general counsel. A couple days ago, Tom came to us with a proposal." He paused. "Tom has a client who's interested in purchasing the hardware store."

Dahlgren was surprised. He'd not heard of any interest in the store, not that he'd ever contemplated selling it. "Who is it?"

Fletcher shook his head. "I don't know. Tom said it's confidential. If the sale doesn't go through, his client doesn't want his identity revealed. The offer is twenty thousand dollars, all-cash, close in ten days."

Fletcher leaned forward. "Jim, I got the board to agree that, if you go along with this and allow the entire purchase price to go to the bank, we'll forgive the balance of the debt. You'll keep your house. Your membership here in the Lodge will be safe. I think it's a fair offer."

Dahlgren took a sip of water and sat back. Dahlgren's Hardware had been in his family for three generations. It would be a huge blow to lose it. But, then, again, what options did he have? If he turned the bank down, he'd very likely lose everything. He had to agree with Fletcher. It was, under the circumstances, a fair offer.

He put a hand up to his face and, with thumb and forefinger, pinched the bridge of his nose, massaging gently. Finally, he looked at Fletcher.

"Tell Tom to write it up. You've got a deal."

#

After the election, Mary returned to school. It was really more just to get out of the house and to feel a part of the world again than to further her education.

On a sunny December morning, she and Sam drove to the school. Sam was full of news about the school play. This year, she would again have a prominent role, but not the lead. Instead, Mrs. Bell had turned over the directorial duties to her.

Listening amiably, Mary steered the Packard into the parking lot and pulled up to a spot near the building directly in front of the bicycle rack. She set the brake and turned off the engine. She saw that there were a couple of bikes in the rack, and a group of students mingled nearby. Something about the whole scene caused her to pause, a hand still on the wheel.

Sam, who had been chattering happily, was already out of the car. She leaned back in.

"Mary?"

Mary turned to her. "Hmm?"

"Did you hear what I said?"

Mary shook her head absently.

"The fundraiser is a week from Saturday. I can bring a guest, and, seeing as how I'm currently unentangled, if you know what I mean, I was hoping you would come with me. We're doing it right this year. It's going to be out at the Lodge."

As she said the last word, Sam seemed to realize something. She stood frozen, one hand on the door, a stricken look on her face.

Mary nodded slowly and turned back to look at the bicycle rack.

A cold tingling sensation started at the back of her neck and spread down through her body. She drew in a sharp breath. Vivid images swirled in front of her. Wonderful images. Horrible images. She hunched forward, then sat back.

She turned to Sam, who now looked very frightened. "Mary, I..."

"It's ok," Mary said immediately. Then she repeated, "It's ok."

She let the images settle. She took a deep breath. Focus, she told herself. She sat as still as she could, heart beating rapidly. What seemed like a long time passed.

The driver's door opened. Sam, who had come around, put a hand on Mary's left shoulder and the other on her left thigh and gently started pushing. "Mary, I need to take you to the doctor."

Mary pushed her away. "No." She stared at Sam, whose face had become a study in panic. With as much calm as she could muster, she said, "I'm all right."

Sam stared back, fear and concern battling in her eyes.

"Sam, I understand now." Mary thought for a moment. And then it became even more clear to her. "I have to go." She reached forward and started the engine.

"I don't think you should..."

"It's all right," Mary said, calmly, but firmly. "Please, Sam."

Uncertainly, Sam stepped back. Mary closed the door, but she rolled the window down half way. "It's all right," she repeated. "I know where I have to go."

She released the brake, put the car in gear, and, leaving Sam standing in the middle of the parking lot, pulled away.

#

It had taken Ben much longer than he'd expected to complete the repairs on the Cessna. By early December, however, he was finally ready to test the engine. On this Tuesday morning, the sun had come out, and the mercury on the thermostat climbed well above freezing. It was an auspicious sign.

A motion in the distance caught his eye, and he looked up over the cowling of the Cessna to see a vehicle coming down the lane. He stepped down off the ladder he'd been straddling and watched as the car reached the end of the drive and pulled off, coming to a stop next to his truck. The driver's side door opened, and a small figure emerged. Ben was surprised to see that it was a woman, though he did not immediately recognize her. Whoever it was, she left the door open and began running toward him. He took a step in her direction and realized suddenly that it was Mary Dahlgren. He took another step toward her, but, by then, she'd covered the distance between them, and she flung herself against him, wrapping her arms around him and squeezing tight. Awkwardly, he returned the embrace, and they stood that way for a long moment.

Finally, Mary pulled away, looked up at him with glistening eyes and said, "Ben, I remember everything now."

He studied her face. She wore an expression of profound sincerity. The comment was so odd, though, he didn't know how to respond.

And then he understood. He pulled her close again, and she clung to him. "You couldn't remember things after your injury," he said, as much to himself as to her.

Her head nodded against his chest.

It had never occurred to him. In retrospect, though, it was the only explanation that actually made sense. He thought back to the day in Jim Dahlgren's office when Jim had told him Mary didn't want to have anything more to do with Jon. With Mary here now, he realized that was completely preposterous. All of a sudden, he felt like an old fool.

"What do you remember now?" he asked.

She stepped back again and used both hands to wipe her eyes. "Everything."

"You remember what happened…" He wasn't sure how to put it.

She gave him a direct look and nodded solemnly. "I remember what they tried to do to me. Those animals. The last thing I remember was Jon. Oh, Ben, he came for me. He came to rescue me. And," she paused, thinking, "and then I was falling backwards. That must have been when I hit my head, because I don't remember anything after that until I woke up in the…" Her voice trailed off.

"Ben," she said abruptly, her eyes imploring him, "where is Jon?"

13

Colonel Mark Halliday set down his pen and rubbed a hand across his face. He'd been writing letters for almost two hours, and he was exhausted. It wasn't because of the physical exertion. Rather, his fatigue was attributable to the emotional wear that the letters extracted.

Each of the letters was addressed to a relative or loved one of a man in his group who had failed to return from a mission. The addressee was the official next of kin who would have earlier received a telegram from the Department of the Army bearing the tragic news that the son, husband, fiancé or other special person for whom he or she waited had been killed in service to his country. Halliday, as the commander of the 96th Bomb Group, had the duty to follow up the telegram with a personal message. In each letter, Halliday tried to bring a recollection of the recently deceased and, if possible, explain why the man's sacrifice was a worthy and noble thing.

In the five months he'd had this command, Halliday had made it a point to meet each of the air crewmen in the four squadrons that made up his group and try to get to know them, at least on a casual basis. They were all fine, young men, tasked with a duty that was, for a commander, exceptionally difficult to order them to do.

Daylight precision bombing was something its critics had said would never work. The British employed a strategy of nighttime bombing, the cover of darkness shielding their planes to and from targets on the mainland of Europe. Bombing at night, however, involved a compromise in accuracy. The United States had plotted a different course. It's plan was to send planes, armed with multiple guns capable of shooting down enemy aircraft and flying in tight formations, that would fight their way to and from their targets in full daylight, placing their bombs directly where they would do the most damage.

In the summer of 1942, the U.S. Army Air Force moved a handful of heavy bomber groups onto bases constructed in the English countryside, and bombing operations commenced in the late fall. Initially, the targets consisted of military installations in France. The distances to the targets were within the range of fighter planes flown from England, and these first formations of bombers were accompanied by escorts of British Spitfires, small nimble planes capable of engaging the German aircraft sent up to challenge the bombers.

Nothing could be done, of course, about the fire from ground-based anti-aircraft weapons. The majority of casualties suffered in the initial raids were a result of bursts from the deadly 88 millimeter shells fired from cannon placed around the targets being bombed.

As the bombing campaign moved into the winter months, the distances to the targets exceeded the capacity of the smaller planes. Once out of escort range, the bombers were completely on their own. Not only did they have to endure the murderous barrage of anti-aircraft fire over the target, they had to slog their way to and from the target across skies patrolled by German fighters.

Too many of the planes under Halliday's command had not made it back to England. Some went down in fiery balls, with all ten crewmembers aboard perishing. Occasionally, some of the crew managed to escape their doomed craft by parachuting out. Most of those men, if they survived the fall, were captured by the Germans and interred in prisoner of war camps. Of the planes that made it home, many were badly shot up and full of dead or wounded men.

The tour of duty for each airman was twenty-five completed missions. At the rate his crews were currently suffering casualties, the odds of any one man making it safely through even half of his twenty-five missions were statistically insurmountable. And yet, mission after mission, his charges manned their craft and took to the air.

The men were extraordinarily young. A few were in their mid to late-twenties, but most were still, or had recently just been, teenagers. He consulted a list of replacements that were expected to arrive within the next couple of days. Here was one, he noted, who hadn't even reached his eighteenth birthday. And, unfortunately, the likelihood of his ever reaching that eighteenth birthday was now exceptionally slim.

#

The troop transport lurched to a stop, and the corporal who had been driving jumped down and came around to the rear. "End of the line, sarge. Welcome to Stanbridge."

Jon had slid the large duffle bag holding his gear from under the bench and put it by the rear of the truck bed. He retrieved the B-4 bag containing his rumpled Class A uniform from the spot on the opposite bench where he'd set it earlier that morning.

The corporal lowered the tail of the truck and Jon hopped down. He reached back, gripped the handle on the duffle, and hauled it out. "Thanks," he said.

Jon stretched his sore muscles. It had been a long journey, the last leg of which had been a bumpy three-hour ride in the truck he'd just exited. He'd caught the ride from the base at Dunston Heath where, early that morning, he had landed with the crew of Plane 532. The trip from the States to his new posting had taken over three days.

The real journey, however, had begun the previous April, when he'd boarded a bus in Ridley, bound for Indianapolis.

In Indianapolis, he'd been put on another bus with about forty other young men, and they'd been driven to the train station, where Jon got his first lesson in the army way: Hurry up and wait.

They remained in the station for a day and a half before a special military train pulled in. By that time, their number had swelled to over three hundred. They boarded and, with stops at various points along the way, finally arrived in Clearwater, Florida, where the army had set up a training base for new recruits.

While in Clearwater, Jon received his first pieces of correspondence. One was a letter from Ben, written a week after he'd left. Ben reported that Mary was still in a coma, but she'd been transferred to the hospital in Terre Haute. Jon wrote back, letting Ben know where he was and asking that Ben keep him apprised of Mary's condition.

A couple of days later, Jon received a letter from his grandmother.

"Dear Jonathon," she had written, "I hope you don't mind my using your full name. I know you like a more informal version, but it's such a noble name I think it is a shame not to use it. I had the same issue with my Ernest. I hope, as Ernest did, that you will indulge me this idiosyncrasy." She went on to give him gossip about people in town, many of whom he didn't really know.

Jon also replied to this letter, informing his grandmother that he had no problem with her use of his full name, and that, in fact, he found it endearing. He told her he was well and that he welcomed her news. He did not mention Mary in the letter to his grandmother. He had seen no reason to trouble her.

His stay in Clearwater lasted six weeks. After completing his basic training, he was ordered to report to gunnery school in Las Vegas, Nevada. After another long train ride, he arrived in Nevada to learn that the next class wouldn't begin for another two weeks.

On the train ride out from Florida, Jon had befriended another young enlistee, Gene Sandler, who was also on his way to gunnery school. Gene's home was in Barstow, California, a three-hour bus ride from Las Vegas. Gene invited Jon to accompany him on a visit to his family. They both wrangled furloughs, which weren't hard to get considering they had nothing to do for two weeks, and Jon spent an enjoyable few days with the Sandlers.

Gene's younger sister, a cute, freckled-face girl who had just turned sixteen, developed a huge crush on Jon, a fact that Gene revealed to Jon a couple of days before they left. Jon was flattered. However, he made it clear that his heart belonged to Mary Dahlgren of Jackson, Indiana. He did not say anything about Mary's condition.

At gunnery school, Jon was once again able to get into an airplane. Of course, he was not given an opportunity to fly. His task was to learn how to operate the 0.50 Browning M2 machine gun against airborne targets. It was at gunnery school where Jon got his first exposure to the B-17.

Known as the "Flying Fortress," the B-17 was a heavy bomber that bristled with multiple machine gun installations. It carried a normal crew of ten, four of whom were typically officers: The pilot, copilot, navigator and bombardier. The rest of the crew were enlisted men like Jon. All of the crewmen on a B-17, with the exception of the pilots, were expected to man the Browning and know how to shoot it.

Jon found the training interesting, and he enjoyed tracking and shooting at moving targets. His marksmanship scores were exceptionally high. Unfortunately, Gene Sandler had struggled, and, after three weeks, he received orders to ship out.

Near the end of gunnery school, Jon was taken aside, along with two others, and they were administered a written examination that tested, as near as Jon could tell, nothing in particular. However, at the end of the gunnery course, instead of being sent, along with the rest of the class, to Salt Lake City for crew assignment, Jon was ordered to report to San Antonio, Texas, where he discovered he'd been tapped to learn how to be a radio operator.

By this time, Jon had been promoted to corporal. It wan't an exalted rank, but he put the dual chevrons on his sleeve with pride. When he got to Texas, there was a letter from Ben, written near the end of June. It had taken almost a month for it to catch up to him. Mary, Ben reported, was still in a coma. Ben had gotten several of the letters that Jon had written, and he was pleased to hear that Jon was being exposed to flying, though he expressed some concern about the nature of Jon's training and what it portended. Jon wrote back telling Ben not to worry.

Jon had been in radio school for a week when a letter arrived from his grandmother. Buried in the litany of news was something that made Jon's heart leap. "I've heard that poor Mary Dahlgren has finally awoken from her coma. That's wonderful news, don't you think?" Two days later, a letter from Ben confirmed Mary's miraculous recovery. Ben reported that Mary was still extremely weak and confined to her hospital bed, but that the prognosis for full recovery was good. Jon's spirits were elevated exponentially.

After completing the course in San Antonio, Jon was finally ordered to Salt Lake City, where, by now, he knew he would meet up with the men who would be his crewmates. When he arrived in Utah, however, he was surprised to learn that he would not be assigned to a regular crew. Instead, the army had decided, for reasons that Jon could not fully expain, to have Jon serve as a "rotating crewman." In that capacity, Jon would fly with different crews as they went through their training exercises, sometimes assisting the crew's regular radio operator and at other times simply serving as the radio operator.

Jon missed out on the camraderie that was developing within the crews. However, his role did give him exposure to many of the men, and, as a result, he was well known. There also seemed to be a certain elevated status associated with the role. Jon was promoted to sergeant a week after his arrival in Salt Lake City and several weeks before others with the same time in service received similar promotions.

From Salt Lake City, they moved on to a base in Sioux City, Iowa, from which they embarked on an extensive series of training flights taking them all around the country. It was an intense period of learning, particularly for the pilots, navigators and radio operators. Jon got to know the various navigators well, and he enjoyed working with them. In the process, he inevitably picked up on certain navigation skills himself.

One day, after a long cross-country flight, the navigator on the crew with whom Jon had just flown put his arm over Jon's shoulder as they were walking back to the crew assembly room. "You know," he said, "if we'd switched positions, you'd have gotten us here quicker than I did. Of course, I would have fouled up all the radio transmissions, seeing as how I can't tell the difference between Morse code and bongo drums."

While in Sioux City, Jon received a letter from Ben that troubled him. It had been written a couple of weeks earlier, and it reported that Mary was home from the hospital. That part was welcome news. However, Ben said nothing about any conversations he'd had with Mary, and, more importantly, there was no message from Mary.

Jon rationalized that she must still be weak, and he convinced himself not to read anything negative into Ben's message. Instead, he wrote back to Ben. With that letter, he enclosed a letter to Mary sealed in another envelope. He asked Ben to deliver the letter to Mary. Ben's reply arrived two weeks later.

"Dear Jon," Ben had written, "part of me had hoped never to have to write this letter, but it was a silly hope. What I didn't tell you in my last letter, but I now realize I should have said, is that, apparently, Mary has decided to move on with her life. I guess the ordeal at the Lodge was too much for her, and she doesn't want to be reminded of it in any way. It's terribly unfair, I know. I am so sorry to be bringing you this news. Please understand that, as painful as this must be, you will get through this. I know you, Jon. You're very strong. Keep your chin up. You'll meet someone else soon. I just know it."

Jon had thought that, after all he'd been through, nothing could hurt him. He had been wrong. The pain this news brought was excruciating.

In mid-December, Jon received orders to report to a base in New Jersey, from which he'd be given further orders for transport to his permanent assignment somewhere in England. Jon wrote to Ben, letting him know he would soon ship out, though he didn't yet know exactly where. Jon's orders had included an APO address to which correspondence could be sent, and he gave that address to Ben. He did likewise with his grandmother.

Two days shy of Christmas, Jon arrived at Fort Dix in south-central New Jersey. He spent a very lonely Christmas sleeping in a barracks room containing twenty beds, none of which, other than his own, was occupied.

On New Year's Eve, he finally received his orders. He was to be attached to the 598th Bombardment Squadron, which was part of the 96th Bomb Group, based at Stanbridge in Suffolk, England. He would get there by hopping a ride on a B-17 that was being flown over by her new crew and was leaving that morning. He'd not previously known any of them. They'd gone through their training in Idaho and Washington. Jon loaded his gear into the plane and settled into the radio compartment with the regular radio operator, a kid from the Bronx. The kid was a big Yankees fan, and they filled a large part of the long flight talking baseball.

From Fort Dix, they flew to Goose Bay, Labrador, where they spent the night and rang in the New Year in a subdued way. From there, they flew to Reykjavik, Iceland, where they refueled and then continued on to a base in Prestwick, Scotland. They bunked down for a few hours in Prestwick before taking off early that morning and finally landing at Dunston Heath, where the 302nd Bomb Group was headquartered. From there, Jon caught the ride on the troop transport that had been returning to Stanbridge.

Jon turned to face the headquarters building, bent and picked up his duffle bag. He took a deep breath, climbed the two steps and entered the headquarters of his new unit. Just inside the door, he found the orderly, to whom he gave his name. The corporal consulted a list, then announced, "Deuces Wild."

266

"I beg your pardon."

"You've been assigned to the crew of the Deuces Wild, sergeant," the man amended. "You're in hut 51." He pointed to the door Jon had just entered. "Around to the right. Go straight down the side of the building. Third hut on the left. They're all numbered."

Jon said his thanks and turned to go.

"Hold on a second, sarge," the orderly said. He held out a piece of paper. "Congratulations. You've been promoted to staff sergeant."

Jon located the hut with the number 51 stenciled above the door. Like all of the other huts, it was a prefabricated building, consisting of corrugated steel sheets fashioned around semi-circular wooden ribs. From a distance, it looked like an upside down water trough.

He took a step up and into the hut. Midway down on the left, four men had set up a makeshift table, and they were sitting on a couple of the bunks playing cards. Jon set his duffle down and slid out of his jacket.

One of the men called out, "Can I help you, sergeant?"

Jon gave a nod of acknowledgement. "Meyer. Jon. I understand I've been assigned to the Deuces Wild."

"Well, you found the right place Meyer Jon," the man said, setting down his cards and standing up. He was tall and thin, with a long neck and a large Adam's apple. He took a step toward Jon, put out his hand and said, "Gooch." Jon must have looked confused, because the man pointed to the strip of cloth above his left breast pocket. It read, "de Gouchand." He smiled and said, "Don't even start. The first name's worse. I go by 'Gooch,' and I refuse to answer to anything else. I'm the right waist gunner."

"And a right waste of a gunner he is," said another man who had also stood. He reached out a hand. "Tony Reyes. Flight engineer. I assume you're our new radio operator."

Jon nodded.

"Welcome aboard," Reyes said. He stepped aside to make way for the man who'd been sitting next to him, a short, squat, muscular fellow with a powerful grip.

"Art Graham," he said. "Ball turret." He waved a hand around. "Any of these guys give you a hard time, you let me know."

"He's our enforcer," Gooch explained.

The fourth man stepped up. Jon could see that his name tag read, "Szymczyk." The most salient features on the man's face were his eyes. They appeared to Jon to be bright and alert. There was something about him that Jon took an instant liking to.

"Ivan Szymczyk," he said. He pronounced it "shim-zik." "Tail gunner. You can call me 'Shim.' Everybody does."

"No we don't," Gooch said. "We call him 'Vowels,' 'cause he hasn't got any."

Shim gave the man a sideways look. "Is that the same reason we call you 'Balls'?"

The other two men laughed, and Jon couldn't help chuckling himself.

"Very funny," Gooch said.

Reyes pointed to the bunk at the end of the row. "I guess that's yours."

Jon looked at the empty cot. "That belonged to the previous guy?"

Reyes nodded.

"Can I ask what happened to him?"

Reyes looked uncomfortable. After a moment, he said, "He bought it on the last mission. Very sad."

They were all silent for a moment. Then Gooch said, "Oh, let's not get carried away. The man was a first-class jerk."

"Still," Reyes said, "he didn't deserve what he got."

"What did he get?" Jon asked.

Reyes shrugged. "A cannon round from a Focke Wulf caught him in the gut. We dosed him up with morphine, but it didn't seem to help. He was screaming the whole way back. He didn't die until we touched down."

They were all quiet again, the four of them obviously remembering. Finally, Jon said, "Was he really a jerk?"

"Yeah," Gooch said, quietly. The others nodded.

Shim put a hand on Jon's shoulder and gave him a wry look. "Welcome to the war."

#

At the main entrance to the Lodge, Vernon left the truck with the parking attendant, and he and Jeff ascended the steps to the front porch. It was a Saturday night, the day after New Year. They were attending a party being thrown in honor of the boys who had played on the back-to-back district championship teams at Jackson High the past two years. District champion, Vernon reflected, sounded so much better than loser in the regionals.

The party had been timed to take advantage of the holidays and give the boys who were away at college a chance to attend, the most significant, Vernon knew, being him. They couldn't possibly celebrate those two teams without including its brightest star.

The party was in the Conservatory. As he entered the room, the first people Vernon saw were Caleb Pratt and Cyrus Clayton. The boys went through a boisterous round of hand shaking and back slapping.

Finally, Vernon said, "Where's Billy? This party can't be official until all five of us are together."

Clayton shrugged. "I know he's here. I saw him a few minutes ago."

Vernon felt a tap on his shoulder. He turned and was surprised to see Tom Anderson. "Oh, hi, Mr. Anderson."

"Hello, Vernon," Mr. Anderson said in his deep baritone. "Can I borrow you and Jeff for a moment? Some of the boosters have a special presentation they'd like to make."

"Sure," Vernon said, as always, pleased with the attention. He turned to the others. He held his right hand up close to his mouth, pretended to blow on the tips of his fingers, and then rubbed his fingers on his chest. He gave them a big grin. "See you in a bit, boys."

He and Jeff followed Mr. Anderson out of the room. Anderson took a few steps down the hall and opened a door on the opposite side. A brass plaque next to the door read "Founder's Room."

"In here," he said, and he stepped back to let the boys pass.

With a broad smile, Vernon stepped across the threshold. He'd never been in this room, though he'd heard about it. It was richly paneled and ornately furnished. In the center of the room was a small table, around which sat a series of high-backed leather chairs. The two chairs facing him were occupied at the moment by men wearing dark suits. One of them Vernon had never seen before. The other, however, looked familiar, though it took Vernon a moment to realize that the last time he'd seen him, the man had been wearing a sweater, and he'd been asking questions about what had happened to Mary.

Then Vernon realized that, in the far corner of the room, sitting side by side on a small settee, were Billy Hamilton and Gwenda Barnes. They both wore ashen looks.

The door closed behind him.

No one said anything for a moment. Vernon's mind was churning. He opened his mouth to speak, but stopped when there was a movement in front of him. Someone who had been sitting in the nearest chair with its back to the door stood and turned to face him. It was Mary Dahlgren.

Her eyes blazed. She raised her right arm and pointed a finger directly at Vernon. In a low, even voice, she said, "You tried to rape me."

Then she moved her hand and pointed it at Jeff. "And you helped him."

Jeff said immediately, "I didn't do it." He took a step away from Vernon. "He did it. It was all his idea. He's the one who hit her. He threw her on the bed."

"Are you that stupid?" Vernon snarled. "You think that's going to help you?"

The door opened behind him. Vernon turned and flexed, thinking that he might make a run for it. A uniformed sheriff's deputy stood in the doorway. Vernon could see another standing behind him.

"We found the bike," the first deputy said. "It was about fifty yards downstream. It's too dark to get it now. We'll have to come back for it in the morning. But it fits the description."

"Thank you," said the man who had been wearing the sweater. He had stood and now indicated Vernon and Jeff. "Please cuff these two." The two deputies stepped into the room, removing handcuffs from their belts.

As they were snapping them on, the man who'd worn the sweater said, "Vernon King, I'm placing you under arrest for the assault and attempted rape of Mary Dahlgren. Jeff Fletcher, I'm placing you under arrest for accessory to assault and attempted rape, both before and after the fact."

He tilted his head toward the other man who was still seated. "This gentleman is Murray McAllister. He's the Winamac County prosecuting attorney. I feel confident he will prosecute these crimes with the vigor they deserve."

McAllister nodded. "You can count on that."

One of the deputies put a hand under Vernon's upper arm and turned him forcefully. "This way," he said, and he half led, half pushed Vernon to the door. When they stepped out, Vernon could see that many of the party goers had come out of the Conservatory and were now standing in the hall, watching.

The deputy marched Vernon toward the front door. As they reached the foyer, Vernon saw Ed Spitzman. It looked like he had just arrived.

"Spitz," Vernon called out, "can you help me?"

Spitzman stared back at him, a look of incomprehension on his face.

"Spitz," Vernon called again, but the deputy was now pushing him through the door.

A pair of black and white sheriff's cars sat in the circular driveway. The deputy led Vernon to the one in front. The deputy opened the back door, put a hand on top of Vernon's head, and pushed him firmly into the back seat. The deputy closed the door, came around the vehicle and slid behind the wheel.

As the car began to move, Vernon turned and looked out the window. Spitzman was standing just outside the front door to the Lodge, shaking his head.

#

After Vernon and Jeff were led out of the room, Mary expelled the breath she'd been holding. Her knees felt suddenly weak; she began to shake. Mr. Anderson came around the chair, put his hands gently on her shoulders and turned her. "Mary, why don't you sit down."

She did as he suggested and sat. She took a couple of deep breaths.

She'd been anticipating this moment for almost three weeks. After regaining her memory and driving to Ben's place, she and Ben had sat down and discussed, among other things, how to deal with the two boys who had attacked her. It was Ben who suggested they consult with Tom Anderson.

They drove to Mr. Anderson's office later that afternoon. The lawyer came up with the idea of luring Vernon and Jeff together into a confrontation, in the hope that they would be caught off guard and would incriminate each other. Jeff, it turned out, had done a nice job of accommodating them.

In the meantime, Mary pretended not to have remembered. She explained away the scene in the parking lot as a panic attack. Sam accepted it, though she insisted on doing the driving to and from school for a few days.

It was an emotional three weeks for Mary. One of the hardest things for her was dealing with her father and Gwenda, both of whom, she now knew, had done dastardly things. These were people she cared for, she loved. And they had taken advantage of her. It was a bitter pill to swallow.

She avoided both of them by feigning fatigue. It wasn't particularly difficult with her father, who was depressed over the loss of the hardware store and avoiding everyone else anyway. Gwenda accepted the explanation, and she'd arrived this evening with Billy, completely unaware of what was in the offing.

Mr. Anderson brought in Billy and Gwenda first. The moment Mary revealed the return of her memory, Gwenda broke down and confessed to lying about the phony party. She tearfully explained that she had been trying to protect Billy when she'd denied it. Billy likewise came clean. He explained the visit he'd received from Vernon the morning after the attack and his honest belief that Vernon would wrongly implicate him as a willing accomplice.

Mr. Anderson now cleared his throat. "I think," he said, quietly, "we need to come to some decisions about Billy and Gwenda."

Mary looked at him. "What do you mean?"

He, in turn, looked at Mr. McAllister. The prosecuting attorney nodded. "I don't know whether they're telling the truth about not knowing the plan. I'd like to believe they are."

"We are," Gwenda said, weakly, from the corner. Billy had put his arms around her to support her, and he nodded his agreement.

"Nevertheless," McAllister continued, "they are, by their own admission, guilty of covering up the crime. They could be arrested and charged right now."

"Oh," Mary said, alarmed. As mad as she was with Gwenda, she couldn't imagine her being arrested. She turned and looked at Mr. Anderson.

He put a hand up and nodded. "May I make a suggestion?" he asked, turning again to McAllister.

The prosecutor seemed to know what the other was going to say.

"This has been a horrible ordeal for Mary," said Mr. Anderson. "None of us want to see it made worse for her. Perhaps, we won't be doing too much violence to the rule of the law if we allow Mary to decide whether and to what extent this needs to be pursued."

McAllister looked at Sheriff Jansen. The sheriff tipped his head slightly. The prosecutor then turned his attention to Mary. "Mary," he said, "how would you like this to be handled?"

Mary thought for a moment. Then she stood and walked over to where Billy and Gwenda sat. Quietly, she said, "Because you were so selfish, Jon is not here. You put him through a horrible ordeal."

Gwenda sobbed softly.

"It's going to take me a long time to forgive you," Mary continued. At the mention of forgiveness, Gwenda raised her head, a desperate look of hope on her tear-stained face. "If Jon is hurt, however, I never will."

Gwenda nodded, fresh tears rolling down her cheeks.

Mary turned to Mr. McAllister. "I don't want them to go to jail."

The prosecuting attorney thought for a moment. "All right," he said, finally. "I'm going to look the other way," and, with a glance at Anderson, "this one time."

Mr. Anderson gave him a slight gesture of acknowledgement.

"Ok," Sheriff Jansen said to Gwenda and Billy, "you two can go."

Billy helped Gwenda up, and they walked to the door.

"Son," the sheriff called out, and Billy stopped and turned.

"You stay out of trouble, do you understand?"

Billy nodded. "Yes, sir."

Mary returned to her seat, folded her hands in her lap, and gave Mr. McAllister a direct look. "So, when can Jon come home?"

The prosecutor's brows creased. He looked at Mr. Anderson, who, after a long moment said, "I'm afraid it doesn't work that way, Mary. Once you're in the army, you're in the army."

"But he shouldn't be in the army," she protested. "It was a mistake."

The two men both nodded. "It was a mistake," McAllister said. "And for that, I'm truly sorry. But, what's done is done."

Mary's shoulders slumped. Poor Jon, she thought. Her heart ached for him. As she'd done constantly over the past three weeks, she wondered again exactly where he was and how he was doing.

#

During Jon's first night at Stanbridge, a massive winter storm rolled in over most of Great Britain and the European mainland. He awoke to find a foot of fresh snow on the ground and the welcome news that flight operations were suspended until further notice.

The evening before, he'd met the rest of the men with whom he shared his living quarters. The other crewman from the Deuces Wild turned out to be Calvin Rogers, the left waist gunner. At twenty-six, he was much older than most of the other air crewmen in the squadron. He was fairly taciturn, and tended to be a loner, but he was nice enough when Jon introduced himself.

The six other bunks in the hut belonged to the enlisted men assigned to the crew of the Silver Bullet. They'd arrived together from the States a week earlier and had yet to go on an official mission, having spent their time on training flights.

Jon had decided to write a letter to his grandmother, and he'd just pulled out a piece of stationery, when one of the other men suddenly called out, "Ten-hut," indicating that an officer had just entered. Jon immediately jumped up and braced at attention.

A voice from near the front door announced, "Gentlemen, I need an enlisted man for a special duty. Who here has got the least time in?"

"That would be Meyer, sir," one of the others called out.

Jon spoke up. "Yes, sir."

There was something oddly familiar about the voice of the officer, which made no sense to Jon, inasmuch as, with the exception of the men in his hut, he knew no one on the base.

Jon could hear the footsteps of the officer approaching and then the man stepped in front of him. The first thing Jon noticed were the two parallel silver bars on the collar of the shirt beneath the man's leather jacket, indicating that he was a captain. The officer leaned forward, putting his face a few inches from Jon's.

In basic training, Jon's instructors had drilled into him the fact that an enlisted man was not to look directly at an officer while at attention. He tried to keep his eyes focused forward, but the man simply wasn't going to let him do it. The officer moved his head sideways and tilted it. Jon's eyes finally focused on his face.

The grinning mug of Tommie Wheeler stared back at him and winked.

Tommie straightened. "All right, Meyer," he said in a commanding voice. "You got the duty. Follow me."

Jon grabbed his jacket and followed Tommie out of the hut. Tommie headed straight for a jeep that was parked out front and,

with a pointed finger, indicated that Jon should get into the passenger seat. Jon complied, while Tommie hopped in behind the
wheel. Tommie fired up the engine, threw the jeep into gear, and
pulled away with an abrupt jerk.

"Thought we'd go somewhere we could chat," Tommie called
out above the sound of the engine and the air whipping by.

Tommie steered the jeep down through the row of huts and
out onto the open area beyond. He seemed to know what he was
doing because, even though the ground was covered in a uniform
blanket of white, making it impossible to tell where the tarmac
ended and the dirt began, he managed to stay on what to Jon felt
to be level pavement. Tommie drove out one of the taxiways,
turned, and headed for a bomber parked on a hard stand by itself.
When he reached it, he came to a stop, set the brake, killed the
engine and looked at Jon.

"Yours?" Jon asked.

Tommie nodded.

Jon considered the plane. "I like the name."

On the side of the fuselage, near the nose, the cartoon silhouette of a man had been painted. He was crouched in the carica-
ture of a boxing stance, two arms held out in front of him, bent
upwards at right angles. The figure sported a pair of immense
boxing gloves, turned knuckles forward, and had a cigar clenched
in his teeth. He was wearing a set of coveralls similar to those
worn by ground crewmen, and a large rag hung from his back
pocket. A baseball cap was perched backwards on his head. Above
the whole thing, in block letters that curved slightly up and over
the figure, was the word "Widowmaker."

Tommie shrugged. "It seemed appropriate."

Jon studied the cartoon. "Don't tell me that's supposed to be
your dad."

"Do you see a resemblance?"

The two of them sat there a moment, squinting at the thing.
Then, in unison, they both said, "No," and laughed.

"Come on," Tommie said, "we can talk inside."

Jon followed Tommie up through the forward hatch and into the cockpit. Tommie took a seat on the left hand side, and Jon slid into the copilot's seat.

Jon had never sat in the cockpit of a B-17. He'd poked his head in the cockpits of a couple of the planes he'd trained in, but he'd never really had a chance to study the controls. It was an impressive collection of dials, knobs and levers.

"This is quite a change from the Jenny."

"Yep," Tommie said. He pointed to one of the knobs. "This one makes the coffee." He tapped another. "This is for calling the butler."

Jon smiled. He put a hand out, a few inches from a series of dials in front him. "Fuel pressure, oil pressure, oil temperature."

Tommie nodded.

Jon slid his hand over to the series of levers that sat between them. Touching them lightly, he said, "Throttle, mixture, and," he hesitated, "propeller pitch?"

Again, Tommie nodded.

"What's this?" Jon asked, pointing to a console below the propeller pitch controls.

"Autopilot."

"Really?" Jon leaned down and studied the black face of the panel.

"You know," Tommie said after a long moment, "you remind me of my brother. A lot. You even look like him."

Jon sat back. "It must have been hard when he died."

"It was," Tommie said, nodding heavily. "For me, I lost my best friend. It was the worst thing that ever happened. But, for my pop." He stopped and was quiet for a long time. Finally, he said, "It was devastating. That's one of the reasons I've got to make it through my twenty-five. Of course," he smiled, "I want to make it for myself. But," and his face became serious again, "I also worry about my pop. I don't think he could take losing both of his sons."

The two of them were quiet for long time. Finally, Jon said, "You'll make it Tommie."

Tommie gave a half nod, half shrug. After a moment, he turned and punched Jon lightly on the shoulder. "You're supposed to be back in Jackson taking care of my pop."

Jon gave him a rueful look. "Something came up."

"Yeah, I heard about that. You got a raw deal."

They were both quiet for a moment. "Have you heard from your dad?" Jon asked.

Tommie nodded. "He writes about once a month. I try to keep pace. I've never been very good about that. I got a letter from him a couple weeks ago. He was getting ready to test the Cessna. How about you?"

Jon nodded. "He's been writing regularly. I haven't seen anything in a while, though. I think it's going to take some time for the mail to catch up with me here."

"Yep," Tommie said. "It'll take a while."

#

Mary knocked lightly on the front door. After a moment, Marvella Wilson opened it. "Mary Dahlgren, come in out of the cold right now."

Mrs. Wilson offered Mary a seat on the divan and sat on the chair opposite her. She arranged her shawl, sat up primly and gave Mary an attentive look.

Mary took a deep breath. "I'm not sure where to start."

"Well, I've always found it best to start at the beginning. I've got plenty of time."

After a moment, Mary began, "It all started a year and a half ago, when Jon arrived in Jackson."

Mary told Mrs. Wilson how she and Jon had met, but had been kept apart by misunderstanding, explaining, but not dwelling on, her father's role in it. She went on to tell Mrs. Wilson how she and Jon had finally begun seeing each other a year earlier and some of the things they'd done. She knew her face flushed a little, but she unabashedly explained how he made her feel and how extraordinary it was when they were together.

"You love him," Mrs. Wilson observed.

Mary nodded emphatically. "Very much."

Mrs. Wilson nodded.

It was hard for Mary when she got to the story about the incident at the Lodge. However, she told it as thoroughly and as accurately as she could, concluding with her suddenly waking up in the hospital with no recollection of what had happened.

She explained how the memory of Jon had come back, but how it had been isolated and devoid of recollection regarding anything else. She then posed one of the important questions she'd come to ask.

"Did my father visit you in October and ask you where Jon is?"

Mrs. Wilson shook her head. "No. I don't remember the last time I spoke to your father, but I know it hasn't been any time in the last several months."

Mary nodded. She had pretty much assumed that to be the case, but she'd wanted confirmation.

She told Mrs. Wilson that her memory had finally returned three weeks earlier, but, at the suggestion of Mr. Anderson, she'd kept it under wraps until Vernon King and Jeff Fletcher could be confronted. She concluded with the events of the evening before and the arrest of the two boys who had attacked her.

"Well," said Mrs. Wilson, "I am very pleased to hear that those two have been apprehended. And I am so sorry for the difficulties you've had to go through."

Mary gave a nod of appreciation. Now, it was time for her to ask the most important question. "Mrs. Wilson, do you know what has happened to Jon?"

When Mary had finally regained her memory and driven to Ben's place, Ben had explained to her that Jon had been undergoing training and was expecting to be assigned to a unit in England. But, he'd explained, he did not know exactly where Jon would be going or, for that matter, exactly where he was now. Together, they had sat at Ben's kitchen table and composed a letter. On their way to meet with Mr. Anderson, they'd posted it to the last address Ben had for Jon. That had been three weeks ago, and there had been no response.

"Oh, dear," Mrs. Wilson said. "I'm afraid Jon has been sent to England. He's going to be flying in a B-17. I'm," she hesitated, then continued, "worried about him."

Mary nodded. It was consistent with what Ben had already told her. "Have you received any letters from him?"

"Of course," Mrs. Wilson said, immediately. She stood and walked to the fireplace. She retrieved a box from the mantle and handed it to Mary. The box was finely constructed of dark wood. On the lid, the initials "MW" had been carved and inlaid with a contrasting light material.

"My Ernest made that for me years ago," Mrs. Wilson explained, "to hold important things."

"May I?" Mary asked, and Mrs. Wilson nodded.

Mary opened the box. Inside was a stack of envelopes. She reached in and lifted them out. She recognized Jon's handwriting.

"Would you like to read them?" Mrs. Wilson asked.

"If it's ok with you, I'd like that very much."

"Of course, dear. Why don't you take your time. I'll make us some tea."

Mrs. Wilson returned with a tea set on a tray just as Mary was finishing the last of the letters. Mrs. Wilson was very discrete, and she said nothing about Mary's tear-stained face.

As Mary was buttoning her coat to leave, Mrs. Wilson excused herself for a moment, then returned with a bright blue scarf in her hands. She reached up and wrapped it around Mary's neck. "This is Jon's. It'll help keep you warm."

"Thank you," Mary said, her hands running softly over the material. She hesitated, then asked, "Do you mind if I give you a hug?"

Mrs. Wilson shook her head. "No dear, not at all."

They embraced, and Mrs. Wilson gave her a squeeze. "Don't you worry. He'll come back."

#

When she got home, the house was empty. Mary slowly climbed the stairs and walked to her room. She opened the desk drawer and retrieved the envelope. It was the same envelope Ben had given her three weeks earlier.

She paused a moment before pulling out the single page. It was worn now, the edges showing the results of being handled multiple times each day over the past three weeks. She'd read the thing so many times, she'd memorized it. Still, when she took it out of the envelope, it gave her the same thrill it had when she'd sat at the table in Ben's kitchen and seen it for the first time.

"Dear Mary," it began, "I have heard the wonderful news that you are home. I am so happy and grateful. You cannot imagine. Believe me when I say that you have been in my thoughts every moment. Now, there is something very important I have to say. I've known it for a long time. But, I didn't know the right way to say it, so I never did. Not out loud. Then I thought I might never be able to say it to you, and I felt so lost. I cannot let another moment go by. I love you. I love you with all my heart. I cannot imagine life without you. It is the thought of you that keeps me going. I pray you feel the same and that we will be together again soon. Please know that I will do everything I can to find my way back to you. Love, Jon."

Mary laid the letter on her chest next to her heart, closed her eyes, and said a prayer for Jon.

14

As quickly as the winter storm that had suspended flight operations at Stanbridge rolled in, it moved out, and, that evening, the entire base was placed on alert. There would be a mission the next day, and the Deuces Wild and the Silver Bullet would participate. The guys in Hut 51 turned in early. They would all need to be up at 4:00 the next morning.

Jon had a difficult time falling asleep. At once excited and nervous, he wondered how he would perform under pressure. People would be trying to kill him, and there was a chance he wouldn't return. And, yet, strangely, the only fear he felt was a fear of letting down his crewmates. It seemed as though he had just nodded off when the lights in the hut came on, and it was time to get up.

After breakfast, Jon accompanied the officers of the Deuces Wild to the primary briefing. As the radio operator, he was the lone enlisted man expected to sit through the session during which the plans for the mission were revealed.

Jon had met the officers the previous afternoon. Gooch had taken him over to Hut 34 and introduced him to Bob Roth, the pilot and commander of the Deuces Wild. Gooch had explained on the walk over that Roth was a no-nonsense kind of guy. Before the war, he'd been studying to be an accountant. Gooch reported that Roth was a good pilot and well-respected, not just by his own crew, but by the other pilots in the squadron. Roth, in turn, had introduced Jon to Phil Murphy, the co-pilot, Vince Ambrose, the bombardier, and Jonas Kovalesky, the navigator. They'd seemed like a decent bunch.

At the briefing, Jon learned that the target would be the Lille Fives Company Locomotive Works in the City of Lille, which was located in northern France, near the border with Belgium. The planes would be carrying 1,000-pound bombs and would drop them from an altitude of 23,000 feet. The Deuces Wild would be in the second flight of the lead section. It would be a good place if they were attacked by enemy fighters, as it was well tucked in to the formation. The spot would be irrelevant when it came to anti-aircraft fire.

While the officers attended their supplemental briefings, Jon filled in the enlisted men.

"Lil," said Gooch, using the phonetic pronunciation. "I dated a gal named Lil once."

"Yeah?" asked Shim, "Did you drop any ordinance on her?"

Gooch wagged a finger and arched an eyebrow. "A gentleman never tells."

When the officers joined them, all ten crew members climbed onto the jeep that had been assigned to them, some seated on the hood and others standing on the running boards. Perhaps reflecting the natural order of things, Roth got behind the wheel. It took the overloaded jeep about three minutes to drive out to their plane.

The inspiration for the name the crew had given the bomber had come from the aircraft number, which ended in 222. A hand of three playing cards, the two of hearts, the two of clubs and the two of diamonds, had been painted on either side of the fuselage near the cockpit, and the words "Deuces Wild" were printed below.

When they reached the plane, the crew scrambled off the jeep. The men split into two groups, half of them climbing up through the forward hatch, while Jon accompanied Gooch, Rogers, Graham and Shim around to the rear hatch. He tossed in his parachute pack, hefted himself up, and made his way forward to the radio compartment. He first checked his equipment. Then, from the canvas bag he'd slung over his shoulder, he retrieved his log book and set it on the small desk. Satisfied that all was in order, he hunkered down and waited.

Jon had been told that it was not uncommon for the crews to have to wait as long as a couple of hours for the go-ahead to start engines. Frequently, weather over the target would be bad, and they'd need to delay their departure. A number of missions for which the Deuces Wild had been scheduled in the past had ultimately been scrubbed, so there was always some uncertainty as to whether they'd actually take off.

It was cold inside the plane, though nothing like it would be at 23,000 feet. Jon, however, was relatively comfortable. He was dressed in a pair of long underwear. Officially known as the F-1 heated suit, the fellows called it the "blue bunny" because of its incongruous blue color. At altitude, Jon would plug the suit in for added warmth. Over the F-1, he wore a pair of fleece-lined leather pants and his leather B-3 jacket.

From his spot in the radio compartment, Jon could look back through the plane and see the others seated, with their knees up. They were close together, yet alone with their thoughts. If they took off, Shim and Graham would take their positions after they were airborne. There was the pungent smell of cordite in the air from the past firing of guns. It was oddly quiet.

They didn't have to wait long this morning. Jon heard the sound of an approaching jeep and something was shouted. After a moment, there was a whirring sound, then a cough, and the first of the four Wright 1,000-horsepower engines roared to life. One by one, the other three followed suit.

After the engines settled into rhythm, there was a slight lurch, and the plane began to roll. Through a window in the radio compartment, Jon could see several other 96th Group planes with their propellers turning. He tried to pick out the Widowmaker, but he couldn't distinguish it from the others.

It took several minutes for the Deuces Wild to wend its way along the series of taxiways to the end of the runway. When it was their turn, Roth guided the plane out onto the runway, where he set the brakes and ran up the engines for one last test. Then the brakes were off, and the plane began moving again, quickly picking up speed. There were loud creaking sounds as the craft hurtled down the runway, bumping and grinding along the slightly uneven surface. Then, suddenly, the bumping stopped, and they were airborne.

At 10,000 feet, Roth ordered them all to hook up to oxygen and report in. Jon adjusted his mask, confirmed that the hose was connected to the supply, and checked in using his throat mike. "Radio operator. Roger."

It took about half an hour for the planes of the 96th Group to reach the designated altitude of 23,000 feet. They rendezvoused with the planes of 302nd Group, which had taken off from their base at Dunston Heath. The 302nd planes would be flying above them, and just to the right. Below them to the left would be planes from the 90th Bomb Group. In all, there were close to sixty aircraft in their formation. It was a clear day, so it made the assembly relatively easy.

Out over the ocean, the gunners checked their weapons by firing a few rounds. All were in working condition. Through the port side window, Jon noticed one B-17 drop out of formation and turn for home. Must have been some sort of mechanical problem, he thought. The crew of that plane would not receive credit for a mission.

As they crossed over the coast of the mainland, Jon got his first glimpse of flak, the bursts of anti-aircraft shells fired from artillery pieces on the ground. They looked like small harmless puffs of black smoke. However, what each of those little innocuous looking puffs actually represented, Jon knew, was a powerful explosion that sent hundreds of irregularly shaped pieces of metal out in all directions, metal that would, depending on the proximity of the explosion, tear through wings, engine cowlings, fuselage skin and, worst of all, flesh.

They were now over German-occupied Europe, and everyone in the crew was searching the skies around them, looking for enemy fighters. Jon manned the .50-caliber machine gun mounted in the radio compartment facing up and aft. His was a limited view of the sky. In comparison, Reyes, in the top turret, had an unobstructed 360-degree view from above the plane, while Graham in the ball turret had a similar view below.

The interphone was quiet, a good sign, as it meant no German aircraft in the vicinity. Kovalesky finally announced that they had reached the initial point for the bomb run. The voice of Reyes came on. "Top turret. Flak ahead. Sorry, boys, looks heavy."

Around them, the tell-tale puffs began to appear. These were much closer than the ones they'd encountered over the coast, and there were a lot more of them. The plane suddenly jumped, then dipped. It leveled, but then shook side to side. Jon could hear the explosions now. Some muffled, others loud and sharp.

There was a sudden cracking sound, and a hole about the size of Jon's fist appeared in the right fuselage wall, two feet away from him. Above him, a B-17 from the 302nd took a direct hit on its number two engine. Flames appeared beneath the wing, and the plane began to drop back and lose altitude. As Jon watched, the left wing dipped, and the plane began to nose over. It dropped out of Jon's view. Jon wondered if, by chance, the stricken plane was the one he'd flown out on from the States. He hoped not.

The bomb bay doors opened, accompanied by a grinding sound, and there was a sudden drop in the plane's airspeed. The engine roar increased as Roth sought to compensate for the additional drag. Roth, Jon knew, would set the autopilot in preparation for turning over controls to Ambrose for the bomb run. The pilot then announced that the bombardier had control of the aircraft.

The plane continued to buck and roll as the flak burst around them. Suddenly, a bright light filled the window on the left hand side of the plane, and, when Jon turned to look, he saw with horror that the B-17 next to them had just disintegrated into a huge fiery ball. It hung, suspended for a moment, then fell away.

"Aw, man," he heard Graham say over the interphone, "that was the Silver Bullet."

"Any 'chutes?" Gooch asked.

After a moment, Graham's voice came over again. "No."

"Pilot to crew, keep the chatter down. Do your jobs."

"Bombs away," came Ambrose's voice, and Jon could hear a rattling sound as the bombs in the compartment just forward of his slid out of their mountings. The plane jumped with the sudden lessening of weight. The wings waggled, then settled back into smooth flight, or as smooth as possible given the concussive effects of the flak bursting around them.

Jon heard the bomb bay doors closing, and, a moment later, the entire formation began a long, slow turn. After another few tense minutes, the bursts from the anti-aircraft guns fell away behind them, and they were in the clear.

Roth's voice came over the interphone. "Pilot to crew. Keep a sharp eye out for enemy planes."

The words were no sooner out of his mouth, when Jon heard an excited cry. "Bandits. One o'clock, low." It sounded like Kovalesky. It meant he'd spotted German fighters ahead of them slightly to their right—where the one would be if the face of a clock were laid horizontally around them and they were flying toward twelve o'clock—and below their current altitude.

Shim's voice announced, "Bandits six o'clock high. I count at least a dozen."

The interphone became alive, several men talking at once. "Bandits. Twelve o'clock level. Coming straight at us. Bandit at four o'clock. Get this guy coming by. Passing on the right. That's a hit. Flight of three coming in at eight o'clock level. Passing overhead."

Jon rotated in anticipation of the planes in the last report. A trio of fighters appeared above him, traveling fast. He picked the lead plane, squeezed the trigger and watched as the tracers reached out from the end of his barrel and stitched a pattern in the belly of the German plane. Swiveling quickly, Jon kept the fire on the fighter as it soared past, moving from Jon's right to left. There was a loud whoosh, and the plane that Jon had been shooting at exploded. The suddenness caused him to jump back. He lost his grip on the gun and almost fell.

Jon straightened quickly, grabbed the gun and swung it back up, looking for more fighters. As he did, the Deuces Wild shuddered, and there was an abrupt change in the engine sound behind him to his left. Jon shot a glance out the window on the right hand side, and he could see smoke trailing along the base of the wing. Fortunately, as he watched, the smoke petered out. He realized with a shock, however, that they'd lost the use of the engine.

They were now flying on only three engines. Roth, he knew, would have feathered the dead engine, flattening the pitch of the blades to minimize power absorption. Jon could hear the other engines being throttled up, as Roth struggled to keep the plane with the formation. The last thing they wanted was to drop out from the protection of the other bombers, where they could be picked off by the German fighters at will.

Somehow, Roth managed to keep them in the formation. The attacks from the fighters continued for another several minutes, but then they all suddenly seemed to vanish, and the skies around them were clear again.

"Pilot to crew," Roth's voice came across the interphone, "check in."

One by one, each of the crew reported in. They'd avoided casualties. Gooch, Jon would learn when they landed, had a piece of flak rip open one of the sleeves on his jacket, but he'd not even received a scratch.

Back at the base, the Deuces Wild was given priority for landing as a result of the damaged engine and a dangerously low fuel situation. One of the tanks in the right wing had been punctured, and Roth had used a lot of fuel running the other three engines at war emergency levels.

When the engines were finally shut down, the men of the Deuces Wild made their way to the hatches and jumped to the ground.

"How about that," Gooch said, waving his torn sleeve around for all to see.

"What about Meyer?" Reyes exclaimed. "Gets a Messerschmitt on his first mission."

A couple of the guys thumped Jon on the back.

Try as he might, however, Jon could not join in the revelry. In his mind, he kept seeing the fireball that had been the Silver Bullet. One moment it was there. The next, it was gone. And now there would be six empty bunks back in Hut 51.

How, he asked himself, could he possibly go through that another twenty-four times?

#

Mary opened the front door, and, when she saw who it was, she cried out with delight.

"Penny!"

Penny reached out her arms, Mary stepped into them, and they embraced.

It was only when she stepped back that Mary realized how differently Penny was dressed. She was wearing a brown overcoat, double breasted, with two rows of gilt buttons down the front. Perched jauntily on top of Penny's head was a cap with a short brim and a stiff crown. Mounted on the front of the cap was a gold insignia.

"Penny, what's this?" she asked. Then she immediately amended, "Oh, where are my manners? Please come in."

Penny bent her knees slightly, gripped the handle of a suitcase sitting at her feet, and followed Mary into the house. Mary showed Penny to a seat by the fireplace. When Penny removed her coat, Mary could see that she was dressed in a uniform of some sort.

Mary perched herself on the edge of the opposite chair.

"Penny, tell me everything," she said, and she waved a hand indicating Penny's outfit. "Starting with this."

Penny laughed. "No, Mary. First, you have to tell me how you're feeling. You look good. You got your color back."

Mary raised a hand to her cheek in a reflexive gesture. "Oh, I feel fine. All the dizziness is gone."

"And you've got your memory back."

"Yes," Mary said, brightly. "You received my last letter."

Penny nodded. "So, have you heard from Jon?"

Mary shook her head. "No. And it's killing me. He must think I'm awful, ignoring him for so long."

"But you couldn't help it. You'd lost your memory. He'll un-derstand."

Mary looked down at the floor. "If it's not too late."

Penny reached a hand out and put it on Mary's knee. "Don't worry, he'll understand."

Mary nodded uncertainly. Then she straightened. "So tell me. Have you heard from Andy?"

"Yes," Penny said, smiling. "He's on an island called New Caledonia. It's somewhere in the South Pacific. He says he's very safe, though I don't know whether to believe him or not." A som-ber look washed over her face. "Anyway, I finally realized that, if I want to get Andy home soon, I need to do something to help fin-ish this darn war. That's when I joined up."

"What, exactly, did you join?"

"The Women's Auxiliary Army Corps. For the last four weeks, I've been in Des Moines, undergoing basic training."

"You're in the army," Mary said with surprise.

"I am," Penny said, nodding. "I'm on my way to New York. From there, I go to England."

"England," Mary repeated, her heart pumping faster. "Really?"

"Yes. I wanted to go to the South Pacific. I had this crazy idea that maybe I'd wind up somewhere close to Andy. But they don't let wives do that. So," she shrugged, "England it is."

Mary sat back. The wheels in her head were spinning.

#

"So," Sam said, studying Mary, "your plan is to go find Jon."

Mary nodded as she continued folding the clothes she'd laid out on the bed.

"Do you have any idea where he is?" Sam asked.

"Yes."

"Really? And where is that?"

"England."

"England," Sam repeated, nodding. After a moment, she said, "You do know that's a pretty big place, right?"

Mary took a sweater that she'd folded and set it in the open suitcase. "I'll find him."

"Uh huh. You'll just hop off the boat and say, 'Hey, anyone seen Jon Meyer around?' That ought to work. I can't believe you didn't think of it earlier."

Mary gave Sam a wry smile. "Ok, I know it sounds a little far-fetched. But, I have to do something. It's been almost two months. I haven't heard anything from Jon. I can't just sit around twiddling my thumbs. There's nothing for me here in Jackson."

There must have been something in her expression, because Mary suddenly leaned over and touched her shoulder. "Oh, I don't mean it like that. Of course I'm going to miss *you*. Very much. But otherwise, really, what is there to keep me here? And my father? I'm so angry with him, I'm afraid of what I might say next." Mary shook her head. "So, no, I can't just stay here doing nothing."

"Ok," Sam said, deciding she'd try a different tack, "how about the fact that you're still only seventeen? Has it occurred to you the army might think that's just a tad too young?"

"They didn't think it was too young for Jon. And anyway," Mary said, a sly smile playing on her lips, "I've already taken care of that."

"Really, how?"

With a mischievous look, Mary reached for her purse, took out an envelope, and handed it to Sam.

Curious, Sam opened the flap and extracted the single sheet of paper. Unfolding it, she could see that it was an official looking document.

"Your birth certificate?"

Mary nodded. "Look at the date I was born."

Sam ran her eyes down the page until she found the appropriate entry. It was smudged, but she could just make out the date. April 23, 1921. She started to look up at Mary, then she quickly looked back down at the certificate. "What. How can that be?"

Mary pointed to the square in which the date of birth had been typed. "It took me a while to get it just right. I used an eraser and my father's typewriter. Then I blurred it a little with my finger. If you look really closely, you'll see the last digit isn't quite the same as the others."

Sam looked at it again, and, sure enough, she could see it now. The vestiges of the number 5 were just visible under the darker number 1.

"Don't you think they'll notice that?"

Mary grinned. "They didn't."

"What?"

"I already showed it to them. That's where I was yesterday. In Indianapolis. I'm all signed up. I've got my orders."

"The army thinks your twenty-one?"

Mary shrugged. "They didn't seem to care all that much. They were happy to have me."

Realizing she was out of arguments, Sam sat back in her chair. "When do you leave?"

"Tonight. I'm catching the 6:10."

"And you're on your way to England."

"Well, no. First, I'm on my way to Georgia for basic training. A place called Fort Oglethorpe. That should take four weeks. From there, hopefully," she held up a hand with fingers crossed, "I'll go to England."

"Where you think you'll be able to find Jon."

"I'll find him," Mary said quietly.

#

Jim Dahlgren stared absently into the fire. The flames in the firebox seemed to him to be dancing on top of the logs, brightly colored figures gyrating merrily to a tune only they could hear. He took another sip of scotch and envied them their apparent happiness.

The past two and a half months had been a blur aided, in large part, by alcohol. Thank God for alcohol, he mused, and he raised his glass in a mock toast.

Silently, he took inventory of all the things he'd managed to lose in that short period of time. His dream of national office and all the status and respect that went with it. Check. His standing in the community. Check. His hardware store, the birthright from his father. Check.

It was, he reflected, with bitter self deprecation, quite an impressive collection of things to lose. He decided that merited yet another drink, and he took a large sip.

What more, he asked himself, could he possibly manage to lose?

A door opened upstairs, and he heard footsteps. Someone began descending the stairs, and he turned to look.

Sam Parker appeared. He hadn't known she was here. Behind her came Mary. It took him a moment to realize that Mary was carrying a suitcase. He thought carefully. Had he known Mary was going somewhere? He mulled it over and then came to the conclusion that, in fact, he had *not* known Mary was going anywhere.

Having solved that mystery, he asked the obvious question. "Where are you going?"

"Sam is driving me to the train station. She'll bring the car back and drop it off later."

Dahlgren considered the new information. It didn't seem adequate. He tapped his glass for a few seconds. Then it dawned on him. "You're catching a train?"

"Yes. I've joined the Women's Auxiliary Army Corps, and I'm on my way to Georgia for basic training."

Dahlgren wasn't sure what he'd expected her to say, but he was certain that wasn't it. He shook his head, realizing, belatedly, that he needed to be thinking a bit more clearly. He reluctantly set down the glass of scotch.

"Hold on a second. I never said you could do that."

Sam spoke up quickly. "You know what? I think I'll just wait in the car." She went to the door, opened it and stepped out. She turned, pointed with her finger and said, "I'll be right over there." Then she closed the door.

"That's right, Dad," Mary said, when Sam was gone. "You never said I could, and you never would have if I'd asked. That's why I didn't bother."

"Now wait just a minute, young lady," Dahlgren said. "You're still my daughter."

Mary considered that. Then she said, "Yes and no."

"I beg your pardon?"

Softly, Mary said, "Dad, you'll always be my father. But you no longer have control over my life. You've forfeited that right."

He started to say something, and she stopped him cold.

"I got my memory back. All of it."

His bluster evaporated.

"I know what you did after I was attacked. Those boys tried to rape me, and you let it all get swept under the rug. You let them send Jon off to the army, and you just forgot about it."

Dahlgren quickly cast about for a rejoinder, but she didn't wait for a response.

"I called Dr. Hudson," she continued. "I know he told you I should get back to my normal routine. You told me the exact opposite. Why was that, Dad?"

He tried to come up with an answer.

"Don't bother. We both know why. Your campaign was more important to you than your daughter." She fixed him with a direct look. "That's why you no longer have a daughter."

Mary bent to pick up the suitcase. "Oh," she said, almost as an afterthought. "I paid a visit to Mrs. Wilson. And guess who I found out never went to see her in October, like he said he did?"

He knew he had no reply to that, and he didn't bother to try to come up with one.

She walked to the door, opened it, and turned one last time to face him. "I'll always love you, Dad. I can't help that. But I've lost my respect for you. Good bye." She closed the door behind herself.

Dahlgren stared at the door a long time after she'd gone. Finally, he reached down and picked up the glass. You had to ask, didn't you, he said to himself. Then he took another drink.

#

"You're in luck, sarge," the duty sergeant said, holding out a pair of envelopes. Jon had made inquiry regarding his mail, concerned that, in the three weeks he'd been at Stanbridge, he'd yet to receive any correspondence. The quartermaster had told him he'd look into the situation, that there might have been a foul up with his APO address. "Should be more coming. It looks like they got things straightened out."

One of the letters was from his grandmother. She'd posted it shortly after Thanksgiving. It contained the usual news, nothing of import.

The other letter, Jon was surprised to discover, was from Walt.

"Dear Jon," it began, "I bet you never thought you would get a letter from me. Do you remember your old English teacher, Agnes Tremaine? Oops. I do not mean that she is old. I mean that she used to be your English teacher. Agnes is helping me write this letter. I finished the book you gave me. It was good. Agnes gave me another book to read. I like it very much. I hope you are safe. Do not let the Germans get you. I hope I see you soon. I have a big surprise for you. Well, I guess I will finish now and mail this letter tomorrow. Your friend, Walt."

Below his signature, Walt had scrawled a postscript.

"PS. Agnes dont know I am writing this part. She is great."

Jon smiled to himself. He pictured big, affable Walt, then thought fondly of his former English teacher. He'd give a month of his meager salary to see the two of them together.

#

On Jon's fifth mission, the squadron was ordered into Germany for the first time. Their target, the railroad marshalling yards in Hamm. With their homeland being attacked in broad daylight, the Germans took umbrage, and they sent up waves of fighters to challenge the bombers.

From the moment the formation crossed the coastline, they were subjected to fire from enemy fighters. During a particularly intense part of the aerial assault, a Messerschmitt Bf 109 launched a frontal attack on the Deuces Wild. Closing at a speed of almost 400 miles per hour, the German pilot just barely avoided a head-on collision, passing a few feet over the top of the bomber. The fire from his guns overshot the cockpit, where he appeared to have been aiming, and instead traced a pattern down the left side of the aircraft, beginning in the bomb bay and continuing aft. Fortunately, none of the bombs had been ignited.

The spray from the Messerschmitt's guns tore through the radio compartment, destroying Jon's radio and shredding the chair Jon would have been sitting in had he not been manning the Browning. Jon was lucky. Calvin Rogers was not. At least five bullets slammed into his body, one of them taking off the top third of his skull and depositing bits of bone, hair and brain matter amid the spent shells that lined the floor of the fuselage.

Jon came back to see if there was anything he could do to help, but it was immediately obvious that Rogers was dead. The sight of his destroyed head nearly caused Jon to be sick, and he had to fight back nausea. Gooch did likewise, but without the same success, and he barely managed to get his oxygen mask off before vomiting his breakfast all over the blood and gore.

When Gooch finished voiding his stomach, he and Jon dragged Rogers' body back toward the rear of the plane so Jon could man the left waist gun.

The flak over the target was exceptionally heavy and accurate, knocking several of the planes out of formation. The Deuces Wild, fortunately, avoided damage from the anti-aircraft fire. After dropping their bombs, the planes fought their way home, sustaining attacks by what seemed to be an endless supply of German fighters. The onslaught did not let up until they were well out over the North Sea. A squadron of British Hurricane fighters finally appeared and drove off the last of the Germans.

When they landed, there was none of the banter that had accompanied prior completed missions. Each of the crew members seemed to retreat into himself, and it was a somber group that made its way back to Hut 51.

The day after that mission, Jon lay on his bunk, staring at the rounded ceiling of the hut. The rest of the crew were out. Jon didn't know where, nor, for that matter, did he care. There had yet to be any new occupants to take the beds that had belonged to the men of the Silver Bullet. He was alone with his thoughts, and they were bleak.

He heard the door to the hut open, and Shim called out, "All right, Jon, let's go."

Jon sat up slowly and swung his legs over the side of the bunk. "What's up?"

Shim walked in and waved a couple pieces of paper in the air. "You and I have overnight passes."

"We do?"

"Yep," Shim said with a smile. "And I'm going to get you drunk. Or laid. Preferably both."

Despite himself, Jon felt his face flush.

"Oh, buddy," Shim laughed, giving him a knowing look. "Time's a wasting."

With a mixture of misgiving and anticipation, Jon packed an overnight bag, and he accompanied Shim to the main gate of the base, where they showed their passes to the guards on duty. A forty-five minute bus ride brought them to the city of Norwich, the home, Shim explained to Jon, of the Mustard Club, where they would be spending the evening.

Leaving the bus station, they walked past a huge marketplace, then down a series of ancient streets that Jon found fascinating. Shim stopped the first few times Jon lingered, studying an old structure or marveling at an architectural detail. Finally, however, Shim said, "You do understand, this is just an overnight pass, right?"

Jon nodded sheepishly, and they continued on.

Eventually, they arrived at an impressive brick structure occupying almost an entire block of the city. Above three stories of an intricately detailed facade, a series of gargoyles held up a steeply pitched roof lined with massive dormers.

"Home, sweet home," Shim said. "At least for tonight."

They entered through the large front doors into a reception area. A pleasant woman in a Red Cross uniform greeted them, and, when Shim told her their names, she stepped behind a reception desk and located their record in a reservation book. She gave them a key and directions, and they made their way to the third floor, where they found a small but comfortably furnished room with two beds and a wash basin. A communal bathroom was just down the hall.

They washed up. Then Shim led Jon back down to the first floor and into an immense, gaily decorated room with a large stage in front of an even larger open area that was obviously for dancing. A band was playing a Tommy Dorsey tune, and there were several couples out on the dance floor. Numerous tables and booths surrounded the dance area, and Jon could see they were filling rapidly.

They found an unoccupied booth, and Shim excused himself. He returned a couple minutes later with two large glasses full of a dark amber liquid topped with white froth. He set one down in front of Jon.

"Have you had a lot of beers?" Shim asked.

Jon shook his head.

Shim looked at him a moment, then asked, "Have you ever had a beer before?"

Again, Jon shook his head.

Shim smiled. "Ok, here's the drill. You've got to drink the whole thing. You can't just take a couple of sips and decide whether you like it. Wait until you're done before you draw any conclusions. Got it?"

Jon nodded.

Shim held up his own glass. "Here's to the 96th."

Jon picked up his glass and touched it to Shim's.

Jon was surprised to find the beer at room temperature. He'd always heard beer referred to as being cold. It tasted a little bitter, but not terrible.

"I'll be back in a couple of minutes," Shim said. Jon nodded, and Shim stepped away, blending into what was now turning into a fairly good-sized crowd as the room filled up.

Jon took another sip of the beer. He knew, of course, about its alcoholic properties. He'd seen people tipsy before and, on a couple of occasions, downright drunk. He wondered what it would feel like. This beer, however, did not seem to carry with it the same potency as other alcoholic beverages. He concluded it was unlikely he'd be much affected by the drink.

He looked around the room. There were more men than women, but, he noticed, there were still a lot of women. It suddenly occurred to Jon that it had been weeks since he'd last seen a female. That struck him as funny.

With the exception of the members of the band and a handful of waiters, all of the men wore uniforms. He saw several in brown Class A uniforms similar to his, with insignia indicating that, like Jon, they were in the U.S. Eighth Air Force. Many of the men, he saw were officers. There seemed to be no distinction being paid between officers and enlisted men.

He saw quite a few men wearing the blue uniforms of the Royal Air Force. There were even a few naval uniforms. The mood of the crowd was exuberant, a far cry from the environment he'd left a couple of hours before. He was glad Shim had arranged this. He began to feel himself relaxing.

He took another drink from his beer and was surprised to discover he'd already consumed most of it. He'd obviously done so without thinking about it. The taste was beginning to grow on him.

Shim reappeared, and, somehow, two young women had attached themselves to either side of him. Speaking above the music, Shim said, "May I present Miss Olivia Hendley." He nodded to the dark-haired girl on his right arm.

"Livvy," the girl said quickly.

"Of course. Livvy," amended Shim, and he gave the girl a quick peck on the cheek.

She giggled. Jon thought that was very nice.

"And," Shim continued, "Miss Victoria Addington." He indicated the blond girl on his left arm.

"Ladies," Shim announced with great formality, "this is Sergeant Jon Meyer of the United States Army Air Force."

With friendly smiles and nods, the two girls slid into the booth, one on each side, Shim following Livvy, so that, once they were settled, the two girls were sitting to either side of Jon. It was a small table, and Jon realized with a start that their knees were touching. He wondered if anyone else noticed.

Shim leaned forward and tapped Jon's beer glass with a finger. Looking directly at Victoria, he said, "This beer is Jon's first," he said. Then, with emphasis, he added, "Ever."

Victoria arched her eyebrows and asked, "First ever?"

Shim nodded solemnly and said, "First ever."

"First ever," Jon repeated, agreeably.

Still talking to Shim, but looking at Jon, Victoria said, "He's awfully cute, but he's a bit young." She reached out a hand and brushed back some hair that had apparently fallen across Jon's forehead. Jon found the touch of her fingers thrilling.

"Old enough to fly," Livvy said, "old enough to…"

"We know," Shim and Victoria said, in unison.

Livvy giggled again.

Shim turned to Livvy. "Livvy, darling," he said, "would you care to dance?"

Livvy nodded enthusiastically, and the two of them slid out of the booth and headed in the direction of the dance floor.

A waiter walked by, and Victoria caught his eye with a raised hand. She pointed to Jon's glass and made a circular motion. The waiter nodded and continued on.

"So," she said, returning her attention to Jon, "exactly how old are you, luv?"

Jon found her accent enchanting.

"Seventeen."

She nodded, still looking at him. She had pretty lips. They were painted red. Jon wanted to reach a hand out and touch them, but he knew it would be wrong, so he didn't.

Finally, she shrugged. "So, I'm a couple of years older than you are. I don't think that's a tragedy, do you?"

Jon shook his head. It didn't seem like a tragedy to him.

The waiter returned carrying four glasses of beer. He set them on the table and left before Jon could retrieve the money in his pocket.

"Your friend said he's got everything covered," Victoria said, picking up one of the glasses. "Bottoms up," and she lifted the glass to her red lips. Jon followed suit and took a drink. He was definitely getting the hang of the beer.

"Would you like to dance?" Victoria asked.

Jon looked out at the crowd on the dance floor. The band was playing a peppy tune, and there was quite a bit of twirling and leg kicking going on. Jon was suddenly very embarrassed.

"Let me guess," Victoria said, "you don't know how to dance, right?"

After a moment, Jon nodded. "I'm sorry."

She smiled. "That's ok. We'll wait for a slow song."

When she smiled, Jon noticed, dimples appeared on both of her cheeks. Jon thought they were adorable.

Shim and Livvy returned, and Livvy took a long pull on her beer. Shim asked, "How's it going?"

"Excellent," Jon said.

Shim leaned forward and looked in Jon's eyes. "Yep," he said after a moment. Apparently satisfied, he sat back and put an arm around Livvy.

The band began to play Glenn Miller's *Moonlight Serenade*. Victoria put a hand on Jon's arm, stood and pulled. "They're playing our song," she said with a smile. He allowed himself to be half dragged out of the booth, then he followed her onto the dance floor.

She turned to face him, took his right hand and placed it on her hip. Then she gripped his left hand and held it up near her right shoulder. She began to sway with the music, and, after a beat, Jon did likewise. She moved closer to him and lay her head on his shoulder. Jon wasn't sure whether it was her perfume, the music, or simply her proximity, but he felt a little dizzy. He didn't mind the feeling.

After a moment, he felt her lips on his neck, just above his collar. She kissed him there, and it felt wonderful. He closed his eyes. She slowly moved her lips up his neck until she'd reached his ear lobe, which she began to tickle with her tongue. Jon had an immediate physical reaction, which Victoria seemed to notice. She pushed herself against him harder, and her tongue slid into his ear.

She pulled it away after a second and murmured, "Follow me." Then she stepped back. Still holding his hand, she led him through the crowd. He followed willingly, walking as casually as he could given his excited condition.

They came to a door. She pushed it open, and they stepped into a dimly lit stairwell. There was another couple just inside the door, locked in a passionate embrace. She led him past them and up the first flight of stairs. On the landing was yet another couple, similarly ensconced. At the second floor, she turned and asked, quietly, "Do you have the key, luv?"

Jon wasn't sure what she meant. Then it dawned on him. After they'd checked in, Shim had given the room key to Jon and asked him to hold on to it. He fished in his pocket. located it and pulled it out.

Victoria held Jon's hand with the key up to the light, then said, "One more floor."

They ascended to the third floor and exited the stairwell. Jon found that they were in the hallway where he and Shim had been earlier. Victoria led him the short way down the hall to their room. She took the key from Jon, put it in the lock and opened the door. Then she stepped inside and pulled Jon in after her.

Before the door had even closed, Victoria had pressed her face to Jon's. Jon felt her tongue slip between his lips, probing. It was an incredible sensation. He met her tongue with his, and she pressed her body up against him. She lifted one of her hands and ran it through the hair on the back of his head. The other she slid across his shoulders and down his back. He wrapped his arms around her and reveled in the intense thrill that engulfed him.

After a moment, however, something began to intrude on his pleasure. It started deep in the recesses of his mind. He tried to push it away, but it was extraordinarily insistent. It began to distract him. Not now, a part of him said. Whatever it was, however, stood its ground.

Victoria pulled back and looked at him. There was a wild intensity in her eyes. "Don't stop now, lover, you're doing great."

He looked back at her, but he was confused. Her eyes searched his. He blinked a couple of times. Her brow furrowed.

And then he knew.

His arms went slack. He realized with a stunning clarity that he couldn't do this. Not because he didn't want to. He most certainly did. But the undeniable reality was that he didn't want to do it with Victoria.

She realized it too. Her shoulders seemed to slump, and some of the fire left her eyes. She stepped back slightly, though she did not let go of him.

"There's a girl, isn't there?" she asked softly.

Jon said nothing, but he nodded slightly.

She looked away for a moment. "Brilliant." She took a deep breath and looked back at him. She pulled her arms around from behind him and put both hands up to Jon's cheeks. "Whoever she is, she's very lucky."

#

Shim didn't heap any grief on him when Jon and Victoria returned to the table a few minutes after they'd left, Victoria giving Shim a slight shake of her head. They ordered more rounds of beer. Jon danced with Victoria and Livvy and even tried some of the crazy steps they taught him. He suspected that he probably looked a little foolish, but he didn't care, and no one else seemed to mind.

Shim and Livvy excused themselves and left Jon and Victoria alone for about half an hour. Victoria told Jon a little bit about herself. He learned she was from Essex and was studying art at the Norwich School of Design. Victoria pressed Jon for details about his life, but he was reticent to provide any. What she really wanted was the story about the girl whom she was sure waited for Jon at home. Unable to bring himself to tell the truth, Jon instead said nothing and let her believe whatever she chose.

The next morning, when they returned to Hut 51, Jon was pleasantly surprised to find a letter from Ben sitting on his bunk. He checked the postmark and saw that it had been mailed in early December. Oh well, he thought, it only took about seven weeks to get to him. He'd have to tell Ben he'd discovered yet another aspect of the army way.

He opened the envelope and took out two pages. He propped up his pillow and settled onto the bunk. The first line got his attention.

"Dear Jon," Ben began, "I hope you're sitting down, because I have some incredible news for you."

Jon contemplated his reposed figure and smiled.

"I'm sitting at my kitchen table, and there's someone here with me who has something very important to tell you. I know you will be as excited and happy as I am. I won't steal the thunder. Just know that I am thinking of you. Fondly, Ben."

That struck Jon as odd. Ben was usually much more voluble, but he'd cut this letter short. Curious, he reversed the two sheets and saw immediately that the second page was in a different handwriting. His eyes slid to the bottom of the page, and his breath caught.

It read, "With all my love, Mary."

Heart pounding, he turned his attention to the top of the letter.

"My dear Jon," she had written, "I am so sorry not to have tried to reach you sooner. When I awoke at the hospital, I had no memory of anything that had happened to me over the past year. The doctors said that it was unusual, but not unheard of. Several weeks ago, I suddenly regained my memory of you, but I couldn't remember anything about how we met or the things that we did. All I knew was that I loved you dearly.

"This morning, thank God, everything came back in a rush. I haven't yet put it all together, but I am embarrassed to say that I think my father had a lot to do with keeping me in the dark.

"Oh, Jon," she continued, "I am so distressed to think that you might believe I don't want to have anything more to do with you. That is so wrong, it makes me angry. I love you. I want desperately to be with you. Know that you have all my heart."

Jon closed his eyes and said a brief prayer of thanks.

"Ben and I are going to see Mr. Anderson to get some advice about how to deal with Vernon and Jeff. If they think they are going to get away with what they did, they have another think coming. You saved me, Jon. Thank you. I'm going to fix everything.

"Please tell me that I'm not too late. I would die if that was the case. I will be waiting for news from you. Be safe and come home to me."

Jon closed his eyes again and held the letter to his heart. He breathed deeply. Then, with a sudden start, he realized that Mary had written this letter seven weeks ago. For seven weeks, Mary had been waiting for a reply from him! With shaking hands, he retrieved his tablet and pen, and he began to write.

15

"Bandits, twelve o'clock high." The call carried with it a jolt of adrenalin, and Jon's heart started beating faster. It was followed immediately by several others. "Bandits, six o'clock high. Bandits, eight o'clock level. Two coming in at five o'clock level."

Jon squinted and peered through his sights. There. He fired a sustained volley. A twin engined German fighter flashed by, its cannon spitting deadly shells. All of the guns on the Deuces Wild were firing.

"Navigator to pilot. We're at the I.P. Prepare to execute turn on my mark. Three, two, one. Mark." The bomber banked slightly. They were in lead position. The others in the formation would follow.

The crew of the Deuces Wild were on Jon's eighth mission, and, from the moment he'd learned what the target would be, he'd known it would be deadly. They were bombing the Focke Wulf factory in Bremen, where many of the German fighters they'd faced on previous missions had been constructed. He knew the Germans wouldn't take kindly to it. The danger was even greater for Jon and his crewmates because today they were in the lead plane, a favorite target of the German fighters.

Gooch's voice came over the interphone. "Jesus, look at the number of fighters out there. It's like a swarm of bees."

The Germans had been trying different tactics lately. Sometimes they would feign an attack from one quarter, only to charge in from a different direction, shielded by either the sun or the contrails of the bombers themselves. When they massed like they were doing now, it was a bad sign.

At the moment, the formation was on the final run into the target and would soon be within the range of anti-aircraft fire from below, so Jon knew it was unlikely the fighters would try any more attacks until they were through with the bomb run. For that reason, it came as a shock when he heard Reyes exclaim, "Shit. Two o'clock high. Three bandits." As he was saying it, the wings of the Deuces Wild rocked and the all too familiar sound of shells striking the bomber reverberated through the fuselage. The fighters delivering the deadly fire passed without crossing into Jon's field of vision, but most of the other guns roared. It struck Jon belatedly that the twin .50's from the top turret had not been among them.

There was a sudden bang, and Jon looked back in time to see flames shoot out of the number three engine.

An obviously stressed Roth called out, "Pilot to top turret, report."

There was no response.

Jon looked with concern out the starboard window and saw that Roth had feathered the damaged engine. There were no more flames that he could see, which was a good sign. Still, they'd lost the engine.

Roth's voice came again across the interphone. "Pilot to navigator. Jonas, check on Reyes."

Bursts of flak appeared outside the windows. The plane started bucking.

After a moment, Jon heard Kovalesky. "Reyes is hit. At least two wounds, one in the chest, one in the hip. He's in shock."

Several seconds passed. Then Roth came on again. "Do what you can."

"Roger that," said Kovalesky.

"Pilot to bombardier. You have the controls."

There was a crunching sound as a shell burst close by, and the plane jumped a few feet, lurching forward. Then it settled back to level flight.

"Bombardier to pilot. Roger. Target in sight. Stand by."

Jon listened to the explosions around him. Spent pieces of flak clanked off the sides of the fuselage. The seconds crawled by. Finally, the voice of Ambrose came over the interphone again. "Bombs away."

As soon as the words had been uttered, there was a huge explosion near the front of the plane, and it was as if the Deuces Wild had hit a wall. Jon was thrown forward, and he slammed into the bulkhead that separated his radio compartment from the bomb bay, falling in a heap to the floor.

He shook his head, trying to clear it. Kovalesky came over the interphone. There was a strain in his voice that Jon had never heard before. "Murphy's dead," Kovalesky said. "The skipper's hurt bad. Oh, God, I think the whole front of the plane's gone."

Jon was already on his feet with his hand on the lever that opened the door to the bomb bay when Gooch came over the interphone, giving voice to the very thing that had so galvanized Jon. "Who's flying the plane?" It was the last thing Jon heard before pulling the jack that connected his headset to the interphone.

Jon yanked open the door and found himself looking down at the City of Bremen passing 25,000 feet below him. The bomb bay doors were still open, though the bombs had been released. As Jon stepped out on the catwalk that led forward through the bomb bay, the only thing between him and the ground was the narrow width of steel on which he was standing.

On either side of the catwalk, there were two pairs of metal rails, one at waist and one at knee level. Gripping the upper rails, and telling himself not to look down, Jon stepped quickly across the gaping maw. At the far end, he grabbed the handle of the forward compartment door and twisted. The door immediately flew open, violently striking him in the chest and the side of his face. He was thrown backward several feet. His back struck the catwalk, and he immediately slid off. As he fell out into the open space of the bomb bay, Jon instinctively threw out his right arm, and his hand slapped the catwalk. He closed his fingers and just managed to catch the far edge of the narrow platform. With a sudden jerk, it arrested his fall, but left him hanging by one hand, his legs dangling out of the bomb bay. Through the panic, Jon realized he was not wearing his parachute.

Jon's purchase on the edge of the catwalk slipped, and his leather glove began to slide across the surface of the walkway. He was a fraction of a second away from falling out of the plane. The instant before he lost contact with the catwalk, Jon did a scissor kick, lunged upward, and reached out blindly with his left hand, trying to grab the lower support rail. As his right hand separated from the platform, his left closed on the narrow rail. He dangled by one arm for a moment. Then he flung his right arm over and managed to grab the rail with his other hand. He was now hanging from the rail out into space.

He tried to swing his right leg up onto the catwalk. but he couldn't get it high enough, and it dropped back down. He knew he couldn't keep his grip on the support rail for much longer.

He gritted his teeth, took a deep breath, and, with all the strength he could muster, he pulled hard with his arms to raise himself, at the same moment kicking his right leg up and over. The back of his shoe thankfully struck the catwalk. Hanging awkwardly now by two hands and a foot, he used the leverage of his right leg to bring his other leg up, and he planted his left heel on the metal walkway. Then he slid his right foot over, feeling for the far edge. He found it and hooked it with the toe of his shoe. With the last of his strength, he swung himself to the right and, using the purchase that he had with his right foot, threw his body onto the walkway. Shifting his right hand to the opposite support rail, he found his balance and stood shakily.

He knew he had two choices. Return to the radio compartment, strap on his parachute and jump, or try to reach the cockpit. He thought of Reyes and Roth. They would probably die if he made the former decision, though he had to consider the possibility they were already dead.

He wasted no more time. Fighting the blast of cold air rushing through the opening at the front of the bomb bay, he pulled himself forward along the catwalk and stepped through the doorway.

He looked toward the front of the plane, and the sight that greeted him was completely disorienting. The area below the cockpit, which should have been the nose compartment where the navigator and bombardier sat, was open to the sky. Kovalesky had been right. The whole front of the plane was gone.

Lying in two heaps at his feet were Reyes and Roth. Neither man was conscious. Jon did a quick check to see if their oxygen masks were attached and hooked to the supply. They were, and he could see that both were taking breaths, though they were very shallow. He realized that he had been unconnected to oxygen since he'd left the radio compartment. He didn't know how long that had been, but he would certainly pass out soon unless he was reconnected.

Leaning into the rush of air coming through the gaping hole in the front of the plane, Jon lifted himself up into the cockpit. Blood had splattered the instrument panel. Below it, beyond the throttle controls and rudder pedals, he could see more daylight. Kovalesky had taken Roth's seat. His head was darting back and forth as though he were reading the controls, but he did not have his hand on the yoke, nor did he appear to have his feet on the rudder.

Murphy was still strapped in his seat. A piece of shrapnel had almost decapitated him, and his body was soaked in his own blood. Jon reached across, unhooked Murphy's oxygen hose and connected his own. He did the same thing with his interphone jack. As soon as it was plugged in, he was greeted by multiple voices.

"I don't know," he heard Kovalesky saying. "We've got to jump," said Gooch. "Watch for fighters," came Shim's voice.

Kovalesky had noticed Jon and had turned toward him. "I can't fly this thing," he said.

Jon reached down and undid the straps still holding Murphy in the copilot's seat. He put his hands under Murphy's arms and pulled as hard as he could. The man's body slowly slid out of the seat. He allowed it to drop down through the narrow passageway leading to the nose compartment.

Jon climbed up and into the blood soaked copilot's seat. He looked down at the autopilot control panel. All of the switches were toggled to the "on" position, where Roth had set them prior to the bombing run. Despite the damage to her nose section, the plane was still flying straight and level, though, as Jon looked at the altimeter, he could see they were slowly losing altitude. They were now down to 18,000 feet, a drop of 7,000 from the mission altitude.

The remainder of the formation would have turned following the bomb run, the second plane in their element moving up to take the lead in place of the crippled Deuces Wild, all in accordance with operating procedure. Jon looked, and as he expected, he could see no other bombers.

The Deuces Wild was flying alone and headed deeper into Germany.

If they were to have any chance of survival, Jon knew, he had to turn the plane around. He put his feet on the rudder pedals and gripped the yoke with his right hand. With his left, he reached down and flipped the master bar on the autopilot control panel to the left, disengaging the autopilot. He now had control of the aircraft.

He banked the plane slightly to the left and began what he hoped would be a full turn. Compared to the Jenny, the response from the bomber was incredibly slow. He was relieved to see, however, that it did appear to be reacting as it should.

"Meyer's flying the plane," Kovalesky announced over the interphone.

After a moment, Gooch's voice came over the system. "Jon, do you know what you're doing?"

Jon wasn't sure how to answer to that. His exposure to B-17 controls had consisted of a few minutes quizzing Tommie Wheeler. But, if ever there was a time for on-the-job training, he figured, this was it. Finally, he said, "We'll see. In the meantime, make sure your chutes are strapped on. Be ready to bail at a moment's notice. Keep your eyes peeled for bandits."

Jon turned to Kovalesky. "Sir, you might want to man the top turret."

Kovalesky looked at him blankly for a moment. Then it registered. He nodded, unhooked his oxygen and interphone, and awkwardly climbed out of the pilot's seat. Jon did a quick check of the instrument panel. Number three engine was out, but the other three seemed to be ok.

Jon was surprised they hadn't yet been attacked by any of the German fighters. He figured they must have decided the Deuces Wild was finished and stayed with the formation. The minute any fighter noticed the plane flying under the control of a pilot, all bets would be off. The Germans, of course, would have no way of knowing the pilot was a non-commissioned radio operator with less than twenty hours at the controls of a Curtiss JN-4 Jenny.

Jon knew the protocol for a bomber separated from its formation was to drop down to tree top level to avoid detection from both anti-aircraft gunners and enemy fighters. However, from that altitude, the men would not be in a position to bail out. Uncertain what he should do, Jon was about to poll the crew when there was an abrupt shout.

"Bandits, three o'clock, high." It was Kovalesky.

Gooch chimed it. "I count two. Look like Ju 88s."

After a moment, Kovalesky said, "I think they're planning to come at us from behind."

"Works for me," Shim said.

Not that it was of much comfort, but Jon thought the German pilots were making a tactical error not attacking the plane head on. From the front, a lone bomber would be most vulnerable, particularly one whose nose had been blown off, taking away the two guns mounted in the forward compartment that the bombardier and navigator manned when not otherwise engaged in their primary duties.

Jon looked about for cloud cover. Below him at his eleven o'clock was a series of fluffy cumulus clouds, not the solid blanket he was hoping for, but better than nothing. He allowed the plane to continue turning until he'd lined the clouds up directly ahead.

"Radio operator to crew. I'm going to put us in a dive. Don't panic. I'm going to try to get us into some clouds ahead and below us."

"Good," Gooch said.

Jon pushed the yoke forward. The plane's nose, or, rather, the mangled stub that now passed for its nose, dipped, and they began to pick up speed.

"Here they come," called Shim.

After a moment, Shim's guns began to yammer. Jon could also hear Kovalesky firing bursts from the top turret. He saw tracer fire from the German fighters arcing over the left wing, and then the shells found the number two engine. The Deuces Wild shuddered from the impact.

The Germans passed directly overhead, apparently overshooting the bomber, and Kovalesky rotated the top turret, trying to bring fire to bear.

The oil pressure on number two engine began to drop precipitously. Realizing he had to act before he lost all pressure, Jon quickly reached over, shut the engine down and adjusted the pitch to feather the propeller as Tommie had shown him.

"The bastards are coming around again," Gooch said.

The tips of the nearest cumulus cloud reached up and tickled the Deuces Wild. Jon flattened out the dive and gratefully eased the bomber into the protective cover of the clouds. The world around them went white.

"All right, Jon," Gooch shouted. "Way to go."

It was a short-lived respite. The bomber suddenly burst through the other side of the cloud and into the clear. Jon aimed for the next cloud, which appeared to be about a mile away.

Again, the bomber's gunners opened up, and, again, Jon felt the plane shudder as the fire from at least one of the German fighters found the right wing and began tracing a path to number four engine. Then they were again in a cloud, and Jon immediately banked to throw the Germans off target, allowing the bomber to slip slightly in altitude before bringing her level again. It worked, as the shells from the German fighters stopped impacting the wing.

Jon looked anxiously at the dials indicating the status of the number four engine. He wasn't sure he could get them back to England on two engines, but he knew he'd never be able to do it on one. The pressure and temperature seemed to be holding.

They slipped once more out of the clouds, but, almost immediately, they were back in. Jon noted their heading. They were flying almost due west. This course would take them across the Netherlands and out over the North Sea, assuming they were able to stay in the air that long. Their altitude was just under ten thousand feet.

"Radio operator to crew. We're under ten thousand, so you can remove your oxygen masks."

He checked his gauges. The oil pressure on number four had dropped slightly.

There was movement behind him. Kovalesky climbed down from the upper turret and crouched by the bodies of Reyes and Roth. Then he came forward and tapped Jon's shoulder. Over the noise of the wind and the engines, he shouted, "They're alive, but in bad shape. What do you think we should do?"

Jon pointed to Kovalesky, then up at the top turret. Then he brought a finger to his ear, indicating the interphone. Kovalesky nodded, and he climbed back up into the turret.

When he was confident Kovalesky was settled in, Jon keyed his microphone.

"Radio operator to crew. Here's the status. Roth and Reyes are wounded badly. There's no way they'd survive a jump. We're down to two engines, numbers one and four, and number four is running rough. If we lose it, we won't have a choice. We'll have to bail and take our chances. I don't know how long this cloud cover will last, but I'm inclined to stay at this altitude for as long as it does. If we lose the cloud cover, then it's decision time. I can take us down to tree top level. Problem is, it'll be dangerous trying to bail out from there, so, if we do drop down, at that point, it's do or die with the engines. I'm prepared to take the chance, but nobody else has to. You don't have to make the choice now. But if we pass into the clear, everyone will have to decide for himself. Jump or stay with the plane."

There was a long silence. Then Gooch's voice came over the interphone. "Waist gunners understand."

"Roger that." It was Shim.

"Understood," Kovalesky said.

"Ditto," Graham said.

They managed to stay in the clouds for about forty-five minutes, finally breaking out into a magnificently clear blue sky. Jon immediately nosed the plane down. As near as he could tell, none of the crewmen had elected to bail out.

Jon brought the Deuces Wild to the point where the plane was just skimming over the tallest trees. The land below them was, for the most part, flat, and Jon hoped it meant they were over the Netherlands. They were flying at about 150 miles an hour, and, at this level, Jon was truly able to appreciate the speed. She may be a big, ungainly thing, he thought, but she still moves almost three times as fast as the Jenny. Despite the tension, it was exhilarating.

They crossed directly over a couple of military installations, but they were moving so fast that no one on the ground was able to bring any weapons to bear. Then, with no warning it was about to happen, they were suddenly out over water, and Jon could see the white caps of the waves below them.

The oil pressure in number four engine was getting close to critical. If they were to lose it, Jon's plan was to buy as much altitude as possible with the last remaining engine, then order the crew to bail out. Unfortunately, after a few minutes, the fuel and oil temperature for number one engine began slowly creeping up, and he realized he soon might not even have that option.

Finally, Jon decided that, whether or not they were near the English coastline, he had to allow the altitude to increase. He began a slow climb.

Kovalesky's voice came over the interphone. "Sweet mother of God, isn't that a beautiful sight?"

Jon looked forward, and, sure enough, land appeared ahead of them. He breathed a huge sigh of relief. "All right," he said, into the interphone, "let's find a place to land."

#

Wing Commander Douglas Townsend was studying a map laid out on the large table in the operations room when one of his orderlies stuck his head in and said, "Sir, you might want to come see this."

Townsend set down the pencil with which he'd been making marks on the map and stepped over to the door. It led out to a viewing platform overlooking the landing field at Queen's End. Several officers stood along the rail, many with binoculars, and they all had their heads raised, following an aircraft that was flying directly over the base.

All of the Mosquito bombers of Townsend's No. 73 and No. 132 Squadrons were on the ground at the moment, though several would be flying sorties later that night. This plane was obviously not one of his.

He joined his adjutant at the rail and said, "What have we got, Mark?"

"An American B-17. It flew over at about five hundred feet and has now circled back. It's very badly damaged."

Townsend nodded. He'd had a couple of Yanks put down at Queen's End in the past, planes unable to make it all the way back to their own bases. "Have you scrambled the emergency crew?"

The answer came in the form of a pair of fire suppression vehicles that suddenly appeared from across the field, heading for the end of the runway. They were joined a moment later by a couple of ambulances.

"May I?" Townsend asked, pointing to the binoculars in his adjutant's hand. The junior officer immediately handed them to Townsend. The wing commander put the binoculars up to his eyes and adjusted the focus. "Badly damaged" was an understatement. The entire nose of the American bomber was gone, the fuselage ending just forward of the cockpit in a mangled mess of twisted steel. The plane was flying on the two outboard engines only, smoke trailing from one of them. Massive holes peppered both wings. He had no idea how the craft was still in the air.

As he watched, a parachute opened, then another. In all, he counted four 'chutes. He wondered if that was all that remained of the crew, but realized after a moment there was still someone flying the plane as it banked and made a controlled turn. The pilot, he realized, was going to try to land the thing. A red flare appeared over the damaged aircraft.

Townsend lowered the binoculars for a moment. "He's got wounded on board," he said, to no one in particular. "That's why he's trying to bring the thing in. That's one crazy Yank." And one damn brave one, he said to himself.

He retrained the binoculars and noticed that the third engine had been shut down. The American was now trying to come in on only one engine. Then he noticed something else. Only the left landing gear had lowered. Where the other should have been, a loose piece of metal dangled uselessly below the right wing. What the American should do, he thought, was retract the gear and attempt a belly landing. Then he realized that, most likely, the American pilot couldn't get the gear back up.

"This is not going to be pretty," he said.

#

In the cockpit, Jon set the flaps. He'd finally had to feather number four and boost power to the one remaining engine to keep the bomber aloft. That engine was threatening to seize at any moment.

They'd tried to raise the left landing gear as soon as they realized the right gear was not extending. It had jammed, and, though Kovalesky had attempted to get it up manually with the crank, it simply wouldn't budge. They'd have to set the plane down on the one wheel and then drop the right wing. It would take a miracle to survive the landing.

Jon had ordered the crew to bail out. Everyone but Kovalesky had jumped, and Kovalesky reported that, thankfully, four parachutes had opened. After checking again on Roth and Reyes, Kovalesky had climbed back into the pilot's seat, explaining to Jon that, as the last functioning officer on board, he felt he had an obligation to help Jon get the plane down. He'd made it clear, though, that Jon was in charge.

As Ben had taught him to do, Jon noted landmarks as he came downwind in order to help himself line up on the runway. Now, as they approached the field, he went through the instructions one more time with Kovalesky.

"As soon as we touch down, pump the brakes. I'll try to hold the wing up as long as I can. When I say 'now,' lock the brakes. Got it?"

Kovalesky nodded.

Jon forced himself to be calm. He imagined he was approaching Ben's field. Easing back on the throttle, he allowed gravity to draw the plane down slowly. He kept the wings dead level. At the outside barrier, he shut down the number one engine. If they missed this landing, they would not be going back around.

In sudden eerie silence, broken only by the whistling of the wind passing through the opening at their feet, they crossed over the threshold of the runway. Jon eased back on the yoke, and the big bomber skimmed along the surface, finally settling onto its one wheel. Jon let the tail come down.

Kovalesky began pumping the brakes as Jon had instructed him to do. With all the concentration he could muster, Jon kept the wings level, as though he were still flying the plane. They were slowing, but not quickly enough to avoid running out of runway. Jon held the right wing elevated as long as he dared. Then he gradually allowed it to dip. With a grinding sound, it made contact with the surface of the runway.

"Now," Jon said, and Kovalesky locked the brakes on the one usable landing gear. With a squeal of protest, the rubber slid along the tarmac. The tip of the wing acted as a fulcrum, and the heavy plane performed a slow languorous turn, pivoting majestically around the wing tip. The wheel dropped off the edge of the runway into the adjacent grass, and, with a last few creaks, the Deuces Wild slowly came to a stop.

There was dead silence.

Jon closed his eyes and let out the air that he'd been holding in his lungs. He was suddenly shaking, but, after a couple of deep breaths, he steadied himself.

He turned to look at Kovalesky. The man had his eyes closed, and Jon could see that he was also shaking. After a moment, Kovalesky opened his eyes and turned to look at Jon. A grin split his face, and he emitted a short laugh, almost like a cough. Suddenly, they both dissolved into an uncontrollable fit of laughter. It was as if someone had just told them the funniest joke they'd ever heard in their lives, and, for several seconds, they laughed so hard tears began running down their cheeks. The moment passed, and Jon drew in another deep breath, his chest shaking as he did.

He heard noise behind them, and, turning, saw a couple of men in coveralls bent over the bodies of Roth and Reyes. They appeared to know what they were doing, so Jon decided not to get in their way. He looked again at Kovalesky, who nodded solemnly. After a moment, Kovalesky held out his right hand. Jon took it, and they shook. Kovalesky did not seem to know what to say. Neither did Jon.

Jon looked back again to see that the men behind them were easing the body of Reyes out of the forward hatch. Roth's had apparently already been taken. An officer in a blue uniform with three stripes on his epaulet appeared and climbed up into the area immediately behind the cockpit. The man's eyes took in the blood splattered across the instruments and soaking the seats. He looked below the flight controls, where the ground was visible through a large hole. Finally, he whistled.

The officer turned to Kovalesky and said, in a clipped British accent, "Lieutenant, that was some of the finest flying I have ever seen in my life."

Kovalesky nodded. "Got to agree with you there, sir. But don't look at me." He nodded toward Jon. "Sergeant Meyer flew this plane home and landed it."

The officer stared at Jon with a shocked expression. After a moment, he put a hand out, and Jon took it. "Nicely done, sergeant," he said.

16

Mary returned to her desk and took a seat. From one of the drawers, she retrieved two pieces of plain white paper and a sheet of carbon paper, arranged them, and set them behind the roller on her typewriter. She scrolled them through and gave the carriage return lever an efficient smack. Referring to the notes she'd just made on her pad, she began typing.

It was a busy Friday afternoon, but Mary was hoping to get away early, and her fingers flew on the keys.

Known as Wealdon Manor, the building in which Mary now sat had been constructed in the early nineteenth century by the seventh earl of Wealdon. It was a massive structure perched on the north bank of the Thames River, a short distance from the Tower of London. Having served variously as a royal residence, guest quarters for visiting dignitaries, and, during the Great War, a hospital, it was now headquarters to the British Home Defense Agency, a joint services group charged with coordinating and overseeing development and logistical support for all military installations in the British Isles.

Mary worked for the senior American officer assigned as liaison to the Department. She had been in England two weeks.

After completing the basic training course for enlistees in the Women's Auxiliary Army Corps, Mary had been taken aside by her commanding officer and encouraged to enter the officer's candidate school. When she learned that the school would involve an additional twelve weeks of training, she graciously declined, saying she felt an immediate need to apply herself to the war effort. When it became apparent to the officer that Mary was not to be dissuaded, she'd offered Mary her choice of assignments.

Mary had carefully reviewed the list of available postings, immediately rejecting all but the handful that involved assignment to England. The opportunity to work in the office of the American liaison to the Home Defense Agency had seemed, to Mary, to offer the best chance for finding Jon. It also had the benefit of having been tagged as a priority assignment, which meant Mary would be sent immediately, without any opportunity for leave following her training. That was perfectly fine with her. Mary's insistence on getting to her post without further delay had impressed her commanding officer, and she'd approved Mary for the assignment.

In New York, Mary had boarded the RMS Queen Mary, an ocean liner from the Cunard White Star Line that had been converted to a troopship. The trip across the Atlantic took a week and was a surprisingly enjoyable experience. Mary was invited to dine with the captain the first night at sea, and he subsequently arranged for her to be a permanent guest at his table for the remainder of the voyage.

The ship docked in Gourock, Scotland, and, from there, Mary traveled by train to London, where she reported in at the headquarters of the European Theater of Operations, United States Army, at 20 Grosvenor Square. She was assigned a billet at the Staunton, a hotel in Mayfair that had been turned over to the U.S. Army shortly after the United States had entered the war. It had become the barracks for most of the women assigned to WAAC units throughout London. There Mary was reunited with Penny, who was working in the office of the Chief Surgeon for the U.S. Eighth Air Force.

It had taken Brigadier General Lloyd Kimbrough about a minute to review Mary's personnel file and all of a five-minute interview to decide that Mary would be his new personal assistant. He'd immediately reassigned the sergeant who had been filling that role, and Mary was given the desk that looked down the former main reception hall, with the big windows to the right that afforded views out over the river, and she now sat typing up a memorandum General Kimbrough had dictated minutes before.

Mary liked her boss. In the two weeks she'd known him, he had never raised his voice, never spoken to anyone in a cross or mean fashion, and treated all with whom he came in contact with respect and courtesy. He was what she imagined a grandfather should be. He, in turn, seemed fond of her.

Mary had waited a week to get settled into her job before broaching the question of Jon's whereabouts. General Kimbrough had arched an eyebrow. "This young man is important to you, I take it."

Mary nodded, realizing her cheeks were flushed. General Kimbrough promised to make some inquiries, but warned her it might take some time to locate him.

After work today, she and Penney were planning to go to the Rainbow Corner, a service club in Piccadilly Circus operated by the Red Cross. Mary had overheard a few of the ladies raving about it and had finally convinced Penny that they should go. Penny would meet Mary here at Wealdon Manor after work. A few minutes before five, Mary glanced up to see Penny making her way through the crowd in the main hall. Penny's uniform now sported the dual chevrons of a corporal.

"Are you able to get away?" Penny asked when she reached Mary's desk.

Mary nodded. "I think so. Let me check with the boss." She pulled the memorandum she'd just finished out of the typewriter, removed the carbon, and stood. "I'll be right back."

She tapped at the door to General Kimbrough's office, then immediately walked in. He had made it clear that Mary did not need to wait to be invited. He read through the memo quickly, then said, "Perfect."

He looked up at her. "That's all I've got for now. I'm guessing you probably have someplace you'd like to be other than here on a Friday evening."

Mary smiled and nodded toward the door. "My friend, Penny, has arrived. We're planning to go to the Rainbow Corner. There's a big dance tonight."

General Kimbrough nodded. "Enjoy yourself."

#

"When you think about it," Jon said, "we've gone to some incredible places."

Shim nodded. "Yeah, we've gone to incredible places," he said in a deadpan, "and blown them up."

Jon gave a slight wave of one hand. "Well, ok, there is that."

They were walking down Cannon Street, which paralleled the north bank of the Thames. They'd just left the Tower of London, to which Jon had dragged a somewhat reluctant Shim.

Jon and Shim were in London on a forty-eight hour pass. The trip offered Jon his first look at the capital of England, and he was excited about seeing all the sites. Shim was less enthusiastic about playing the tourist, but he'd agreed to humor Jon.

Six weeks had passed since the final flight of the Deuces Wild. The damage to the plane had been so severe the army decided to write it off. A team of mechanics drove out to Queen's End and spent a couple of days removing what components could be salvaged. They had, however, at the request of the Royal Air Force, left the shell of the aircraft. The Brits considered it so extraordinary that the plane survived a safe landing they decided to keep the thing, and moved it to a prominent spot on the Queen's End base for display.

Though Jon's actions hadn't saved the plane, they had, much more importantly, saved the lives of Bob Roth and Tony Reyes. The doctors found it necessary to amputate one of Roth's legs, but they managed to save the other. Roth would never fly again. He would, however, be able to return home to his wife and young son. Reyes likewise recovered, though, as a result of the hip wound, he'd walk with a limp for the rest of his life. He also was taken off of flight status and was due to be sent home in a few weeks.

Jon, Shim, Kovalesky and Gooch went to visit Reyes at the hospital, and he was so effusive in his thanks that Jon became embarrassed. They also tried to see Roth, but he was sedated and unable to receive visitors.

In addition to saving the lives of the two wounded men, Jon's actions had also spared the other survivors of the Deuces Wild the prospect of bailing out over Germany and likely becoming prisoners of war. Ironically, the plane on which Art Graham flew his very next mission was shot down, and that fate, delayed by Jon, had inevitably visited Graham. A few weeks after his plane went down, the group received word that, fortunately, Graham had survived. He'd been captured and was now a prisoner at Stalag VII-A, where a number of other flyers from the 96th were also incarcerated.

With the Deuces Wild no longer in service, the surviving crewmembers had no permanent assignment, and, in the following weeks, they'd been slotted onto other crews as needed.

Jon became a hot commodity. In the superstitious world where the men who flew bombers lived, his fellow airmen viewed him as a good luck charm, and all the other crews in the 96th requested he fly with them. It didn't hurt that he was also considered one of the best radio operators in the group, if not *the* best. And, of course, it was a plus that Jon could fly the plane in an emergency. He'd been on a dozen missions following the demise of the Deuces Wild, and there had, thankfully, been no casualties and no serious battle damage on any of the planes to which he'd been assigned. Belief in Jon's good luck status grew exponentially.

Airmen on crews with which Jon was not assigned began seeking Jon out before each mission to shake his hand or touch his shoulder for good luck. Tommie Wheeler had dispensed with all military protocol, and, before each of his last six missions came to

Jon and rubbed the top of Jon's head. He'd yet to get Jon assigned to the Widowmaker, but it wasn't for lack of trying.

A couple of days before Jon and Shim got their furlough, Jon returned to Hut 51 to find two airmen from the 302nd who had taken the three-hour ride from Dunston Heath to see him. After some good natured ribbing from Gooch and Shim, Jon allowed the men to rub his head. They left for the long ride back to their base with satisfied grins.

Because of the demand for his services, Jon was assigned missions quicker than would otherwise have been the case if he'd been assigned to a regular crew. Not every plane in the group flew every mission, but, due to Jon's somewhat mythical status, he'd flown on almost every sortie the group was assigned over the prior six week period. As a result, Jon had already completed twenty missions.

However, the irrational confidence in Jon's ability to ward off misfortune began to wear on him. Jon was as superstitious as the next guy, and part of him worried he was tempting fate by going along with all the hoopla. He'd had trouble sleeping the prior week, and this trip to London could not have come at a better time.

It was this thought that occupied his mind when he heard Shim suddenly call out.

"Miss," Shim was saying, holding out a hand and pointing a finger. "Hey, miss."

Jon, who had been absently looking at the buildings on the other side of the street, glanced back at Shim, then looked in the direction his friend was pointing. About twenty yards ahead of them, a cab sat idling on the curb, and a young woman in an army uniform was just getting in. The woman paused and stepped back out. She wore the stripes of a corporal.

Shim quickened his step, and, when he reached the back end of the cab, he crouched and picked up an item from the gutter.

"This fell out of your purse," he said, handing it to the woman.

She looked at it and said, "Oh, my goodness." She glanced at her handbag, then back at Shim. "Thank you so much. I would not have wanted to lose this."

As Jon reached them, Shim nodded and smiled. "My pleasure."

She returned Shim's smile, then looked at Jon. The woman had a pleasant countenance. She was not classically beautiful by any stretch, and the side of one of her eyes drooped slightly, but, to Jon, she exuded a sense of warmth and friendliness. He smiled back at her.

"Well," she said, turning her attention to Shim, "thank you, again." Then, after another brief look at Jon, she slid back into the cab. The driver put the car in gear and pulled away.

Jon watched the cab as it merged into the flow of vehicles traveling down Cannon Street and eventually was lost in the traffic. He couldn't shake the feeling that there was something important about it.

#

Penny looked down at the object the young soldier had retrieved for her. It was the silver compact Andy had given her shortly after they were married. He'd had it engraved with what were, at the time, her new initials, "PR." Andy had told her when he gave it to her that he never wanted her to forget they were married. As if she ever could do that. She looked again at her handbag and this time saw that one of the straps had come loose.

"What was that about?" asked Mary.

Penny held out the compact. "I almost lost this. Fortunately, a soldier saw it fall out of my purse." She was about to say something else about the other young soldier she'd seen, but she didn't know how to put it, so she demurred.

"Oh," Mary said, "I know how important that is to you. I'm glad you didn't lose it."

Penny nodded, still distracted.

After a short drive, they arrived at the entrance to the Rainbow Corner, a Victorian structure fronting Piccadilly Circus. As they pulled up, Penny saw quite a bit of activity, as uniformed men and women came and went. Most, she noticed, were arriving, rather than leaving. Penny paid the fare, and they got out and joined the crowd making its way into the club. Inside the entrance, they turned and headed toward the main room, where Penny heard a band playing.

As she did whenever she and Mary went out, Penny steeled herself. Mary, bless her heart, had no idea the effect she had on men when she walked into a room. It was as if their heads were on swivels, and, by some irresistible force of nature, they were all immediately drawn toward Mary. Their reactions triggered all of Penny's maternal instincts.

And, of course, she had to acknowledge, she had, somewhat inadvertently, managed to pour gasoline on the fire.

From the moment the WAAC had been formed, it had suffered from a variety of poor decisions made by the army with respect to its uniforms. Most of the articles of clothing issued to the women were based on designs adapted from those intended for men, and they did not remotely flatter a woman's body. This, Penny had heard from her fellow servicewomen, had proven to be a source of great consternation throughout the ranks of the auxiliary service.

Fortunately, the women assigned to duty in England had a relatively accessible alternative. As soon as Mary arrived in London, Penny took her to Savile Row, where she knew a tailor who would, for a reasonable price, alter, or more accurately recreate, uniforms for men or women. Though Mary had not brought a lot of money with her from Indiana, she had more than enough for a complete overhaul of her military wardrobe, and Penny had encouraged her to take advantage of the opportunity.

Utilizing a much nicer cloth that draped in a more flattering manner, and allowing for the curves that so gracefully characterized Mary's body, the tailor to whom Penny had brought Mary produced a wardrobe that was the complete opposite of the stiff, manly uniform most WAAC personnel reluctantly tolerated. Instead, Mary sported a chic, classy outfit that looked, to Penny, to be straight out of the covers of Vogue magazine.

In short, if you were male, and you didn't notice Mary when she walked into a room, you were blind.

Penny steered Mary to a table at the side of the dance floor, and they took a seat. A number of men immediately approached, but Penny held up a hand. "Hold on, boys. We just got here. Give us a little time."

Mary chuckled. "Don't you want to dance?"

Penny nodded. "Sure, but let's have something to drink first."

The Rainbow Corner had real Coca Cola made on site from syrup shipped from the States, and they ordered two glasses. They were sipping their drinks when a burly sergeant with three stripes up and three stripes down stepped to the table.

Putting a hand out, he said to Mary, "Would you do me the honor of this dance?"

Mary smiled brightly and said, "Yes, of course."

As Mary slipped out of her seat, Penny reached out and gripped the sergeant's arm. He turned toward her.

"Keep your hands where I can see them, sergeant," Penny said, evenly.

The man opened his mouth as though to say something. Then he apparently noticed the look in Penny's eyes. "Yes, ma'am," he said.

#

As they approached the Rainbow Corner, Jon put a hand on Shim's shoulder. His friend turned, and Jon gave him a level gaze.

335

"I'm here to have a good time," he said, "I'm not here to meet girls. Fair enough?"

Shim nodded agreeably. "We'll just take what comes."

They worked their way through the crowd in front of the club and stepped into the lobby. From the main room, they could hear a band playing Genn Miller's *In the Mood*. At the reception desk, Shim gave the attendant their room number. The woman stepped away and returned a moment later with a key and a small piece of paper, folded in half. She handed them to Shim, and Shim unfolded the sheet of paper. A scowl appeared on Shim's face. Wordlessly, he handed the page to Jon.

The note was short and to the point. Their furlough had been cancelled, and they were to report immediately back to Stanbridge using the quickest available form of transportation. Jon knew it could only mean that there was to be a maximum effort the next day, and that all crews must report for duty. It also meant they wouldn't be attending the dance.

He had the irrational thought that they could pretend they'd never gotten the message. They'd spend the night in London, return the next morning after the planes had departed and express the appropriate level of surprise. He knew, of course, neither of them would do that.

Still, it was a devilish temptation.

He looked at Shim, who shrugged. "Not much we can do, is there?"

Jon shook his head. "Let's go get our stuff."

#

"Good morning, General," Mary said.

It was just before noon on Monday. General Kimbrough had attended a meeting at 20 Grosvenor Square that morning, and he had only now arrived at his office.

"Good morning, Mary," the general replied, stopping by the side of her desk. "Would you mind stepping into my office?"

Mary grabbed her pad and followed the general. He set his briefcase down on his desk but did not remove his jacket. Instead, he pulled a sheet of paper out of the briefcase, turned and considered Mary for a moment. Curious, Mary was about to ask him if there was a problem when the general began reading from the sheet.

"Staff Sergeant Jonathon Meyer," he read. "96th Bomb Group, Stanbridge, Suffolk." Mary's heart began to pound rapidly. The general looked up. "I believe we found your fellow."

Mary suddenly felt weak. Having trouble finding her voice, she said, "He's ok?"

General Kimbrough nodded. "He was as of this morning. He's completed twenty-one of his required twenty-five missions. I know his group is assigned to a mission today, but I don't know whether he's flying."

"Oh, God." Mary put a hand to her mouth. For the longest time, she had worried herself sick about whether Jon was safe, but the immediacy of this information was overwhelming.

She took a deep breath and steadied herself. "This place," she said, "where Jon is. Is it far?"

"It's about two hours away. By train."

Mary was already turning over plans in her mind when General Kimbrough chuckled. "However," he said, "it just so happens I have some business in that area." He cocked an eyebrow. "Perhaps you'd like to ride out there with me this afternoon?"

"Oh," Mary said, not daring to believe what she'd just heard. "Yes. Yes, I would. Very much."

"My car is waiting for us out front."

"Oh," she said again, surprised. She turned toward the door. "I just need to get my…" She turned back. "I mean, if it's ok, sir. I just… my… my purse and jacket. I just…"

"Why don't you get your purse and jacket," General Kimbrough said, with a smile. "Then we'll go."

#

The target for the mission that shortened the furlough for Jon and Shim had been Hamburg, and the mission was, as Jon suspected, classified as a maximum effort. Over one hundred Eighth Air Force bombers, mostly B-17s, but a few B-24s as well, massed for the purpose of knocking out the shipyards and submarine pens in the historic city. Heavy cloud cover and poor visibility broke up the formations before they could reach the target, and there was no way to bomb with any accuracy. The 96th Group wound up turning northwest and dropping its bombs over the shipyards in Wilhelmshaven.

On Monday, they were ordered back to Hamburg, and it was an exceptionally difficult mission.

On the way to the target, they were attacked by waves of German fighters. Over the target, the Germans set a heavy smoke screen, forcing the formation to go around a second time before dropping its bombs. It meant two deadly trips through heavy flak. Then, when they turned for home, they were hit again by enemy fighters.

In all, the Americans lost twenty bombers, three of which belonged to the 96th. The plane in which Jon flew, the Miss Medearly, was struck on the tail by a burst of flak that took out her rudder and badly wounded the tail gunner, a young man from Montpelier, Vermont named Harrison, who was on his very first mission. Jon left his position to come back and tend to the man. He managed to stem the bleeding from two deep wounds in Harrison's back and leg. Then he administered morphine, bound the wounds, and made Harrison as comfortable as possible. For the remainder of the flight, Jon manned the tail gun.

The pilot managed to keep the Miss Medearly in the formation without a functioning rudder by carefully working the other flight controls and adjusting the fuel mixture and propeller pitch. It took a skillful job of flying, and Jon thanked his lucky stars that the pilot had been as good as he was.

As Jon gratefully jumped down onto the tarmac, he wondered if his string of luck had finally come to its end. He had three more missions to complete. The way he felt, they might as well have been thirty.

The crew of the Miss Medearly, with the exception of Harrison, who had already been taken away by ambulance, piled onto a jeep and drove to the operations building for debriefing. When they finished, Jon made his way to the door, prepared to walk back to Hut 51. With his hand on the knob, he felt a tap on his shoulder. He turned to see a corporal he didn't know.

"Sergeant, you're wanted at group headquarters."

"Do you know what it's about?"

The corporal shook his head. "Sorry, sarge."

Jon trudged heavily down the gravel path, his mind filled with images of crippled B-17s falling from the sky. As he neared the headquarters building, he noticed an army staff car parked out front. Some big wig, he thought, had come out from wing headquarters. He stepped up and into the building. The corporal on duty looked up.

"Meyer," Jon said. "I was told to report."

"Yes, sergeant," the orderly said, immediately, "Colonel Halliday would like to see you in his office." He nodded in the direction of the hall that led back to the colonel's private office.

Jon walked down the hallway, wondering why the group commander had asked to see him. When he reached the colonel's office, he heard voices and saw the man seated at his desk, speaking to someone on the other side of it. Because of the position of the door, however, Jon couldn't see the other person. He paused at the doorway, hesitated, then rapped lightly.

The colonel looked up, saw him, and said, "Sergeant, please come in."

Jon pushed the door open, and the colonel stood, as did two other people who had been sitting in chairs across from him. The man standing nearest to the door, Jon saw immediately, wore the star of a brigadier general. This was the closest Jon had ever been to a general. Instinctively, he straightened.

Jon couldn't immediately see the other visitor, who was shielded from view by the general. Then the figure slowly stepped back from the colonel's desk and into view.

Jon drew in a sharp breath, and the rest of the world melted away. As impossible as it was, he found himself staring into Mary's brilliant blue eyes.

He stepped forward as she threw out her arms. He reached for her, she fell against his body, and he gathered her to him. A wave of wondrous emotion broke over him. He closed his eyes and allowed himself to be swept away.

"Oh, Jon," Mary said, quietly. He knew she was crying, and he realized there were tears spilling down his own face.

He couldn't say how long they stayed that way. Time had stopped. Eventually, Mary leaned her head back to look up at him. She put her hands on his face, caressing him. Her eyes seemed to be soaking in every detail, as if she were memorizing them. She brushed back the hair from his forehead, and ran her hand along his cheek.

Suddenly, she giggled. "You have whiskers." Then she again threw her arms around his neck and pressed her body to him.

Finally, Colonel Halliday coughed discretely. "Sergeant?"

Reluctantly, Jon straightened and turned slightly. But he did not let go of Mary, nor did she give any indication that she was prepared to release her grip on him.

"Sergeant," the colonel said, "this is General Kimbrough. He was kind enough to give Private Dahlgren a ride up here this afternoon."

He suddenly remembered he was in the presence of two senior officers, one of whom was a general. He turned toward the general, bringing his right hand down to his side and, in a way he hoped wasn't obvious, gripped Mary's hand. She immediately brought her other over and placed it on Jon's, so that she was holding on with both of hers.

"I'm sorry, sir," he said to the general.

"No apologies necessary, son," said the general. "I don't get to do a lot of things in my job that I truly enjoy, but this was certainly one of them."

The general glanced down at Jon's side and said, "I would offer to shake your hand, but I see Mary's pulled rank on me."

"Oh," said Mary, and she pushed Jon's hand out in front of him, toward the general. She released it and shifted her grip to Jon's upper arm.

General Kimbrough smiled, reached out and shook Jon's hand.

"Thank you, sir," Jon said.

The general nodded. Then he turned to Colonel Halliday. "Is everything ready?" he asked.

"Yes, sir," said the colonel. "We'll do it in the conference room across the hall."

The general turned back to Jon. He inclined his head toward Mary and said, by way of explanation, "When Mary asked me if I could locate you, I made some inquiries. This weekend, I heard back from one of my colleagues at the Eighth Air Force headquarters. I had a meeting with him this morning. In addition to providing me with the information I was looking for, he explained there was something that needed to be done here. When I learned what it was, he granted my request that I be allowed to perform the duty. And, for that, I'm going to ask that we all step across the hall. Colonel," he said, glancing at Colonel Halliday, "would you mind leading the way?"

The colonel nodded and walked to the door. "Please follow me."

The general motioned for Jon and Mary to precede him. Jon looked at Mary, but she shrugged. With Mary still clinging to his arm, Jon stepped out of the office. The colonel stood a short distance down the hall next to a door on the opposite side. He waved Jon and Mary in.

Four people were already in the room. Three were officers. The fourth man was a corporal, and he had an immense camera hanging from a strap around his neck. The general walked to the head of the conference table that dominated the room, looked back at Jon and waved him over. He and Mary joined him.

The general reached out and put his hands on Mary's, gently prying them away from Jon's arm. "Mary," he said, softly, "I'm going to ask you to stand right over here," and he led her a couple of steps away. "Don't worry. I'll let you have him back in just a moment. I promise."

Mary complied, but her eyes did not leave Jon.

General Kimbrough removed from his briefcase a leather-bound folder and a small box. He placed the box on the table, opened the folder and cleared his throat. "Attention to orders," he said, and the officers all came to attention. Jon did likewise.

"The President of the United States," he announced, "in the name of Congress, has ordered that Jonathon Meyer, Staff Sergeant, U.S. Army, Eighth Army Air Force, 96th Bomb Group, 598th Bombardment Squadron, be awarded the Congressional Medal of Honor. I will now read from the official citation."

Jon was stunned. No one had said or even intimated anything about this. Out of the corner of his eye, he glanced at Mary. Her eyes were wide.

"For extraordinary heroism and courage above and beyond the call of duty," he continued. "On 3 February, 1943, while he was serving as the radio operator on a B-17 during a bombing raid over the City of Bremen, Sgt. Meyer's plane was struck and severely damaged by enemy anti-aircraft fire. The copilot and bombardier were killed instantly. The pilot was gravely wounded and unable to continue to fly the plane. With no previous experience flying a multi-engine aircraft, Sgt. Meyer nevertheless took control of the damaged plane, which, at this point, was flying on only three engines. Enemy fighters then attacked the plane and destroyed one other engine and damaged a third before Sgt. Meyer was able to guide the aircraft into cloud cover. Realizing that the pilot and the top turret gunner, who had also been gravely wounded, could not survive a parachute drop, Sgt. Meyer opted to stay with the plane and attempt to fly it to England after giving the remaining crewmembers the option to bail out. When he reached England, Sgt. Meyer ordered the crew, who had all remained with the plane, to bail out. Then, though he was down to only one remaining engine, and though only one of the landing gear had lowered and would not retract, Sgt. Meyer skillfully and successfully landed the damaged aircraft. Through his actions, and at the risk of his own life, he saved the lives of the pilot and top turret gunner."

Mary's eyes, Jon could see were still wide, and she'd covered her mouth with one of her hands.

General Kimbrough closed the folder and set it on the table. He picked up the box, opened it, and removed a long blue silk ribbon, from which dangled an impressively large gold medal. He stepped behind Jon, draped the ribbon around Jon's neck and fastened it from behind. The corporal snapped several pictures with his camera.

The general stepped back around in front of Jon, put out his hand and said, "Congratulations Sergeant. And well done."

"Thank you, sir," Jon managed.

One by one, the other officers stepped up and shook Jon's hand. Each had brief words of congratulations. Then Mary had her arms around him. She kissed him on the cheek and whispered in his ear, "You don't need to be so brave all the time."

Colonel Halliday ushered everyone out of the room, leaving Jon, Mary and General Kimbrough. He stepped out, closing the door quietly behind himself.

The general turned to Mary. "I'm going to ask Colonel Halliday to give me a short tour of the facilities. Unfortunately, we'll need to start back in a few minutes. I'm sorry that's all I can give you."

Mary nodded. "I understand. Thank you."

General Kimbrough turned to Jon. "I'm told you have an important birthday coming up."

That caught Jon by surprise. He hadn't been thinking about it, but the general was right. His birthday would be in a couple of weeks. "I do. Yes, sir."

"You'll be eighteen, right?"

Jon nodded.

The general looked at Mary and gave her a wry smile. "Mary?"

"Yes, sir?"

"Exactly how old are you?"

Jon saw Mary's face flush, and she was suddenly having trouble looking the general in the eye. "Well," she said, slowly, "I, um…"

The general put a hand up. "You know what," he said, still smiling, "I don't think I really want to know."

He picked up his briefcase and walked to the door. He opened it, then paused and turned back. "Mary," he said, "please meet me at the car in fifteen minutes." Then he gave the two of them a long look. He shook his head and chuckled softly. "Amazing."

When he was gone, Mary turned to Jon. He looked for the first time at her uniform and said, "How did you…"

She put a finger up to his lips. "We only have fifteen minutes," she said. She put her hand behind his head, drew him to her, and they kissed.

17

On Wednesday, two days after his reunion with Mary, Jon went on his twenty-third mission, and it was the easiest one yet, what the airmen called a "milk run." They were dispatched to bomb the marshalling yards in Rouen, France. British Spitfires provided fighter escort most of the way to the target and, again, on the way back. The flak was light and inaccurate, and no German fighters attacked the formation.

It was the twenty-fifth and final mission for Gooch. He became the first of the old Deuces Wild crewmen to complete his tour of duty. A few weeks earlier, Shim had spent time in the hospital with a mild respiratory infection, so he, like Jon, was left at the end of the mission two shy of the twenty-five necessary to finish up.

There were a lot of handshakes and backslaps when the planes returned to Stanbridge, and that evening several of the men who had flown with Gooch accompanied him to the enlisted men's club, which was really just an oversized Nissen hut with a phonograph, a few tables and a bar. Gooch proceeded to get roaring drunk. He was hilarious, cracking jokes, readily allowing himself to be the butt of jokes and explaining in detailed and graphic nature all the things he was going to do with and to the ladies of Rochester, New York when he got home. Jon finally learned that Gooch's first name was Étienne-Marie, and he had to acknowledge that Gooch had been right when he'd said it was worse than his last name.

Mary had given Jon the telephone number for the Staunton. It was a communal phone located in the first floor lobby, and they'd made plans for Mary to be standing by at seven o'clock each evening. To make calls off the base, one had to go to the group headquarters building and talk the orderly into letting him use the phone. Most of the guys who served in the headquarters outfit were decent sorts, and they could be convinced to look the other way for a few minutes if there were no officers around, especially if there was a cigarette offered. The arrangement made for short, awkward conversations, with the orderly sitting two feet away. But, for Jon, it still represented heaven to be able to hear Mary's voice.

Jon received approval for another forty-eight hour pass to make up for the one that had been shortened the previous week. He and Mary arranged to meet at Victoria Station on Saturday. First, however, he had to fly his twenty-fourth mission on Friday. It was another maximum effort.

They were ordered back to Bremen, where the Deuces Wild had been mortally wounded in February. Jon and Shim were assigned to the Widowmaker after Tommie Wheeler pulled some strings. Weather was bad over the target, so they dropped their bombs on the shipyards in Rotterdam.

Jonas Kovalesky stopped by Hut 51 early Friday evening to say goodbye to Jon and Shim. The mission that day had been Kovalesky's twenty-fifth. His infant daughter, who'd been born after he'd shipped out to England and whom he'd yet to see, had developed an illness the doctors were having difficulty diagnosing, and she was in the hospital back in Amarillo. As a result, the army had approved him for priority transport home.

Kovalesky had been awarded the Distinguished Flying Cross for his actions on board the Deuces Wild during its final mission. He wore the ribbon proudly above the left pocket on the jacket of his Class-A uniform. He and Jon exchanged addresses and agreed to keep in touch. Just before leaving, Kovalesky shook Jon's hand one more time and said, quietly, "Thanks." Jon simply nodded.

Jon and Shim were in the enlisted men's club when the duty officer stopped by and shut down the bar, announcing that all leaves were cancelled and the group was on alert for a mission the next day. Jon tried to call Mary, but the headquarters building was crawling with officers, so he was unable to get word to her. He was more concerned about her waiting in vain at Victoria Station than about his having to fly the next day.

It was just one more mission. One more mission, and he'd be done.

#

"Bombs away."

Jon could hear the bombs rattle out, and the Widowmaker jumped as the plane was relieved of its load. "All right," Tommie said over the interphone, "let's go home."

"Amen to that," came Shim's voice.

Not only was this Jon's and Shim's final mission, but it was also Tommie's. They had, unfortunately, not drawn a milk run.

They'd been re-assigned the mission to Bremen that the weather had stymied the day before. Today, the skies over Germany were crystal clear. It made the submarine slips they were bombing easy to target. Unfortunately, it also made things easy for the large number of German fighters who were sent up to meet them. The formation had been under attack from the moment it had crossed the coastline. During one fierce assault, shells from a Focke-Wulf Fw 190 stitched a series of holes across the wing and fuselage of the Widowmaker. They came inches from striking Jon as he was manning the machine gun in the radio compartment. Jon knew they could expect similar attacks on the way back.

The formation had turned for home and was just leaving the flak field, so Jon again took up his station with the Browning.

"Jesus," he heard one of the other crewmen say, "look at that poor bastard." It sounded like Turner in the top turret.

"I don't think there's anyone flying it." It was Mustain, the right waist gunner.

Jon looked out the right window but could see nothing out of the ordinary. The planes in their element were all flying normally, as were those he could see in the top group.

"You're right," came Turner's voice, again. "There's no one at the controls."

"'Chutes," said Mustain. "Two. No, three."

"Bombardier to pilot. That thing's getting awful close."

Jon felt the Widowmaker bank slightly to the left as Tommie adjusted course. As the right wing came up, Jon strained to see what the others were talking about. It finally slid into view.

Ahead and to the right of them, a B-17 in the top group had fallen out of formation. It appeared that both the number one and number two engines were on fire. The plane was no longer flying in the same direction as the formation. Rather, it had begun to drift to the left, taking it back through the rest of the planes. On its current course, it would pass directly over the Widowmaker. Jon could feel their altitude slip as Tommie sought to provide for more clearance.

Suddenly, to Jon's horror, the entire left wing of the stricken plane folded upward and broke off from the fuselage, spinning away like a flaming top. The damaged plane immediately lost all semblance of flight. For a moment, it seemed to hang, suspended in the air. Then, slowly, the remaining wing rose and the tail slewed to the right, bringing the fuselage almost perpendicular to the path of the formation. The nose dipped, and the plane began to fall.

With the numbers three and four engines still providing propulsion, the right wing swung around the tip of the doomed plane, and one of the huge Wright Cyclone power plants, its propeller spinning at full revolution, came straight at Jon from above. He reflexively ducked, and, with his eyes closed, he tensed, waiting for the blades to bite into him.

There was a deafening shriek of metal on metal. The sound lasted only a couple of seconds, and then, as quickly as it had started, it stopped, replaced by a strange whooshing sound. Jon opened his eyes and found himself staring up at the Browning, which was now dangling from its mount at an absurd angle. It took him a moment to realize that, to his right, there was nothing. Or, rather, nothing but sky. From Jon's radio compartment back, the rest of the Widowmaker was simply gone.

"Bail out. Bail out," he heard someone call over the interphone. It might have been Tommie. Jon had no idea.

He rolled onto his stomach and scrambled forward, his hand reaching out for his parachute pack. He found it, sat up, and, with fumbling fingers, snapped it onto the harness that he wore over his leather jacket. The floor tilted, and Jon was spared the necessity of jumping, as he slid right out into space, his power, oxygen and interphone lines snapping off as he did.

With a disorienting feeling, Jon tumbled through the air. He reached for his chest, found the D-ring and gave a hard yank. A jumble of cloth and lines streamed out in front of him. With a sudden jerk, he felt as though he had been pulled upwards, and then he was no longer falling. Instead, he found himself dangling beneath a broad expanse of white. After the noise of the plane, the world around him was remarkably quiet.

He twisted his body to look about. High above where he now was, he could see the formation of bombers receding in the distance. As he watched them, another parachute abruptly popped open, perhaps a hundred yards away from him and a little above. Then another appeared beyond that, followed shortly by a third. There were no others in that direction, so he looked around. He could see nothing but empty sky. And, of course, the ground, which he belatedly realized was rising up at a rate of speed he had not anticipated. He had just a second's warning before his feet struck. He tucked in his chin, and he allowed his knees to come up and his body to roll forward.

He went through at least two revolutions until he came to rest lying on moist ground between rows of what smelled like potatoes. He was tangled in his lines. He knew from the escape and evasion lectures he'd attended that the first few moments following a parachute landing were critical to the question of whether he'd be captured. With a sense of urgency, he picked at the lines. It took him about a minute, but he finally got clear. He stood and looked about.

He'd landed near the edge of an immense field, about twenty yards away from a line of trees. He scanned the field, but did not see anyone. Shrugging off his parachute harness, he ran to the tree line and slipped into the relative cover it provided. He could see that, in actuality, he was now in a forested area.

His first thought was to find the others who had gotten out of the plane. He'd been completely turned around by the landing, and he wasn't sure in which direction he'd seen 'chutes. However, thinking logically, he realized he'd been looking at the retreating formation when he'd seen them open, so the others had to be somewhere to the west. It was after noon, so he looked straight up, then drew an imaginary line to where the sun currently stood in the sky. That wouldn't necessarily be due west, he knew, but it would be generally correct. The line led deeper into the wooded area. He set out in that direction.

The further he walked, the thicker the overhead canopy became. He was soon picking his way through semi-darkness, even though it still had to be mid-afternoon.

He heard a rustling ahead and froze. After a second, he scrambled forward as quietly as he could, and, at the base of a moss-covered trunk, he cautiously peered around. He was greeted by the sight of a man dangling from the cords of a parachute a few feet off the ground. The rustling he'd heard had been the attempts of the man to free himself.

"Hey," Jon called out in a hoarse whisper. The man's head jerked around, and Jon could see it was Abernathy, Tommie's co-pilot.

"Oh, thank God," Abernathy said, in his own whisper. "Can you help me down?"

Jon nodded and hurried over to him. He put his hands under Abernathy's feet and pushed up. With one hand gripping the lines from which he dangled to steady himself, Abernathy used his other hand to yank the cords that had caught up in his harness. Just as Jon was concerned he'd have to let go, Abernathy got the straps free, released himself, and then fell in a heap on top of Jon.

Abernathy rolled clear and sat up. "Sorry about that," he whispered. "But thanks."

Jon nodded. "Have you seen or heard anything?"

"Yeah. About five minutes ago, I heard voices coming from over there." He pointed to the right of the direction Jon had been traveling when he'd come upon Abernathy.

"Germans?"

"They weren't speaking English."

"Who else got out?"

"Pilot and top turret."

Jon was relieved to hear that Tommie had escaped the crippled bomber. "Navigator and bombardier?"

Abernathy shook his head. "I don't know." A look of sadness crossed his face. "But I don't think so. What about the guys in the back?"

Jon winced. He thought about his friend, Shim. "I don't know how they could have. That other bomber cut the whole back of the plane off."

Abernathy grimaced, but said nothing.

"We should try to find the others," Jon whispered.

Abernathy nodded.

"This way," Jon said, and, with Abernathy in tow, he struck out in the same direction he'd originally been walking.

They'd been at it for about twenty minutes when Jon felt Abernathy's hand on his shoulder. He looked back, and Abernathy pointed off to the left. Through the trees, Jon could see a sliver of white. They switched directions and worked their way over to it.

What they'd seen had, indeed, been the canopy of a parachute. However, as they got closer, Jon could see that the fabric had torn and was practically in two pieces. At the base of a nearby tree lay an American airman. He was not moving.

Afraid of what he might find, Jon put a hand under the man's head and gently turned his body. It was Turner, the top turret gunner, and he was obviously dead. When Jon let go of his head, it lolled sideways at an unnatural angle. Jon guessed that death had come instantly.

The sound of a loud snap startled Jon. He looked at Abernathy, who tipped his head in the direction they'd been traveling. Jon pointed to Abernathy, then to a large tree behind him. He tapped his own chest and pointed to another tree. Abernathy nodded, and they both moved quickly to take cover behind the trees indicated by Jon. Keeping low and offering as small a profile as possible, Jon carefully looked back around the trunk.

He heard some faint sounds. Then, after a moment, a figure appeared. Jon breathed a sigh of relief. It was Tommie.

Tommie was carrying a pistol, and he held it out in front of him at the ready. Jon didn't want to be accidentally shot, so, from behind the tree, he whispered, "Tommie. It's me, Jon."

"Jon?"

Jon stepped from behind the tree. Tommie lowered the gun. "Thank God. Anyone else?"

Jon nodded in the direction Abernathy had gone, and the co-pilot emerged from behind his tree. "Unfortunately," Jon whispered, and he pointed to the body of Turner.

Tommie looked, and his shoulders slumped. He looked back at Jon. "Turner?"

Jon nodded.

Abernathy joined them. "What's the plan?"

Tommie squatted, and Jon and Abernathy did likewise. Tommie jerked his head back in the direction he had come. "I landed in a field, near the edge of these woods. The place is crawling with German soldiers. I was able to get into the trees before they started shooting."

Jon pointed to what he assumed was southwest. "I say we head that way. If I'm right, Belgium and France are in that direction, though it's a long walk. I think our only hope is to try to meet up with the Resistance."

Tommie thought for a moment. "I don't have a better plan." He looked at Abernathy.

"Works for me," Abernathy whispered.

Jon started to stand, and Tommie grabbed his sleeve. "Jon, give me your dog tags."

Jon wasn't sure why Tommie was asking for the identification tags he wore around his neck. Then he remembered. The last line on each tag was stamped with an initial identifying the religion of the wearer. Jon's tags were stamped with an "H," indicating he was Jewish. Because of concerns about how captured Jewish flyers might be treated by the Nazis, the army recommended that they dispose of their tags if capture was imminent.

Jon nodded. He slipped the chain containing his tags off his neck and handed it to Tommie. Tommie rose, walked to Turner's body and crouched over it. He returned a moment later and handed a set of tags to Jon. A quick glance confirmed they were Turner's.

Jon put the chain over his head and tucked the tags under his t-shirt. "Ok, let's go."

They struck out, Tommie leading the way with the gun.

\#

Jon was awakened by the sound of voices. His eyes flew open, and he was immediately aware that he was in danger, though it took him a moment to remember where he was and how he had gotten there.

The prior afternoon, Jon, Tommie and Abernathy had worked their way through the forest until it ended at a spot overlooking a small town perched on the banks of a river. They'd halted there to rest and wait for the cover of darkness. Though, on several occasions throughout the afternoon, they had heard the sounds of men calling out to one another behind them in the woods, those sounds had faded as they'd put distance between themselves and the place where they had come down. They'd fortunately encountered no other people.

When the sun set, they made their way down the incline and around the town, giving it a wide berth, for the most part keeping to the fields. At one point they almost walked right into the side of a farmhouse. They retreated quickly and worked their way around the structure. A dog started barking, but it didn't come after them.

They stumbled across a carrot field and dug up several of the vegetables. When they came to a small stream, they gulped large handfuls of water, then washed the carrots in the current and ate them. It was their first food since breakfast the previous day.

Shortly before sunrise, they found a thicket of shrubs surrounding a large tree on a knoll by the side of a field. It seemed to offer good concealment, and they stopped. Jon was dead tired. He'd been awake for over twenty-four stressful hours. He gratefully stretched out in a crook formed by two large tree roots and apparently dozed off.

Above him now, bright mid-day sun was filtering down through the branches of the tree overhead. Jon rose slightly and saw that Tommie and Abernathy were also awake and alert. Tommie pointed beyond the tree, and, when Jon looked, he saw three people walking in their direction. The approaching figures were on a well-worn path that would lead them directly to the spot where Jon, Tommie and Abernathy were hiding.

Now that it was light, Jon could see that, from the knoll where they were crouched, they had a view down a lush valley. In the distance, he could see the steeple of a church and the roofs of a few buildings. He guessed it was the town they had skirted the night before.

The sound of laughter reached him, and he realized it came from a female. As the trio approached, Jon could see that all three were women. Two were carrying baskets, and the third had what appeared to be a rolled-up blanket under one of her arms. Great, he thought, they'd managed to hide in the exact spot where these women now intended to have a picnic.

Knowing that he and his colleagues were moments away from being detected, Jon stood and called out, "Guten tag."

The three women stopped suddenly, startled expressions on their faces. Jon could see they were young, probably in their early twenties, if that.

"I'm sorry," Jon said in German, smiling broadly. "I didn't mean to startle you. My friends and I," and he turned slightly, putting a hand out and making a quick gesture to indicate they should stand, "were just resting a moment and admiring the beautiful view."

Behind him, Tommie and Abernathy stood.

"We didn't mean to take your picnic spot," Jon said. "We were just about to leave."

After a moment, one of the young women stepped forward and said, "You're wearing strange outfits. Are you soldiers?"

"We're pilots," Jon said, immediately. "Fighter pilots."

"They must be stationed at the airdrome," another of the girls said to the one who had stepped forward.

"We are. We've been given passes for the day, and we've been out walking."

"You've walked a long distance," the first girl said.

Jon nodded. "Yes. It's good exercise. When you spend as much time as we do sitting in a cramped cockpit, you appreciate the opportunity to stretch your legs."

That seemed to be an acceptable answer. "I can tell from your accent that you're from Bavaria," the first girl said.

"You have a good ear for accents. I'm from Munich."

The girl looked at Tommie and Abernathy. "Your friends are very quiet."

Jon chuckled. "They're shy. When it comes to flying planes, they know exactly what they're doing. But they don't know how to talk to pretty girls."

One of the other girls giggled. She reached out a hand and touched the arm of the first girl. "Ask them to join us," she said.

For the first time, Jon saw the hint of a smile on the face of the first girl. "Yes," she said, after a moment. "Won't you? We have plenty." Her smile widened. "And you can tell us your flying stories."

As improbable as it was, Jon had the sudden sense the girl was flirting with him.

He smiled and shook his head. "That's very kind of you, but we must be getting on. As you know, we have a long distance to walk."

She seemed disappointed.

"Well," Jon said, turning to Tommie and Abernathy, "we'd better get going." He motioned for them to follow, and he stepped down the path, nodding as he passed the girls. "It was very nice meeting you."

After they had walked a short distance, the first girl called out from behind them. "What is your name?"

Jon stopped and turned. "Meyer," he said. "Johan Meyer."

The girl gave him a friendly smile. "Perhaps I'll see you another time, Johan Meyer."

Jon returned the smile. "Perhaps."

When they were far enough away they couldn't be heard, Abernathy whispered, "What the hell was that?"

"They think we're German fighter pilots."

"Jesus," Abernathy said.

Jon could see Tommie giving him a big grin. "That girl was coming on to you, Jon."

Jon didn't know what to say, so he simply shrugged.

Tommie snorted and looked at Abernathy. "We better find another hiding place quick, before she comes back after him."

When they'd walked a few hundred yards, they left the path and made their way into a wheat field. They lay down, and the stalks were high enough that they were completely shielded from view. They started out again an hour after sunset, and they'd been traveling about three hours when they encountered the other man.

They were making their way down a narrow country lane, bordered on either side by a line of trees, beyond which were more fields. Off and on, they'd heard the sound of planes overhead. There was a quarter moon out, and the sky was clear, so they had just enough light to pick their way. The hard-packed dirt surface of the lane was scarred with narrow ruts that appeared to have been made by wagon wheels. Those ruts looked to be the only tracks, and Jon hoped it meant they would be unlikely to encounter a fast moving vehicle.

They were in single file, Jon leading the way, followed by Abernathy. Tommie was bringing up the rear. They were moving quietly, and they stopped every couple of minutes to listen for noises.

Jon felt a tap on his shoulder. He stopped and turned. Tommie had stepped up and stood next to Abernathy. "I think we're being followed," Tommie whispered.

"Followed?" Abernathy whispered. "That doesn't make any sense."

"I'm not making it up."

"How long?" Jon asked.

"Not sure. I thought I heard something a few minutes ago. Then I decided it was my imagination. But I was looking back just now, and I swear there's someone back there."

"All right," Jon said, softly. "Let's take cover."

They stepped off of the roadway, and each took up position behind a tree. Nothing happened for several minutes, and Jon was beginning to think that Tommie had, indeed, imagined it. He was about to say something when he saw a dark figure approaching from the direction they'd just come. The man was in a crouch, moving cautiously. When he got to the point where they'd taken cover, he appeared to look around.

"Hey," the man said in a hoarse whisper.

There was a loud distinctive clicking sound, and Jon realized Tommie had pulled back the hammer on his .45. "Jon," Tommie said quietly, "tell him I'll blow his brains out if he moves. Find out who he is and what he wants."

Jon quickly translated. There was a long moment of silence. Then the man said, "Jon, since when do you speak German?"

To his surprise, but overwhelming relief, Jon realized it was Shim.

They huddled by the side of the road, and Shim told them what had happened to him. When the Widowmaker had been struck by the other bomber, the tail section had spun away. Shim had found himself pinned against the side of the fuselage by the rotational pull. He'd been certain he would die. Fortunately, the spinning had slowed, and the tail section had gradually turned so that the open end faced down. Shim had barely enough time to clip on his parachute before he slid out of the severed portion of the plane and found himself hurtling toward the earth. His parachute had opened no more than a hundred feet above the ground, not enough altitude to slow him sufficiently to avoid multiple broken bones. However, he'd been incredibly lucky. He'd landed smack in the middle of an immense pile of dung.

"Now that you mention it," Tommie said, "you do smell kind of ripe."

Shim nodded. "I tried to wash as much of it off as I could in a stream back there. But," he grinned, "I'd rather smell like shit than be dead.

"Anyway," Shim continued, "I'm sure I shocked the farmer. He just stood there watching me climb down from his dung pile. When I realized he wasn't going to do anything, I took off. I figured I'd head southwest. I was pretty surprised when I came up on you guys a while back. I didn't know who you were, but it was obvious to me you didn't want to be seen. I thought maybe we might be in the same boat. Small world, huh?"

Jon put his hand on Shim's shoulder. "Even though you stink, I'm glad you're here." Shim put a hand up and set it on top of Jon's. He nodded.

They struck out again, continuing down the road until it came to an end at a pair of farmhouses. They moved out into one of the fields and stayed well away from the houses. They'd been traveling for a couple hours when Jon realized there was a glow in the sky ahead of them. His first thought was that daybreak was coming, though it seemed early for that. Then he realized it couldn't be daybreak, as they were moving in a southwesterly direction.

Perhaps, he thought, they were nearing a city or a large town. A plane flew overhead, and it was low. It was followed shortly thereafter by another. Then he remembered what one of the girls had said the day before. "They must be stationed at the airdrome." Jon guessed they were approaching an airfield.

They came to a slight rise, and Jon instinctively crouched as he climbed, getting down on his hands and knees for the last few feet. When he reached the top, he peered over and saw his guess had been correct. Spread out before him was a facility that, though it was a mere fraction of the size of the base at Stanbridge, had the same general appearance. He found himself staring almost straight down a runway lined with bright lights.

Shim and Tommie crawled up to either side of Jon. As they did, another plane flew overhead, only a few feet above them. It had twin engines and, instead of a conventional tail, there were two short vertical stubs mounted on the ends of the rear horizontal stabilizer. Jon recognized it immediately. It was a Messerschmitt Bf 110. Originally designed to fill a role as an escort for German heavy bombers and to serve as a light bomber itself, it had been retooled as one of the primary weapons the Luftwaffe threw against the American and British bombers. Jon had seen many of them as they had attacked the formations in which he'd flown.

These were obviously night fighters. Jon guessed the planes landing now had been scrambled earlier in the evening to attack formations of British heavy bombers.

"That's our ticket home," Tommie said, after a moment.

"Oh, really," Shim said. "Are we just going to walk in and check one out? Did you bring your library card, because I seem to have left mine back in Stanbridge."

"How do you think we're going to steal one of those?" asked Abernathy, who had joined them at the top.

Tommie said, "I have no idea." He turned to Jon. "Jon, how are we going to do it?"

#

General Lloyd Kimbrough set the phone back into the receiver and looked at Penny Radkovich. He shook his head. Penny nodded slowly, a profound sadness on her face.

General Kimbrough had arrived at his office earlier than usual that morning. To his surprise, he found Mary already at her desk, her face drawn, dark circles under her eyes. She explained that she'd not heard from Jon since Wednesday, and, what was more alarming, Jon had not kept their appointment to meet at Victoria Station on Saturday. Mary had waited all day and well into the night, as each train had come and gone. She'd not slept for the past two nights, and she had been waiting for several hours at her desk for General Kimbrough to arrive that morning, hoping that he might be able to check on Jon's status.

He had her ring 96th Group headquarters for him. Colonel Halliday had personally called him back an hour later. Unfortunately, the news the colonel delivered was not good. Jon's plane had gone down on Saturday in a raid over Bremen.

General Kimbrough broke the news to Mary. Looking at her stricken face, he added that several parachutes had been observed. What he didn't tell her was that only four 'chutes had actually been seen, dramatically lowering the odds that Jon had survived. Because Mary had been assuming the worse, though, she was somewhat heartened by the general's little white lie. She kept her poise and informed General Kimbrough that she was confident Jon would be ok and would find a way to return to her.

Shortly before noon, General Kimbrough received a second call from Colonel Halliday. This time, the colonel delivered the worst possible news. Jon's status had been modified from MIA, missing in action, to KIA, killed in action. The colonel reported that he did not have any more details, but promised to find out what he could and get back to the general.

Mary, who had put the call through, was waiting anxiously when he came out of his office. He lied again to her and told her that there was still no information regarding Jon. Then he asked Mary to take some papers to 20 Grosvenor Square for him and to wait for them to be signed before bringing them back. When she was gone, he placed two calls.

The first was to a close acquaintance at the headquarters building letting him know that a Private Dahlgren would be arriving with an envelope full of meaningless papers and asking that she be kept waiting until the general called back. His friend readily agreed to do the favor.

Then General Kimbrough called the Office of the Chief Surgeon for the Eighth Air Force, where he knew Mary's good friend, Penny, worked. He wanted Penny to be available when he broke the news to Mary. Penny arrived forty-five minutes later, and the general then called his friend to tell him to return the envelope to Mary.

The general had just received a follow up call from Colonel Halliday. The colonel reported that Jon's body had been recovered by the Germans from a wooded area to the west of Bremen. Apparently, Jon had, in fact, been one of the crewmen who'd bailed out of the damaged plane, but he had not survived, his neck having been broken in the fall. The information had been passed along through the Red Cross.

There was a tap at the general's office door, and Mary entered, carrying the envelope he'd given her earlier. She had a momentary look of confusion when she saw Penny. Then her eyes went wide, and the color drained from her face.

"Oh, no," Mary said. "Oh, God, no."

Mary looked as though she might fall, but Penny moved quickly. She reached out and put her arms around Mary, pulling her close.

"No, no, no," Mary said, her voice muffled against Penny's blouse. Then Mary drew in a large breath, and she was suddenly wracked with immense sobs. Penny held Mary tightly. She had a stoic look on her face, though the general could see her eyes were moist, and there was a distance to them.

The general glanced away, a feeling of helplessness gnawing at him. He'd faced his share of grief. He'd lost a sister to cancer ten years earlier, and, as a young infantry officer in the first world war, he'd had a number of men under his command killed or badly wounded. Yet, for some reason, this hurt in a way he couldn't have possibly imagined.

#

"That one over there," Jon said, pointing.

"By the maintenance shed?" Tommie asked.

Jon nodded. "Yes. Both nights it's been the last one out. It's in shadow for the most part. And, because it's out of the way, the other ground crew won't have any reason to walk past the spot after the planes have left."

Tommie thought for a moment. "Do we know that plane's scheduled to sortie tonight?"

"It's loaded with ammunition and fuel. They finished up a little while ago. Don't see why it wouldn't be. And," Jon shrugged, "if it's not, we take it anyway."

Tommie nodded. "All right," he said, starting to back up. "Let's tell the others."

Jon put a hand on Tommie's sleeve. "You sure you can fly that thing?"

Tommie gave Jon a grin. "Piece o' cake."

They half-crawled, half-slid down the embankment and rejoined Shim and Abernathy, where they huddled together to review the plan.

After they'd discovered the airfield on Sunday night, the four of them had worked their way south, then west to a spot located along the edge of the German base, across the main runway from the maintenance and personnel facilities. The ridge they'd been on when they first came upon the field became steeper the further they traveled and eventually fell off into a small valley through which ran a stream swollen with winter runoff. They found an ideal hiding place in a thick copse of evergreen trees perched on the side of the slope, a few yards below the crest of the ridge. Aside from a handful of animal tracks, there was no evidence the place where they were hiding was ever occupied or visited.

Perhaps because the base was situated in Germany, as opposed to occupied territory where there would be concerns regarding possible sabotage, there appeared to be little security. Or, at least that had turned out to be the case on the side of the airfield where Jon and his fellow crewmates were hiding. As far as they'd been able to tell, the precautions the Germans had taken to safeguard the perimeter consisted of wooden posts placed at thirty foot intervals and strung with three lines of barbed wire. The fence would keep out large animals, but not a person. They'd seen no guards and no patrols.

On Monday and Tuesday, they carefully observed the activities at the airfield, taking particular note of the procedures followed by the air and ground crews getting the fighters into the sky. On both days, the planes were fueled and armed in the late afternoon and early evening. Then a quiet descended over the field.

On Monday night, about an hour after sunset, a claxon sounded, and there was a sudden swarm of activity. Men emerged from the wooden structures at the far side of the field and sprinted toward the planes. At each aircraft, two men scrambled up into the cockpit and fired up the engines. Two ground crew members per plane stood by near the outer edge of each wing, ready to pull cords that would release the stops from under the front wheels. The planes had not taken off, however. Fifteen minutes later, there was the sound of another horn, and the crews stood down, returning to the buildings from which they'd emerged.

Around midnight, the same thing occurred, only this time, the planes taxied the short distances from their dispersed locations along the far side of the field and took off one at a time.

On Tuesday night, the claxon sounded a couple of hours after sunset, and, following the same mad scramble of personnel, the planes took off again. While Jon and Abernathy conducted a vigil from their observation spot at the top of the ridge, Tommie and Shim went reconnoitering, working their way counterclockwise around the perimeter fence to see what kind of security was present. They returned a couple hours later to report that the boundary defenses appeared to be identical on the other side. Shim had even slipped into the compound for a few minutes. When Tommie recounted that detail, Shim had, with a devilish look on his face, reached into his jacket and pulled out an enormous wrench. "I figured it might come in handy," he announced, holding it in one hand and slapping it against the palm of his other.

They decided to make their move on Wednesday night. The plan was simple. The four of them would work their way around the perimeter to the far side, slip through the fence and hide in the shadows behind one of the wooden structures from which they'd seen men emerge during the scrambles the two nights before. They'd wait for the claxon to sound, then they'd start running and join with the others pouring out of the buildings, heading for the plane they'd selected. Their hope was that, in the darkness, no one would notice their uniforms were different.

They'd each been assigned to shadow one of the four men who crewed the targeted plane. Shim and Abernathy would take the ground crewmen. The plan was that, in the confusion, each would step up behind his man and deliver a hard blow to the back of the man's head. Shim would wield his wrench. Abernathy had found a rock whose shape allowed him to grip it, but was big enough to get the job done.

Jon and Tommie would take the air crewmen. They'd have to use their fists. Ben's Widowmaker was going to come in handy. If they could get to the pilot and radio operator before they boarded the plane, so much the better. Otherwise, Jon intended to grab one of the caps the ground crewmen wore, put it on his head, and climb up on the wing, announcing that there was a fire below the fuselage and the men needed to get out quickly. Once they'd gotten the men away from the plane, they'd disable them. If they couldn't get the men to leave the plane voluntarily, they'd have to deliver the blows to the men while they were seated in the cockpit and then drag their bodies out. It would delay things and increase the chance of drawing attention from others, but it was the best plan they'd been able to devise.

The last resort was Tommie's .45. They hoped not to have to use deadly force, but they were prepared to do so if necessary.

Although only two crewmen manned the plane they intended to steal, the aircraft had been originally designed for a crew of three. The pilot sat in the forward portion of the cockpit. Behind him was a space intended to accommodate the remaining two crewmembers. It would be a tight fit, but they'd be able to squeeze in three. Shim would take the rear seat. Jon and Abernathy would share the middle section. Since Jon might need to assist Tommie reading the German controls, Abernathy would go in first and make himself as small as possible.

Once they had control of the plane, their plan was to taxi to the end of the runway, take off as if they were heading out on the mission with the others, and, once airborne, simply turn west and slip away under cover of the darkness.

It was by no means a perfect plan. There was a very good chance they'd be caught or, worse, killed. But they'd all agreed it was worth trying. For Jon, it offered the only reasonable chance to get back to Mary, so, no matter the odds, he would take them.

As soon as the sun set, the four of them left their hiding place, and, moving in single file, they quietly followed the curve of the ridge around the perimeter of the airfield. Because there were no flight operations at the moment, the navigation and runway lights were off, so the glow that had been in the sky when they'd first discovered the base on Sunday night was not present. There was, however, an almost full moon, so they were able to pick their way easily through the trees and underbrush.

When they reached the point at which Shim had passed through the wire the previous night, they huddled together at the tree line, listening carefully for any sounds that would indicate the presence of sentries. They heard nothing. Finally, Jon and Tommie crawled forward. Tommie stood in a crouch and put his foot on the lowest of the three wires. He gripped the second wire and pulled it up, making an opening large enough to accommodate Jon. Jon had put one leg on the other side of the wire and was just swinging his body through when the silence was shattered by the sound of the claxon.

Jon froze momentarily, his heart beating rapidly. He quickly reversed himself, stepped back outside the wire, and he and Tommie scrambled back to the safety of the trees.

After a moment, Jon heard the first of the planes' engines firing up. Soon the air around them shimmered with the roar generated by a combined force of over twenty four thousand horsepower. From where they lay, the planes were shielded from view by structures, so Jon could not tell whether they had started taxiing. He listened carefully for a variation in pitch that would indicate the first of them taking off. If they did take off, the plans for the night would be a bust, and the four of them would have to return to their hiding place to wait another day.

Several minutes passed, and there had been no change. Jon looked at Tommie, who shrugged. Suddenly, the horn blew again. Almost immediately, the sound of the engines began to diminish until, a minute later, relative quiet had returned. In the distance, Jon could hear men calling to one another, and he heard someone laugh. It took a few minutes for the voices to stop. When they did, the area was once again plunged into silence.

They waited, listening. When he was satisfied the Germans had returned to wherever it was they congregated while waiting for word to man their planes, Jon tapped Tommie on the shoulder and nodded toward the fence. Silently, Tommie crawled forward and again held the wire for Jon.

Jon slipped into the compound, followed in rapid succession by Abernathy and then Shim, who held the wire for Tommie. They moved quickly to the rear of the nearest building, which they had concluded was some sort of storage facility. Led by Shim, who'd previously been there, they crept along the back wall until they came to a gap between it and the next structure. To reach the building beyond, they would need to cross approximately fifteen yards of open space that was, in comparison to the shadow in which they now crouched, brightly illuminated by the moon. No one spoke. They'd worked out the details in advance.

Jon and Tommie stood upright, and, as casually as they could manage, they walked across the gap between the buildings, Jon holding his breath the entire way. When they reached the other side, they melted into the shadow behind the building and listened intently. All seemed to be quiet. Two minutes after they'd made the crossing, Shim and Abernathy came strolling over. Again, they listened for any sound that would indicate trouble, and, again, they detected nothing.

The next three buildings were close together, so they did not need to leave the shadows. However, these buildings were either living or working quarters. They had no idea whether the first two were currently occupied. But, the last one they knew for sure contained several men, as it was one of the structures from which members of the crews would emerge if the signal again sounded. Their intent was to wait behind that building.

Crouching to stay below the windowsills, they moved as silently as possible along the rear wall of the first building, Shim still in the lead, followed by Abernathy and Tommie. Jon brought up the rear. When they came to the far end, they squatted. Shim leaned out and peered around the corner. He then rose, and the others followed suit, preparing to step across to the next building.

Suddenly, a voice behind them said, in German, "Stop where you are and put your hands up."

Jon turned and saw a German soldier with a rifle pointed at them. The German stood just outside the shadow cast by the building. In the moonlight, the weapon in his hand looked enormous.

Jon straightened, and, in German, he said, "Excellent." The soldier shifted his rifle so that it was trained on Jon's chest. Jon turned his head toward the other three and said, still speaking in German, "I told you those reports were exaggerated." He looked back at the sentry and said, "We are here testing the security. My name is Meyer. I am with the Gestapo."

At the mention of the feared secret police, Jon saw the barrel of the gun waver. Smiling, Jon casually reached out his right hand

and, as he did, said, "I would like to shake your hand soldier." Fearing at any moment his chest would be torn open by a bullet, Jon extended his arm to its fullest length, and he leaned forward. When his hand reached the point at which it was even with the tip of the barrel, Jon jerked it up and to the right, catching the end of the barrel in the crook formed by his thumb and forefinger and shoving it up and away.

The rifle discharged with a thunderous crack, and Jon was certain he felt the rush of the bullet as it passed by his ear.

Tommie moved the instant Jon's hand shot up. He took two steps and, throwing the weight of his entire body behind the punch, drove his fist into the German's jaw. The soldier crumpled into a heap.

"Let's go now," Jon shouted. The words were barely out of his mouth when the others were up and running.

The four of them raced through the gap between the buildings, and they emerged on the other side in the open. The plane they had targeted was about fifty yards away.

Jon yelled, "Shim, pull the stop on the right wheel. I'll get the left. Tommie, get us out of here."

As they reached the plane, Shim bent and yanked away the angled piece of wood that served as a stop for the right wheel. Then he followed Tommie and Abernathy, who had already ducked and passed under the fuselage. Jon sprinted around the nose of the plane and the left propeller, reached down, gripped the rope attached to the left stop and jerked it away. Both engines coughed and roared to life simultaneously, and the plane was already rolling when Jon jumped up on the wing. He put his hands on the metal supports to either side of the cockpit opening, hoisted himself up, and dropped in on top of Abernathy, who grunted. He twisted back and pulled up the side panel of the canopy, then reached above him and pulled down the top section, sealing the cockpit.

As they rolled across the grass, Jon looked over and saw men spilling out of the buildings from which the flight and ground crews had emerged the previous night. In the light of one of the doorways was a uniformed officer. The man reached down to his side, unsnapped a holster at his hip, and lifted up a handgun. Jon saw a muzzle flash, and the gun jumped in the officer's hand. The man brought the gun level again, and Jon saw another flash. This time, there was the sound of a bullet striking metal somewhere on the plane. With a third flash, a hole opened in one of the Perspex panels on the right side of the canopy, with another appearing opposite it high on the left side.

Then, fortunately, they were on the runway, and, even though he'd not yet lined the plane up, Tommie had already thrown the throttles to their stops. The plane rapidly picked up speed, bouncing along the uneven surface. The instant the bouncing stopped, Tommie retracted the landing gear, and the plane jumped forward. Jon looked back and could see that two of the other fighters had their engines running and were moving. Only one of them, however, was near the runway.

Tommie leveled out just above the trees and turned to a due westerly heading.

"We got company," Shim called out. Jon looked back, and, in the moonlight, he could see another Bf 110 rising up above the tree tops and turning to their heading.

Abernathy shifted uncomfortably. Then he drew a hand up from beneath him and looked at what he'd retrieved. "I knew I'd sat on something."

It was a cloth cap with a set of headphones sewn into it. A throat mike dangled from one side. Jon took it from him. "Perfect."

He slipped the cap on and immediately heard excited voices speaking in German. It took Jon only a second to realize it was the pilot in the plane behind him speaking to someone on the ground. "I'm gaining on him," the pilot said. Jon looked and saw that he was right. Must be the weight of the two extra bodies, Jon thought.

"Do I have permission to fire?" the German pilot asked.

There was a pause. Then the ground controller came back on. "Permission granted."

"Tommie," Jon said, "take evasive action now."

Tommie banked left. Behind them, what appeared to be headlights on the nose of the pursuing plane blinked as the German fired his cannon. Tracers reached out toward them, but the German had been thrown off by Tommie's sudden maneuver, and the deadly fire sailed off to their right.

They leveled out. The German was firing again, but they abruptly dipped, and Jon came up out of his seat. Tracers flew harmlessly overhead.

Jon looked forward and saw they'd come to a large valley. Tommie had dropped down heading for the valley floor.

Suddenly, there was a new sound. Shim had begun firing the rear mounted machine gun. Over the radio, Jon heard the German pilot swear. Then the pilot reported to the ground controller that the stolen plane was returning fire. After a moment, the controller instructed the German to stay on their tail and report their position. He announced that fighters from a Dutch base were being scrambled to intercept.

"Tommie, we've got to lose this guy. He's leading others to us."

Tommie just nodded. He'd turned up the valley, which was narrowing. With quick movements, he guided the plane along the path of the river that flowed in a serpentine pattern no more than a hundred feet below them.

The German behind them had dropped back slightly, and, in the face of the fire Shim was delivering, he seemed to have decided that, rather than shoot them down, he'd be content simply to follow. Jon could hear the reports he was delivering to the ground controller. They were now apparently heading up a valley known as the Madeleine. Jon could see the sides were closing in and becoming steeper. The abrupt banking Tommie had been doing in order to avoid the fire from the German was now necessary just to stay within the course of the valley.

They came roaring around a sharp bend and, with a sickening flood of realization, Jon knew they'd made a huge mistake. Looming ahead of them was a bridge spanning what had now become a narrow gorge. They were too close to pull up and over the span. And, unfortunately, the distance between the vertical supports for the bridge was far too narrow to accommodate the wingspan of the fighter. There was also insufficient clearance from the ground to the underside of the bridge to allow them to turn sideways and slip through.

Tommie dropped the right wing and without hesitation headed for the gap between the two center support towers at a diagonal. It was, Jon saw, a brave but futile gesture. There was no chance they could make it through. It was the equivalent of trying to toss a thread through the eye of a needle from across the room. Bracing for the final impact, Jon watched with morbid fascination as they plunged into the gap.

There was a teeth rattling screech to their left as the tip of the wing scraped along either the underside of the bridge or the side of the left support tower. Or, Jon realized, probably both. Inconceivably, though, they were through, and Tommie was pulling them up out of the valley.

Jon jerked his head around to see what the German would do. He likewise tried to squeeze through the narrow gap. However, his wing clipped the support tower and sheared off, sending his aircraft into a cartwheel. It exploded on contact with the valley floor, and brilliant flames snaked along the bottom of the narrow gorge.

"Tommie," Jon said, "turn north."

Tommie immediately banked the plane hard to the right and pulled back on the stick. Jon felt himself pushed downward by the additional g-forces. Then they were level again, skimming above fields of wheat shimmering in the moonlight.

"Stay on this heading for two minutes. Then turn west again."

Tommie nodded.

Through his radio headset, Jon heard the ground controller trying to reach the pilot of the plane that had been chasing them. After a minute, he heard a new voice checking in with the ground controller. From the exchange, Jon could tell it was a pilot in another plane, likely one of the fighters that had been dispatched from the base in Holland. The new pilot reported that there were flames lining the bottom of the valley floor and no sign of any aircraft.

"It looks like they tried to go under the railroad bridge and didn't make it," said the German pilot.

"One or both aircraft?" asked the ground controller.

There was silence for several seconds. Then the pilot came back on. "Impossible to tell. But I don't see how anyone could have flown through that opening."

The ground controller acknowledged the information, then vectored the pilot to a new location to stand by.

Tommie banked the plane again, this time not quite so violently, and they were now heading due west. They could see no other aircraft. Tommie kept the course steady for several minutes. The terrain below them gradually flattened out. They flew directly over a few small towns and, at one point, passed through a cloud of steam rising from a locomotive crossing their path and pulling a long line of box cars. Suddenly, they were out over water.

Jon rotated the dial on the radio, setting it to the emergency frequency used by returning allied planes, or, at least what he hoped was still a current emergency frequency. Their big problem now was going to be convincing the Brits that they weren't what they obviously appeared to be: A German fighter bomber approaching England to attack British targets. All allied aircraft emitted signals known as IFF, or Identification Friend or Foe. Any plane approaching the British coastline and failing to emit such a signal would be assumed to be hostile and, if its pilot couldn't make a convincing case to the contrary, would be shot down. It would be a tragic irony, Jon reflected, if, after all they'd been through, they were taken down by friendly fire.

Jon keyed the microphone. "To any allied radio operator receiving this signal. This is Sergeant Jonathon Meyer, United States Army Air Force. I am in a stolen Messerschmitt Bf 110 on a heading of 270 degrees, flying at an altitude of three hundred feet over the North Sea. We are not hostile. Repeat, we are not hostile. Please acknowledge."

There was no response.

After a minute, Jon repeated the message, and, again, the radio was silent.

Jon adjusted the frequency, and tried again. Over a period of twenty minutes, Jon tried his message on several frequencies. The atmosphere in the cockpit was becoming tense.

Jon set the radio to a new frequency and delivered the message. Almost immediately, a man's voice with a British accent said, "Stand by."

"Got something," Jon said.

A long moment passed. Then the voice came back on the radio. "Increase your altitude to one thousand feet and lower your landing gear."

"Roger," Jon replied. "Tommie, take us up to a thousand feet and lower the landing gear."

Tommie immediately pulled back on the stick and eased the aircraft up to a thousand feet. He leveled off, reached forward and toggled the landing gear. There was a whirring sound as the wheels came down, and the plane's speed dropped with the new drag.

"We are now at a thousand feet," Jon said into the radio. "Our landing gear has been extended. We are still on a heading of 270 degrees. However, I am not sure of our position."

"Don't worry, Sergeant," the voice came back, with a much friendlier inflection. "We know where you are. Check your six o'clock."

Jon looked back and, after a couple of seconds, a British Mosquito fighter bomber slowly rose into view, approximately fifty yards behind them.

"Hot damn," Shim said. Then he added, "I hope that guy doesn't get trigger happy." He raised both hands up next to his head, palms facing the Mosquito, and waved them. After a moment, the British pilot raised a hand and waved.

The British ground controller came back on the radio. "Turn to a heading of two eight zero." Jon relayed the instructions, and Tommie altered their course.

Over the next twenty minutes, they received a series of instructions, adjusting their course and altitude. Finally, the ground controller came on and said, "Well, Sergeant, you're on final approach to the main runway at Queen's End." Jon could see in the distance a series of lights in a straight line, the first few red, the rest white. Tommie allowed the left wing to dip slightly and they slid a bit to the left, where they were perfectly lined up.

Jon keyed the microphone one last time. "Runway in sight. Thank you for all your assistance."

"My pleasure."

Tommie eased the Messerschmitt down, and, as they passed over the end of the runway, he allowed the plane to flare. The two main wheels and the small rear wheel made smooth contact with the runway at the same moment. A perfect three-point landing.

"Show off," Jon said.

Tommie glanced back. He had a big grin on his face.

At the end of the runway, a jeep appeared, and a ground crewman signaled for them to follow. Tommie taxied behind the jeep, and it led them across another runway and down a short taxiway to an apron sitting in front of a hangar. Tommie set the brakes and shut down the engines.

There was a moment of silence. Then, from below him, Abernathy said, "Jon, you know you're not that light." Smiling, Jon reached for the latch to open the canopy.

Tommie said, "Yeah, let's get out of here. This place is starting to smell like manure."

"You had to bring it up," Shim said, "didn't you?" And they all four laughed.

As they climbed down from the cockpit, another jeep materialized out of the darkness. A man hopped out of the passenger seat and walked briskly over to them. As he got closer, Jon could see it was the same officer he'd met after landing the Deuces Wild.

"I had to see this with my own eyes," the man said. He peered at Jon, then nodded. "When they told me the name, I said it couldn't be. I should have known better."

Jon smiled. "This time, sir, I didn't fly the plane."

The officer laughed. "Well, all right, then," he said, and he put a hand out. "Congratulations gentlemen." As he shook their hands, he said, "This is a story I'm dying to hear. And something tells me you boys are probably hungry. Let me give you a ride to the mess."

As they accompanied the officer to the jeep, the man put his hand on Jon's shoulder. "You know, sergeant, I have only a finite amount of room here at my base. You're not planning on bringing me back any more airplanes, are you?"

"No sir," Jon said, with sincerity. "I'm happy to report that I'm all finished. I have only one more very important thing to do before I go home."

18

"Mary," General Kimbrough asked, "don't you think you've done enough for today?"

It was late on Thursday afternoon, and Mary had just offered to transcribe the general's notes from the meeting he'd concluded a few minutes earlier. It was her first day back at work.

After Mary had been given the news about Jon on Monday, Penny had taken her back to the Staunton. General Kimbrough had arranged for Penny to be excused from her work, and Penny had been with Mary constantly for the next three days. Mary had been grateful for Penny's presence. Still, it had been an awful time.

On Thursday morning, Mary had awakened with the realization that she had to get control over her life. She knew she couldn't spend the rest of it crying. It wouldn't bring Jon back. And it was something Jon wouldn't want her to do. What she needed, she knew, was a routine, something to make her feel part of the world again. When she'd arrived at work that morning, General Kimbrough had been surprised, but pleased, to see her taking steps to get beyond the grief. He'd given her a little work to do, but she knew he was holding back.

"No, sir," Mary said. "The day's not over."

Then she noticed the look of worry on the general's face, and she smiled weakly. "Sir, I appreciate your concern. I just need this to occupy my mind. Otherwise…"

The general nodded. "I understand."

Mary carried the notes out to her desk. She fit some paper into her typewriter, then paused, taking a deep breath. She looked down the hall in front of her. Late afternoon sun streamed in from the windows to her right, and the bustling crowd before her moved in and out of the light and shadows.

The work was helping, though, try as she might, she could not banish Jon's image from her thoughts. For example, just now, as she had gazed down the teeming mass of people in front of her, she could have sworn that, for the briefest of moments, Jon's face was there, at the far end of the hall.

Of course, when she blinked, it was gone.

She took another steadying breath. Get hold of yourself, Mary, she thought. You can't keep doing this.

And then it happened again. For a just a fleeting instant, a gap in the crowd, and Jon's face appeared, a little closer this time. She closed her eyes and squeezed them tight. When she opened them, all she could see were strangers coming and going up and down the hall, darting left and right.

How long, she wondered, would this go on?

She looked down and put her fingers to the keys. She was just about to begin typing when something compelled her to look up again. All she could see before her were uniformed personnel moving through the hallway, scurrying to and fro.

But then, as though it were the Red Sea being commanded by Moses, the crowd in front of her suddenly parted, and there, striding purposefully down the hall, his hazel eyes locked on hers, was Jon.

Mary was standing, though she had no idea how that had occurred. Then she was around her desk and running toward him. And, then, with an ecstatic leap, she was in his arms, and he was drawing her close. She clung to him fiercely.

"Sorry I'm late," he said softly.

Through her tears, her face burrowed into his chest, she laughed and squeezed tighter.

The door to the general's office opened, and General Kimbrough stepped out, speaking as he did. "Mary, I've just gotten some…" and he paused at the sight of the empty desk. Then he saw Mary in Jon's arms, and he finished with a broad smile, "wonderful news."

Mary turned her head and placed it against Jon's chest. She could hear his heart beating. "Promise me one thing, Jon," she said. "Promise me we'll always be together."

He lay his head on top of hers. "I promise."

Around them, the crowd continued to swirl, people as they passed looking curiously at the young couple locked in passionate embrace. Jon and Mary neither noticed nor cared.

#

A distant whistle sounded, and Marvella Wilson stood. That will be the 3:20 crossing the gorge at Middleburg, she thought. It won't be long now.

A noise from behind caught her attention. She turned just as Tom Anderson stepped out onto the platform. He tipped his head amiably and said, "I heard there might be a couple of special people on this train. If it's ok, I thought I'd join you."

She nodded. "You're quite welcome, Tom."

The sight of Anderson reminded her of the day the previous November when the lawyer had come to see her with an intriguing business proposition. Jim Dahlgren, he'd explained, had borrowed a lot of money for his failed campaign, and the bank needed a substantial payment that the man simply couldn't make. As a result, Dahlgren was facing imminent foreclosure of his home and his hardware store. He would be completely wiped out. Anderson had cast about for a solution that would keep his friend from losing everything. He'd convinced the bank to accept the payment they were demanding as full satisfaction for the debt, noting they'd likely not do better if they had to take the assets and try to re-sell them.

Walt Gallagher, who had worked for Dahlgren for almost two decades and had essentially been running the hardware store for the past several years, had saved almost every penny he'd earned. It was a good sum of money, but it still wasn't enough to cover the amount the bank needed. Anderson suggested to Marvella that she might consider the investment. Walt, it turned out, had become quite close to Jonathon, and Jonathon was familiar with the store, having worked there for a time. If Marvella was of a mind, Anderson explained, she could, on Jonathon's behalf, put up half of the investment. Jonathon and Walt would be equal partners. Walt was delighted with the prospect. And, to sweeten the arrangement, Anderson was prepared to offer his services to the new venture for a modest two percent share. They struck the deal. Though Jonathon didn't yet know it, he owned essentially half of Dahlgren's Hardware.

Marvella's thoughts were interrupted by another noise, and, when she looked, she saw Ben and Tommie Wheeler step onto the platform. They both nodded pleasantly. Tommie had arrived home two weeks earlier, and he and his father had visited Marvella shortly thereafter. Tommie told her the breathtaking story of how he and Jonathon and two of their comrades had managed to make their escape from Germany after the harrowing loss of their airplane. Marvella had been relieved to hear of it well after the fact. She was not sure how she would have dealt with the knowledge that Jonathon was in such grave peril.

Tommie also told her about Jonathon's wild business scheme. Apparently, Jonathon had decided there was a big future in travel by airplane, and he intended, with the assistance of Ben and Tommie Wheeler, to pursue the establishment of a venture that would offer flights from city to city and across the country. Marvella could not imagine anyone would prefer traveling in the tiny space of an airplane when they could just as easily travel by train, but she had long ago learned not to underestimate her grandson.

A young dark-haired woman followed the Wheelers onto the platform, and it took Marvella a moment to realize it was Samantha Parker. She hadn't seen the girl in a long time. Samantha, she noticed, had filled out quite nicely. The young woman gave a friendly nod to each of the gathered group. When her eyes met Tommie Wheeler's, he gave her a broad smile in return, and Marvella saw the girl's face flush. Tommie's smile widened and, after a second, so did hers. Oh, my, Marvella thought. I know that look.

To Marvella's surprise, Walt Gallagher arrived. Walt, she knew, was supposed to be on his honeymoon. He and his new bride, Agnes, had been married a few days earlier at St. Luke's. After the ceremony, they had traveled to Chicago, the first time in Walt's life that he'd ever been out of the state of Indiana. When she saw him, Marvella raised an inquiring eyebrow. Walt said, "There wasn't no way I was gonna miss this." Agnes, who had her arm linked in Walt's, smiled and patted her husband's shoulder tolerantly.

Marvella turned and looked down the tracks. She had a sudden flash of déjà vu. No, not déjà vu, she realized. It had been almost exactly two years before that she had stood on this very platform waiting for her grandson to arrive. How extraordinary life could be. How wonderful it could be. She wished dearly that Ernest could be here now.

There was another loud whistle, and suddenly the 3:20 emerged from between the trees lining the tracks, and, amid a cloud of steam, rolled into the station. As it came to a stop, there was an expectant hush on the platform. Then, in the doorway of one of the cars, Mary Dahlgren Meyer appeared, her brilliant blue eyes shimmering in the June sunlight, a radiant smile on her face. She stepped down lightly, and then, behind her, Jonathon filled the doorway.

Marvella's breath caught. Her grandson had grown at least two inches since she'd last seen him. His face bore a more angular and mature look. But what had captured her attention was the mischievous twinkle in his eyes. He looked just like Ernest.

She closed her eyes for a moment and said a silent prayer. Then she stepped forward. Mary reached out her arms and gathered her in a wonderful embrace. "Oh, Mrs. Wilson, it's so good to be home." They hugged for a long moment. Then Mary released Marvella and turned to Jonathon. Marvella looked at her grandson. He gave her a solemn look in return.

"Ma'am," he said.

Marvella gathered herself. "You will address me as Grandma Wilson. Understood?"

He gave her a broad grin and nodded.

"Now," she said, "are you ready to go home?"

"Yes, ma'am."

A Note from the Author

Though this story is one I've had rattling around in my head for quite some time, I was reluctant to try to tell it, for fear I'd fail to do it justice. Whether I ultimately succeeded or not will be up to you, my reader. But this I can say with confidence: My attempt would certainly have fallen short if not for the assistance of a number of others.

Please allow me a moment to acknowledge them.

First, my profound thanks to renowned editor and publishing executive, Hillel Black. I'm extremely fortunate to have had the opportunity to work with such a consummate professional—and a nice guy to boot. In his over forty-year publishing career, Hillel has, among other things, edited best-selling books that I count among my personal favorites. After I'd completed my initial draft (and realized it might be just a tad too long), I reached out to Hillel for guidance. He read the book, enjoyed the story, and encouraged me to pursue its publication. More importantly, he offered to edit it. How great was that! Being no dummy, I immediately took him up on his offer. Starting with a (perhaps slightly bloated) 600+ page manuscript, Hillel brought to bear his considerable skill, and, after what amounted to a number of (admittedly painful) cuts, what emerged was a much leaner, smoother and compelling novel. I am, and will forever be, grateful for his assistance.

But Hillel was not the only professional editor to work on this book. Before I finally let it loose on the public, I reached out to Kathryn Johnson, who, in addition to being a talented novelist in her own right, operates an editorial service for writers. I knew from past experience that she would bring to bear exactly what I needed: A disciplined eye that would catch those unintended—but inevitable—variances from smooth story-telling that tend to infect even the most heavily-scrutinized draft. She helped me clean up what stubbornly remained after countless read-throughs. I not only thank her, but heartily recommend her to other writers who are serious about taking their manuscripts to the next level.

Of course, I needed the feedback (and support) of my early readers. They're the ones who slogged through the initial drafts, putting up with the typos, the well-intentioned (but sometimes badly executed) segues, and the ill-conceived focus on minor characters. And yet they still found merit in the manuscript. God bless them. My sincere thanks to Cathryn Cormier, Damon Jespersen, Geri Hunter, Seth Pierce, Reuben Mack and Hal Light.

And last, but by no means least, allow me to acknowledge my wife, Martha. I honestly don't know where to begin to explain how important she has been, not only to the development of this book, but to everything else in my life. She is, at once, my audience, my champion, and my prize.

So, back to you, dear reader. I sincerely hope you enjoyed the telling of this story. If I brought some enjoyment, I'm happy. And I'm grateful for the fact that you indulged me, not only through the book, but the acknowledgements! To be honest, you are the reason I took the time to write all of this. Thank you, and I look forward to the next one!

Also by Marty Steere

Sea of Crises

What really happened to the crew of Apollo 18 in the Mare Crisium, the Sea of Crises? The last of America's manned lunar forays, the mission was conducted in eerie silence following the inexplicable loss of all communication during the astronauts' first moonwalk, and it ended in tragedy when the heat shield on the command capsule failed during re-entry, leaving the dead bodies of three astronauts inside burned beyond recognition. With them died the answer to a great mystery: What was the meaning of mission commander Bob Cartwright's last words, "That shouldn't be here," uttered just before the loss of communication? Thirty-six years later, Cartwright's sons make a shocking discovery: The capsule that came down in the Pacific Ocean with three charred remains was *not* their father's capsule. And the body they buried all those years before was *not* their father.

Praise for Sea of Crises:

"Steere's high-octane suspense tale takes off with all the intrigue and honor of the best Space-Age Westerns and political thrillers... A stellar thriller that handily juggles its formulaic elements to achieve near-perfect liftoff."

— *Kirkus Reviews (starred review)*

"Author Marty Steere is brilliant!... The action is non-stop and fast-paced and is mixed with just the right amount of mystery to make a perfect thriller... [The] plot is plausible, the characters are realistic, and the writing is superb...so stunning a read that you will be unable to stop reading until the very end."

— *Readers Favorite*

"Steere's assured prose is compelling, and the book's intriguing plot will keep readers turning pages until the very end."

— *Publishers Weekly*

"Sea of Crises is a mystery set amongst exploration, very highly recommended."

— *The Midwest Book Review*

"Marty Steere's Sea of Crises drew me in, held me at the edge, and gave my hand a comforting squeeze when I couldn't stand to see what happened next. This is a thriller with heart that will leave its readers satisfied they followed the Cartwright boys into a dangerous adventure."

— *Bookideas.com*

"[P]ulse-pounding... I highly recommend you check out Marty Steere's novel Sea of Crises!"

— *Bestsellersworld.com*

www.ingramcontent.com/pod-product-compliance
Lightning Source LLC
Chambersburg PA
CBHW051552250626
47157CB00001B/274